Praise for

King of the Forgotten Darkness

I loved this book ... Goodwyn's *King of the Forgotten Darkness* maps the lands of heroic quest and enchantment known to C. S. Lewis, Tolkien, Philip Pullman, Ursula Le Guin, and J. K. Rowling. We follow Liam who has been severed from his love, his fate, his imagination and his home. Can he find his way back into the world of terror and delight, of magic, of creatures that prophesy and dragons that promise annihilation or deep being? With a blend of Celtic culture and fantasy so sinuous it enters our dreams, *King of the Forgotten Darkness* reads like a key to a new series as gripping as it is revelatory. For surely The Forgotten Darkness is our own.

Susan Rowland (PhD) Author *The Sacred Well Murders* and *The Alchemy Fire Murder*

King of the Forgotten Darkness

A Raven's Tale Fantasy

Every story is a magic spell
The most recent magicians I know
Being Lily and Rowan

King of the Forgotten Darkness

A Raven's Tale Fantasy

Erik Goodwyn

ROUNDFIRE
BOOKS

London, UK
Washington, DC, USA

CollectiveInk

First published by Roundfire Books, 2025
Roundfire Books is an imprint of Collective Ink Ltd.,
Unit 11, Shepperton House, 89 Shepperton Road, London, N1 3DF
office@collectiveinkbooks.com
www.collectiveinkbooks.com
www.roundfire-books.com

For distributor details and how to order please visit the 'Ordering' section on our website.

A CIP catalogue record for this book is available from the British Library.

Design: Lapiz Digital Services

UK: Printed and bound by CPI Group (UK) Ltd, Croydon, CR0 4YY
Printed in North America by CPI GPS partners

We operate a distinctive and ethical publishing philosophy in all areas of our business, from our global network of authors to production and worldwide distribution.

For Von
My inspiration
My soulfire

The real problem is the following: we have paleolithic emotions, medieval institutions, and godlike technology.

E. O. Wilson

Preface

Human beings are storytelling animals, perhaps more than any other species. It is telling that so many of our oldest stories are so wild and fantastical. Some might say that the outlandish imagery of fantasy *obscures* the truth, but I disagree. Rather, I feel the symbolic imagery of fantasy is the *best* way to depict the emotional and complex truths of trauma, recovery, and indeed life itself, which is why I wrote the stories of the Raven's Tale series the way I did.

EG

There have always been two worlds: our beloved Midworld, an advanced realm of reason, logic and peace. And Erentyr, a primitive realm of dark magic and war. After ages of Erentyr inflicting conflict and suffering upon us, the Magnolent Council finally managed to shut all twelve gates between the worlds. Peace reigned in Midworld for decades.

9-year-old Liam Panregon was the last refugee to cross the worlds before the last gate was closed, putting Erentyr's horrors behind him.
Fifteen years later, those horrors could be ignored no longer.

Chapter 1

Liam's Nexwork device buzzed in his pocket. He ignored the call, and increased his pace, crossing the glass bridge toward the gym-plex facility, modern white squares and winding tram tracks rising over the green woods below. Through the glass, he saw the beginnings of autumn, the pale aspens' bright flames in the shadow of the housing towers. Trees … how long ago had he actually walked among trees? No matter. Walkways were cleaner. Safer, as always. No threats from anywhere stalked him now. Yet inwardly, he buzzed with dread. Muscles twitched, on a pulsing edge. A big difference from the numb emptiness of most days. Much worse today. He focused on the walkway — no flashbacks, no flashbacks, no flashbacks. Not today. He shook his head, as if to force them away, as he passed by another free *orinol* dispenser. An animated ad flickered on it: *GG Industries Universal Medical Initiative. Live stress-free! Cost: $0!* He slowed as he approached it. One button push and he could have an entire bottle of the white pills in a green container. Free for anyone and everyone.

Heart pummeling his chest, he paused before the animations of people frolicking in open fields of golden light. The flashbacks, the memories, the guilt, and the panic would all dissolve for the rest of the day. Relief. He breathed out through his teeth and sped up, so he couldn't change his mind. No. Not today, not ever again. Two parents and six brothers, all dead. Taking any more orinol would be like erasing them. He decided years ago to stay away from that stuff. He didn't *care* if his trauma and losses were two decades ago. Just because today was a rough one was no reason to break his promise to himself. His family deserved better than to be erased! Who cared if they were all from Erentyr? No. There *had* to be a way to live a normal life without that stuff.

1

That said, today was wearing down his resolve.

His breathing quivered, stomach aching. He pushed on, brushing past countless pedestrians chatting or tapping on their Nexwork-d devices. He scoffed, the crowd agitating him as usual. He kept the urge to punch people away from him in check. They wouldn't understand anyway. Nobody did. Not even Mia.

Thinking of her caused a pang of regret he quickly buried.

Though sweat trickled down his cheek, he powered forward, eyes glaring. He knew the 15th anniversary of him escaping Erentyr would be tough, but today was proving harder than he'd expected. Above him white, bland buildings towered into the murky sky, a tram track heading from it toward the cluster of monotonous, monument-like housing towers webbed with their own cross-tracks. He entered the elevator, and the usual ads for Raythera hair supplements and skin treatments scrolled endlessly on the walls. He drew out his Nexwork-d after it buzzed again.

The program was ready! He pocketed his device quickly, scanning for cameras. *Finally! The timing couldn't be better ... at last I can have a REAL challenge.* His breath quickened, the restless energy which threatened to blossom into panic channeled into a powerful fist.

He walked into the gym-plex main area, a wide room of Real-Plastic™ planters separating the exercise machines. No longer sweating, the promise of executing his plan swept away the dread and crackling muscle energy almost eerily quickly. He showed his company badge to the cylindrical Secura-bot and passed the front desk where bored attendants scrolled through Nexwork screens. "Machines? Aerobics?"

"Martial arts trainer." *And we're not playing nice today.*

He clenched his jaw and pushed toward the main rooms filled with exercise machines. Screens played hundreds of AI-generated shows from the Raythera-net streaming platform.

Weeks of the endless routine of work for six days a week, workout at the gym, drink himself to sleep each night was about to turn on its head, knowing what he was about to do. Phony smiling models scrolled on billboards attached to the high walls of the divisions as new songs from AI musician "Tanzi's" 174th album, *Lonely*, blared.

His hands opened and closed into fists absent-mindedly as he went into the changing area. Fifteen years ago today he escaped from Erentyr. Fifteen years, barely evading the bloodbath, with only the clothes upon his 9-year-old back, a magic Stone from his mother, and naught else but horrifying flashbacks and nightmares as luggage. He neared his locker. For *this* training session, he would have to be sneaky. Mia wouldn't like him breaking the law, but then they'd been broken up for years now. What did her feelings matter? He scowled. They still mattered, but never mind.

After changing into loose, grey workout clothes, Liam furrowed his brow and the world seemed to shrink into tunnel vision. His plan was really going to happen. After weeks of working on it. He took a few breaths next to his locker and stretched his arms and legs as gym members grinded workouts like hamsters on wheels. He tied back his long, wavy red hair, splashed his face with water and pat dried his trimmed auburn beard.

Tonight I finally get to push the limit. Scanning the locker-room, he hid from the security cameras. It was on. Just knowing what he was about to do was already helping.

Loosening up with jabs and elbows in the air as he marched forward, bare feet on the floor mats, he pressed into the individual martial arts challenge-room where the mechanized trainer waited. No one looked, so he swiped his badge across the side of the screen and the program activated.

He reached the panel. Years of advanced tech-work taught him that most screen-ports hid a compartment in the back for standardized memory devices and maintenance. Popping the nearly invisible cover out of place, he took the NW3 from his blue jacket and inserted it. A security clearance box appeared on screen, asking him how he wanted to program the auto-trainer.

He was ready to do this. Robot-therapists and years in the Childcare Plex never quite quelled the inner hurricane like a good pummeling session, especially since he'd given up orinol, but the trainer could not satisfy him anymore. Years of "expert" mode left him bored. Last time he accidentally destroyed the trainer on that mode. Luckily the expense was covered. Anyway, that was in the past. He would get to take it up a notch today.

Easily passing three layers of security logins, he changed the settings, but paused at the final step. This was the illegal part. Probably earn him five years in the Containment Facility if he got caught. But the clobbering still needed doing. CC335rp-TRNR martial arts auto-trainers had been modified from earlier versions made before the Magnolents' rise — two hundred years ago when actual wars were fought. But those changes meant the newer programs just pandered to students who didn't like a *real* challenge.

Liam paused, tapping his fist against his leg, second thoughts plaguing him. This was *not* healthy. But what else was? More orinol? More endless sessions with therapy-bots? He persisted. Something within him refused to be denied.

With a few keystrokes and finger swipes, he set the trainer to full-contact. He smirked and stepped back, flexed his knees and arms, stretching his powerful 6 foot 4 frame. A surge of energy coursed through him. Today was a full-on war. Finally a *real* fight. For once. Panic and fear had melted away. It felt *good*. He took a fighting stance, coiled like a spring. "Trainer."

"Welcome back, Mr Panregon," said the robotic, reassuring voice. "Warning. This trainer is set to full-contact combat-mode.

Battle to knockdown. Risk of injury: high. Do you agree to continue?"

He put in a mouth guard, charged toward the padded, human-like trainer-bot in the center of the egg-white exercise room and punched the TRNR unit hard in the chest. "Yeah, I agree." The trainer recovered and charged, fists up. He darted about, the machine adjusting to each step, its body shifting into position with each movement, electric eye scanning, analyzing. Much faster than before. It closed in, striking and kicking with speed and ferocity.

The TRNR swept past his guard and blasted him in the gut with a gloved mechanical fist, sending him stumbling back. Pain flooded his stomach and flank. He dropped to one knee, whereupon the trainer backed away and waited, bouncing like a restless boxer of old.

Liam winced, then smiled.

Now we're talking. He snarled and sprang forth, now much harder, but each time the TRNR bested his advances, anticipating his moves and landing solid blows on his jaw, flank, and chest. Liam growled and shook it off.

He took a deep breath. No more playing around. A couple wandered over to watch. He advanced on the TRNR and feinted, creating an opening, and swung at the TRNR, but the robot had anticipated this move and countered, kicking him in the chest and knocking him to the ground again. It all happened so quickly he couldn't tell if he had hit the head.

Suddenly memories flashed into his mind. Erentyr. 9 years old. Fifteen years ago.

Harsh hands, yanking his young body. Mail-clad soldiers. Binding his and his mother's hands. His chest tightened, lungs quickened, pulse hammered in his head. Death closed in on him, and he could barely gasp for breath. The memory came unbidden — one man was dragged to the iron chair, red-hot coal glow beneath it. One man who meant more to young Liam than any other man.

No! I am not reliving that day ever again. He closed his eyes and forced his breathing to slow. He knew the robot had defeated him. A storm of terror rocked his frame, yet he held it, muscles tense, like weathering an earthquake.

"Do you yield?" asked the sweet-voiced TRNR.

He tasted the tang of blood from a cut inner lip despite the mouth guard. Something shifted within him, and panic melted back into anger. He *liked* that. He glanced at the onlookers. Some of them gaped in horror, others with brows wrinkled in concern. But this only angered him more, for some reason he couldn't place. He snarled. He didn't want or need anyone's pity!

He slowly stood up, glaring at the TRNR. He wanted to try again, seeing its weakness. It had anticipated his feint perfectly. *Too* perfectly. That meant he could count on it. Feign a false opening, then feint *knowing* it would counter it. Counter the counter.

He wiped the blood from his nose.

Concerned faces waited for his decision, murmuring to each other. Embarrassment flushed his face. He swallowed and forced himself to relax.

"Yeah," he pushed out. "I suppose I yield." He absent-mindedly tapped his gloved fists together as the onlookers asked him if he was all right. "I'm fine. Just got a little winded."

"What level did you set that thing to?" asked a man in sweats.

"I just passed level 36. Been on this program for a while." He tried to cover his embarrassment with bravado. "I'm good, just another damn fine day, that's all."

"Oh. Cause I started the martial arts program last week. I'm on level 4. Is that, uh, what I have to look forward to?"

Liam scratched his neck and looked away. "Well..." he stammered, taking off the gloves. "Um, yeah."

The man nodded slowly. "I think I'll go back to you-go. That looks painful."

"Well," Liam said, "I mean, it *is* kind of painful sometimes, sure. It's *fighting*, after all, not..."

He trailed off as the man wandered away to the exer-bikes. Liam sighed.

The trainer voice chimed in: "Sir, sensors indicate minor injuries of face, mouth, abdomen and left flank. Two possible minor rib fractures. Are you feeling all right?"

He growled. "No worries." He tossed the gloves aside, and logged off the trainer, but the injury report worried him. He contemplated heading to the medical facility on the second floor.

Then the TRNR caught his attention. Knuckle-shaped dents wrinkled the blank face.

He smiled. He *had* landed the head hit. He released a satisfied chuckle now that the onlookers left. He stroked his beard, looking over the TRNR. His plan had worked, even though it beat him. So what if he'd lost? He admired his handiwork as the robot removed the face plate and repaired the dents he had caused.

Chapter 2

Liam washed up, tugged on a t-shirt and button-down shirt, and left the gym-plex. He passed the atrium, the usual crowd shuffling, staring at their Nexword-ds as if being pulled by the nose. He beamed inwardly at those knuckle-dents as he started toward the apartment complex along the moving walkway. The rainstorm sweeping down on the autumn woods outside the glass made no sound. He assessed his recent self-made "therapy" and nodded to himself as he turned a corner. The feelings of being on edge were a little better. But he furrowed his brow. The fight triggered a bunch of flashbacks. That was brutal. And risky. What if it got so bad, he started having *the nightmare* again?

He shuddered. God forbid. He slapped his cheeks, as if to snap out of even *thinking* of that. The fight was good. He had to focus on that.

He neared an escalator that climbed past more tall windows, sunset lighting the advertising screens on the walls. *What would Mia think, though?* His smile faded. But then, why keep asking himself that? They weren't a thing anymore. He let out a breath and took out his Nexwork-d. Not a thing. Her face was on the lock screen.

He engrossed himself in the photo as he rode the escalator. Her turquoise jewelry shined brilliantly against the autumn background, and her thick, black hair blew behind her as a ray of sunlight glared next to her contagious, squinting, half-silly smile. The smile that had caused his heart to race from the moment he met her as a kid in the Childcare Plex almost fifteen years ago. He breathed in the memory and ran his finger along the screen, as if caressing her face. The random photo captured her well — a rare glimpse of the zany magic tiger that was normally hidden behind long black waves and strict daily calendars. Despite her complaints that it was awful, he refused to remove the picture from the home screen. His head lowered, heart sinking. How bad was it to hang on so long to an ex-girlfriend's picture on your Nexwork-d?

That thought stung. By all rights, he should have been back in the dating scene years ago. He stroked his short red beard, then brushed dust from his shirt, tucking a hand into his jeans pocket. The catharsis of the TRNR dwindled as he absent-mindedly muscled through the crowd and contemplated downloading the latest GG-ware dating program. Sure, he'd get plenty of request-backs, but then he would have to actually *talk* to whoever she was. He curled his lip, feeling a bit nauseous. *Hard pass.*

He strolled alongside the windows as Raythera-on clothing advertisements flashed on the walls of the well-maintained lower building tunnels. Normally he loved the look of those clothes.

Today he wasn't interested. He hopped on another escalator and resisted the temptation to send Mia a message. Then he remembered *why* he lost the fight with the TRNR. No way he was going to mess up her life *again* with his post-traumatic ass. No, she was better off without him. Much happier, too, no doubt. Her happiness was more important than his longing anyway. He folded his arms, nearing the top of the escalator. In *that* conclusion, he would never budge. He got on the elevator and looked through the glass down at the city. His eyes followed the cars that zipped over the surface roads where Nexwork roadsters chauffeured the sub-Magnolents around ComCorps city 335.

His side stung from the fight, snapping his attention back to where he was: the elevator of residential tower 17A. He exited it and marched down the cream-colored hall to unlock the door and enter his apartment: a modest Identi-plan studio with a small living room, kitchen, single bedroom and bath. Abstract smear-pattern art and pared-down trimming decorated his walls. Coming home always reminded him of being stuffed into a decorated crate, but it safely cocooned him, nonetheless. No crime here since the building came up — like most new city projects. Near zero crime rates were one of Midworld's greatest achievements. Erentyr certainly could never say that. He shuffled through the door across the parquet floor and pocketed his Nexwork-d, then wandered to the grey cabinet that opposed his favorite faux-leather recliner.

The cabinet. That's where the figurine was. He had always kept it, even against therapy-bot advice. Today, especially, the drawer it was in tempted him. He stared at the cabinet for a while, his thoughts still stewing about the near panic attack he'd suffered at the gym-plex. Venting with the martial arts trainer only helped for a little while. The flashback lingered in his mind, hence the cabinet beckoned. *Haven't you dwelt long enough on Erentyr for one lifetime? Should you really re-open that wound?*

He studied that question with a long breath, in and out.

Yes. He pulled out the drawer with the small wooden figurine in it. A medieval warrior (in Midworld terms) with mail-coat and sword carved, and a hole in the helmet so one could make a necklace out of it. He had made it out of a chunk of aspen wood in the first days of arriving in Midworld. It comforted him, paradoxically, when it should have triggered the traumas. But Mia noticed it hanging from his neck when they met as kids, and that started their friendship. They both loved art. Not prompting AI programs that made art but actually *making* art themselves. Everyone else grew out of the childish habit, but he and Mia never did. Creating art together kept her tears at bay, too. He *understood* that.

He caressed the wood. Maybe it was time to make another necklace out of it? Luckily someone "higher up" stopped the Monitors from making them destroy it. He wondered who that was.

He slumped and set down the figurine on the night table. *That's enough, Liam. This isn't helping.* He settled into his recliner near a bottle of Jameson and a glass. Pouring himself a double, he turned off the lights and took a deep sip as the night-lights filled the room with dim red. The apartment hazed over as he sipped, hoping to fall asleep and forget the bloody images still engraved in his head, threatening to break through his defenses. End the day normally.

No. He let out a sharp breath. The fight helped some, but he knew it wouldn't be enough. He had to get more help.

He picked up his DRN-slim tablet. Many more days like today and he would be in trouble. It was time to get back into therapy again. The thought nauseated him. He pinched the bridge of his nose and closed his eyes. Despite it all he would have to.

His Nexwork-d buzzed. He took it out. Mia — calling. His heart jumped. "Um, yes? Mia?"

"Thought I would join you in the drink you're having right now. Irish whiskey, right?"

He coughed, mostly to hide how good her voice felt. He laughed nervously. "Am I that predictable?"

"Kinda."

Awkward pause. "So...um. Good to hear from you. Is everything ok?"

"Yeah. I just knew today might be hard on you," she said. He noticed the tiniest lilt in her voice. She'd been drinking, too. "With it being, you know —"

He blanched. "The 15th anniversary of ... all that?"

She breathed. "Yeah, all that. I know nobody else has called you."

"I'm ... no, I'm ok. Thanks for calling," he said, voice tight. "I really appreciate it. I mean that." He opened the screen on the tablet on his lap.

"Did you have an ok day?"

He laughed ironically. "Well ... I mean, I decided to go back to therapy, actually."

"That bad, huh? But, well, that's good, isn't it? You're taking the initiative. Another therapy-bot?"

"I'm thinking of trying a live one this time, assuming there are any left." He scrolled through the tablet screen. "At least I'd like to. The AI ones helped, but I've never tried a live one. Even with years of treatment it was hard to share the, uh, 'old stuff', you know?"

"Like the recurrent nightmare? That's still gone, right?"

Liam shuddered, forcing his mind *not* to go there. Thank everything holy *that* nightmare had not returned. Flashbacks were bad enough. *That creature* haunting his nightmares, triggered by all the traumas, he was told, was another thing entirely. "Yeah, still gone." He laughed without humor. "I'd go back to orinol again if that nightmare ever came back."

"Really? Wow. But then, I don't blame you."

He realized a bead of sweat had formed on his forehead. Better change the subject. "So anyway, how about you? Last we talked you were thinking about trying the...," he paused and took a long sip of whiskey.

"The dating scene again?" she finished.

He swallowed, rubbing his forehead, wondering why he took the conversation in this direction. "Yeah," he said with fake cheerfulness.

"I have a date tomorrow night, actually," she said, her voice somewhat tentative.

Liam cleared his throat. Didn't want to think about that either. "Hm, here's something." Search results for available psychiatrists only yielded one name. Tomorrow availability — how often did that happen? "Some new guy named Dr Morderan."

Mia fell silent.

"What?" He clicked through the links to nearly finalize the appointment.

"Ah, it can't be," she said. "Never mind. I just … I saw a Dr Morderan all those years ago when I was in therapy at the Childcare Plex."

"Wait … the one you said was crazier than you?"

"Yeah. But he left C-City ages ago."

"Weird coincidence?"

"Maybe. Probably nothing. So … how do you feel about going back to therapy?"

He took another long sip and stared at the tablet screen. All he had to do was click "confirm" to make the appointment. But his hand froze and began to tremble. Erentyr wasn't just about knights and happy quests. It was all that *other* stuff that provoked such dread. The stuff he never told anyone — not even confidential therapy-bots. And yet here was a live therapist. What a stroke of luck! He felt crushed from both sides. But he *had* to try again. A chance to live a normal life? Orinol free? No need to get beat up by training robots? But that meant dredging up all that … *stuff*. Yuck.

"Liam? Did I lose you?"

A memory surfaced. Something his mother told him when he was a little boy, afraid of the Fairywilds that surrounded their homes. Where did *that* memory come from?

"No." His voice cracked. "I was just thinking of something Mom told me once."

Long silence. "You … don't normally talk about her."

He ground his teeth. "Don't let fear take your heart, she said."

"That sounds like pretty good advice," she said softly. She inhaled, as if to say more, but didn't.

He breathed slowly out, then pursed his lips against the tension, forcing his hand to move and finalize the appointment. "Yeah. Well. She believed it. Want to know how I know?"

"Liam, you don't have to — I didn't mean —"

His pulse quickened. "Even with hunters bearing down on her, she only thought of getting me to Midworld. She got *shot* by a crossbow and kept going. She didn't let fear take her heart, down to her last breath."

And I left her there to die with the rest of my family, he wanted to add. But guilt choked those words. He cleared his throat. "And to answer your question, I'm feeling great about it. I'm looking forward to rehashing my entire life story again with a stranger."

Mia sighed at the sarcasm. "Good night, Liam."

His defenses tightened his neck and shoulder muscles. "Good night, Mia."

Liam hung up, then glowered into the red darkness, finishing the whiskey. He gripped his glass. The day churned in his mind, closing in on him like a vise. His hand trembled. Frustration, dark memories. Images not only of his family's deaths, but the terrifying creature that had haunted his nightmares the moment he escaped Erentyr. It had gotten so bad the Monitors got permission to give him children's orinol to stop them. That worked except on days he forgot to take it. His forced his breathing to slow.

Then he hurled his Jameson into the corner, smashing it against the floor in a spray of booze and broken glass.

Chapter 3

All around him loomed twisted woodland. He was alone, rustling leaves beneath him. Darkness lay upon the world like a cold blanket. Just as it did when he was a boy, fleeing Erentyr. Trees, covered in wildly colored mushrooms dulled by night air, towered over him like menacing, spindly giants, branches clawing, purple fireflies drifting through distant shadows. Drips of silver fell from the odd pine cone. A Fairywild. How could this be? He'd escaped Erentyr. This was impossible. He patted his jeans and button up shirt. No weapons. No Nexwork-d. How the hell did he get back here?

Red-orange light glowed upon the trunks, a dull roaring sound permeating, a burnt cedar smell in the wind.

Fire.

Hot air flowed past him, and he turned to see silhouettes of the trees against crackling tendrils. His whole body began to shake with fear.

Then Liam could feel *his* presence, trickling up the hairs of his neck. Blood drained from his face, stomach twisting in knots. Liam turned slowly from the fires, and standing silently between two dark oaks, *he* stood.

The Woodsman.

He stood 7 feet tall, at least. Tattered, thick leggings waved in the wind above heavy, worn boots; a rope belt about his heavily muscled waist. His bare, massive chest heaved slowly, covered in runes of nearly glowing dark red. A crimson cloak flowed from his neck, swaying in the smoky wind, and a deep, seven-layered hood concealed the top half of his face. But the bottom half was visible — a wolf's snout, snarling, fangs baring, breath frosting in the air. Upon his shoulder, a long, sharp bearded axe rested.

Liam froze, his blood chilling to ice. He took an involuntary step backwards, toward the heat. He tried to cry out but his voice failed him. Panic clamped upon his chest; eyes wide. He began to wheeze in horror.

The Woodsman finally raised an accusing, taloned hand. "Why are you here, Liam?" he said, his voice deep, growling, seemingly echoing in Liam's mind. Liam shook his head ineffectually, unable to answer, as he had so many times in the Childcare Plex. He backed up another step. "You should be dead with your family! You do not *deserve* to be alive." The Woodsman gripped the axe with both hands, red light glinting on the blade.

His heart pounding was the only sound Liam could hear. He turned and bolted. Toward the flickering blaze. Sparks drifted past him as he sprinted, gasping, glancing back to see the Woodsman, lips curling in a menacing snarl, sprinting after him swiftly, axe brandished. His growl dominated all other sounds. Fire surrounded Liam.

***

He gasped deeply, drenched in sweat, and sat up in his room. Breathing staccato and shallow, hand on his chest, he covered his face with his other hand.

No.

Not again. After everything he had been through. All these years free of it. He fought the urge to weep in despair. It came in waves. "Just a dream, just a dream, just a dream," he whispered. He wiped his forehead of sweat. He would *not* give in to this. No more weakness. No more. He slammed his fist into the wall, caving in the drywall.

He roared and stood up, slowly catching his breath. Beside his bed, Jameson awaited. He poured a double and downed it straight, burning his throat. He coughed and poured another.

His nerves calming, he watched the swirling golden-brown liquid in the glass. No ... that was enough whiskey for now. He set it down.

The figurine caught his eye — the one he'd left on the table instead of putting it back in the drawer. He returned it and glowered at the clock. Forty-five minutes before his alarm would go off. No sense in trying to go back to sleep. The very idea made him shudder. He huffed, trying to center himself, then stormed off to get ready for work.

***

After work the next day, Liam passed the 24-hour Graves-stim dispenser in the red-and-white hall of the NAC Medicost complex. A new ad flashed on it. An AI-generated model smiled, words forming under her. *Stressed at work? Relationships? Give yourself the peace of mind you deserve! New orinol 6-month injectable formulation now available. Scan this code today for a free consultation!*

He shook his head. Of course they had that now. Just so easy. But there had to be a better way than that. Desperation closed in on him.

He inhaled deeply. Remembering his mother's quote the previous night triggered memories of that last day in Erentyr. Memories he knew he would have to dive back into today in therapy with the new doctor. Jitters fluttered through his body. He pushed past the dispenser, and the sun shined through the glass of the windowed hall, falling on the abstract line-art of the carpeting. Thankfully his side no longer ached from the TRNR bot, and the additional double-shots of whiskey last night (and this morning) had no ill effects. Mia always said he healed too quickly to be "natural." Too bad that did not help him now.

He entered the empty waiting area. No one was at the front desk either — there was only a Nexwork screen with a welcome message. Weird. Everburn faux fluorescent lights lined the ceiling, and framed paintings lined the egg-white walls in between pricey shoe advertisements on screens. One of the paintings was entitled "Disquietude, by artificial artist LZ." He tapped the screen at the desk.

"Welcome, client," a computer voice answered. "Who are you here to see?"

"I'm here for my appointment with Dr Morderan."

"Dr Morderan does not exist."

He blinked. "Excuse me, what?"

He barely noticed the screen flicker. "My apologies. System error. Fixing … Welcome, client. Who are you here to see?"

"Um … like I said, Dr Morderan."

A long pause. "Please follow the prompts on the screen."

He scratched his head. What the hell was wrong with Nexwork today? He shrugged. Anything, even more painful therapy, was worth trying to have a normal life without just taking orinol forever. He opened his left palm … the one with the long nasty scar across it. The one he had gotten crossing into Midworld as a boy. It itched for some reason, all along all the additional, smaller scars on top of the older, larger one. Now those scars had long healed. He stared at the screen, resolve growing. *Here we go.* He started filling out the forms.

An old man's voice came from somewhere within the office. "Oh good. He's here! Never thought he'd call."

Liam put his head through the open window to peek. A man with salt-and-pepper hair sat on an office chair looking away. He tapped the silver head of his cane. There seemed to be nobody else in the office but him — who was he talking to?

Finally, footsteps, interspersed with the clack of a cane against the beige tiles, like an approaching street repair robot. It stopped at the door. Liam pretended to be distracted with his Nexwork-d.

More waiting. He tapped his foot. What was the doctor doing?

The knob turned, and the door opened. A tall man in his sixties entered, suit classic and well-tailored, though scruffy with ragged elbow patches and a worn collar. A face, creased with many lines, smiled at him. The doctor's right eye was clouded over, giving his cheerful, snaggle-toothed expression an eccentric air, like an old tenured professor who loved to shock new students with unfiltered sarcasm. "And you'll be Mr Panregon?" he asked in a Scottish-sounding accent.

Liam stood up, jitters in his lungs. "Doctor?"

They shook hands. "Follow me." He hobbled toward his office. They passed sterile-smelling empty rooms. Dr Morderan's office was cluttered with books and bric-a-brac, along with a viewing screen on a roller, a huge reclining office chair and a lush, ancient leather couch by a mahogany coffee table. More cluttered, forgotten attic rather than medical office. A window offered a little view of the pink concrete buildings of the ComCorp City Medicost sector.

The doctor sat down and offered Liam a seat on the couch, then looked piercingly at him with an odd smile. Books buried the tabletop: an analysis of *MacBeth*, some neuroscience texts, and something called *I Claim Them All* by J. Savage. Liam sat comfortably, returning this strange doctor's penetrating glare with a curious eyebrow.

Here he was. Maybe this time he could figure life out. Just being here caused memories he had pushed away to surface with force. The final moments with his mother haunted him, when she gave him the last Dream Stone. Her face dripped with blood that trickled down the lines of her rounded cheeks. Her long, wavy hair tossed from the winds of an oncoming storm over the purple glow-fly meadows. She winced at the pain from the crossbow bolt in her leg, her russet kirtle rustling in the cold.

Bring the Dream Stone back to me, she said. *Or our homeland will die.*

That was the last day he saw her alive. How could he finally get past all that and move on? He took a deep breath, in and out, and waited.

"So there you are," said the doctor finally, breaking the silence. "After all this time. I cannae believe it."

It was a strange way to start. "I'm sorry, have we met?"

Morderan smiled. "Not exactly, Mr Liam Trendari Panregon."

No one ever used his Erentyrian middle-name. Interesting choice to start out. More silence. "I guess I don't really know how to begin. All my previous therapists have been bots, actually." He crossed his legs.

Morderan smiled. "It's about trust, Mr. Panregon. Trust is necessary for healing, and in fact for life itself I believe. Trust in a bot is easy. Trust in a human? Well..."

"So ... what shall I trust you about?"

He raised a finger. "Ah. Let's not be twiggy. Let's take our first step." Morderan's good eye twinkled. "I want to show you something."

"Twiggy? Ok. Usually we start off with 'therapy goals' and a list of 'incorrect cognitions' and so forth. What's your approach? Should we talk about my relationship problems? My career stresses? My time in the Childcare Plex? Stuff like that?"

Morderan nodded. "Patience, lad. We will talk about your past. Not of the Childcare Plex, but how about before that?" He turned on the screen and it faded into the image of a little boy being interviewed — video footage stopped in a freeze-frame.

A wet chill climbed his spine. He cleared his throat. "W-Where did you get that? That footage was archived — well ... they said it was." He leaned forward. *It's me.*

"I was granted special access to the Magnolent archive by a very high authority. It took quite a bit of work to get to treat you, Mr Panregon. You're quite a special case as you must know, lad."

A creeping, dreadful stillness crept up Liam's muscles. What kind of therapy was this? Who was this doctor? "All right," he said, tentatively. "What are we doing, then?"

The doctor turned to the screen. "Take another look at this old footage, Mr Panregon. But now through the eyes of an adult." A look of fatherly concern crossed his face. "Does it bother you to see this, young man?"

He wavered, torn between pulling away and leaning further in. "Well, no ... I ... no, go ahead, I don't care. I can handle it."

Morderan nodded and started the video.

The little boy had an accent like the doctor's ... where had that gone? "My name is Liam Trendari, and I'm the seventh child of Ynwin and Cormac Panregon. New squire for Thane Finn of the Shoreland Tuath. But he's dead now. I ... came here to escape the Nurnian invaders ... but now I can't get back home. They took me Dream Stone." The little boy was rocking back and forth, not looking the interviewer in the eye, as if reciting something to a wall. He was clearly in shock.

Liam shook his head, riveted to the screen, breathing shallowly. *Jesus, I was screwed up.*

The off-camera interviewer asked: "And how did you hurt your hand?" The feed closed in on his bandaged hand. Liam held up the scarred palm before him as he watched the video.

"A dragon bit me deep in the Fairywild. Mama's prayer to the Ocean Mother didn't save me from it."

"A dragon? Wow, that's scary. Tell me more."

"Look at me," said Liam, watching as the little boy on the screen seemed to shrink, shutting down. "I'm so afraid ... petrified. I can barely talk."

"The code of the knight?" said the boy, the interviewer having coaxed him to talk again. "I can recite it by heart. It goes: I swear to honor the Fairy Queen and Her children, uphold my lord and liege, and protect all those in need. And then the lord strikes you across the face."

"Strikes you?" The interviewer sounded aghast. "Who?"

"I told you. Your liege lord. Don't you know anything? Then ye say: I swear to seek the greatest glory, achieve equan— equanimity of spirit, and fight for purest Good. And then finally —" Morderan paused the video.

He had to finish it, like a musician needing to play the last note of a melody.

"Finally, as a knight," Liam said softly, "I swear to hunt for naught but Truth, humbly keep the courtesies..." The words were still there, stirring something cruel that lurked just out of reach. "And avenge all wrongdoing."

"Ah, you remember!" said Dr Morderan.

"Yeah," he said softly, shaking his head, shifting uncomfortably on the couch. "I remember all that about honor and courage. Hmf. What does all that matter if you still lose in the end? I mean, it didn't do my family any good, did it?" He wrinkled his nose. "Nobody stresses about it in Midworld, anyway."

The screen held the frozen image of young Liam, holding up his bandaged hand to the camera, his eyes haunted, his face concealing deep wounds.

"How much of your life in Erentyr do you remember?"

Nervousness pushed more words out of him. "Not much, thank goodness. Probably would have driven me nuts, like my roommate in the Childcare Plex. Tommy — that poor guy. He once bit his own tongue off because the voices told him it was evil. His tongue." He shook his head, mesmerized by his younger self. "Poor guy. He used to mumble this weird rhyme after his surgery ... what was it? *Oho,* he would say ... *When the pale moon dies in the autumn night's glen ... three days, three nights, it rises again.* Over and over he mumbled that. I covered my ears as he repeated it." The calming white air-conditioned halls of the Childcare Plex stretched over him in his memory. Safe and secure.

"Indeed ... sounds like you're thankful to be here in Midworld, and not the land of your birth."

Liam rubbed the knuckle that hit the TRNR yesterday. "Of course! Unlike most people here in Midworld, I actually *know* what Erentyr is like. Midworld has no war and no want – the Magnolents did their job well. What do these people know about any of that? Locking away the Dream Stones was the best thing anyone ever did. Me, I'd just as soon forget Erentyr ever existed." But his voice faltered at that last word. The image of his mother on that last day appeared in his mind. But then he also remembered why he was here. He had to move past all that.

The doctor raised an eyebrow and seemed to study his expression. "Aye. Well, I encourage you to keep an open mind."

Liam squinted. "About what?"

Dr Morderan smiled. "What might you say to me if I said you could go back, right now?"

Liam furrowed his brow. That was an odd question. No therapy bot *ever* entertained such hypothetical scenarios. He ran a finger along the scar on his left palm, tapping where the dragon bit him. Memories of cutting the scar on purpose in the Graves Childcare Plex surfaced. Along with the feelings that brought the urge on. Grief. The nightmare about the Woodsman. Cutting the scar distracted him. Until he met Mia, anyway. She helped. He cocked his head and leaned back in his seat. "I guess I never ask myself that, now. I mean, the Magnolents have the Dream Stone locked away, so even if I wanted to, I couldn't —"

Morderan removed a small object from his pocket and handed it across the table slowly, as if presenting something fragile.

Liam blinked and leaned forward. He took the oval-shaped dark grey Stone into his hand. Carved expertly onto the surface was an eye with three spiral pupils. A sinking feeling overcame him. His scarred hand trembled holding it, and his breath shortened, as if snakes suddenly coiled around him. He lifted it closer. The weight and smoothness of the Stone was perfect. Precisely how he remembered it when his mother gave it to him before she fell.

It was tangible, weighty in his scarred hand. His fingers tingled as he caressed its contours. He glanced at the doctor, flushing. "How the hell — is this the real one? Or is this some kind of exercise?"

Dr Morderan smiled and nodded encouragingly, both hands resting on his walking stick. "It's the original, lad. Hold it. Re-familiarize yourself with it."

"How did you..." Liam caressed its solid contours. He never thought he would see this thing again. That triple-spiral eye stared right into him. Piercing. But this was not right. This had to be a trick! *Somehow the doctor must have gotten hold of a very detailed replica.*

The sight of the Stone triggered a memory to burst into his mind. He ran, gripping the Stone in his unscarred hand, the overgrown castle before him, howling twisted forests behind him. His mother's prayer echoing in his head.

He rubbed his eyes. *No! This is what your therapy programs warned you about.* Years of therapy bot sessions flashed past him.

Morderan pointed, voice sharp. "That Stone is an ancient item with very special qualities. With it you can—"

"This was my mother's Stone," he said, fending off the flashback. "It wasn't really supposed to go to me. She told me to brave the dragon and flee to Midworld, but to one day return it to her. Seemed very important."

Dr Morderan nodded solemnly, seemingly working out what to say next. "Liam ... a lot has happened since you escaped. Do you remember how to use the Dream Stone?"

He gripped it and raised his eyes to the doctor. "Use it? To go back? Are you nuts? No, I don't remember! And I don't want to."

Morderan leaned forward. "When you are at the appropriate location, you can close your eyes, and concentrate on the gate. Imagine it, and it will open up for you ... then you must go through it."

He laughed, incredulous. "Why would I do that, Dr Morderan? I barely escaped that hell. My mother handed me the Stone and then died. I'm the only," he said, clearing his throat sharply, "survivor."

The doctor jutted his jaw out for a moment, furrowing his brow in thought. Then he shook his head. "Aye, but that's just it, lad. There's something you don't know. Something you couldn't know. *Your mother, Ynwin, did not die that day.*"

Liam blinked, not registering what the man was saying. "Wh-what are you talking about? Yes she did."

He raised a hand, as if to calm him. "Now, I know it is a shock to hear it, lad. But she is still alive. And she needs you. And she is in trouble, now more than ever. She and your homeland are dying."

Liam assessed this bizarre doctor. He seemed genuine behind that crooked smile. But Liam's whole body tensed, belying his calm. A black storm of memories roiled within him, just out of reach, but threatening to burst through any time. He scoffed. "This is nuts. I can't go back there. My life is here in Midworld, doctor. What the hell am I supposed to do about all this? This is *Erentyr* we're talking about, man. You might as well tell me to jump into a volcano, it'd be safer. You *do* remember why I left, right? I could barely save myself from that place! Why don't *you* return if it's so important?"

He furrowed his brow. "I cannae return it to her. It's complicated."

Liam clicked his tongue. "I'm sure." He sat up. This was absurd. Surely some kind of trick. "Ok, so ... you're insane. This is not ok, and I've had enough of this. I don't know what you're trying to pull but you're nuts and I'm done." He stood. "I'm out, and with any luck you're going to have your license revoked, and they'll throw you in the containment facility for meddling with the Magnolent Mandate."

"Aye, and what of your mother? Will you turn your back on her?"

He ground his jaw. "Erentyr nearly destroyed me. I lost everything."

"Aye, I know, lad!" shouted Morderan. "You were stabbed in the heart!" Liam stood still as a stone at the sudden outburst. "Stabbed. I understand, son. The blade broken off in your soul. Believe me, *I know* what that is like," he said, voice sharp and piercing, as if commanding. Liam instantly believed it. Morderan's expression softened. "But for all that pain, all you gained here in Midworld was a lifetime supply of painkillers. That blade still lies buried. But your mother needs you. Your homeland needs *her*."

Liam cleared his throat, forcing himself to stand strong through sheer force of will. "No," he rasped. "My whole family died there. Going back would be suicide." His lips curled into a snarl. He tapped the doctor on the chest with a finger. "And how dare you use my mother's memory to —"

"It's nae a lie, lad."

"They shot her in the leg," he growled, voice rising. "They stabbed and shot every one of my brothers," he continued, voice straining, He swallowed and closed his eyes for a moment, looking away. "And then," he said, turning back to the doctor. "I fled that world. Left her," he added, voice cracking and low, throat tight, "in a pool of blood on the glow-fly meadows of Caldbana. There is *no way* she survived Arrius's hunters. Think I didn't remember it right? Because I've re-lived that day a hundred thousand times, my friend. So don't tell me she still lives."

Morderan's eyes softened into pity. Liam hated that look, but unlike others, he sensed a deep understanding from the doctor. "All right, Liam. But at least keep the Stone. Study it. Feel its energy. It's bound to her. You'll know," he said, putting a hand on his shoulder, making Liam's eyes dart uneasily to his thick hands. "She is alive. But you must feel it right deep down. 'Tis fair enough. The years have passed, and the danger grows. You say your life here now is in Midworld. Maybe 'tis so. But I owe you this much; your entire homeland will be destroyed and your mother executed soon. The Fairy Queen Herself sent me here to ask this task of you. This is our last chance, Liam. Please reconsider."

Liam stood speechless. Gaping, his mind a whirlwind. It was far too much. All utterly impossible. He clenched his scarred fist and shook his head, as if to fling the confusion from his mind. But the doctor's plea wrenched his heart. His chest ached. What if it was really true? "Look, doc, w-what are you trying to do? I was the last one to cross the gates — everyone knows that. The Magnolents took the Stone from me almost as soon as I got here. His Grace, Damien Raythera has it now."

Morderan scowled. "It's not Raythera's Stone, lad. It's *yours*. It's *your* blood kinsmen who need you. Your homeland. If you'll give me time, I'll explain everything. Come, at least have a seat and we'll talk about it."

Memories stabbed at him from within, struggling to make their presence known. His heart hammered his chest and a deep pain pinched his temples. "I'm not your guy, Doc. His Grace, Mr Raythera is. He went to Erentyr and returned a hero. I ran screaming from it, remember? I'm sorry."

The doctor straightened, his expression almost scolding. "With respect, Mr Panregon, you have no idea what you're capable of. Midworld has left you no room for it."

But Liam shook his head. Thoughts swirling, he turned abruptly and walked out. Leaving the Medicost tower, he noticed he still clenched the Dream Stone close to his heart, taking it with him.

Chapter 4

For hours, he considered looking up the C-City Medicost board to report Dr Morderan for trying to breach the gates — punishable by life in prison. Every time he opened up his Nexwork-d, he stopped. Something kept him from reporting him. An inner pressure ... a desire to *know*. What if it was true? Maybe Mom really was alive. He paced the halls, wandering aimlessly from the Medicost district to the tram station. He got on and sat down in the egg-white car, closed his eyes, and rubbed his temples, barely noticing the shuffling citizens about him staring at their Nexwork-d's. Everyone politely sat without talking. The twelve-person tram car sped along the city back toward the residential center. *I barely escaped that nightmare! Why would I go back?* He kept on for hours, staring at the Dream Stone, inwardly pacing about like a wolf that wanted to chew a bone but couldn't decide where to lay.

Bring the Dream Stone back to me, she said, *or our homeland will die.*

But she *died*. Right? He punched his scarred palm absent-mindedly as he stepped off the tram, but instead of getting off at the residential sector, the station opened into the market district. The session with Morderan replayed over and over. What if she really was still alive and needed him in Erentyr?

An involuntary shudder arose. An image of her flashed. *She knelt, took his freckled hand in hers and showed him the Dream Stone. "It's just us now," she whispered, wincing in pain — one of the hunters' arrows in her calf.*

The memory refused to go away. His breathing became ragged.

She held him close as the hunters closed in. "Ocean Mother please protect my only remaining son," she sobbed. "Keep him safe from harm, I beg you."

He mouthed her final words.

A constable of ravens scattered into the sky from the camphor trees above the blue standing crystals of Drenhai, beyond the glow-fly meadows — that seemed to encourage her. But then came the Nurnian hunters — angry mailed men-at-arms — from the forest, crossbows readied.

He shook his head, as if to fling such thoughts down the corridor leading to the market center, where they couldn't hurt him. Several deep breaths. The idea of going back to Erentyr, even for that, sent shivers down his back. He grimaced. *Damn it, stop. If you go back there and get killed, then she sacrificed herself to save you for nothing!*

He stared at the Stone. It seemed to pulse in his mind when he pondered it. Within its weighty heft carried the key to opening gates between worlds. Its contours, Mom had told him, were crafted by the Fairy Queen Goddess Herself, older than time.

What if.

He needed a drink. He left the bathroom and got on the escalators, and the light of flashing clothing and restaurant advertisements bathed the tunnel. He emerged into the sprawling market sector known as The Dome™. The great silver hemisphere soared above him as he pushed through a maze of bars and dining — all subsidiaries of Raythera Industries. Endless flashing screens lit the bustling streets, distracting his eyes. Advertisement drones swarmed above him through the haze, peddling beauty products, health supplements, and jewelry. He descended the stairs and uneasiness seeped into his skin. Crowds … yuck. But going home would have just meant he drank himself to sleep. He needed to walk it off. Let his thoughts chew on everything for a bit.

What the hell am I going to do about this?

Something flickered out of the corner of his eye as he passed a restaurant called *Circuits*, right past the entrance tunnel. The silhouette of a hooded figure with a wolfish snout crossed the blinking lights inside the restaurant. The fleeting image sent a jolt through him. He straightened, taller than most, and watched it turn and disappear into the shadows inside. He rubbed his eyes and looked around. Not dreaming, definitely. Had to be an illusion? He pushed through the noisy crowd, the weird encounter with Dr Morderan still churning in his head.

This was getting out of control. Whatever was happening, the idea Dr Morderan proposed tugged at him, like a pesky raven picking at his hair. And now he was hallucinating the damn Woodsman while he was awake. He sighed through his teeth. Erentyr had obviously beaten him and made him a freaking nutball. He entered the noisy restaurant, dancers to the left, large screens blaring to the right, and squinted. He brushed past a waiter, nearly dumping a tray of glasses, and powered through full dining rooms with cartoonish tropical scenes painted on the walls to reach her.

No Woodsman. He scoffed at himself.

Doubts and turmoil were edged out by leap-frogging jolts of worry. Screens surrounding the dining area played events from the recent Sports-Bot Olympics at the bar, where fans howled at the game like chattering monkeys at the humanoid robots competing.

"Liam?" a woman's voice called. He whirled.

Mia.

She sat at a table in the corner, setting down a tablet. Working on her artwork? Here?

"Hey," he said, faking calm. "Fancy meeting you here," he said lamely. He looked around. "Um. Is your date not coming?"

Jitters buzzed within him as he neared. Fighting murder-bots was fine but trying to figure out how to talk to Mia about all this? Terrifying.

She rolled her eyes and went back to her artwork. "Stood me up. Come on over."

He tilted his head. "Should we?"

She raised an eyebrow at him. "Can't old friends share a dinner?"

He shrugged and quietly neared her as she swiped and shaped a scene: a fantastical castle built on sea-stack cliffs by the wine-dark ocean. Huge wolves, soaring falcons, stormy mountains. Dense and elaborate. Incredible talent — not as technically slick as AI art, but he much preferred its soul. He looked closer as she continued.

No fiery, slashing demons, unlike her old drawings.

His eyes went back to her as she finished up a corner of her painting. Maybe she had outgrown the darker stuff she used to make.

The sweeping movements of her hands caused her frilly blouse to wave in the low light. She still chewed her bottom lip when painting, just like when she was 11. He rarely saw her like that anymore.

He sat down. Her hair tumbled about in thick waves, and her mahogany eyes, behind small, round glasses, darted between him and the tablet. The faux-candlelight made her coppery skin glow, revealing faint birthmarks he used to call "skin perfections." Tension at seeing her in person immediately tightened his neck and chest. It was good to see her, but impossible to forget their inability to live together. Sudden moods. Long silences. Short, sharp conversations. Knowing she would never be able to understand his pain. Knowing she could do far better than him. Still, she was beautiful, in a deep way. He gave her a tentative smile. "So ... hi."

She put the menu away. Her eyes met his, as if measuring his emotional state. "Hi."

Awkward silence. Liam's insides felt like a beehive buzzing. He didn't want to fight. "I recognize that painting you were working on. That's from our plays, right? From the Home? The great fortress at the cliff. Remember the name?"

Mia pursed her lips to one side. "Of course. Caer Lannican. Forget ... seriously? Who learned your native language in secret when we were kids? Who helped you make that old wooden figurine of, what was it? King Brendan of Ancient Kaledon? Or did *you* forget?"

"Touché. I'm sorry your date stood you up. That's annoying. What was this one's problem?"

She set the tablet down, slumping, her hair drifting in front of her face. She shrugged. "I don't know. Probably scared him off."

Liam scolded himself for being relieved her date didn't show. It obviously hurt her feelings. Much more important than their ex-relationship. "Scared him off?"

"Oh, you know. Last night I started blabbering on about my research with some timberwolves we just got? See this?" She lifted her hand, the one with her grandmother's ring, to reveal a bandage. "Got a little love nip from one of them," she said with a chuckle. "And then I started going on and on about their habitat and how they're so endangered." She sighed, tapping the table. "I bored him silly, just like I always do. Must make *me* silly."

He opened his palm to her. "No sillier than my memorizing dusty old poems. Or Shakespearean monologues. Remember that phase?"

She laughed. "Let this be the whetstone of thy heart," she said dramatically.

He laughed, forcing a smile. She obviously noticed and her own smile faded.

"So," she said, twirling the stem of her glass, "How did the therapy session go?"

A black cloud overcast his mind. He was dreading that question. He looked down and frowned, guilt weighing on him. The waiter served their drinks and left quickly, sensing the tension — a red wine for her and a tall Wycom beer for him.

He sipped. He absent-mindedly gripped the Dream Stone in his pocket, forcing away memories of his mom. "I actually walked out on him."

She took her glasses off and hung them on the cut of her blouse, then rested her chin on interlocked fingers, leaning in. "Why?" she asked, concern in her eyes.

"It was so weird," he said, going through it. He clenched the Dream Stone. Her eyes went to his hand in his jacket pocket. She was always too smart to hide things from. He knew he had better tell her now. The idea was horrifyingly risky — she might reject him for even *having* the Stone at all, and then he wouldn't even have her as a friend. Why didn't he force the doctor to take it back? Still he gripped it despite himself. Then he got angry. *Am I a coward?*

Muscles tight, he forced himself to move. He looked around, then cupped his hands to briefly show her the Dream Stone.

Her eyes snapped to it. "What's that?"

He tucked it away. "The Dream Stone."

"Wait. You mean — *the* Dream Stone?"

"That thing I always talked about. Yes. From the old stories."

She leaned back in her chair, eyes narrowing. "How?"

He stayed eye-to-eye with her, steady. "Dr Morderan gave it to me. I don't know how, but I *know* it's real." He leaned in, voice to a whisper. "He didn't say as much, but I think he stole it from Mr Raythera himself, to give to me."

Her expression was inscrutable. But he knew her — she was processing. She tilted her head to the side. "To do ... what?"

"Go back to Erentyr and save my mother. Yeah," he said, reacting to her skeptical eyebrow, "not only is she still alive, but she is in great danger and needs me. So *he* says, anyway."

The waiter interrupted them and they hastily ordered dinner — steak and fries. He rubbed a hand through his hair as his mind tossed back and forth. She glared at him, holding herself close, lips moving silently, as if unable to find words.

She tapped her cheek and blinked. He felt he teetered on the edge of a cliff. What was she thinking? He didn't rush her. Her shoulders were tense and squared. "And this isn't some kind of test or trick?"

"Mia," he said, licking his lips, mouth suddenly dry, "I don't know how to explain it. But it *felt* like he was telling me the truth. He said he was from Erentyr and that's how he knew. What's more," he glanced at his pocket, "the Stone. It's like it's telling me she's alive."

She placed a hand on her turquoise necklace as she took a deep breath, her grandmother's ring reflecting the neon light. Finally she raised her eyes to him, a mixture of resolution, resignation, and a hint of a smile tinged with sadness. She leaned in. "Maybe. Maybe you should go," she said softly, looking about, as if to avoid someone overhearing.

That didn't register immediately. His heart rate leapt despite the terror the idea invoked. "Seriously? It's illegal. I mean, unless I turn it in to the Magnolents. I can put this all behind me."

"I'm not really sure that's a good idea." She reached across the table and took his large hand in hers, dark hair reflecting the faux candlelight. "You say put it all behind you. I say how the hell is that possible with your home and your mother still needing you?"

He did *not* expect this from her. Not in a thousand years. "So, let me get this straight — you're *encouraging* me to go back to Erentyr? After all these years?"

She nodded, slowly at first, then more resolutely. "I don't like it, but I don't see how you really have a choice. Look, I remember the stories you told me. Sure, they were scary, but this changes everything. Maybe it's a pipe dream, but you'll never forgive yourself if you don't at least get more data. At least go back to Dr Morderan and see what he has to say. Grill him about Erentyr. If you catch him in a lie, you'll know. And you better go soon — maybe after work, tomorrow?"

He raised his eyebrows. "I–I don't know what to say. You're really something else. Truly."

She shook her head. "Tsk. You think you're the only one to feel like going on a grand, perilous adventure? It's part of why I had such a crush on you when we were kids. I loved your stories. I just," she said, sitting back wistfully, "I know it sounds crazy, but I wish I was strong and tough enough to go with you. But from everything I've heard about Erentyr, I think I'd die in five minutes. Especially if I had to hurt someone to save myself."

His smiled faded. "Mia, you *don't* want to go there. Trust me."

She nodded, downcast. "Yeah, of course you're right." She clacked the silverware absent-mindedly, eyes following the metal. "I wouldn't last a day there."

"There's a lot I never told you about Erentyr. I would never want to plunge you into that world." He pinched the bridge of his nose, a headache brewing. Was he seriously considering this? He nodded to himself. "All right. I'll at least hear him out. Right after work, tomorrow."

Her eyes met his. "I'm in the area tomorrow afternoon. I'll go with you. Would that be ok?"

He regarded her quietly. "It would be an honor, Mia."

She held out a fist. "Friends always?"

The seriousness of what he was about to consider overpowered him. But he swallowed his misgivings, powering through the growing dread. His eyes drifted to the knuckles where he struck the martial arts robot. Dark hunger moved within, but he didn't show it. He tapped her fist with his. "Friends always."

Chapter 5

Liam did not sleep that night. Any time his eyes closed, his mind churned. If he began to drift off, the image of the Woodsman erupted in his head and his eyes popped open. He stared at the Dream Stone in the dim red light and sighed. *I think I liked it better when I was numb all the time.*

Exhausted, he arrived at his workplace in the data complex of ComCorps City 335 the next day already on his third cup of coffee, the forest of repeating grey concrete skyscrapers cluttering the morning skyline visible through the windows, bleak and dull. Drained from shaking off the images of last night, the weight of what he was considering bore down on him that much harder. He barely noticed the maze of identi-plan buildings running with flocks of NW-d85 drones, analyzing traffic patterns and making deliveries to the pneumatic system. At the entrance to his office, he stopped before the hallway garbage disposal. A solution to all this slunk into his mind. He took the Dream Stone and held his hand over the opening. *Drop it in. Get rid of it.* With a turn of his wrist, he would never be bothered by the Stone again. Life would go back to normal.

But the image of his mother flashed, kneeling in pain to hand him the Stone. *Bring it back to me, or our homeland will be destroyed.* He bit his lip. He stood rigid, glaring at the disposal, wrestling with a giant inside. Too strong for him. He couldn't do it.

He closed his scarred fist and pocketed the Stone. "This isn't healthy," he muttered. *Think only healthy thoughts,* he repeated inwardly, executing the cognitive exercises he'd learned at the Childcare Plex. *Bad feelings come from incorrect cognitions.* He pushed through the drills, but that offered no comfort. As he walked through the bustling work area, he thought he saw something out of the corner of his eye in the window reflection. A snarl of canines under a seven-layered hood. His head whipped to the wall of windows. No. Just another drone floating by. He let out a weary breath.

A voice snapped him out of his reverie — his co-worker, a paunchy, well-dressed man named Danny eating a chocolate muffin. He suppressed an eyeroll. Today would be difficult enough without Danny's nonsense. At least he was consistent. He'd always been there. *Like sock odor in a gym.* Back at the window, the drone was gone.

"Hey Wonderboy." Danny clicked on his computer in his cubicle, "new boss wants to see you."

People milled around him, tapping their tablets. He swallowed and tried to forget about the Woodsman. "Dude. Wonderboy? You realize you killed the joke."

Danny chuckled and Liam smiled, then Danny indicated with his eyes for him to go to the elevator. "Better just go see the boss, he's asked about you twice."

"Wait, *the* boss? Mr Raythera? Top floor?"

"Yeah. Didn't I just say that? Come on, man, don't get distracted on me. He didn't say what it was about. Congratulations."

He sighed. "Yippee."

Liam started for the elevator but activity in the back caught his eye. Four police officers questioned his coworkers, coffee mugs steaming. Why were they here? A chill permeated his thoughts. Maybe they caught wind of his antics at the gym. It *was* illegal, after all. They made their way toward him. Maybe he could slip out unseen. The doors were not easily reachable, and the cops were closing in. They stopped Danny and murmured, and Danny pointed at him. He gulped and turned, trying to play it off.

"Sir!" one of the cops called.

Liam walked toward the elevator, pretending not to hear.

"Sir, Mr Panregon, a word?"

He froze. He was cooked. How many counts of tampering with CC335rp trainers? Violating safety precautions? He turned and mustered a smile. "Yessir?"

But the man was talking on his comlink. "Say again, ma'am?" He indicated for Liam not to go anywhere, sipping and listening.

Liam's heart pounded but he stayed put. He looked the cops over. *Actually ... I'm pretty sure I can take 'em. Probably only need about five strikes and a knee.* He pinched the bridge of his nose. *Damn it, Liam, what the hell? Stop.*

"Yes ma'am, Ms Papilio-Castor," said the cop. "Roger that." He put away the comlink. "False alarm. You enjoy the rest of your day, Mr Panregon."

Discomfort tightened his throat. "Sure. Will do, sir." He saw himself out of the office and into the hallway. What was that all about? He didn't have time to ponder it. He still had Mr Raythera's Dream Stone in his pocket and was supposed to meet him right away. *Should I hide it before I visit him? Damn it! Why did I break the rules with that stupid robot?* He glanced at his cubicle, where he worked every day inserting product placements into mainstream media entertainments. He was going to lose his job. What would Mia say about that? Maybe he should give the Dream Stone back to Mr Raythera. His mother's eyes flashed in his mind. He stiffened. No way. He headed toward the elevators.

***

Liam fidgeted with the Dream Stone in his jacket pocket as he waited for the elevator to reach the top floor — Mr. Raythera's office. His heart raced, but he forced a calm exterior, though his palms sweated. This Dr Morderan had put him in a terrible position. *I should hand it right over to him, along with Dr Morderan's information.* Violating the Magnolent's Mandate bore steep penalties. Much steeper than tampering with martial arts robots. If he chose poorly today, he could be locked up in a Containment Facility for the rest of his life. He was lucky enough to have been released from the mental hospital as it was. That freedom had felt good, allowing him to live a normal life. He gripped the Stone tighter. It was normal, wasn't it?

Bring it back to me, or our homeland will be destroyed.

His head ached. The top floor was near. He breathed deeply.

Ding!

He entered the office of Damien Dromenhar Raythera, Magnolent of ComCorp City 335. The office was cavernous and immaculate, with giant windows that overlooked the city and tasteful Realplastic™ plants placed perfectly. Cloudy skies splattered rain upon the windows and patio beyond as his Grace stood tall and powerful in a perfectly tailored suit. He sipped his coffee, gazing out the window, gently tapping the glass.

Liam entered and stood quietly before the massive desk that separated them. Mr Raythera's computers and stacks of papers sprawled about its expanse. Liam's insides crackled with nervousness, and it took effort to smooth out his ragged breathing. He let go of the Dream Stone and clasped his hands before him respectfully, waiting for the Magnolent to finish gazing into the distance.

Far to the left, the CC335h tram track peeked through a light canopy, the occasional white oval car coursing toward the distant aspen grove on the far side of Cauldron Lake where the sparsely populated new living quarter was. For a long while Damien stared, not through the glass door, but seemingly at his own reflection, shifting his face left and right. His chiseled image floated before the scenery beyond. He swept his long fingers through his blond hair. "It strikes me as odd that we have not met in person before, Liam 'Trendari' Panregon."

The use of his Erentyrian name struck him off-balance. "Indeed, your Grace."

A distant helicopter caught Damien's eye. "After all, of the free people on this earth, only you and I have actual first-hand experience of Erentyr. Everyone else only knows about it from books."

That was interesting. Did Mr Raythera not know about Dr Morderan? Surely not, if this Stone was stolen. That proved it. Liam forced himself to stay cool. "Quite so, your Grace. Video equipment doesn't work in Erentyr, after all, does it?"

"Indeed not. It's been five years now since I went there as part of the Magnolent Mandate. But for you it's been fifteen, hasn't it?"

"Yes sir."

Damien set down his cup and turned to him. Liam gave his best poker-face and stood straight and still. Mr Raythera brushed something from his lapel, then gazed at him squarely. "So much death ... by now I'm sure you know your mother is gone, too."

Is she, though? He blinked, forcing a pleasant smile. "May she rest in peace."

"It would seem the chaos and evil of that world spared you no pain," he continued. "I can't imagine *anyone* longing to return there. But it has happened to many. That is why we try never to use the Stones, you see. We have found that Erentyr has a way of seducing people. Making you think that suffering and torment can be good things," he said, chuckling indignantly. "The allure of Erentyr is very powerful. But, of course, it leads to nothing but misery."

Liam's smile faded. It seemed he already knew everything. "Well I have no such insane desires, your Grace. Compared to that world, the Magnolents have built a paradise."

Damien's eyes narrowed into a knowing smile — a bit too broad. "Few know that so well as you." Damien gestured for him to sit down. Liam did so uneasily. What was his angle? The Magnolent took a seat at his huge swivel chair behind the desk and steepled his fingers thoughtfully. "This year marks the two hundred and sixty-third year of the Magnolent Council, Liam. Hardly anyone now alive actually remembers anything about Erentyr save you and me. We were spectacularly successful in closing the gates and vaulting the stones, and it has brought us peace and prosperity." Eyes glinting, the Magnolent held up his hand; his left palm was scarred, just like Liam's. "My expedition was the last. And like you, I had to brave the dragon to pass the gate."

Liam remembered that day all too well. He shivered involuntarily but clamped down on it immediately. The day the dragon bit him, injecting the venom that tested his young life and nearly snuffed it out. He nodded in pleasant agreement but suppressed a squint. Sure he survived Drelthun the dragon, but was Damien a 9-year-old boy when he did it? He stiffened against such anger. He needed to hold it together. "Nothing quite like the agony, is there, your Grace?"

Damien shook his head. An almost imperceptible shiver coursed up him as well. "Certainly not. And yet we both lived, unlike most." Mr Raythera frowned, giving Liam a cold chill. "And it was worse than when you left. A curse has befallen the land of your birth."

Liam raised his eyebrows and looked at the table, feigning disinterest. Dr Morderan mentioned something like that. "A curse, your Grace?"

"Indeed. It seems the Unseelie King himself decided to cover the kingdom of Kaledon in his choking Fairywilds. Devouring the lands from one end to the other. Pushing out those loyal to the Fairy Queen. Does it bother you to hear this?" asked the Magnolent, genuine pity in his eyes.

Liam hated pity.

His pulse and temperature were rising. Dr Morderan hadn't lied, it seemed. "No, your grace," he said, fighting off the grip of bitterness, "I barely remember it. I mean, it's sad to hear all that, but what do you expect from that world?"

Mr Raythera nodded, leaning back and crossing his arms. "Well you certainly don't seem like you want to return. Which is why your recent behavior at the gym-plex is most puzzling."

Bingo. Liam lifted his eyes to meet Mr Raythera's, his heart jumping. "Oh that?" He laughed nervously. Just what *did* the Magnolent know? He swallowed. Raythera had access to the city's Nexwork. Surely he knew. "Just a lark, your Grace. An overzealous moment. Here." He retrieved the NW3 quickdrive from the pocket that also held the Dream Stone and slid it across the desk. "This is how I did it. I'm returning it to you in good faith. Won't happen again."

Raythera snatched it with fine-honed reflexes. He looked it over and glanced at him. His eyes fixed upon him for an uncomfortably long while. Liam licked his lips, mouth suddenly dry.

"The Magnolent Mandate is absolute, Liam. You know that."

"Your Grace, I—"

He stopped Liam with a raised finger. "It's only because of your history that we're concerned. In any other case, I'd chalk it up to mere mischief. But you're different. You were the last refugee from Erentyr in generations. That's why I asked you here. To judge you myself. So I have your word that you have no interest in returning to Erentyr? Seeing the Dream Stone?"

That was the question, wasn't it? Liam mustered the most relaxed smile he could, crushing the firestorm inside him with sheer will. Now it came to it. Telling the Magnolent of the City about the stolen Stone was the right thing to do. He knew that. Lying about it would get him locked up forever. More importantly, it was the morally right choice. Erentyr *was* dangerous and locking away its insidious influence *had* allowed the Magnolents to build a better world.

And yet … putting his faith into the mysterious Dr Morderan might wind up giving him the only chance he ever had to see his mother again, where as a child he failed to protect her. He *owed* it to her.

Bring it back to me.

Liam smiled nervously and spread his hands about him. "Your Grace, why on earth would I want to return to the place that almost killed me?"

Mr Raythera regarded him intensely for a long moment, forcing Liam to control his breathing. Smoothly in, smoothly out. Then the Magnolent nodded, pocketing the NW3 and smiling. "Good. I'll set aside any legal action. Have no fear of that."

A huge relief. "Thank you, your Grace."

They sat in silence for a moment, eyes locked.

"That will do, then," said Mr. Raythera. "You are free to return to your floor. And do try to stay out of trouble, this time. I won't be able to protect you again."

Liam stood up and nodded. "You won't have to, your Grace. I promise." He whirled and left, the Dream Stone nearly pulsing in his mind, his pace even and measured, despite wanting to run.

He could scarcely believe what he had just done. He entered the elevator, nodding one last time to Mr Raythera. The doors closed and he let out a huge, exasperated sigh. Why did he have to do everything the hard way? Now there was no time to decide what to do. He paced the elevator, tapping his knuckles absent-mindedly. He took out his Nexwork-d. He had to meet with Dr Morderan. Now. Before Raythera realized he had the Dream Stone. He texted Mia.

***

Damien Raythera leaned back in his chair and sipped coffee as he watched Liam leave through the elevator. The patio beyond the balcony sprawled beyond the sliding glass door into a manicured lawn high among the city skyscrapers. The distant aspen grove caught his eye again, removing him from the reverie. That's where they found him as a boy. Broken and permanently damaged. Even now. He smiled and shook his head. *I should have known, even you wouldn't be so stupid to return to that shithole of a world.*

A presence crept into his awareness.

One he had not felt in many years. He slowed instinctively and straightened, alert.

A rumbling voice seemingly emerged into the room — inhumanly deep, its source invisible, resonating. Deeply unsettling. "I findeth myself disappointed, Damien Dromenhar," said the voice, "in thy slipping resolve."

Icy prickles crept up his spine at that name. None called him 'Dromenhar' but those from Erentyr. How many years had it been since he'd heard that name? He scrunched his nose at it. It nearly made him vomit.

He cleared his throat, scanning the room. He could never get used to the way Remembering Ones were invisible in Midworld. "Good morning, Drelthun. Good to hear your melodious voice again." The hand which had suffered the dragon's bite pulsed softly. He forced it to stop shaking. What the hell was the gate guardian doing here? "To what do I owe this pleasure?" He sipped coffee.

"Thy recent visitor. Didst thou know he possessed the last Dream Stone?"

"Don't be ridiculous." He laughed shakily. "We confiscated it from him the moment he arrived here fifteen years ago. I've had it ever since."

"So certain art thou?"

He furrowed his brow, smile fading. Drelthun was always difficult, but he knew when the dragon was being serious. *Something* prompted the being to speak to him again after all these years, after all. That *never* happened without a dire need. Blood drained from his face. "Why are you asking me this, Drelthun?"

"For thou art deceived."

His pulse raced. Now his status as Magnolent was in question? The idea! But being a Remembering One — in their own language, a Kosithi — Drelthun never lied. Damien swept to his computer and logged into his files on Liam. He opened the data on his recent medical encounters — no Dr Morderan, but something urged him on. He ran a changelog dedicated to account admin. Dr Morderan's account had been there, but was then deleted! *What trickery is this?*

His expression tightened. Something about Liam's behavior *had* been off. He recounted the meeting. He charged to the back elevator beyond the fireplace in his office and took it to his basement. He crossed his arms and tapped impatiently as the elevator dropped onto his private floor — a cool, dim complex of chambers in brown concrete. Almost running, he went to the vault where he kept the precious Dream Stone. His jaw ground, his pulse rising. He opened the vault.

There, where the Stone had been, now sat a silver grinning skull.

"Morderan!"

This evoked a bone-rattling growl from the Unseelie dragon. "I told thee before. The good doctor ... treacheroussss. He hath stolen it to undo thy good works."

"Indeed," he said, rushing back upstairs. "I don't know how he did it, but he did. Damn!" He opened up the command panels for the city Nexwork grids back at his desk. "I bet Panregon had it on him! That's why he looked so nervous. Only a Dream Stone would inspire such behavior."

"What wilt thou do of it, mortal?"

He paced, hands behind his back. The Dream Stone was under *his* charge. If it went missing, the Magnolent Council would hold him responsible. "Morderan will teach him to open the Gate. I'm not letting that happen on my watch."

He went to the sliding glass door as his computers powered up. "Why would the Fairy Queen choose him for this?" he asked, more to himself than Drelthun.

"Mayhap, the Queen seeth in him some strength," said the dragon.

He snorted. "He is the broken son of an enslaved people. What has he proven but that he is weak and insignificant? I alone was able to journey into that world unscathed," he added slowly, those old emotions stirring in him again. Feelings he thought he had buried since he escaped Erentyr. Rage. Bloodlust. Intoxicating élan. He mastered himself. "She would choose *Liam* to champion this cause against me?" He scoffed. "What a waste. Damn that Morderan! Curse that old man to hell."

"Morderan is no man, Damien." Damien felt a sudden chill. "He is far more than he appeareth. He hath sought long of a twelvemonth before he came to thee, seeking the Stone."

Damien punched his scarred palm hard in frustration. "Indeed. He no doubt has the Fairy Queen Alyia's help."

"E'en so," said the beast, his voice now seeming to invigorate the very air around Damien with more intense colors when the creature spoke. Sharper contrasts. Richer tones. "And so again, I asketh thee — what wilt thou do on't?"

Damien scowled at the computer screen. "The Mandate is absolute." He felt as if teetering on a tightrope. His reputation was in question! To a Magnolent, was *anything* more valuable? "There's no time for an official report." His jaw tensed, his heart thundering, not only with anger at being lied to, but outrage at the imminent danger to the Magnolent cause. "I have no choice but to act unilaterally. Liam is a fool. Nevertheless ... I can't risk him fleeing Midworld with the Stone. It was too hard won for us."

He opened the tram controls on his desktop and looked down at the hub. Liam was likely heading to the aspen grove via the tram. He would need to make it look like an accident, then cover up his tracks. Then he could retrieve the Stone himself, and that would be the end of it.

The Unseelie dragon laughed slowly, seemingly sensing his plan, then his unsettling presence disappeared.

Damien let out a ragged breath. Murder in Erentyr was one thing. This was different. But the bastard lied right to his face. He brought all this on himself. He recalled the day he took up the mantle of Magnolent from his father. No duty greater than the Mandate. And as one of the Council of Magnolents, Midworld's safety, and the integrity of the World Democratic Union depended on it. He calmed himself and let ice trickle into his veins. He shook his head. *The ends justify the means.*

He began clicking furiously.

Chapter 6

Liam brushed through the bustling, glass-enclosed station on the outer preserve of C-City. The crosswalk overlooked the large plate-glass windows of a central hub in the data processing quarter. Hypo-allergenic air breezed past him as he frowned at the buzzing activity on the close-cut lawns below. Sunlight glinted off Raythera tower, which overlooked the hub from high above, temporarily blinding him. He shouldered through waiting customers distracted by their Nexwork-d devices under the shadows of the criss-crossing tram tracks. One man, about his age, looked up at him as he passed by, squeezing his Raythera emotional support robot. The strange conversation with the Magnolent ran through his mind as he leaned against a concrete column to wait for his tram. Why didn't he just hand him the Stone? Stay out of trouble?

But he knew why. The image of his mother emerged, blood-stained, green eyes stern but loving, weary and sad.

Dr Morderan's words churned in his mind, as did the haunting image of himself as a little boy on video. He gripped the Stone in his scarred palm within the pocket of his jacket. He had to be sure his entire life in Midworld had not been a lie … he shivered. That he hadn't abandoned his homeland and his mother. He closed his eyes and let out a sharp breath.

The digital sign flashed above him as his tram neared. He marched toward the entry point, but Mia came seemingly out of nowhere behind him. "Liam! Thank goodness I didn't miss you." She touched his arm to keep him from moving away. He stopped in his tracks.

"Mia. You got my text."

She wore the very blouse and turquoise jewelry she had in the picture he constantly mooned over. It was so good to see her.

"Yeah, sorry I didn't respond right away. Flustered, I guess," she laughed nervously. A CC335 hx tram car whooshed quietly above them.

She absent-mindedly rubbed the skin "perfections" on her arms. "So what happened with Mr. Raythera?"

The gravity of what he had to do punched him in the chest. He raised his eyes to her. The wind blew her hair back, and he lingered on her brilliantly dark eyes shining behind her glasses — the bittersweetness of her presence stung deeply. It dawned on him. Now there was no escaping it. He would have to either leave her here or face a life sentence.

She pursed her lips to one side, hands in her jeans pockets. "That's a very concerning look, Liam."

He tugged at his beard, releasing a weary breath. He wanted to caress her cheek but thought better of it. "Remember our conversation at the restaurant?" She blinked and nodded slowly. "I ... didn't tell Mr Raythera that I had the Stone."

She looked around as the tram approached. "You *lied* to him?" she whispered.

A pang of sadness hit him. "You don't know what it means to me that you support my going back there. I have to see if my mother really is still alive."

She nodded, a sad smile on her face. "If my grandmother still lived and she needed me, I know you'd support me, too."

"You're damn right," he said, holding out a fist. "I'd go there *for* you. Friends always."

She half smiled and tapped it with her fist. "Always."

The tram car arrived and the automated door opened. He hopped in. "You coming along?"

She nodded. "Dr Morderan wants to meet at the aspen grove. He's on his way — we should get there first."

He took one last glance at Raythera tower and the garden patio high above them and entered the tram behind her. With a wobble they left the station. Liam settled into the familiar terrain of the tram car. The plastic-steel compartments and screen tables, velour padded seats and sterile conditioned air were comfortable and bland, but the air was pregnant with tension.

Mia chewed her lip, deep in thought. Her eyes searched, as if playing chess against a master-level bot. He knew that look. "So I guess this means you're really going through with this."

He nodded, wrinkling his brow. He stared at the Stone. So familiar. A dozen bloody images threatened to force their way into his mind. He clamped down on muscles that threatened to shake, locking himself into a tense stare. "You going to try to talk me out of it?" he asked, half hoping she would. As if to answer himself, he added, "I'm not a coward, you know. I'll do it."

She put a hand on his, locking her mahogany eyes on him. "There's courage, and there's insanity." He opened his mouth to defend himself, but her raised index finger stopped him. "This is courage." He relaxed a little, blinking at her. She turned away, eyes downcast. "Courage I wish I had myself."

He thought to object, but a flashing red light caught his eye. The tram's speed soared unnaturally. "Hmm." He got up and made his way to the front of the vehicle. The speed increased.

"Incoming transfer" popped up on a screen.

Mia followed him. "What is it?"

"What the hell?" Treetops flew by. A chill fell upon him.

"Liam? I don't like that expression. What?"

He turned to her. "This isn't right."

She looked at him sidelong as the trees blasted by. "Why...?"

"It seems like someone — or something is overriding the tram system." Scrolling through pages on his device as the car shuddered, she grabbed a stabilizing pole. Tree tops zipped past, and they dropped down a track decline, making his stomach rise before leveling and speeding toward the aspen grove. "See that curve in the track?"

She wrapped her arm around him and latched onto the pole, "Yes?"

"This tram uses the same Nexwork system the martial arts robots do. A million times I've ridden home on this tram and it's never done this." Blood ran from his face. "Mr Raythera! Damn ... he must have figured out I lied to him." He gazed at her square-on. "Mia," he whispered. "I ... think we're in big trouble." He growled. "I should have just handed him the Stone."

She curled her lip in horror, eyes wide. "You don't think he would—"

"He's authorized to use deadly force to secure Midworld. Why didn't I give him the Stone?" Guilt crushed him. Alarms buzzed, and the computer screens blared "malfunction."

She scanned the controls, utterly lost, searching, reading. "Isn't there some way to stop it?"

He scrambled with his Nexwork-d, trying to hack into the server somehow. Impossible. Her face went wan. She chewed a strand of black hair, eyes darting, and a death grip on the standing bar. This was going to hurt. A lot.

But he would be damned if he was going to let any wreckage or debris touch her. He pulled them both close to the beeping, shuddering front panel and braced for impact, another tear trickling down his enraged jaw. "So sorry, Mia," he whispered into her hair. "I...I..." He couldn't say it. She shrank into his embrace, terrified.

"I know, Liam," she whispered back.

***

The brakes slammed. They bashed into the front. Debris, equipment, and bottles crashed around them as the car tore from the track. Noise exploded all around them. A brief silence followed as they floated, alarms cut off, the car hurtling. Then impact thundered — a chaotic swirl of blows, tumbling, burning, tearing. He roared as his body was slashed and hammered. He shielded Mia, until his head crashed into something solid and darkness overtook him.

***

The sound of his Nexwork-d buzzing woke him up. Pain tore through his body. Sunlight settled upon the lake shore, now scattered with burning debris. Rust-tang spread through his mouth. His clothes were torn and bloody, but in his embrace Mia's body lay still — but she was breathing! Blood trickled from her nose. Welts and cuts covered their skin from pummeling, glasses shattered, and on her bare stomach, between tears of her blouse, rested the Dream Stone.

Liam struggled to a sitting position as the lapping sound of the shore permeated the air, small flames crackling in the wind. The aspen trees flittered above them, autumn leaves circling in the smoke. Images swirled in his mind unbidden. His strong brother Rendan, the oldest, run through with a spear. An arrow striking his swift, brown-haired brother Arran; huge gashes through the twins Declan and Aidan. His huge brother, the dark-bearded Banner, gutted after killing three men, and the musical Ewan, smashed in the head. All dead from the purges that *he* survived.

He sat up, shaking, coughing up blood, terror pummeling his head, dazed. He cried out, head in his forearm, as if trying *not* to see what his mind forced him to see. He grasped the Stone, and found his hand was cut the exact same way it had been years ago as a child. His breathing ragged, he focused on the Stone and forced the storm to calm enough to think more clearly. Mia needed him! He checked again. Still breathing. That was something. Blood continued to pound in his neck and sweat dripped down his cheek. He blinked at his mobile device — still ringing. Strange that it survived with only a cracked screen. He answered it, his vision too blurry to tell who it was.

"Liam?" said Dr Morderan. "Are you there?"

He turned the device to speaker and cleared his throat. "Doctor," he rasped, "Raythera discovered us … tried to kill us."

"Fie on't! He is a sciolist and a crookback! Where are you now?"

"We crashed by the aspen grove." He spat blood. "Mia and I…" He winced with pain in his stomach. "He may have killed us yet."

"Mia is with you?"

"Yes, she's hurt!" Nothing else mattered. He pulled her into his arms, cupping her scraped face. She breathed weakly. Probably bleeding internally. He looked up at the tram track — a long fall at maximum speed. "She's dying."

"Liam, hearken to me. Damien is not playing games. Willing to kill for the Stone. He should hang by the scrag! But never mind that. You need to get out of there. You can use the Stone to escape. It's a strange fate that made Damien try to kill you here. Use the Stone and go through the gate."

"I don't remember how to use it!"

"Liam, Damien's men will be there any minute. Don't be twiggy. He wants the Dream Stone. But the Stone is the only way out of this, now. No questions!"

The shore was quiet with manicured forest and walking paths, the smoking wreckage in the clearing. Then distant sirens wailed, and … a helicopter? He shook the blurriness out. Across the lake — at Raythera's mansion — a boat sped toward them along with airborne drones. They would be there in mere minutes. Vans sped along the old road by the lake as well. He angrily tried to force himself to stop shaking and was minimally successful.

"Liam? You still with me? Talk to me, lad."

"I'm here. All right. I have to try. So all I do is close my eyes," he winced as pain tore through his flank, "and picture the opening of the gate while holding the Stone, and that's it?"

"Aye, that's it."

This is madness. It had taken Mom years to master this. He strained to remember the stories of how she did this. The sound of the aircraft grew louder.

"What will they do with Mia?" He wiped more blood from his eyes.

An uneasy silence. "Best not to worry about that."

He snarled. "That's all I needed to know. I'm taking her with me."

"Hold on, now, lad. There are some things you don't know yet. Get yourself out of there. Leave Mia. EMS will tend to her — Damien's got no quarrel with her. She wasn't the target — you were. They'll only kill you and cover it up. That's what they do to those they can't 'rehabilitate'."

"Then they'll kill her just as sure! There's no way I'm risking it."

But taking her to Erentyr of all places might be even worse! *Damn!* He placed his Nexwork device on her stomach and scooped his aching arms beneath her small body, refusing to rush despite Raythera nearing.

He took a deep breath and summoned every ounce of his strength to stand, Mia in his arms. Pain wracked every limb. He probably had multiple fractures. He clutched the Dream Stone in his fist and faced the upward slope of the aspen grove opposite the shore. Speckled trees towered above him, interspersed with bare, jagged rocks where a gentle fog still lingered over the autumn leaves. "You'd better be right about this, doctor. Tell me what to do."

"Go to the edge of the grove, right near the shore."

"I'm almost there." He hobbled toward the misty lake, straining to carry her. Sirens blared louder.

"Now use the Stone," said Morderan, his voice excited, like a scientist on the brink of discovery. "Close your eyes and focus your mind, as I told you before, facing the grove itself."

He pulled Mia closer and clutched the Stone. He closed his eyes, trying to picture — what? A circle? A square? An old barn door? He opened his eyes. Nothing. He sighed in frustration. "It's not working!" He suppressed a panic attack, holding a fist to his forehead. "I'll try again!"

He closed his eyes, but the sirens and sounds of the boat tearing across the lake broke his concentration. Mia's breathing became more ragged. He opened his eyes.

Still nothing.

"Doc? This is starting to look like a good time to freak out, man. You better talk to me!"

"No, no, lad, you're too stressed right now. Try to focus through that."

"How?" Pain threatened to cause his knees to buckle as the siren-blare rose.

"The Stone was given to you by your mother. Focus on that."

That was true. Ynwin's tired, thoughtful eyes glinted in the purple glow-fly light of the Fairywild in his memory. An odd tingle swept up his body. "All right. I'll try again."

Liam closed his eyes and breathed deep, pushing through the pain ... through the sirens blaring ... through the oncoming helicopters and the drones and the boat. The feel of the Stone and his mother's hand covering his returned to pierce the chaos. Her gentle touch, the weary wisdom-lines around her green eyes settling upon his young face. This was that very Stone indeed — in another life. From before, when he lived in that *other* place.

A sudden wave of élan ignited his spirit, flying through him like a mischievous wind.

He opened his eyes.

Before Liam stood a perfect circle of mist, wound in a swirling knotwork design. Some ten feet in diameter it opened into a circular tunnel of moss-covered blue stone that led, after fifty or so feet, to a dark place.

He swallowed. "Whoa, Jesus! Doctor?"

"You did it, didn't you, Liam?" asked Morderan, "You see it, don't ye?"

"Yeah, I see it." He nearly laughed hysterically. "I see it!"

"Good! We don't have time to chit-chat about it. Now go in. Don't let Raythera get hold of the Stone."

"That rat bastard can pound sand." He stepped closer to the gate, marveling at both the solidity and translucence of the misty cords that created the opening.

"Now. Since you insist on taking Mia, know this, lad. You'll be able to heal her with the Dream Stone once you cross the threshold. But beware the dragon. Drelthun may not let her pass."

He looked down at Mia's unconscious body. Blood trickled from the side of her mouth. "Wait, what do you mean 'heal' her?"

"The Dream Stone has healing properties in Erentyr, lad. Use it on her. Don't worry about your own wounds — remember your scar? You were bitten by Drelthun. It just didn't kill you ... ach! If I only had time to explain it all — here I am again, only able to pray for you. But hearken, you can heal her with the Stone, but the dragon blood that flows in your veins will heal you. Follow?"

His head swam. "What? You realize how ludicrous that all sounds?" And yet, he *did* remember the bit about the Stone being able to heal from the old days. The sirens wailed louder — they would be here in mere seconds.

He bent to pick up Mia. Her chest was still. "Oh, shit! I'm losing her, Morderan!"

The copper-tone of her scraped skin paled. "I'm not leaving you here." He limped toward the Dream Gate, pushing through the pain. Behind him helicopter blades roared and sirens crooned. Vehicles scrambled along the lake road directly behind him.

He took a deep breath and stepped through the gate.

He nearly lost his footing on the wet stone, for the air immediately changed — lighter, clearer, sharper. The stone tunnel lit strangely from within, and not from the daylight behind. A surge of power flowed into him, burning from his scarred hand into the rest of his body. Everything whitened over. Then he was back in the tunnel with Mia in his arms. His suit was gone, replaced with a wool tunic with belt, large wolf pelt resting on his shoulders, a claymore sheathed in a baldric atop it. Mia's clothes had changed as well — gone were the jeans and shirt, replaced with a skillfully hand-made side-fold, double fringed sheepskin dress with elk teeth sewn into buckskin, and on it were brightly colored diamond and animal designs. Upon her shoulder was slung an empty leather satchel. She still was not breathing. He furrowed his brow at the ancient clothing.

He knelt down gently and vehicles drove into view from the gate behind. The boat neared the shore and helicopters and drones coursed beside.

Instinctively, he took the cut hand that held the Dream Stone and placed it on her stomach. The Stone hummed with warmth — unlike before. He breathed in deep, pouring his will into the idea — somehow — of healing her. It seemed insane, and yet natural, in the way insane things seem normal in a dream, only he was not dreaming.

He felt like an idiot. Was this right? He needed to hurry. She still wasn't moving! His heart raced. He steadied his hand and held it there as the vehicles screeched to a halt. Then burning coursed through his hand from the now hot Stone and flowed into her body. He felt her spirit, then, along with the life-force within her body. The power of the Stone did not touch her spirit, however. He puzzled over that as the power pulsed and whirled into her. His eyes widened and he gritted his teeth, holding the Stone in place.

She gasped for air, her eyes opening wide as she coughed and groaned, as if shocked by paddles. Liam held her close and laughed almost hysterically. "You're alive! You're alive! Thank..."

"God?" she said, smiling at him weakly.

He caressed her forehead, sweeping away waves of black hair. "God, the Cookie Monster, anyone will do!" She laughed, then winced in pain, but she smiled through it. So good to see her alive! Past the Dream Gate, security personnel hopped out of an ambulance and headed toward them as Damien's yacht neared the shore. "Come on, let's get out of here. Can you stand?"

She struggled to her feet, flexing her hands before her. "I think? Wait, what is this place? Where are we?" She puzzled over her dress.

He shook his head. "Remember our plan for me to enter Erentyr alone? Well..."

"What is that?" she narrowed her eyes on the Dream Gate and the curious light effect — the Lakeshore now seemed distant, and the sunlight did not illuminate the tunnel. Her eyes tracked to the other end, where the tunnel opened into a large, dark chamber of stone.

"Come on, no time to explain." He offered his arm, not trusting the healing.

She nodded, blood trickling from her nose, as the impeccably dressed Damien exited his boat and approached, pistol in hand. Armed drones and security forces followed him.

"Don't do this, Liam!" shouted Damien, the sun reflecting on his sunglasses. Damien's men approached apprehensively, uneasiness in their eyes. "There's no hope where you're headed. Erentyr will only kill you both."

He glared at the man who had nearly murdered them. Mia snarled at him weakly, like a wounded wolf. Damien's men raised their rifles. Liam and Mia shrunk back.

"Don't be idiots," Raythera told his men, "your weapons can't pierce the gate." They complied. "Your mother's dead, Liam. There is no reason for you to keep that Stone. Give it back and I won't pursue you."

Liam opened his palm. His mother's Dream Stone was now cool to touch after healing Mia. Curious. Nevertheless, the Stone still seemed to whisper through his blood. Mom once spoke of the bond the Dream Stone had on her. She was given a great task to do with it. She was *not* dead, and she *needed* this Stone. He could feel it.

Bring it back to me.

He shook his head. "Sorry, your grace. I'm out. Have a good life." They limped down the glowing blue tunnel.

"Fool!" shouted Damien. "After them, now!" he commanded. His security forces charged forth, but a rumbling growl emanated from within, causing even Damien to halt in his tracks. "Stand down," he muttered, "don't move." The men froze in place, squinting into the shadows beyond the dark tunnel opposite the gate. Blackness yawned and a cool wind tossed Liam's hair back. The rumbling growl rose, sending creeping, crawling sensations along his body.

Drelthun.

Within the blackness beyond the dripping stone tunnel of bricks, in a dark expanse of a chamber, barely visible in the dim light, two malevolent purple slits opened, glowing in a reptilian gaze within a pitch-black silhouette, huge and looming. The slow breathing of a massive beast silenced all else.

Mia's eyes widened in horror. She gripped his arm tightly.

Liam stood his ground. With Mia here, his own terror shoved down. He took her hand, stood slightly ahead of her and glared hard into the darkness. Huge eerie eyes stared back. Liam and Mia stood like taut springs, locked between certain death behind them, and uncertain death before them. His heart hammered against his chest.

A huge gaping maw opened, the same unsettling glow emanating from within the creature. The dragon leered at them hungrily, causing the mercenaries to shuffle backward.

"Come back, Liam," whispered Damien. "I will grant you mercy. Drelthun will not. You know this."

Liam set his jaw and glanced at Mia. She was pale with terror and sweat formed beads beaded on her forehead. Her nostrils flared with fast breathing. But she nodded at him, already knowing what he was thinking.

He returned with a slow nod of his own and took a step forward. Dozens of memories, flashes of death, and spikes of burning horror blasted him from within like a hurricane, nameless, faceless. Blood dripped from his nose, and a massive pain wrenched his head. The smell, feel, and wind of this place hadn't touched him in fifteen years. It all flooded back. He pushed on. "Come on, Mia," he said as they walked together, voice quivering but persistent. "Welcome to Erentyr. Let me introduce you to the guardian of the Gate."

Mia glanced back. Damien had entered the tunnel, now clad in a polished coat of heavy mail, with an ice-blue brigandine over top. On his shoulders hung a fur-lined traveling cloak, and at his hip hung an exquisite arming sword, gauntleted fist preparing to draw it, its metal far richer than the sword Liam carried. But Damien did not attack. He stood still, seemingly awaiting the dragon some fifty paces away. Behind him the Dream Gate already wavered — his men too terrified to follow him. He cast a disdainful glance at them but said nothing, apparently waiting for Liam and Mia, eyes locked on them like a predator.

The breath of the beast clouded the chamber of blue stones, tangible shadowstuff swirling in the air. The ground shook with the great creature's shifting, the beast's form silhouetted in the torchlight. Liam and Mia entered a centrally lit area of the high chamber, where red light beamed down.

"Who dareth to enter my gate house?" rumbled the dragon, his reptilian face shifting up — he seemed to loom some thirty feet above them now.

Within Liam pounded decades of fury and horror. For so long, Erentyr had been a nightmare haunting his past — but only that. Now he was here again, after so long; Mia counting on him. The brave little boy who faced this beast long ago stood full grown now. Had the years made him any stronger? "You k-know me, Drelthun," said Liam, holding up his hand. "I passed your test, even as a boy."

"That is true. But that woman beside you — she hath not."

"She was unfairly targeted by Damien back there."

"Thy complaints concern me no more than that of a bleating goat."

Damien half smiled, but concern belied his amusement.

Liam searched his memory, trying to recall anything relevant that might help him get out of this mess. "Fine. Then what about ... the Old Ways of the Fairy Queen? Don't they matter anymore?"

The dragon narrowed its eyes upon them. Mia shrunk back. "Some still holdeth the ways of the Great Fairy Queen. What of it, young mortal?"

"It means you still owe me a boon. For passing your test of courage."

The dragon chuckled, making the crisp air reverberate. "So I do. But I shall not honor it for respect of the Old Ways, but rather because thou art interesting, Liam Panregon. As is the friend who hath chosen to join thee."

Liam pulled her closer. Interesting could mean many things — he chose not to ponder that. He glanced at Damien, who still stood at the ready. He was obviously waiting for the dragon's judgment too. Damien's eyes narrowed on them, as if to say, "the moment I get a chance you're dead."

"So," said Liam, "does that mean you'll honor my request, great dragon?"

"I shall gift thee but a single bequest. What shall it be?"

He exchanged glances with Mia, who looked too bewildered to have any ideas. He glanced at the Dream Stone. He was finally here. For better or worse. After all these years, now he had a chance to fulfil his mother's last request. His heart soared at that chance, despite the terror it evoked. Despite fear that he might be too late. Despite *everything.* But how? Where was she in this huge world? He pushed down the rising panic. *I have to start somewhere.* "We ... ask only for safe passage to the homeland of my birth: to Kaledon. So I can return this to my mother."

Drelthun laughed, thundering in their ears, practically shaking the walls. He shifted his massive frame and caused the darkness to swirl about. "So shall I grant thee as the one *single* boon. Ask for more at thy peril." The beast lifted a giant head. "Doth any object to this judgment?"

"I do not," said Damien from the tunnel, taking his hand off his sword, eyes fixed on the dragon. Behind him the Dream Gate closed, trapping all without a Dream Stone in Erentyr. "But don't worry, Liam. I'll find you anyway."

Liam gritted his teeth, neck twitching. This wasn't the time for a fight — too many variables. The dragon, the fact that Damien had superior battle-gear; Mia would be at risk. Nevertheless, he glared at the man, fists clenched, his mind clouded by fear and anger.

But the dragon laughed again, filling the chamber with darkness. Then all went black.

Chapter 7

Liam swirled wildly through a sea of blackness, battered in a fathomless nightmare. He swam hard to the surface, but the storm tossed him back under many times.

Darkness.

Pain.

High waves and sudden rains hammered him.

Then he found his feet. They were small; he was a little boy, running along the beach. The crisp, salty breeze of the ocean triggered a tidal wave of memories that flew through his mind. He stood on the shore among the black-rock sea stacks. Behind were the crannogs of the Shoreland people, teeming with fishmongers, herders, and traders enjoying the rare sunny day before the journey to the hilly pastures of Cwen Dreorig, where everyone would participate in the spring fire festival in less than a fortnight. Dozens of families gathered on the shores, clad in tunics tightened with leather belts; most people wrapped in cloaks of green, blue, red and other colors, trimmed with braids and clasped with brooches. Traders equipped themselves as *kerns* — light footmen, carrying axes, darts, dirks, and the occasional targ. Young Liam trailed behind his scruffy twin brothers Aidan and Declan, holding his fishing line high with a mackerel at its end, boasting of its size. Ewan played flute music as Father discussed serious matters with his two oldest brothers; thick-limbed and keen-eyed Banner and tall and eldest brother, Rendan, behind them. Father wore his fine mailcoat and arming doublet, in full gear as a Kaledonian knight, leading his horse. The second youngest, quick-legged Arran, still three years older than Liam, chased after another knight down the Snakeroot Road that led into the forest ahead.

"That's no sized fish," taunted Aidan in their native tongue of Gaelsh.

"Aye, 'tis naught but a shallows wiggler," added light-haired Declan.

Liam shrank, resentment swirling in him even as an adult.

"Lads!" snapped Father in a commanding bellow. "Don't tease your little brother, now. He's still learning."

"Yes, sir," said the twins, bowing their heads, but then sneering at Liam before pushing ahead toward Arran.

"It's plenty big," protested Liam, pressing forward in his child's body. "Some day I'll be strong as St Brendan and pull up the Choinchenn monster itself!"

"The Choinchenn hasn't been seen in the Shorelands for nearly five centuries, little red," said Mom, as if from nowhere. He looked up at her as she strode beside him, her many-wrapped cloak wafting in the salty breeze. She held out her left hand — the one which bore the Calling Brand: a tear shaped mark of interleaving swirls. Liam wiped the fish oils off his hand and took hers.

She smiled warmly at him. "Come, little red. Time to make offerings to the good folk of the forest for safe passage. Want to help?"

He shrank, glancing at the daunting forest ahead, where everyone awaited his mother to approach. The strange trees of the Tyaku woodland stood hundreds of feet tall and sprawled southward. Each trunk sprouted spiky growths, and the canopy burst with cottony pods that scattered fluffy seeds across the softly lit undergrowth. Before the Snakeroot Road, however, the roots gnarled to a stop, as if to part for it. He swallowed his fear and smiled. "Yes, Mama, I do want to help. I want to see the fairy folk."

**

The blackness faded and he found himself on the dark beach, no longer lost in memories. The surf breathed loud, sea mist hanging in the air. He wrapped himself in the wolf pelt and dusted the sand off his high-laced boots, emptiness consuming him from within. So much loss. He thought he'd accepted it. Inside felt like an old wound ripped open. His face bunched up. He hardened a fist. The moment dashed him in an icy wave, forcing the emptiness down for the moment. He was in Erentyr again, for better or worse. No turning back now. After all these years, the world of his birth opened up before him. No longer in his memory ... *out there.* Everywhere, as before when he was little. Lifting his chin, he faced southward. The horizon loomed, a jagged boundary of shadow against the midnight blue.

Mia stirred ahead of him, her breathing heavy, her body curled on the sand, long black hair a wet tangle about her.

Mia! He swept to her side, hands ready to help if she needed it. He furrowed his brow. Her birthmarks, the "skin perfections," were darker and more vivid here. And they seemed to move subtly, unless it was a trick of the dawn-light. He blinked in confusion. He reached down to her, squelching a rising panic. Everything happened so fast — she wasn't supposed to be here! He held her in his arms. She rested peacefully as indecision fluttered in him, her wounds knitted closed from the power of the Dream Stone, now cold in a sporran hanging on his belt. Before him wound the old Snakeroot Road to the ancient Fairywild they used to walk when he was a child — once in harmony with the Shorelanders of Kaledon such as his family, but now ... who knew? The road was overgrown. Forbidding mist oozed from its depths. He let Mia rest and rubbed his temples, trying to piece together what to do next. *Damn all this! She knows almost nothing of this world. I only half remember it!* He sighed. It was so long ago, and now everything had changed.

He caught his breath as dawn rose upon the new and ancient world. To the east rose the two Erentyrian suns: one large and yellow, the other smaller and red. What were their names again? Above them shineda crescent moon — all three aligned and equidistant from each other, floating over a snow-capped mountain range of islands that encircled him. Liam's aches and pains faded, and the air quelled the stitches in his side. Just as Morderan had suggested, his injuries were already beginning to heal. He opened and closed his scraped and bruised hand with the dragon-scar on it. In only a few hours they would likely be healing well. At least that was something good, even though the scrapes and cuts tingled, making him hiss; the quicker healing concentrating the pain.

He examined the sword which had fallen from his shoulder. A fine long sword, with forward leaning quillions and a ring pommel, all tempered steel, in a fur-lined baldric. He shouldered it, puzzling over its origin.

All around, the colors of grass, sky, mountain and ocean were brighter and more vivid than he remembered. It saturated his senses. The cool-warm, early autumn wind raised prickles on his skin, making his dripping red hair tickle his face. Watery life filled the air with scent, and gentle waves rushed behind. His insides quivered with electricity and his breathing quickened with the sense of danger, though there were none he could see immediately. But he was in Erentyr — the world of danger and darkness, barely remembered in Midworld. His eyes darted about, looking out for anything that could bring blood and death without warning.

Billowing clouds brought a quick thunderstorm. He let it fall on him, his massive weatherproof wolf-pelt shielding him and Mia from light rain spraying his back. His heart was pumping, on guard for attack. The sting of seawater on his scrapes and cuts barely touched his awareness. Then his heart grew cold when he saw the crannogs behind him — rotted and abandoned. The piers, where there once flourished many posts on which to tie fishing currachs, hides stretched across their bows, their square sails flapping in the sea breeze, were all gone. Empty ruins and rocks. And to the south, past the sea stacks, the forest of Tyaku loomed ominously, a crowded tangle of giant trees that towered over sprawling mushrooms and thorny branches making him shiver, for he knew he would have to enter there.

Drelthun ... bastard. The dragon had granted them passage to Kaledon, all right. But he had done them no favors returning them here. His old homestead was gone, and the dragon knew it. His blood boiled. He scanned the ruined crannogs, squinting through the mist conjured by frothing waves that crashed into the sea stacks. *I could try to scavenge for fishing gear in a crannog ... remember how to fish, maybe? That would keep her safe.* He patted a scrape on her cheek with some of his tunic. No way she would go for that. *But that's only because she grew up in Midworld — never in fear for her life. Never wanting for food or shelter.* Even thinking such things threatened to summon memories of slaughter and death. Mia was near. That's when walling himself off was most important. For her sake.

They could live in hiding, learn to survive, the Shoreland way. As much as he could remember it. It was tempting. He narrowed his brow, watching her twitching, unrestful sleep. They were going to have to figure out how to get along together here. That failed miserably in Midworld, how the hell were they going to make it work in the chaos of Erentyr?

The rain shifted. He shielded her face from it.

Suddenly she gasped and opened her eyes, sitting up, staring at him blankly.

He put a hand on her shoulder. "Mia? Are you all right?"

She wiped her eyes and breathed sharp, quick breaths, calming herself. "I–it was a dream. I dreamt of you drowning at sea. A great bird threw you into an ocean so vast... I'm glad it was just..." she trailed off, mouth agape at the vista before her. She blinked. He watched her closely. What must it be like, having never seen this place? All the years of hinted stories she'd surely heard about Erentyr. During moments of weakness, when he could share, only giving her scraps of his old life because it was so painful to speak about. She pressed him more than anyone else ever did, wanting to know more, when others were content to shrug and go back to their Nexwork devices, never even bothering to ask. That was fine with him, but Mia wanted to know. But he knew he'd done her a disservice. He had shielded her from the raids and rival kingdoms; the servants of the Unseelie King, who hated mortals and prowled the Fairywilds. And the wild beasts of Erentyr, far more terrifying than anything in Midworld. Or the sorcerers, capable of terrifying spellcrafts, possibly anywhere, spying on you with conjury, boring into your mind with magic.

She spoke, as if into the wind. "It's quite a thing to hear hints and little tidbits about something for so long, then finally see it. Feel it. Hear it. For yourself." She turned to him. "So we crossed the gate, then. We're really here?"

He nodded. "I'm afraid so. The dragon sent us here. A cruel joke."

She chewed her lip, trying to sort out what that truly meant. She swallowed, struggling to keep her breathing steady, blowing out slowly, trying to stay calm. Trembling as she spoke. "Ok. Ok. So, where are we exactly, then? I mean, so you're saying this place is your homestead in Erentyr? Th-the Shorelands?"

He let out a long breath, calming himself for her. "It was. Once. Yes."

She worked to her feet and he stood with her, the top of her head coming to his chest. She examined her dress and the marks on her skin. "What—what is this? Where did this dress come from? What's wrong with my skin?"

He furrowed his brow, taking an arm in his hands with her nonverbal permission and examining it. "Does it hurt?"

She shook her head. Her deep brown eyes were wide, dilated with fear. She must have been utterly overwhelmed. The coppery tone of her skin was pale and her chin quivered, yet she kept herself together.

"Yeah, I don't know," he replied. "Crossing the gate put me in this outfit of woolen tunic and cloak. This sword. But that dress looks more like..."

She glanced at it, puzzled. "Like traditional Newe dress. Something my Grandmother spoke about in her letters to me. Our heritage."

He nodded. "Mom always said some people *change* when they enter Erentyr for the first time. I never knew what she meant by that. As for your skin, I don't know what that means either." He swallowed, vaguely remembering a few things it *could* be, and none of them were good. He breathed in frustration. "I just don't remember."

She nodded and turned her gaze back to the Fairywilds ahead of them. "Ok. File that away for later." She turned to him. "So what happens now? Do you remember where to go from here to find your mom?"

He studied the land. "A lot is coming back to me," he said darkly, "but I was only 9 and that was fifteen years ago. It's all so different."

She tensed, obviously trying to calm herself. She laughed nervously. "Well, I *said* I wanted to come with you. Looks like I'm getting my wish — wise or not. Maybe you should tell me everything you remember as we go."

He nodded, pointing to the Snakeroot Road—more a path, now. "I ... think we have to go in there. We used to travel that road to the fire festival every spring. My mother bartered passage through the Fairywild with this," he said, showing her the Dream Stone. "She was ... bonded to it somehow. Maybe she still might be. I don't know. But I'm doubtful that having this will help *us*. If we can get through there, though, we'll be in Kaledon, and we can start looking for her."

"What will happen then?" she asked, staring at the Stone.

He shook his head. "Didn't exactly have time to plan. A lifetime ago she asked me to bring this back to her. We'll start there."

She tapped her cheek and looked up at him.

He raised an eyebrow at her. "You have that look. What is it?"

"You … said once that your home had been conquered," she said softly.

He nodded. "Yeah. I'm guessing that's one of the things Dr Morderan was going to explain to me. Like, how that all played out. He mentioned that and some kind of curse. But now, well, we're a little out of cell phone range, aren't we? So we'll have to figure this out on our own." The Dream Stone weighed in his hand; its contours smooth. Satisfyingly solid. Could he use it to find Mom? It had some healing power. Did it have any others? He closed his eyes, concentrating. He stood in self-imposed darkness, listening for anything. He opened his eyes. Trees, valley and distant rains. He went to put the Stone back in the sporran, puzzled, but then felt something. Mia watched him, calculation in her eyes, but also empathy, reading him. Somehow, as if *coming from* the Stone, he sensed a presence. The image of his mother flashed in his mind. She was alive. He could feel it!

He held it aloft, clenching it tightly. *Mother? Are you there?*

"You okay?" asked Mia.

Nothing emerged but a desperate, yearning, and sad presence. Like the last time he remembered his mother as a boy. She did not answer his thoughts. But instead of recalling the day she gave him the Stone, a new image emerged. She sat in a dark space, turned away, weeping — a woman who had lost the world. It disappeared as quickly as it came. He growled and pocketed the Stone.

Seemingly understanding the exchange, Mia gazed upon him with compassion on her face. She looked him in the eyes. "We can do this."

He gritted his teeth and nodded.

"Come on," she said with a smile. "This could be exciting. It's an entire magical world."

He returned with a grim smile. He remembered that childlike wonder. "Yeah. It is that."

They marched south together.

The huge forest loomed before them like a gaping maw, the path itself a small opening in a whorled and tangled space. She looked at it, then back at him, worry creasing her brow. Excitement melted quickly into fear in her eyes. Guilt stung him. He had dragged her here and it might very well kill her. He felt like an idiot. He dipped his head in resolution, and together they took their first step toward the Snakeroot Road.

Chapter 8

Damien Raythera brooded as he peered from the eastern foothills of the northern Rutala mountain range. Before him stretched the southern reaches of the great Fairywild forest Drelthun banished Liam and Mia to, if he was any gauge of the dragon's games. To his right and left rose great blue standing crystals, carved by long-forgotten hands into ghost-like shapes of moaning spirits. The stones of Drenhai. The story behind them he'd forgotten.

He scowled at the grassy path between crystal and forest, and the too-vivid colors and sharp lines of Erentyr. He sneered at the floating seeds drifting along in clouds from northerly winds. Soaring buzzards and muddy, musky smells from the Fairywild wafted into his nose, sickly sweet and tart. Coyotes gnawed a large bloody carcass, flies swarming near the standing crystal. He recoiled at the smell. No clean tram lines. No walls of white to keep out the filth and blood. Damn that Morderan.

He packed his sloppy, handmade saddlebags and slipped his suit of enchanted torgonite mail over an arming doublet, then strapped a heavy brigandine coat over that. Crude armor for crude weapons. He geared up for another ride from Caldbana, where Drelthun's castle stood amid the purple glow-fly meadows. Wishing that he could finally get used to the stench of the ruddy horse he was forced to ride, he made his way finally into Cwen Dreorig, a border territory of Kaledon. He wore as fine a quality longcoat as could be mustered in this backward shithole and rode steadily onward with only one goal in mind: the capital of Kaledon, to meet the king. With such rude traveling accommodations, it would take days before he could meet the king and begin hunting for Liam and the Stone. He pushed through the nausea.

The mail horse barding rustled as he rode on. He didn't want to leave Midworld the first time he came here and he certainly did not want to be here now. He wrinkled his nose. Down the slope, Cwen Dreorig opened into a mixture of boglands peppered with small settlements. He sighed and curled his lip in derision. Kaledon stretched before him, now even more accursed and wretched than it was ten years ago. Dun, foggy bogs had expanded like a relentless fungus across the land. He felt an involuntary chill at what that meant: the Curse of Vinraith, the Unseelie King, Lord of the Dark Valley to the West. It seemed the Unseelie King had made good on his promise to slowly consume Kaledon should the Dream Stone be lost. What degenerate squalor.

His road meandered through villages and abandoned farmsteads. The sparse denizens thankfully asked few questions of travelers. Rye, bean, and turnip fields withered with blight and lumped with disease-crippled sheep and cattle. The Unseelie King's slow vengeance struck at the very heart of the land itself, it seemed. Brochs that once held Clan Lords and their families were now picked-over ruins. Crannogs now rotted into muddy lochs. *God, it's so much worse than I could have imagined.*

Given his rich cloth, armor, and exquisite sword, few asked who he was or why he traveled the road to Caer Lannican. Hunting dogs gave him a wide berth, as did the villagers.

After a few days of rough travel that brought callouses to Damien's hands, he set out again. That morning three men, and two others hidden in the damp brush, appeared before him, crannequin crossbows trained upon him. Bandits. A haggard leader skulked forward, skin stretched over thin, wiry limbs wrapped in rags. Wrinkled, ruddy skin over sunken cheeks. Twitching eyes. Disgusting, desperate filth. "Hand over your coin," said the man in Gaelsh. "Now!"

Damien sneered, not even bothering to hoist the shield at his side into his hand. "You do know that crossbows were banned by the Myrddian church of Atrogonia, do you not?" They chuckled grimly but didn't answer. "You have but one chance to disperse, or you will regret it."

A gnarled grin. "Just hand over your coin, and we won't nip your mount or your gear to boot. A courtesy for foreign knights."

He considered it. But no. This was absurd. Those barbed quarrels wouldn't even pierce his mail, much less the brigandine. Irritation grew like a biting fly. "No. I cannot accept such terms." He drew forth a beautifully crafted arming sword of blue-grey pattern-weld torgonite. "Behold the blade, Larsorn," said Damian with a smarmy grin. "Boon from the dragon for passing his deadly test at the gate of Erentyr years ago." The bandits squinted at each other, unsure. "What, never heard of it? It's a famous blade, you know."

The bandits stood firm, exchanging glances. "You've not even got your shield up," said the leader. "Just hand over what you've got, and we'll leave you be. We'll even let you keep that gold-gilt blade."

Damien narrowed his eyes upon them and unleashed his rage into the sword, calling forth its power. The force erupted as if from his very blood, straining and shaking his body, but he was able to master and control it. The skill returned to him as if he'd never left Erentyr, but still the effects shocked him. Pulses of energy stretched out, barely visible in the drizzling fog, plunging into them. Their eyes bulged, unsuspecting, overwhelmed by the magic before they could react.

They dropped, contorting in agony upon the grass, their skin covering swiftly with a layer of frost. His hand burned where it touched the hilt, but even so, the pain rejuvenated him as more waves flowed from the sword into their bodies. He hopped off his steed. A bandit rasped at him, blood trickling from his nose and crystallizing on his blueing skin. He placed the sword tip to the man's chest. The bandit mouthed the word, "mercy."

Damien granted mercy by shoving Larsorn down hard. He curled his lip in disgust, as if stepping on a squishy roach. So cruel and pointless. He reminded himself of the Magnolent Mandate he had sworn to uphold no matter the cost. For Midworld. He cooled himself and slaughtered the other two men. The men in the brush fled into the mist.

The last man's eyes deadened. Liam's last breath would have to come soon, just the same way. A quick end to his possession of the Dream Stone and he could be done with Erentyr. He let out a breath and redoubled his resolve. Rain picked up, and he tugged his woolen weatherproof cloak deeper against the elements. *And not a moment too soon.*

***

Damien rode without further impedance over the next few days along the misty roads of Kaledon —Liam's homeland, where walls of stacked stone separated the countryside into steads, the most of which were now overgrown with foul, stinking boglands and misty blackthorn groves twisting with menace. His disdainful lip-curl rarely left his mouth as he continued on, up the long sloping hill-country, to the great keep in the distance, the two suns of Erentyr peeking through a rising haze to reveal a mighty ancient fortress on the cliffs of the northernmost shore of Teralia. *If only this whole place would simply burn to cinders. That would at least help with the stench.*

For the better part of the day, Damien passed up and down the defensive embankments that surrounded the first gatehouse. Trumpeters announced his arrival from the battlements. As the portcullis had been opened for him in the evening fog, he passed through the gatehouse and crossed the dizzying bridge to the main central sea-stack upon which the keep proper had been built centuries ago. From that central keep, nine bridges flared to smaller sea stacks with their own smaller keeps. All these comprised the fortress in whole, upon sea stacks a thousand feet above the churning bluster of the Northern Sea.

He passed through the inner gatehouse, distant ocean surf churning, into the main courtyard complex. Painted sea-stack stone, the strongest stone known, rose about him in the gatehouse, and beyond, as the outer wall material, chosen for its resistance to conjury and ability to withstand giants and war-beasts. Elsewhere, nearly as strong, towers and side-strongholds towered in granite. Each carefully masoned angle bore scars, cracks, and lines of repair told of countless wars; storms weathered for ages. Carven crests, crudely painted in layers up the sides at key overhangs, told a story of the clans that held the great fortress of Caer Lannican since it was built thousands of years ago.

It struck him that so much time and energy had gone into it all. Certainly very hand-labor intensive. No automation could do such things in Erentyr. How much grunt and sweat had soaked into it over the ages?

He stabled his horse, taking care not to wince at the stench of manure and forge smoke which wafted across with the clanging of hammers on anvils. He climbed the wide stairway to the great landing before the tall central keep where he felt a strange chill. He turned, but saw only the bustling Nurnian men-at-arms pacing the walls that looked out over the ever-rotting farmlands sloping southward into a grey mist. Night was falling, and he shook off the chill. He turned to the double door, which was opened for him, men-at-arms in mailcoats standing at attention with spear and axe beside. He entered, and in moments, climbing the levels, he made his way to the great Royal Hall of the central keep. The suns were gone now and candlelight glowed from within the many tunnels and halls.

He rounded the walkway and strode into the throne room, boots clanking on granite. Tapestries of the Nurnian conquest covered the now faded whitewashed stone walls that stretched high, where lit candles dripped wax upon a massive wooden chandelier, the light of which barely touched the dark corners of the flying buttresses. A dozen bodyguards in fine mail and coats of plates stood beside the Nurnian King.

"Sir Damien, Knight of Ozremorn of the South, my king," said a herald.

Damien bit his lip to keep the disgust and disdain to himself. He stood before the king and his retinue. So many crude, boorish men serving no better than a common, dressed up thug. But no matter his feelings about this world, and every part of it, he would never stoop to base and low manners. That would be beneath him. He knelt with a flourish. "Hail, King Arrius, Conqueror of Kaledon."

King Arrius of Nurn turned weathered and piercing eyes below a gnarled brow to him. "I'm surprised you have returned to my home, Lord Damien," said the king, his craggy face older and more rugged than Damien remembered, his voice more gravely and grim. A scar twisted down his cheek to disappear into a full white beard. "We all know how you long for your home in that mysterious world beyond the Dragon's Gate."

"Indeed," said the equerry, eyeing him with suspicion, "I seem to recall you saying you would never return from the world beyond the Gate when last you left. And yet here you are. Come to stir trouble?"

Arrius laughed. "Enough, Fabus. Lord Damien is an emissary. An ally of our master to the south. He is welcome here." He gestured to Damien to rise.

He did. Damien stood slightly above everyone else in the room below Arrius's throne dais. The king's exchequer, equerry, and other officials stood beside him, and several of Arrius's knights stood close by as well. Damien paused, studying the king's features, curbing his irritation with them. "I have news, sire, from Midworld."

King Arrius raised an eyebrow and shifted comfortably in his throne. "Let's hear it."

The candlelight flickered off the whitewashed walls, barely fending off the darkness of night. "Liam Trendari, the so-called 'Lost Panregon,' has returned to Kaledon."

This elicited several chuckles from the knights, and puzzled glances from the younger officials. Arrius grinned. "So he did escape, after all, into your world. Why didn't you kill him there?"

Damien crossed his arms. "Please, highness. My home is a world of peace and enlightenment. We abhor violence."

"Sounds boring," muttered one of the knights, eliciting snickering around the room. Arrius gave them a stern look and quietened the room.

Damien regarded the man coolly. "We tried to rehabilitate him. But he seems to have had too much of his homeland blood in him. He stole the Dream Stone and has returned to your kingdom. For this I am charged with apprehending him and executing him."

All eyes fell upon the king. Arrius stroked his grey beard. "So much for peace and enlightenment, then."

Damien nodded and bit his tongue. "Indeed. But this means I must ask something of you, sire. I suspect Liam is looking for his mother, Ynwin. Is she ... still alive?"

Arrius stared at him, not answering immediately. His retainers turned to him expectantly. "No," he said, his expression opaque. "I had her executed years ago, hoping to end this accursed affliction of the Unseelie King that has befallen my land. Clearly that did not help. But I have learned since then what *will* help. It would seem Vinraith's curse is a *kingslayer* curse." Nodding agreement came from the knights and officials. Clearly, they had heard all this.

"And what is that, sire?" said Damien.

"It means once I kill the leader of the Kaledonian rebels the curse will lift. And so the hunt goes on to find the man. The rebels still cling to the shadows, of course, even to this day."

Damien pursed his lips — lifting the curse was a subject he knew to avoid. "Of course. But did Ynwin pass the Calling Brand blessing to anyone else before she died?"

A pause. "No. And no one could have taken it from her before that. I made sure of it."

Damien nodded slowly. "Good. As such I have a favor to ask."

The king cocked his head to one side and gestured with a palm. "Proceed."

"As the representative of Midworld, I request that you give me leave to hunt Liam Panregon on your land and in the Fairywilds that surround it."

Arrius smiled darkly. "So you can reclaim the Dream Stone he stole from you, eh?" A few laughs circulated through the great hall.

"Pray, great king," he interrupted, "and begging your pardon. But perhaps do not speak of what is to become of the Stone just now. There is need for conjury-level secrecy and discipline, I think. The rebels may be watching us even now with spellcraft."

Arrius nodded knowingly, glancing about. "Wisely spoken, knight. Well enough."

"Your fears are unfounded," said a voice. The soldiers parted, and an open-cloaked man strode into the center of the hall, the candlelight falling upon complex marks upon his bare chest, red garments flowing long behind him, a thin staff of bronze in one hand. A deep hood bathed his face in shadows but for the eerily bright eyes. He moved with deliberation, a mark on his upper chest red and oozing, as if he suffered from an allergic reaction.

Damien resisted the urge to recoil in distaste, masking his expression. *Arrius's sorcerer.* He had been hoping to avoid meeting him. Being in Erentyr at all was bad enough without having to deal with those rare abominations of nature who wielded spellcraft. No one so unpredictable and dangerous would ever be tolerated in Midworld. He mustered a polite smile. "I bid you good evening, Lamon, Royal Conjury Master. Your reputation precedes you."

The bald and clean-shaven man bowed slightly, his expression seemingly in a permanent condescending smirk that pushed through an inner pain of some kind. Damien knew little of those called *magus born*. But that could not be helped. Midworld had no comparable analogy he knew of.

Lamon surveyed the room, making the younger retainers avert their eyes. The wizard then smiled. "The rebels are reduced to petty raiding and hiding in the mountains," he said, his voice gravely and much older sounding that seemed right. Damien heard once that magus born people lived very long lives — who knew how old Lamon really was?

"The rebels have fought hard," continued Lamon, "but are nearly gone. It won't be long now." He turned to Arrius. "Liam has returned far too late to be of much interest, sire."

"Is that so?" asked Damien. The sorcerer Lamon glanced at him, those eerily bright eyes no doubt holding plans within plans.

King Arrius stood, and everyone else straightened. Those seated rose to their feet. The king walked to Lamon. "Care to share?"

The wizard shook his head. "Too much detail *would* require conjury-level secrecy, my king. Suffice it to say I *ensnared* what I needed with the latest ambush of the rebel raiders."

Arrius nodded in satisfaction, seemingly understanding. Damien, having been well versed in conjury theory, knew as well: Lamon had planted a spy. Incredibly difficult magic.

"Whatever it takes," said the king. "After fifteen years, it is worse than ever here ... much more rot and Fairywild spread and there won't be anything left of Kaledon to hold. Therefore, I do not want any wild-cards roaming my lands. Damien."

"Your majesty," said Damien, straightening before the older man.

The king glanced at a batch of his well-armed guard. "Take a full hunting party with you. Let's be done with it."

Damien smiled. A full, seasoned hunting party would make this even easier than he'd hoped. Arrius' smile faded, eyes flickering between the hunters and Damien. "But take heed. If he is roaming this kingdom, you may have to pursue him into the Fairywilds. Servants of the Unseelie King may try to kill you … or worse."

Chapter 9

Waves and wind their only company, Mia marched along the southern surf to the south as dawn came up, with Liam by her side. She padded along with bare feet on the sand that blended into growing patches of grass, leaving the beach where their footprints trailed back to the crashing surf. Rain softly fell. Events of the last few hours swirled about in her head. Everything had changed, it seemed, in an instant. Her eyes fell on Liam. He had that haunted look about him that came when he shut down about his past, only more intense. Brooding, even obsessive. The powerful, extremely handsome lines of his bearded chin pulsed with tension. Those fiery green eyes blazed, hyper-focused, every muscle of his 6 foot 4 frame gnarled with strain.

Best to let him brood when he got like this. But even thinking that only heightened her own regret and pain, bringing up unwanted memories of their long, icy silences when they lived together. She hated him shutting down and hated herself for not being strong enough to 'fix' it. She didn't deserve his friendship. He needed someone much stronger than her. That thought only made her sick to her stomach.

He glanced at her and his expression softened some. He gripped his pelt. "Do you need this? It's windy and cold. How warm is that dress?"

She shook her head, more to clear it of sour memories than answering him. Oddly, she didn't need the pelt. Not only was her dress thick and warm, but even where bare feet touched the earth, or the wind blew against her calves or forearms, she wasn't cold.

But that puzzled her. In Midworld she would have been freezing. Not here — a swirling, dark energy pulsed within her here, barely perceptible. She felt it crackling like electric blood cells. Something lurked deep in her spirit, and heat emanated from within. She swallowed the disturbed feeling that gave her, for she remembered "people sometimes *change* after crossing the gate" they said in warning. If Liam was worried about that, he didn't show it. *Perhaps it's best not to speculate.*

He offered the pelt again. "Mia?"

She blinked at him. "Oh. No, I'm okay." He squinted at her, his face skeptical. She fidgeted uncomfortably under his concerning gaze. But it just irritated her. "Dude! Seriously, stop worrying about me. You've got enough on your plate." And the last thing he needed was to be weighed down by some weepy, jittery little creampuff. She regretted snapping at him but didn't know what to say. She crossed her arms. "I'm fine."

He half-closed his eyes. "Jeez, not this. Not here, we can't do this here, Mia!"

Why was he all the sudden jumping all over her? "Do what, Liam?"

He shook his head, rubbing his forehead. "Look, I know it's just 'what we do,' but we can't afford to be bickering."

She nodded grudgingly. "Agreed," she said, eyebrows raised.

"Are you sure? Because we're in real danger here. There's no free orinol dispensers or painkillers. If we panic or get hurt, we're just screwed. There's no easy transportation. No food stations."

She put a fist on her hip. "Yes, I get it. There's no Raythera streaming services out here to watch your favorite AI soap operas. No five-star hotels with jacuzzis." She breathed and calmed herself, holding her hands out, as if to lower the tension. Something caught his attention.

"What's going on here?" He raised the hand that bore her grandmother's ring. It glowed dimly in the misty morning. She examined its contours, and the blue light that twinkled from it. She shook her head. "Another Erentyr mystery, I guess."

He turned back to the forest, scrunching a cheek, apparently frustrated. "Fantabulous."

She brushed aside trepidation and steeled her nerves, eyes locking on the wild tangle of misty wilderness that loomed closer with each step. She tied her hair back, and they followed a grassy path along the hillcrest that overlooked the ocean. The engulfing sounds of crashing surf faded as they pushed through the drizzle, a forest of sea stacks soaring about them, a dark crystalline rock at the base that the wrathful ocean seemed unable to erode away.

"This was it," said Liam glaring at the ground, then the Fairywild ahead. "This was where we used to walk southwest, to the Snakeroot Road. More like a forest trail, now."

Strange trees hundreds of feet high sprawled southward and towered above them. Tall, spiked trunks grew into a canopy bursting with cottony pods scattering fluffy seeds across the tangled undergrowth. She took a deep breath and let it out slowly, summoning her resolve. "Well. I've never been camping."

He looked at her and chuckled grimly.

They entered the eerily quiet Fairywild. The silence crept into her awareness, intoxicating her, but inflaming her awareness at the same time. They climbed up a natural stairway of roots, the surreal mushrooms stretching to make a tunnel over them, then wound through tangled, giant glowing mushroom patches, the light of which met beams that filtered through the mist of the high canopy to land on their clothes. The hyper-greens, purples and pinks saturated her senses, as did the wafting rose and honeysuckle scents in crisp-thick air.

"Ok," she said softly, heart pounding in her ears, feeling like an ant about to be stepped on, "so I know you don't like talking about your home, but I need data. Is this forest full of ... good fairies? Or...the, um, other kind?"

He ran a hand through his red hair, obviously working through how to answer that. "Unseelie fairies," he said at last, eyes darting from path to treetop to glowing mushroom. "Seelies are friendly. Loyals of the Fairy Queen. Unseelies, on the other hand … don't like mortals. Their king, especially, doesn't like us. Mom always made deals with the fairy creatures of Tyaku." He waved a hand. "This place around us. They allowed us to pass through here to Kaledon, in exchange for offerings to honor them, songs of praise. That kind of stuff. Children of the Unseelie King, however, don't make such deals. Tyaku used to be a Seelie Fairywild But that was a long time ago."

She caressed a fruit-like appendage that dangled from one of the mushrooms — purple, melon-like, and half eaten by … something. "So is any of this edible? I mean, we're going to get hungry and we can't exactly order pizza out here."

"I'm aware," said Liam, gingerly sweeping her hand away from the melon-thing. "But you don't want that. But some of the stuff here is ok. I just hope I can remember correctly which ones. This journey used to take, like, a week, and that was when the path was wide and clear enough for horses."

They left the mushroom tunnel and entered a dense grove, where long-stemmed plants hung lamp-like fruits that glowed dimly in the haze. Liam plucked one, and its pink light illuminated his face. He stopped and she turned to him.

"Here," he said. "These are tor-heedrom." She took one. Its tiny bristles tickled her fingers. The glow clashed with the glow of her grandmother's ring. But Liam paused, eyes on the ring.

"What is it?" she asked.

He looked at her, an expression of half-seriousness, half-mischief on his face. "In the old Midworld stories, they said eating food from the Fairy-world would trap you in it forever. Celtic fairytales, you know. My people, probably, those who'd made it here and returned."

She raised an eyebrow and put the pear-shaped fruit in the satchel. "I don't think I'm quite that desperate just yet."

He smiled and stowed his in his sporran. "Yeah, agreed. We will be soon enough."

They hiked further through the tor-heedrom grove. Butterflies flitted among the spore-filled, swirling air. She stopped. Ahead the path opened to a clearing, in the center of which stood a grassy knoll. Atop the knoll rested a flat rock with a small, black figure on it next to a stumpy, sprawling tree. They exchanged glances. "Is that a bird?" she whispered.

He raised his eyebrows and squinted. "Never easy to tell right away. Come on." She followed him into the clearing. Light from the suns shined through clouds, warming their skin and lighting the grey rock in the center. The black shape came into view. It was indeed a bird sprawled on its back next to an ancient bristlecone pine. Odd position for a bird. Its black feathers shimmered in the light, and it had a small blue tuft on the crest of its head.

"Oh, it's a raven," said Mia. "Corvus corax! Aww, she's hurt."

Mia shot forward, but Liam held her back, suspicion in his eyes. "Could be a trick."

Mia removed his hand, her expression telling him she would not be kept from helping the bird. He nodded, understanding. They both neared and crouched beside the creature. Was it alive? She reached to touch, Liam watching her closely. Its eyes stared, as if dead, but it was breathing. Strange behavior for a bird. It was breathing. She gently stroked it to check if it was hurt. It bit her.

"Ouch!" She recoiled.

"Well serves you right, you wazzok!" said the bird, flittering up to a bristlecone branch. "How'd you like it if some starkey missy pushed her gribblers inta *your* knickers?"

She shook the pain out of her hand, laughing, "What? You bit me! But I'm sorry, miss? I didn't mean to ... um, you're a talking bird."

"Well that's a sharp eye, innit?" Her laughing accent sounded strangely familiar — yet unplaceable. "And what we got 'ere, then?" said the bird, eyeing Liam. "My, my, but you are a specimen, aren't you?"

Liam stepped toward the branch, eyeing the raven evenly. He seemed less surprised.

The raven tilted her head at him. "What? Don't recognize me, old bean? Forget me already, have you, love?"

He shook his head, eyebrows raised. "Forget you? What are you talking about?"

"That's right, you just came from Midworld, by the smell of you — probably having a time making sense of it all."

"Midworld? Yes. The gate guardian sent us here."

"Oh, that Drelthun! Dodgy varlet! Base, common, and popular villain he is! Setting up right there in that castle in Caldbana like that, pretty as you please. Frazzles my feathers, he does."

Mia gaped. "A real, talking bird. Is this a–are you a … fairy creature?"

The raven flittered to a closer branch. "Goodness, child. But you're a pretty one to be so daft! Or maybe you've had conversations with ravens back home in Midworld? Of course I am a fairy creature, you chock-a-block," she added in a light-hearted, but mocking tone. "Or maybe you've been sampling the lemonade, hmm? The both of you? Having a wee sip, this fine morning, a couple of lovebirds?"

Mia and Liam both blinked. Who knew what kind of being she really was? *Best not to offend her.* He laughed nervously at the word "lovebirds", exchanging a glance with Mia, who was stumped as to how to respond. A regretful pain hid beneath that thought.

"Oh, we're not, you know," Liam started, a hint of sadness in his eyes.

"Yeah, no," Mia said, eyes still on his, "not–not anymore."

"Maybe you can help us?" said Liam, changing the subject, to both their relief. "I'm trying to get to my home, Kaledon. Can we pass this way? Is it dangerous for mortalkinds like us?"

"Mortalkinds" she pondered. The language and customs of his old home seemed to be returning to him.

The bird looked them over. "Aye, it can be, love. And if you want to go back to Midworld, you've got to use that Dream Stone that's wobbling around in your pocket. Unless a god wills it, of course." She popped closer to Mia. "Otherwise you're stuck here, aren't you?"

Mia struggled. *Actually talking to a bird* tangled her thoughts. Yet here they were. Best to get with the program.

"What? Old Crook got your tongue?" said the raven on the slender bristlecone branch.

"How did you know about the Stone?" asked Liam.

Mia watched them closely, listening intently. Studying.

"Mm," said the raven. "Relax, love, I'm here to help. You don't remember it, but your mother sent for me to help you."

He squinted. "I'm sorry, what?"

"Now you just watch that tone, young man," she chittered, flying to a higher branch. "You were just a pup back then, but she did. She prayed for help, so I've been waiting about for you to finally leave that dodgy Midworld and come back to Erentyr where you belong."

Liam's expression suggested he was about to protest — Midworld was at least safe, he would say, unlike this insane place. Mia agreed.

Mia stepped forward. "We meant no offense, Ms...?"

"Anundiami. But you can just call me Sea Breeze. Like the zephyr but easier to remember!" She chittered. "Now come along, you two. No sense chin-wagging all day in the suns. There's work to be done!"

Mia and Liam glanced at each other and shrugged. It was the best offer they'd had so far.

"Now look sharp," said Sea Breeze, perching on Liam's shoulder and pointing a wing to the path that plunged back into the forest. "That way. And keep that Dream Stone close."

They entered a path where tall, mottled trees covered in spotted mushrooms towered over them on both sides. Mia swallowed. "So are you telling us all this because you want to help us rescue Ynwin, Sea Breeze?"

"Hmf! So long as you're loyal to the Fairy Queen I'll gladly help. In fact, look at me, chattering on. The children of Alyia will want to know you're here, won't they? Maybe more will help before the Unseelies get hold of you, or Arrius's low-born blackguards. I'd best be off. Well good luck, loves. Follow the trail, and if the Fairy Queen favors you, you'll make it to the outskirts of Kaledon in one piece. Off you pop, now."

With that the raven flittered into the sky, deftly veering through a criss-cross of mossy branches into the hazy glowing canopy.

"Hey wait a minute," said Liam.

Mia watched the bird zip through the branches into the sky. They glanced sidelong at each other. His eyes immediately began scanning the forest, large hands often open, as if waiting for an attack. She found herself shrinking next to him, rubbing her old wolf-bite scar absent-mindedly. Somewhere in the back of her mind she felt a tinge of anger at herself for being so small and afraid. But every towering tree, every gloomy space between plants felt like it had eyes watching them. Her skin felt clammy and her breathing continued to be shallow, mouth dry. Nevertheless, she continued, close to Liam. "Well," she said after a moment, "this is certainly no Midworld, is it?"

Liam unshouldered the baldric of his sword. "Indeed." He pressed on cautiously, following the path further south.

"Think we can trust the raven?" She lifted a branch, peering into the darkness. She pulled back. Too dark that way.

He scoffed. "Maybe. She feels trustworthy, but who can say?"

They crossed a wet patch in the darkening path and rocks began to rise to either side, plunging into the huge trunks as undergrowth thinned in the gloomy forest floor. There a galaxy of glowing mushrooms opened before them, glowing butterflies flitting between.

Mia's eyes darted, gently squinting in wonder. "This place isn't *anything* like I imagined it as a kid. Always thought it'd be all pitch black and flames or something."

A muscle in his temple pulsed. "Yeah, well. Careful. Darkness has many shades, Father used to say. Anything here could be a bloodthirsty fairy creature in disguise or a hostile sorcerer under the cloak of a spell."

"Sorcerer?"

He nodded, eyebrows arching. He held up a wayward branch for her to pass, feet padding on dirt, swirling butterflies mesmerizing in their cloudy dance among the explosion of mushroom growth.

"Sorcerers are another of Erentyr's treacheries," said Liam. "Enemies who wield spell-craft. In Erentyr they can do all sorts of horrible things with a wave of their hand and a word of power. Extremely dangerous. Thankfully they're rare, even in this world."

She shuddered. "Ok, good to know."

He sighed. "I know. Unseelies, Warlords, evil sorcerers." He shook his head, frown deepening. "I never thought I would return to this world. Least of all bring you along. I was hoping to forget it. Mia, I'm so sorry."

"I'll be ok, Liam," she said, feigning courage for his sake. "Worry about yourself. I know I'm just a Midworld softie, but you've got triggers here."

He nodded, ducking under leafy overhang and holding it for her to pass.

They walked closer together now as rain filtered down through the glittering leaves, clear lines dripping through multicolored carpeting of fungi on the trees. She sidled closer, nearly able to fit inside the great wolf pelt on his shoulders. He brought her closer seemingly without thinking, as if protecting instincts in full force, great sword in his other hand. His gesture nearly calmed the ever-rising heat and electric feelings stirring within, pulsing with desire to lash out, not necessarily against him, but just … out.

She wiped a bead of sweat from her brow, making a cool spot on her skin. Liam whacked a vine out of the way with the blade. She pressed on, strength draining from her limbs, just as the growing surge of inchoate emotion rose. She forced herself to focus.

"Pity I didn't get a nice weapon like that sword when I crossed the gate," she said. She held out her hand with the glowing ring. "All I got was some sparkle on the ring I already had."

Suddenly the rising energy in her finally erupted — unstoppable, as if vomiting pure power. Light blasted into her vision and energy coursed through every cell of her being. She reeled with sorrow, rage, bliss, and love all at once, and the air split open with a deafening roar, a thousand smells filled the blazing air, freezing pain and pleasure clutched her entire body.

She collapsed, blinded by a cascade of strange, twisting images, fire and blood coursed in interlocking patterns in her mind, and her body tensed, as if seizing.

"Mia!" cried Liam, holding her. His sword clanked onto the ground.

Her outcry choked to a squawk. Now a spirit arose within her, as if from her very blood, like an entity with a mind of its own. Shrouded in ancient power barely remembered, the energy churned in her mind. It held out a hand, and instinctively she knew she had a choice. In an instant, she had to decide, now or never. Recoil, and it will fade into the shadows, perhaps forever. Or touch it, and see what inner firescapes erupt. She faltered, the spirit closing in on her inner self, mind clouded over with images flashing. A repeating twelve-symbol pattern. Stylized animals, storms, winds, rings, moving bodies. It was now or never! Three heartbeats resounded, slow and thunderous. On the fourth it would be gone, maybe for all time. She shot her hand forth and touched the shadowy spirit.

All went white.

Her eyes burst open and her skin felt like it was burning. She cried out. Liam's expression was panicked, but his voice hardly registered. The markings, which were mere blotches before, formed into shapes that matched the images in her mind. The pain seared, tears streaming.

The marks struck in waves, and tiny droplets of blood oozed from them. On it went, until finally after what seemed eternity, it stopped. Stars sprayed in her closed eyes, tears salting her tongue.

***

She melted into a dark haze of memories blending together. The last day she saw her parents, filling out paperwork in the Childcare Plex. Countless nights curled up, crying in her room night after night. Young Liam checking on her every day and playing make-believe with her. Finding him in crowds when other children made fun of her skin marks and thick glasses, calling her "little nothing"...

The twelve images blazed in her mind again, repeating, as her body was lifted — maybe by Liam, she couldn't tell — then she drifted, drifted, drifted. Into oblivion.

***

Mia woke up with Liam over her, Sea Breeze perched on the low, mossy branch of an oak tree. Red haze floated above them, filling the space between the ground and the high canopy just outside of a cave. They rested, a fire crackling nearby, a stream rustling somewhere.

"My glasses," she said, sitting up with effort. Liam's concerned eyes shot down at her, his arms around her, just like when they were children. His presence calmed her. She awoke, and he released her, seemingly embarrassed by being so close. "I just realized I don't need them here."

"Had a nice kip, have we?" said Sea Breeze. "Nothing like a long nap to give you a new perspective." She flitted into the cave and plopped onto beaten earth, the flames flickering off her shiny black feathers and blue tuft on her head.

"Are you all right?" asked Liam.

Mia nodded, smacking her lips, throat dry.

She took in the earthy, burnt wood smell of the cave. "What the hell was that?"

"You kind of had a seizure. We've been here for several days, actually, worrying about you. Scared the crap out of me," he said without mirth. "Sea Breeze here came back and helped me find this cave, where I carried you. I've been watching over you since. She also filled your satchel. Fruit and nuts, flint and tinder for fires." He glanced at her. "Wouldn't say where she took it."

The raven turned her head up and closed her eyes. "Hmf. That's gratitude, for ya, innit?"

He smiled. "Here," he said, offering her a water flask. She drank, and the water cooled her, the skulking inner shadows now burning like embers, the currents crackling like a distant storm in her soul-depths. The twelve swirling images repeated themselves dimly now, and whispered words, like demon voices speaking a forbidden language, echoing faintly. How could she even come *close* to explaining this feeling to him? She wouldn't bother. There would be no way he could get it.

"You've been out cold," said Liam, apprehension on his face. "Sea Breeze came when I cried out, not knowing what was happening to you. She came."

"In for a penny, in for a pound, I always say," quipped the bird.

Mia sat up and held her arms in the light. The dusk light and the fire danced on the amorphous shapes — unlike any skin markings she'd ever seen in years of training in biosciences. Stranger still, if she squinted, she seemed to catch them *moving*. Liam and Sea Breeze sat silently with Mia, letting her take it in. "Is ... this something Erentyr is doing to me?"

Sea Breeze shook her head. "No ... well, not exactly, little flower. But you're an artist back home, aren't you? What is it? Painting, writing, music?"

"Well, I—"

"And it's not just a dabble here and there, is it? It's a deep, powerful *need* to create, isn't it, love? You feel a huge surge within you, like high tides, and you *must*."

Mia blinked at her, the sounds of frogs and crickets in a dusktime chorus rising. Thunder rolled far off. "How did you know?"

Sea Breeze studied her. Mia shrunk under her scrutiny.

"Well, Liam," said the raven, "I think that answers our suspicions. Had to have been the Enlightening. I must say, I never foresaw that! Didn't figure there was anyone like her *left* in Midworld."

"Like what?" said Mia, heartbeat rising. Wind sailed through the treetops outside the cave. "Is there something wrong with me? Is Erentyr making me sick or something?"

Liam shook his head, thick brows deeply furrowed, concern and amazement on his face. "No, nothing like that. I guess I should have known, honestly."

She frowned at them both. "Should have known what?" Frustration bubbled up to the surface, making the inner lurking shadows pace about within her like panthers. Deeply unsettling. She shoved that disturbing sensation away. Something *was* wrong with her here. No. Couldn't be. "Ok, so this is the part where somebody tells me what the hell is going on. Are we still on for rescuing your mom? What's the deal? I don't care what this is," she said, waving her hand at her skin markings. "You're not giving up on her just because something is going on with me. You know me, Liam. My parents abandoned me and wanted nothing to do with me. I never even did anything wrong!" Her voice caught, but she powered through it. "But your mom needs you, now. I know you're afraid for me, but ... we can't be thinking about that right now. Right?"

"Mia," said Liam, his voice soothing. "Easy, easy. We're not giving up. This just complicates things. Remember when I said we would need to be wary of sorcerers — spellcasters?"

She squinted sidelong at him. "Yes. So, what are you saying? This sickness is because I'm the target of a sorcerer?"

"No love," said Sea Breeze, hopping next to Liam. Both of them gazed sternly at her. "It's happening because you *are* a sorcerer."

Chapter 10

Liam sat by Mia's sleeping form. Outside the cave, dark winds made the spiky trees sway and hiss. It had been hours since Sea Breeze had flown south, having spent a long while trying to explain sorcery to the both of them. Mind runes, gestures, and the dreaded wizard marks filled the conversation. It made little sense to Liam, but Mia seemed to understand some of it already, if only by feeling and intuition if nothing else. All very troubling no matter which way one sliced it.

Brief glimpses of memory were all he could recall. The bent form of the sorcerer they called a Druid he saw only once as a child, shrinking behind the big frame of his older brother, Banner, at a fire festival, during a moment of quiet anticipation. The Druid had waved her hands, swaying in her bull pelt, antler headdress bobbing, weaving a spell to conjure fire to begin the festival while all looked on with fascination. She spoke in a strange language that altered her voice, making it sound as if it came from within your head as well as without. As a boy, Liam popped his hands on his ears, but still watched. She seemed to wince — sorcerers seemed plagued, as if by some kind of disease. But it was her eyes which terrified him most; they burned unnaturally bright, even seeming to glow sometimes. He caught glimpses of them and turned away. She spoke again. A flash came, and thunder rolled. Then the Druid was gone, the bonfire instantly burning into the night sky.

Mia slept fitfully, her face flinching. He swallowed, worries making him chew the inside of his mouth nervously. She looked as if plagued by violent dreams. If only he could protect her. He never should have dragged her here. Outside, thunder carried, echoing. He took up the pouches of ochre clay and charcoal Mia filled the night before. A fey mood had struck her, and recalling her grandmother's letters to her, she decided to get materials needed to make fierce war-paint, "like my ancestors," she said. He said nothing, but it troubled him. Erentyr was already working on her. What was it doing to her? He glowered into the darkness, angry guilt shoving down on him. He didn't deserve to be her friend. He had only poisoned her life. He put it out of his mind. He placed the containers of paint materials in her belt pouch and straightened the wolf pelt that covered her.

A heavy thump came, bending branches. Something moving in the Fairywild. First one, then another far away. Within moments, tromping sounds grew from one to many, scattered across the Tyaku. Liam's heart jumped, and he immediately hopped over Mia to place himself in between the misty night and the dying embers of their fire. He tensed, hand on sword, peering into the night. Patches of glowing lights shimmered in the misty gloom, obscured by dense woodland.

Mia awoke with a start, stirred, then slunk next to him. "What is it?" she whispered.

He searched through his childhood memories for anything useful. "My father told me about this once, I think. Giants, roaming on the nights following summer's end. Look."

He pointed to where moonlight shined on swaying treetops. The movement was haphazard — not like a herd. Individuals tromping in the darkness. Deep, rumbling voices murmured. If it was Gaelsh, he couldn't make it out. But there was no back-and-forth. The beings muttered to themselves, not each other. She shrank down, eyes wide, color draining from her face. The creatures were huge.

"It was something from the old days," he whispered. "They would come from the Land of Giants to the northeast, many miles. Hunting, maybe. Who knows? They always told me giants were solitary. See how scattered out they are?"

She peered intently into the night, reaching for her absent glasses, then blinking, apparently remembering she didn't need them here. "Are they ... dangerous?"

He let out a breath. "I'm not sure. I mean, they're *giants*. So, probably. This only ever happened before I was born, the way they talked. It was the old way."

"Seems the old ways have returned," she said, squinting into the forest, clouds moving in from the moonlit south. She handed him his wolf pelt.

"Are you all right?" he asked. "You didn't sleep very well."

A chill seemed to course through her, and with a slight shudder she turned away. He waited for her reply, fire embers fading beside them. He resisted the urge to pull her close — she wouldn't want that.

She turned to him. "Many dark dreams since yesterday. It's like there are twelve … images … bursting from within me." She shuddered. "It feels like they're … *alive*. Struggling to form in my head. But it's not just images. It's hand and body movements, and words — holy crap the *words* are so strange. Each one connected to one of these markings on my skin."

He frowned, worry and dread slithering like a serpent within. How long would it be before she became … something else? Damien's warning about Erentyr consuming them echoed in his memory.

"Hey," she said looking at him squarely, her voice hesitant, but persistent. "I'm all right. Calm those fiery greens, Liam."

But already the stars seemed to flicker in her own eyes unnaturally brightly. He forced a smile.

It quickly faded. Something wasn't right. A gust of wind blew from deeper in the cave, making the embers flicker. Then a crawling, prickling sensation crept up his pale, freckled skin. His abdomen clamped down, and his muscles became sluggish. He stood slowly, speechless, horror creeping into his mind. The air began to smother him, the very air seeming to rumble in his head with a sense of impending doom.

"Liam, what is it?" asked Mia, eyes following his slow movements.

He glared into the darkness of the cave.

The sound of a single step echoed. Then another.

Liam's breathing became shallow, his heart raced, and he waved Mia to stand behind him. She nodded and quickly obeyed.

Into the light, hoods pulled low, long axe in hand, wolf-snout snarling, the Woodsman stepped into the dim red light. Not in a dream. Not in a fleeting glance.

In the flesh.

Liam was 9 again. His chest heaved with silent screams. Mia gasped and stumbled backward.

The Woodsman's axe glinted in the moonlight. Sharp and deadly. He shook his head, lips curled in disdain, canines bared. "You should nae have returned here, Liam," he said, voice rumbling against the stone. "You, who abandoned your own. Left them to die. And now you come to the Fairywild." He brandished the axe. "You'll pay the price!"

"Run!" said Liam.

They bolted out of the cave into the rainy night, scrambling past thorns, glowing mushrooms, and tangled branches. Liam's eyes darted between misty, whorled underbrush, menacing trees towering, Mia catching up with him as he waited for her, heart pounding like a hammer. Behind the Woodsman leapt from rock to rock, speeding toward them, voice raising in a howl which caused other howls to erupt within the darkness.

***

Then a voice bellowed from above them.

"Me find you," it said.

A huge arm plunged in between tree trunks and grabbed them both in one monstrous hand.

The new voice thundered, "Me hunt good!"

Yanked from grasping mushroom stalks and scratching branches, the barely dawn-lit world twirled. Hung at least fifteen feet above the rocks, a humongous brown face, haggard from a hundred scars, cracked and bumpy, stared at them upside down.

Panic exploded in Liam's body. He squirmed. The Woodsman was still out there somewhere in the darkness. He shoved against the stony grip, trying to no avail to pry the hand loose from Mia. She strained, pulling against the impossibly large hand. The creature let out a monstrous belch, and two small, glassy eyes looked at them.

They stopped wriggling and watched.

"You 'nother bad humans. You come home with me. Me cook you!"

The howling continued through the Fairywild. The giant glanced to the side. "Me leave now." The creature then opened up a massive hide sack he'd shouldered and tossed them into it. Liam landed with a thud on a pile of reeking furs but managed to catch Mia.

"Hey!" shouted Liam as the top of the sack closed tight, blood pounding through his frame.

"Wait!" shouted Mia, yanking at the cloth by him.

Light leaked in from gaps in the sewn musty hides. The giant hefted upward, knocking him into a pile of gnawed bones. Mia toppled. He climbed on top of a pile of squishy things and peeked through a gap and pulled Mia up. She peeked over his shoulder. The sack was slung over the giant's back. The creature strode fast in a thunderous limp, rattling them about like marbles in a child's toy bag.

Liam squinted, looking about for an exit, regaining his breath, the image of the Woodsman still sharp in his mind. Mia pulled apart the cloth, trying to get a better view as they lump-thumped ahead in a jarring gait.

"Is he ... limping?" she whispered.

He glanced, returning to their present problem and tried to feel the movements of the giant. "I can't tell. Maybe?"

Outside the night air gradually gave way to misty forest. No sign of the Woodsman but being trapped in a giant's sack wasn't exactly an improvement. The giant loped up an incline where glittering creeks through autumn-colored foothills passed. Lump, thump, he went, shoving through the forest quickly despite his limp.

Mia closed her eyes, muttering something to herself — trying to remember something? This was bad. Finding Kaledon would be impossible if they were carried off to who-knows-where. That is, assuming they did not get eaten.

Mia opened her eyes. She glanced at him, wordlessly saying "Let me try something." Then she held out a marked hand, twirling it precisely to place it on the sack resting against his back. Was she trying to cast a spell already?

"*Olosynn*," she said, her voice scratchy and odd, as if echoing in a way that was impossible. Her eyes flashed white briefly, then she hissed, her forearm recoiling, the skin red, as if lashed. He leaned in, eyes widening, holding his breath.

But whatever she'd tried failed.

He put a hand on her shoulder. "You ok?"

She nodded, wincing. "Fine, fine," she said waving him off.

He let out a breath in relief. He peeked out of the sack again as they lumbered along. Trees swept by. No Woodsman.

Another solution arose in Liam's mind. He retrieved the sword and drew it halfway out, holding the hide for balance. The steel shined even in the dim light. Anger boiled. The sack was against the giant's back. One stab could possibly cripple him enough for them to escape.

But Mia placed her hand on his. "Wait, before you do that."

"We can't afford to get lost — or get eaten," he said. "What were you trying to do?"

"Distract him long enough to drop us, so we could get away. He doesn't seem dangerous. Just like a big animal."

Another lurching forced them to regain their balance.

"Must keep going," grunted the giant, out of breath. "Fairy Queen say, go back home."

Lump, thump. Lump, thump.

Liam stood, body tense, balancing on piles of random junk the giant had collected, sword ready. With one shove, he could possibly kill the giant and end this disaster. He could at least injure it enough to get away. Each lurching step took them farther away from the Snakeroot path.

Mia simply gazed at him. She did not press the issue. But he knew from her expression that she was going by instinct here. Something felt wrong about just stabbing him.

He nodded, scowling. "Not the knightly way, my father used to say."

Surprise crossed her features. He never spoke of his father. "R-right. Exactly. Let's just see where this goes."

Liam sheathed the blade and shouldered it, and they held hands, peering out the tears in the sack. Hours passed, and night slowly gave way to early dawn. The giant climbed, and floes of mist drifted through empty air outside like slow waterfalls.

How high are we going?

One great hop preceded a loud smash into the stone. The sack flung around and they tumbled into a huge cauldron full of cold garlicky water, floating with half-rotten vegetables.

They swirled to the surface.

A metal circular lip towered over them to a relatively small opening. They were trapped in a massive soup pot. The giant dumped a bag of vegetables on top of them, plunging them underwater.

Liam swam back to the surface, gurgling, only the cloudy sky visible; Mia was treading water beside him. A loud rubbing sound preceded a burning smell. Waves of heat drifted up from below. This was getting serious. First the Woodsman and now this.

"Hey! Giant!" said Liam.

A huge stony face popped over the rim.

"You no trick Lungor." The giant winced from whatever it was, then hobbled off to pile more logs under the pot. He tossed a bag of celery in. "You cook good."

Liam and Mia exchanged glances. She quelled a panicked expression and placed her hands on the metal as the rubbing sound outside the pot grew louder. She began to mumble.

"Can you cast a spell to get us out of here?"

She gnashed her teeth. "I ... feel like I can, but I have no idea what I'm doing!"

Liam swam next to her, searching about for any way out. "Take it easy, just try. Anything would help."

Sweat trickled down her cheek and her whispers grew to chanting, until at last she intoned *"turil-karoth."* But instead of anything happening, her eyes flickered with blue light.

Then she passed out.

She sank below the surface as the heat waved hotter from below. "Mia!" he shouted, diving after her.

He pulled her back up and wrapped an arm around her torso, fighting against dipping under the surface. He gnashed his teeth. He should have stabbed the giant when he had a chance.

"Hey," he shouted, "L-Lungor? That's your name, right? Look here," he said, forcing a laugh, "you don't want to eat us." He dunked below, then surged back to the surface, spitting out water. "I'm just skin and bones!"

"You lie. You full of muscle."

"Hey, wait-wait-wait!" He inched toward the edges where it wasn't so hot yet, holding Mia so her head stayed above water. The soup bubbled and the bottom glowed red. *Oh boy.* "Seriously, here. Let me help. I have to find my mom. You have a mom, right? A, uh, big mom? Wouldn't she worry if you were lost?"

This was about to be the shortest trip to Erentyr in history.

The giant's face scrunched into a scowl, massive hands over his ears. "Me no hear you."

"Giant!" he shouted, his hair now dripping with sweat. "Give me a chance. At least let my friend go!"

Lungor's hand blocked out the sunlight and he pushed him underwater, forcing Mia to float down. The bubbling soup blasted his face, the wolf pelt pulling him down with the weight of huge fingers behind it, baldric and sword swirling away.

Water stung his eyes. He reached in vain to pull Mia up. The sword drifted out of reach. Rage burst forth and he hissed, bubbles erupting from a muffled growl. Slipping out from under the pelt, he shoved against the hot iron and gripped the giant's arm. Lungor pulled away, but Liam clambered up rocky skin, past the elbow as the giant recoiled with a roar. He had no plan but to grapple the massive creature. It was hopeless. The giant's skin scratched like stone, his muscles monstrous. The giant tried to shake Liam off, but he clung like a tenacious cat. He lunged, hooking his legs around a huge shoulder. Each second felt like an eternity.

He pounded fruitlessly on the giant's back, when further down swelled a red area, large as a watermelon. *That's why he's limping!* In the center, a sliver of stone embedded into thick skin, far out of reach of Lungor's groping hands. He hammered the sore, making Lungor emit a thunderous roar. The giant slammed into a stone wall, trying to crush Liam. He held tight despite the wind being knocked from him. Hitting the wall only hurt the infected area more, making Lungor howl again.

Then an image flashed into Liam's mind of before, when Mia had convinced him not to stab Lungor. Fighting was getting neither of them anywhere. An idea emerged. He scrambled for the Dream Stone, hanging with both legs from the giant's shoulder as he fumbled with the sporran, nearly dropping the Stone. He placed it in his scarred hand and stretched forward to yank out the sliver, causing the giant to bellow and whirl, knocking over the cauldron. Mia spilled out with a gush of water that doused the big fire. Once the behemoth paused, Liam reached for the center of the giant's upper back, warm Dream Stone in hand, and he poured his mental energy into the swollen area like before, using the power of the Stone to heal. The cooling Stone flowed into the large infection, coursing through his hand and causing muscles to tense. Lungor groaned.

The giant slowed his bucking and whirling and Liam climbed carefully down, keeping his hand on the swollen area. It popped, covering his hand in stringy pus. He endured, face scrunching from the reek. He kept steady, pushing the healing intent through the Stone into the giant's cobbly back. The giant groaned with relief and settled on his haunches with a thud. The abscess healed over, matching the rest of his lumpy skin. The courtyard of the ruins was littered with a dozen steaming puddles, and the smoldering logs smoked in the new day's light.

He rushed to Mia's side. She coughed up soup and scooted against a stone wall, confused. He sat back and breathed deep, relieved, and washed his hand in a puddle while the giant and Mia recovered. Then as before, the Dream Stone went cold, and he put it away.

Mia caught her breath, smiling in relief. They squeezed their clothing and hair. "I'm ok," she said. He nodded, muscles relaxing, breath deepening.

He clambered to his feet and rounded to the weary giant's front, rubbing his fingers where the Dream Stone's power had stung his hand. Lungor raised his massive face to him. "Well, big guy? How does that feel?"

Lungor roared and grabbed his trunk, rising to his feet to tower over them, snarling. He raised the tree high, blocking the sunlight, and Liam and Mia both froze in place. "You mess up soup. Me smash you!"

Great. This was it. They were dead. He frantically searched for a way out as Lungor waved the tree, but if he moved, he would surely get smashed before they could get out of the way. No escape.

Liam stood his ground. "No, no. No smash. Me friend. See?"

Mia nodded vigorously. "Friend, yes! We like giants! Giants good." He glanced at her and she shrugged slightly, eyes wide, smiling nervously.

Tense moments passed. Then Lungor scratched his head and stooped to their level. "Me no kill you. You friend now." He smiled an ugly, toothy grin.

They laughed out the tension in relief. Liam patted the giant's massive cheekbone. "Yes, yes. You don't eat friends, right?"

He screwed up his face into a frown. "No. That against rules." He looked at Mia. "Me sorry try to eat you."

"Um, no hard feelings?"

He nodded and lumbered back to the courtyard.

Liam heaved a sigh. "Fantabulous." Mia rubbed her forehead in relief.

They took several moments to collect themselves, then Liam climbed a flight of stairs to the battlements, trying to reorient himself. Mia joined him. They rested their hands on the battlements, admiring the ocean of clouds floating by, engulfing the keep on all sides. "Any idea where we are?" she asked.

"None whatsoever. The clouds must be pretty low. Maybe we're getting closer to Kaledon here? Not sure."

"So," she said tentatively, "are we going to talk about the wolfman with the axe who knows your name?"

His neck tightened involuntarily, posture clamping down. He looked away. "Remember the nightmare I used to have all the time as a kid?"

She tilted her head in thought. Then her eyes widened. "You mean–"

He nodded. "Yeah. In Midworld just a nightmare. Here, apparently, flesh and blood." He frowned and tapped the battlements. "As real as you and me." He watched as Lungor stretched, enjoying being free of pain.

"What *is* he?"

He furrowed his brow. "He must be some servant of the Unseelie King, maybe. Hunting mortals for sheer spite. I don't know. I should have known he was real." He scoffed. "Back in Midworld all he could do was terrorize me. Here," he swallowed, that axe blade flashing in his mind. He placed a hand on his neck.

Mia looked at him squarely, serious and still. "Not if I can help it," she said after a moment, putting out a fist.

He looked down at her and smiled, tapping his fist on hers. "Thanks."

The wind flowed calmly, and everything from Midworld seemed a hundred miles away. The safety of his apartment, dinners at The Dome™, the easy life … all gone. He squinted, scanning the horizon.

Mia squeezed more water from her dress and padded over gingerly to the giant. "So … Lungor? Can you tell us where we are, friend?"

Familiar laughter arose — Sea Breeze was perched on a scraggly bare tree by the ruined rookery that overlooked the dumped cauldron. "I see you're getting on chip chop with Lungor here. Found a way to the old ruins of Shin-Arem, didn't we?"

"Sea Breeze!" Liam fanned himself, still hot from the cauldron. "And yes. Did you know about the giants?"

She flitted to the overturned pot. "Land sakes, what the feathers were you three doing?" The giant stretched and flexed his back, still enjoying the lack of pain, lifting his tree up and down.

"We had a slight culinary disagreement," said Liam.

"Lungor!" said the raven. "Did you try to *eat* my new friends?"

The giant gave a blank stare. "Ya."

The blue tuft on her head puffed in indignation. "Ugh! You giants never listen. Thick as oak trees, you are. What did I tell you? The Fairy Queen's words: *no eating humans* on the journey from Giant's Land this year."

"Uh," said the giant, glancing at Liam. "But ... me no eat them now," he said with a toothy grin.

Sea Breeze cawed and flittered closer to Liam. "Well!" she huffed. "Wait 'til the Queen hears about this codswallop."

Liam retrieved his wolf pelt to squeeze water out of it. "It's ok, Sea Breeze. We're just happy to still be alive. Let's just keep going. Where are we? How far from the Snakeroot path did he take us?"

The bird hopped in several directions, getting her bearings. "Hm. Northern tips of Cwen Dreorig are that way, I'd say." She pointed to what looked to be southwest. "That's the border territory you want. You're almost there, but there's still the Tarila Wood betwixt here and there. Best be careful. Got to know your onions to make it through those parts, love. But if you do make it past that, you're onto Kaledon proper then. You'll want your best bib and tucker on when you go there, too, what with the Kaledonians and the Nurnians fighting and all. Well, it's just not going to be easy any way you go it, is it? *Err, err.*"

Lungor, having satisfied himself that he was better, tromped over to sit down, causing the ground to rumble. Mia sat on the battlements by Liam and the bird.

"King Arrius is still in charge there, isn't he?" he asked.

She flew up to his shoulder. "Sorry, old bean. I think he is. And now, I'd just bet he and Damien are working together to capture you and that Stone of yours."

"Wait," said Mia, approaching. "You know Damien too?"

The raven flittered back and forth in frustration. "Ooh, that Damien! He's a wooly coxcomb if you ask me. Yes, I know him. And I hope you budge off his crumpet and look lively at it, that's what."

Liam's scowl deepened, those names evoking nothing but feelings of revenge. "That makes two of us. Does Damien know where we are?"

"I just bet that dragon might have told him where you are, that grumbletonian rattlecap! But anyhows I'm not sure. He *did* carry that Dream Stone of yours for a long time."

"Why does that matter?" asked Mia. "Is there some kind of, um, magic link because of that?"

"Only the Queen knows that, love," said Sea Breeze. "But I think there might be. Now, off you pop, and keep your eye out for wildgnomes and other rough-timble fairy folk, love. They're nothing but chatty quidnuncs and they'll get you side-tracked sure as the suns."

"Where are you going?" asked Liam.

"You're headed for your home, but your home is very sick, remember? Riddled with dodgy bogs. Covered in the curse of the Unseelie King and all that... I'll go ahead of you and see if I can reconnoiter a bit. I only know how to get to Kaledon as the raven flies, old bean. I haven't actually visited these castles of Shin-Arem in a long while. Bad memories for me, I'm afraid."

Liam stood up, glancing about nervously. "What do you mean? It's not safe here?"

Sea Breeze shook her head. "Not for humans like you, loves. I once had a run-in with old Ishanoren Sebec out here."

Mia scrunched her eyebrows quizzically.

"Another Remembering One," he said. "A fairy god. Like Drelthun, Vinraith, or the Queen." She nodded, vague understanding.

"He got cheesed off at me," continued Sea Breeze, "and took the form of an ice-drake. Looks like he hasn't been here in a while, but he might come back. Anyways I wouldn't push my luck staying here for long. He won't bother Lungor, but Sebec doesn't like human squatters. Better be off. I'll keep trying to help — at least until you get to Kaledon. I'm not very welcome there these days."

He nodded. "I understand."

"Well, stay strong, young lad. And you, too, Mia — keep practicing, like I told you last night. Mind the Fairywild." She winked at him. "You dishy wazzok."

She flittered to the southwest.

He turned everything over in his mind. But the bird had been clear. There was no time to dawdle. He stood at the battlements and looked down. Mia glanced down with him, stroking her chin. "That's a long way down."

The cliff plunged into a sea of clouds.

"Yes, it is," he said, gathering himself.

"You didn't tell her about the Woodsman," she said.

He shot her a glance. "One catastrophe at a time. Let's just get to Kaledon. Maybe once we're out of the Fairywild he'll leave us alone."

She raised an eyebrow. "If you say so."

Lungor sat sniffing items in his huge bag. Mia's eyes darted about the stone wall and cliff beneath. He furrowed his brow. "Makes me wish I'd practiced climbing more at the gym-plex. See why I didn't want you to have to come here?"

She didn't answer, her eyes were narrowed, deep in thought, chewing her lower lip.

He glanced at her sidelong. "I know that look. Wheels turning. What are you thinking?"

"I almost had it. The spell."

He strained to understand. "You've only been here a few days."

She shook her head, turning to him. "But that's just it. I feel like I've been practicing my whole life. I should be better."

A dark wave of fear crossed his heart. "Maybe don't be in such a hurry, Mia. In Midworld, whatever this is merely amounts to being seen as artsy or 'imaginative' but not much else. In Erentyr, this fire in the head, this surging spirit ... it can *kill* you, Mia. Don't go too hard too quickly."

She frowned and looked down, nodding. "Hm," she said.

He braced himself for the climb. "I wish I could help, but everything I ever learned about conjury only scared the crap out of me." He let out a short breath and turned to Lungor. "Well, big guy, looks like it's back into the Fairywilds for us. Good luck to you. Farewell."

Lungor scrunched his face up. "Me help."

Liam shook his head. "Sorry, buddy — too dangerous. I don't want to get you mixed up in all this mess. Besides, I have no idea where I'm going exactly. You stay here where it's safe ... you know, for giants."

The giant stared blankly. Liam exchanged glances with Mia. "...ok then. See ya." He climbed over the wall and started down the cliff, heart pounding. He gulped at the dizzying, windy drop. No safety line. He took a few more precarious movements down, gripping for dear life. This was going to take a while. He breathed deeply and steeled his resolve. Mia followed after, carefully stepping down.

"Want to hang on me?"

She pursed her lips to the side at him. "Now, look here, you big lummox. I'm not *that* small and delicate. I can climb. I have strong legs and excellent coordination."

"All right, it was just a thought."

"Stop treating me like a frail flower."

He blinked at her, not used to that. "Ok, of course. I promise–"

Suddenly a mournful wailing arose. Not from below, but above, in the ruins. "Little friends," bawled the giant, "you no leave me alone!"

"Awww," said Mia.

Liam laughed wearily. "You've got to be effing kidding me."

"Friennnds! Me help!" He snorted loudly.

Mia smiled, and they worked their way back up to the sobbing giant.

They popped their heads over the stone. "All right, all right! You big lug," said Liam.

"Yeah, come on," said Mia.

He perked up, like a monstrous puppy. "Lungor help? Yes. Help." The giant unfolded himself to rise up and tromp toward them. Lungor lowered his head to them, then swept with a meaty hand and hoisted a shocked Liam and Mia onto his shoulders — one on each. Liam gripped the gnarly, rock-wood skin of the giant. Palm against the giant's neck, he felt the slow, deep pulse pounding. Warmth radiated from his massive frame. Mia seemed to marvel at the texture of his muscles and the heat emanating from him, running her hands along the giant's cobbly skin, gripping the animal pelt for stability. Liam steadied himself as Lungor stood to look west where puffy clouds flowed into the distance. The giant perched himself with renewed strength upon the battlement where the cliff plunged. "Which way we go?"

Liam shrugged. "Um..." A wall of white peaks broke the clouds southwest. He pointed. "Sea Breeze said that way."

The behemoth bellowed, his mighty voice echoing across the clouds.

"Oh boy," said Liam, steadying himself. Mia's eyes wide, she grabbed Liam's hand and clamped tightly. The height was dizzying.

He leaned forward. "All right, we're hanging on. You can climb down now, big guy."

Lungor cracked a ragged smile. "Lungor no climb. We go down quick way."

Liam raised his eyebrows. "Um ... come again?"

Lungor leapt off the battlements. Liam and Mia gripped the giant's stony muscles and involuntarily howled. Liam's stomach rose as they dropped into the free air.

Chapter 11

Damien rode at the head of the hunting band — six riders in mail coats, with spear, mace, axe and belt-hook crossbows upon swift Sathenite steeds in padded harness. More than enough to capture two lost and starving Midworlders. At the head of the band was Lucius, one of King Arrius's most trusted scouts, his station evident from the fine coat of plates he wore over the middling quality mail. *No doubt here to keep an eye on me.* A middle-aged man with salt-pepper hair hanging around a balding head, Lucius sniffed and nodded to Damien, his ever-disapproving eyes indicating he'd caught a trail. Damien rubbed his clean-shaven chin and pointed near the northern base of a large nearby hill.

They rode, rounding the bend near a foggy landscape of tall hills and sharp draws, lightly wooded. Low clouds hid the tops of the hills and drizzled wind carried the scent of decaying leaves. They had dared the outskirts of the Tyaku Fairywild and would be deep in Fairywild territory if they kept going, the roads now fading under the encroaching flitterweeds — tall stalks of thorny blue-green, topped with vivid flowers shaped like butterfly wings. Their honey-gold scent filled the air, hiding the dangerous nature of the nearing Fairywild territory. These hills contained one of the ancient ruins of the Fallen Dream Empire, lost to time, crumbled, and overgrown in Fairy woodlands.

Damien led the band eastward a few yards and then dismounted. Lucius followed and scanned the ground as the nervous hunters looked about with weapons drawn. Damien nodded — they were now in Fairywild country. He adjusted the strap of the shield on his back and drew his sword out a palms-width to reassure himself it would not stick in its sheath. He sneered at the men, their ugliness irritating him. Time to get this over with.

"Here," said Lucius quietly crouched over large footprints. "A giant, burdened."

"This far southeast?" asked one of the hunters.

"Not uncommon in the last few years," said Lucius. "You saw the huge starling flocks. Something stirred them last night. Giants, I'd wager a month's coin on it. They come for the great gyrfalcons and timberwolves of the old Shorelands. Following them toward Neiten."

"Are there such beasts in Kaledon? Great falcons and timberwolves, I mean?" asked Damien.

Lucius shook his head as he followed the trail up the steep hill. The path climbed into a sheer cliff face before disappearing into the low cloud cover. "The few that migrated this far wandered into the Unseelie bogs of Rathchylde territory years ago and haven't been seen since."

"Hmf," said another hunter. "Good riddance to them."

"Oy, Lucius," said the first, "what's a giant got to do with our quarry?"

Lucius snorted. "Probably nothing."

But Damien wasn't so sure. He opened and closed his left hand, noticing a strange tingle in the fingers. He scanned the clouds where they met the cliff face. *Am I feeling the presence of the Dream Stone?*

A sudden bellow echoed from the other side of the great hill. The hunters drew weapons, turning about, looking for enemies.

"Giant," said a hunter.

"Aye, closer than I thought," said Lucius. "Best leave Tyaku. Head westward to Neiten."

"No," said Damien, pressing south. "You said the giant tracks were 'burdened' didn't you Lucius?"

He squinted at the sky, scanning the hillcrests. "That could be anything, milord. Giants love to lumber about with huge sacks of junk, everyone knows that."

"Aye," chimed in a hunter. "I'd want at least four more spears before I tackled a giant, anyhows."

"I don't intend to kill it," said Damien. "I just want to know what it carries." He pondered the sensation in his hand. "I have a strong intuition that we might be close to our quarry. We should at least investigate."

The men paused, eyes darting between Lucius and Damien. Damien nonchalantly rested his hand on the hilt of the ancient sword. Larsorn was well known. The movement did not go unnoticed. He suppressed a smirk. Carrying a god-forged weapon often accorded one additional consideration. Lucius nodded, a grudging respect in his eyes.

Damien returned to his mount and advanced, and they followed him around the feet of the great hill for several hours, heads darting back and forth nervously, monitoring the oddly twisted spruces and sycamore trees.

The overgrown path dwindled and their horses came to an expanse of muddy ground at the feet of thickening woodland. Damien noticed the others no longer trailed behind. He studied their twitching expressions. "What is it?"

Lucius nodded ahead. "That's the Tarila Fairywild ahead, milord."

"Indeed?" He turned. "So close to Kaledon now?"

"Aye," said Lucius. "It's been ... *growing* ... for the last few years. Curse of the Unseelie King Vinraith, no doubt." Lucius swallowed, nearly suppressing a shudder.

Damien's pulse raced. He knew what creatures lived in Tarila. Unseelies. Very dangerous. But his quarry awaited. More and more he became assured of it. "Hmf," he said, "I wonder. If Arrius were here, would he press on?"

Lucius swallowed, but his expression stayed opaque. "King Arrius is a strong leader. A spear-shaker of great renown. But there is a difference between courage and foolishness, milord."

"Indeed. Which shall I prove here this waning afternoon, I wonder?" He smiled and pushed ahead, until his horse could travel no further. He hopped off and strode into the darkness on foot, glancing occasionally at the gawking hunters. Lucius' brow furrowed in anticipation. A bead of sweat trickled down his temple.

Damien steadied himself, stepping one foot ahead of the other stubbornly, dread rising within him. Still he pushed onward, boots in disgusting mud. Then he halted, muscles tense, heart pounding. In the gloom ahead, small burning red eyes came into view. Dozens, under rag-tousled hair and ugly, twisted features. Fangs protruded and drooled onto torn and muddy tunics. Many raised spears and bows against him.

Spriggans. Very nasty children of the Unseelie King.

One stepped forward, taller than the others, but only half human-sized, though Damien knew not to assume anything from such appearances. Spriggans were said to be the ghosts of giants, and just as strong. None really knew what they were other than Unseelies. Not to be trifled with, having no love for mortals. Taking pleasure in torture and slaughter.

The lead spriggan hissed, then laughed, an eerie, scratching laugh, with a sound that seemed to emerge from *within* Damien's head as well as without. "Tell me why I should not impale you where you stand, human?"

Damien drew Larsorn and planted it in the ground before him. Tension mounted, as the spriggan leader's eyes narrowed on the shimmering blue steel, frost misting off the metal slowly in the cooling wind. Damien fingered the strap of his shield which rested on his back, knowing things would get ugly if this gamble didn't pay off. "Because the dragon of Caldbana castle has granted me his favor. This is Larsorn, forged in the First Stone of Time by the hand of Ilseth herself. A personal gift from the gate guardian."

The spriggan inched forward, spear pointed. Damien refused to budge, nostrils flared, ready to fight, eyes steady. The hairy creature glared hungrily at the blade and cracked a wicked smile. Then it began to laugh, followed shortly by the others. Then, they slowly faded backward, into the darkness. "Follow us."

Damien sheathed Larsorn, relieved his bluff paid off. This might go quicker than he had thought. He turned to an apprehensive Lucius. "Courage or foolishness?"

The barest hint of a smile flickered in Lucius's eyes, but he regarded him coolly, glancing back at the others. "Come on, men. Dismount and follow Sir Damien. For Glory."

"For Glory," they murmured.

Damien pushed in deeper, eyes adjusting to the dark forest, quickening his pace to follow the spriggans. Liam's time was short.

***

Liam, Mia and Lungor plummeted through the white air, until the misty Fairywild below came into view. He clung hard with one hand upon a stony muscle, the other clasping Mia's hand. Her black hair swirled above her head, eyes wide, a mix of terror and exhilaration on her face. The giant slammed gripping fingers into the cliff and slid, nearly flattening them from the impact. They passed the bare mountainside to crash through patches of pine trees. The giant shifted through bumps and overhangs, leaving behind marks in the dirt and stone.

The woodland stretched like a thick green blanket over great waves of earth, with hills rising to meet the low clouds as if they were columns holding up a ceiling of quilted white.

"We in Fairywild now," whispered Lungor. He tromped forth, as the wind swirled orange and red leaves. "Now me be stealthy. Me sing song." The behemoth hummed a deep, rolling tune that followed the rhythm of his thunderous footsteps. Mia's eyes darted everywhere, the marks on her arms seemingly quivering.

"Which way to Kaledon now, Lungor?" asked Liam.

"Me not know. Think that way," he said pointing a monstrous digit to what might have been west. "Must be careful, now. Unseelies here — hydras and squibbits."

Liam unshouldered his baldric and gripped the hilt, shifting to sit upon the giant's wide shoulders.

Mia shifted likewise and mouthed the question to him: "squibbits?" Liam shrugged, just as baffled as she was.

A small person skittered along the tree branches beside them.

Liam squinted at it. "Hey, Lungor, I think we have a visitor?"

"Oy, Lungor!" said the little person. "Wait for me! This looks like fun, where are you going?" A little round-faced, red-headed woman roughly half Mia's height ran from branch to branch, level with him — some 18 feet off the ground. She wore a long, red square-cut coat that flapped in the breeze along with her wild, curly hair. She scurried with uncanny agility, a smoking pipe in her hand. She popped it into her mouth, and underneath the coat peeked black breeches, a button-up white shirt and mud-splattered boots.

She did not seem the "monster" type at all, but what in the heck was she supposed to be? Why hadn't he listened to Mom's lessons about Fairywild creatures? Mia covered an open mouth with her palm, a tentative smile on her face at the newcomer. He wrinkled his brow. She was having fun here, and this place was going to kill her. That would be *his* fault.

The strange little woman hummed along with Lungor's somber tune with a big smile, before she hopped off a branch and scurried up Lungor's arm, hopping over Mia to sit herself on Lungor's gigantic, bald head, feet dangling off a bony protuberance. She turned childishly large eyes to him and puffed her pipe. "Hi there!" she said, in a soft, breezy voice. "'Tis himself! What are you, then?" She turned to Mia, "And you?"

The giant stopped humming and halted by a small creek. "No, no, no. Not you. You go away, Maple." He closed a huge hand around the small woman and tossed her toward the creek.

"What? Hey!" she cried in midair before catching herself on a branch with her pipe and hopping back to her feet. "Now, Lungor why'd you do that? Don't be makin' a holy show with me. Let me come too, you lot. I want to know more about those creatures on your shoulder! Tell me, tell me, tell me. Mm, let me guess. He looks like a scribbly Shorelander, and she looks like an Islander."

"They *my* friends. You go away." He trudged on.

"Oh, Lungor," said Mia, "can't we have another friend? You're our big friend, but we need a *little* friend, now, too."

"Hmf."

The little person kept up, bouncing nimbly along branches. "They've got the smell of Midworld on 'em."

"Excuse me. I'm right here you know," said Liam. "Name's Liam Panregon. I am, in fact, a Midworlder, sort of."

"And I'm definitely a Midworlder," said Mia. "And what are you supposed to be? A … leprechaun, maybe?"

She scratched her wild red hair. "Hm. A wildgnome, perhaps? Oh that's grand, I think I forgot now. Maple Magicwood's my name, anyhows. Pleased to meet you," she flipped back onto Lungor's head with ease and popped her hand out, meeting their palms with a coarse little hand.

"Pleased to meet you, too, Ms Magicwood," said Liam.

He climbed up to sit properly opposite Mia, who, being smaller, more easily held her balance. He held on to the hide tunic to keep steady as they crossed the creek into a shallow ravine. Lungor slowed through thicker trees. Maple plucked a monocle from one of the pockets in her voluminous coat and squinted at them, her little round face wrinkly and yet youthful. "Indeed likewise!"

Lungor waded into a shallow river beneath a natural stone bridge. The trees shined black, with rusty drip lines coursing down their trunks. *Metal?* "What's wrong with those trees over there?" asked Liam.

"Ooh, 'tis the Tarila glade," said Maple, "very special Fairywild place. Planted long ago by the Lyrvian courts. Very mysterious, those Lyrvians. Just the place I've been searching for."

"What on earth are you looking for *here*?" asked Mia.

"I've lost me grand-da, Wattle-bee. He came here seeking the Great Feathered Fluffawump. Have ye seen one?"

Liam blinked. Mia shrugged. "What does it look like?" she asked.

"Nobody knows," said Maple. "But it has square eggs, can change shape and lives deep in the bushes. Maybe you've seen one?"

Liam scratched his head. "Um, can't say that I have."

"I think this little one might be my spirit animal," said Mia, hand by her mouth, as if speaking a secret to Liam. As they crossed the river, she reached out to touch one of the branches, and it smacked against her hand. "Ouch!"

Maple giggled. "Tarila means 'Iron Wood.' Cause of the — well, you know."

"Yes!" Mia rubbed her fingers.

They plunged into a webwork of dark trees that bled rusty colors. Leaves — normal feeling ones — swirled about the air, Lungor carefully navigating the harsh crisscross. Maple laughed as her little walking stick struck the branches with a clang. Daylight penetrated the Iron Wood nearly to its dun-shaded floor where mottled shadows swayed.

"So where are you headed?" asked Maple.

Liam had become so immersed that he'd lost track of that. Sea Breeze warned him not to get distracted by the Fairywild. "I'm trying to get to Kaledon."

"Oh, Kaledon, sure! Erm..." she scratched her head and caused scraggly red hair to flail wildly, "not sure which way that is. It's all so manky and quaggy with wars and curses and such, I hear now. But I've always wanted to go — can I come? Huh? Huh?"

"Sure," said Mia, "but did you miss the part about how lost we are?"

"Oy, bless me before the Fairy Queen," said Maple. "Let's see, at least now I think we might be somewhere north of the hedgerows of Kaledon? Or maybe east."

"No more talking!" rumbled the giant. "He say he find home land. And momma."

Lungor's insight astonished him. "Right, Lungor."

Suddenly an arrow struck the giant's shoulder. He recoiled, though the arrow merely left an indention and did not break the skin.

"Oy! Bad people," said Maple, scampering up the giant's head and hopping into the trees.

Liam drew his sword. Dozens of ugly, rag-tousled creatures with burning eyes and gnarled bows loosed arrows. Four bounced off thick hide. One lodged into his wolf pelt. He pulled it out and tossed it as the giant growled and gathered speed. "Unseelies!" growled Lungor.

Liam instinctively put a hand on the Dream Stone in its sporran. Still there.

"Spriggans!" yelled the wildgnome as she darted through the branches across the river. Lungor sloshed across, peppered with arrows. Liam took shelter on his other shoulder. The spriggans bared their sharp teeth and hissed, releasing more arrows.

Liam snarled. He thought of shouting at them to leave him alone, but all he managed was a roar like a beast. He whipped back and forth, darting, trying to think of a way to fight back. Mia, to his surprise, was not panicking, but glaring at them, her eyes twitching, mouth moving in a wordless chant. "Mia?"

Arrows flew past them as Lungor gathered speed. The spriggans sped along the branches like Maple.

"I can practically taste it! A spell ... something to fight back," she said, her voice containing the barest hint of a scratch, as if the sound came from within her head as well as without. She raised up and weaved her hands, eyes cloudy, as if partially in a trance. He tried to inch closer to her along Lungor's back.

The hint of red smoke emerged from her fingers. She stared at one of the spriggans wielding a bow.

"*Siaklaa!*" she shouted, and the smoke formed into an elongated shape, but then dissipated in the breeze, accomplishing nothing. She snarled in disappointment. Spriggans howled with laughter and hopped on iron logs that spanned the river. They loosed more arrows. One planted itself right between his fingers, deep into the giant's neck. The giant let out a deafening roar, making Liam clamp his hands on his ears. The giant plucked a tree from a jumble of rocks, spewing earth, water and stones at the spriggans and splattering one against a metal tree. Blood dripped from the branches. He winced, but it was one less enemy.

The giant bowled over rusty trees and clanged into the trunks. Liam barely held on, sheathing his sword and shouldering the baldric in time to grip tough skin. The spriggans pursued them and stung the giant with arrows, causing him to barrel into a steep copse of iron trees, but with several great steps, they lost them.

Liam sighed in relief. *Thank goodness.*

Then a group erupted from Lungor's right to let loose a new volley. Mia hissed at one of her marks. An embellished, semicircular mark on her left forearm seemed to burn her. She didn't see the new enemies. Liam instinctively gripped his wolf pelt and shot to her side in desperation. This would be a short, pathetic, and arrow-riddled return to Erentyr.

But the wolf-pelt turned the arrows. Mia gawked at him face-to-face, amazed they weren't both dead. They stared, catching their breath, but then a shooting pain tore down Liam's left arm, where a barbed arrow stuck from his forearm above the pelt. He gritted his teeth and held it with his good arm. Maple hopped to his side and launched a counter-volley of her own with uncanny speed, sending spriggans to dive for cover.

Lungor pushed ahead, making distance from the spriggans by slamming his bulk into the metal trees and bending them as best he could. Behind, the trees slowly unbent themselves, creaking in the growing storm winds.

A glint caught Liam's eye. To their flank, Damien and a half-dozen crossbowmen emerged from the dark tangles. The Magnolent brandished a mighty sword, a scowl of concentration on his face, and Lungor howled. Waves of frost crept up his stony hide, and the disoriented giant slammed his shin into a log, denting the ironwood and tripping. The forest spun and Liam flew off the giant. Mia was also flung away and Maple tumbled into the shadows. Lungor crashed down the slope like an avalanche. "Frieeeends!"

Liam turned just in time to avoid smashing his head but thundered into another branch with his abdomen. Stars splashed in his eyes, and he hurtled into a bush, crashing through it into a mudslide, sliding over painfully knobbed roots into a puddle. Silent darkness settled on his swimming head. His arm roared in pain, the broken shaft still sticking from his flesh, blood dripping. Mia helped him to his feet, dirt smeared and bruised. Lungor's bellowing and spriggan hissing disappeared into the distance, followed by Maple's cursing at them in a rich brogue.

Fog seeped into the dark clearing, the dusk light waning upon a towering circle of tangled iron trees. Damien ducked into the waxing moonlight, escutcheon equipped — an ornate circle with four smaller circles around it, and a three-starred lion in the center — the symbol of Ozremorn, Grand Sovereign of the Conclave of Wizard Kings and King Arrius's master. Hunters followed Damien, with one Sir Lucius. Pain drowned in anger, for he remembered Lucius. He bared his teeth and stared at the man he remembered from fifteen years ago as if it were yesterday. King Arrius's right-hand man. The last time they met, Lucius's hands forced his 9-year-old body onto a chair and bound him, across from his father – Liam choked down that memory. *No. No time for that story. NO.* Rage clenched his fists. Lucius was a little man, now, compared to his memory. But now was not the time for vengeance. They were surrounded. Mia was in danger. He was wounded. Their enemies were better equipped. *Next time, if we survive this.*

"It's over, Panregon," said Damien, waving for the hunters to back off. Much to Lucius's annoyance, they lowered their crossbows without even looking at him for confirmation. The Magnolent approached. "Let's just get this over with, Liam. Give me the Dream Stone, and I'll even bring you back to Midworld with me. We'll forget this hell hole forever, and good riddance to it."

Mia's eyes were lowered, but glanced at him questioningly, as if to ask, "do you want to do that?" He scowled and turned to the armored man, brandishing his sword.

Damien shook his head, lunging forward and smashing his ancient sword into Liam's blade. The impact rattled his injured arm, sending pains shooting up his shoulder, forcing Liam and Mia backward several paces in the dark clearing. Thunder rolled, and rain rose in the distant wind. Liam lifted his sword with great effort — a crack now coursed along the steel, halfway down the blade. "Don't be ridiculous, Liam. You're outmatched in every way, and you're wounded. This is Larsorn. A gift from the dragon. Your steel is no match for god-forged torgonite."

"Aye," Lucius chimed in, stepping forward, smirking. "And where be your father's blade, lad? Why have *you* not the famed sword of Cormac an Brionglóir?"

Liam's nostrils flared. "How *dare* you speak my father's name! Scum!"

"Enough," said Damien, shooting Lucius a hard glance. The old soldier sneered but said nothing. "That blade is likely beyond anyone's reach now, Lucius, you know that. That's the way of such artifacts of the Fallen Dream Empire. But it doesn't matter, Liam. This world chewed you up and spat you out. Be reasonable. You don't belong in Erentyr anymore, and you never did, Mia." He advanced again, forcing Liam and Mia to inch backward, the rising dark tangle behind them. "You may be a magus-born, but you obviously have no idea how to use your soulfire. You'll only hurt yourself if you try to spellweave again." He snorted. "Look, I'm only here to finish the Magnolent's Mandate once and for all. Erentyr will only kill you. So tell you what. We can do this the easy way or the *really* easy way. Give me the Stone and we'll all go home right now. Or I will be forced to kill you both and I'll take the Stone back to Midworld anyway. What's your choice?"

Liam sputtered in rage, unable to answer immediately. He snarled, anger, pain, and frustration slamming at him from within, pulling him in every direction. Sharp breaths escaped his burning lungs. He knew Damien was right. All the hunters had crossbows at the ready, with axes, flails, and daggers besides. Lucius ranked high enough to have *his* own sword. Charging against foes with thick coats of mail and brigandine while wounded was foolhardy, especially with Mia here. He noticed the soldiers eyeing her small and curvy form and gnashed his teeth. "You don't understand, your Grace."

Damien narrowed his eyes on him, blond hair swirling behind him. "What don't I understand? Try me."

"The Stone belongs to my mother. I must return it to her. This is why the kingdom is dying. I think she is the only one who can stop the curse!"

He shook his head, taking another step forward, now only five or so paces away. "Your mother is dead, Liam. King Arrius told me himself."

That hit him like a shockwave. He exchanged glances with Mia, mistrust in her eyes. He took out the Dream Stone. Ynwin's presence still persisted, bringing the image of her alone in a dark corner of the great fortress of Caer Lannican somewhere to his mind. Her cryptic message about saving the kingdom becoming clearer the longer he dwelt in Erentyr: only she could save Kaledon. Damien *couldn't* be telling the truth, could he? He growled. "You lie!"

Damien's eyes darted between Liam's and the Stone, a flash of confusion on his face. He wondered if Damien knew about the way the Dream Stone's "magic" seemed to operate. But it passed, and his expression returned to one of confident forcefulness. "It's no lie, Liam. She's gone. It brings me no joy to tell you this. But there is nothing for you here anymore. Your kingdom is lost. Let it die. Let this whole world disappear into the past."

"Liam," Mia whispered, her hands moving in gestures she concealed behind her dress, the distant wind keeping her voice from carrying even to Damien. "I've got it."

"Got what?" he whispered back.

Damien scowled. "This is your only chance, Liam. I won't offer you clemency again." He offered an open hand. "Drop your weapon and hand me the Stone. Give it up and I will haunt you no longer."

"A spell," Mia continued, "I can feel it. I can get us out of here."

Damien snarled. "The next time I offer my hand, Larsorn will be in it. What is your answer?"

"Are you sure?" Liam whispered, trying not to move his lips. "Do you trust me?"

He glared at Damien, the hunters, and especially Lucius. Then straightened and sheathed his sword. Damien lifted his chin. He turned to Mia. "Yes," he said loudly.

Her lips curled into a half smile, then she lifted her hands, moving palms and fingers in a complex pattern quickly. The whites of her eyes shined unnaturally for a moment, contrasting her dark eyebrows. "*Hirrok*," she said. His body felt it — a quickening of pulse, each muscle now coiled like a spring and practically *itching* to sprint at full speed. The air almost imperceptibly shimmered around both his boots and her bare feet. Thinking she had failed yet again, the hunters laughed and raised their crossbows. But Lucius and Damien both scowled. "Now," she said, "RUN."

They bolted into the darkness, leaving the clearing behind and penetrating the tangle of metal boughs and trunks. Through trails of rusty puddles with the uncanny speed of a windy river in a flood, they sped into the night, the enraged cries of Damien dwindling behind them.

Chapter 12

What the hell am I doing?

Mia wiped sweat from her brow as she and Liam bolted under and around the metal branches of Tarila wood, her spell nearly doubling their speed, the hunters slowed by their horses in the unyielding forest. Blood pounded feverishly in her veins, hammering her head as she strained to contain the magic of the spell. Her feet fled wildly beneath her, and yet she did not stumble. It was exhilarating and terrifying at once.

And here she was, the horrors of Erentyr, horrors she'd shivered to hear about from history class, crashing down upon her from all sides from without ... but also from within.

Who knew merely entering Erentyr could awaken something within her so volatile, so insistent, so *alive* as the twelve spells of her blood? Twelve *entities* which obeyed her commands, and yet also demanded a price. Pain, confusion, blood, sorrow.

Insanity.

The first spell she'd managed to unlock required focus she'd thought previously impossible. But the dire situation forced her to unlock herself in ways she didn't think she could. The words nearly formed themselves, connected to everything in the environment: the smells, the moon, the two suns, the dark trees, even the sneers of their hated enemies. And the hand motions — so critical — also ever changing, but once caught, like a deadly firefly, could be used to enact. To move. To create *magic*. Finally there was the mind-rune — an image she somehow knew needed to be imagined with immense clarity and precision. A complicated webwork of symbolism and esoteric images, coalescing into a unified whole, painful to contemplate. Her soul burned with it. Years of laborious, creative, passionate work that benefitted no one made the mental skills possible within her.

"There's magic in you," Morderan used to say.

It wasn't a metaphor.

But it *hurt*. It roiled and surged. It burned. It lived.

The churning ocean of chaos alight in her blood pounded with her thunderous heartbeat, threatening to tear her from within. But she held it together for Liam. *I will persist for him. He had a thousand chances to walk away from me. Even when I pushed him away. He stayed a loyal friend even after the breakup.*

She charged on, Liam faltering beside her. The envenomed arrow wearing him down. He huffed as he ran with spell-enhanced speed, sweat dripping, drool falling from his gnashing teeth. And even then, his eyes shot to her frequently. His only concern seemed to be her safety.

They emerged from the Tarila wood and crossed a barren, abandoned field as night deepened. No indication of Damien or Lucius any more. Signs stood haggard with sheep skull warnings on them to keep Kaledonians from entering the very wood they just left.

Leaving Tarila brought a noticeable change of air. The eerie, timeless and dark clarity of Tyaku gave way to sodden and foggy wind. They slowed down to walk a rutted road past a slope to their right where stacked-stone walls partitioned pastures and dilapidated houses. Liam caught his breath and wiped his forehead with his palm, wincing at the arrow-wound. Left, past the turf ditches, gloomy groves of unnaturally tangled blackthorn trees encroached, clawing through mud and stretching into the hilly distance.

A rumbling noise echoed from that direction, encouraging them to walk the north side of the road. "Is this..."

"Kaledon," said Liam, voice wavering. He stopped and closed his eyes, drinking in a deep breath. "Home. Even beneath the bog-stench I can tell." He ran his fingers along a cobbled wall. "Never thought I'd see these ragged stones again."

Horses galloped behind from what seemed north. They scampered into the ditch. Two horsemen slowed. Their garb looked Nurnian, like Lucius's hunters. She furrowed her brow. Liam glowered, jaw grinding, eyes burning through obvious pain, hand inching toward his sword.

"Up this road here," said one. "I swear I saw someone — two wanderers. A woman in foreign garb, and a tall man with a wolf-pelt. Did you see them?"

"I did." He scanned the area.

A spell-form clambered into her consciousness. Almost immediately it began to make sense, the energy beckoning her within, wordlessly, to speak the incantation self-organizing, to perform the hand motions, and to envision the mind-rune. A wave of weariness crossed her mind, threatening to black her out again. Her eyes drifted closed and the world faded. But this time she pushed through it with an explosion of will.

"*Tiyarr-nan*" she whispered, and the spell locked together. A wave of power stretched from her hands, making a rare breeze that swept across the Nurnians, turning both their heads.

"That way. Southwest, come on!" They both galloped into the distance.

She smiled as she worked through the emptiness that arose after. Like a lamp full of oil, Sea Breeze had told her, each spell "burns" the soulfire inside. She could feel a relative lessening of the power in her blood. How many spells could she cast before it dissipated completely? Did it replenish? How did it work? She cursed.

Liam nodded wearily at her, not noticing the turmoil. "You're learning! Brilliant."

She caught her breath and smiled, just as surprised as he was. But then she scowled. She probably could have killed both Nurnians with a third spell that now lurked, as if next in line. She wanted to try — that disturbed her. She glanced back. Where were Damien and the hunters? Gone?

Commotion up the hill caught her attention. She padded back across the road and crept near the stone wall, Liam close after. A small garrison stood near a broch — also garbed like the hunters but with poorer cloth. Many marched in tabards over mailed gambesons, geared in gloves and helmets, spear, axe, and hammer. A chill crept up her back, but it changed into anger, for two Nurnian soldiers were taking livestock from the herdsmen. *Here we go.*

A soldier dragged a little boy — he must have been about 10 — and roped him to a post as his mother wept. He sneered and took out a whip, enjoying the horror in the mother's eyes at what was about to happen.

"Oh, hell no," said Liam, drawing his sword from the baldric, hissing at the injury.

Mia hopped over the wall and stole across the grass, so as to align herself with the two soldiers. She paused, looking within. The third spell ... it practically *looked* at her. What was it?

She faltered, vision darkening, then returning, and then she had it. All the elements. Many steps — complicated! But it was like her art. Years of practice sped the process, even under no tutelage or guidance, for such things were barely attended to in the digital paradise of Midworld. Yet she had never given up. Never stopped practicing. She chewed her lower lip, intense concentration forcing the energy to form together.

"What else can you do?" asked Liam. "Can you bring them to me?"

"I can do better," she said, shifting her position in the muddy rut by a turf wall. "*Udrana*" she uttered, conjuring forth the glowing red Bow of Mogdun. Mogdun — the name meant nothing to her, yet the *spell* knew what it meant. The meaning emerged unbidden to her. Mogdun, the ancient Remembering One who had created the spellweave in fathomless ages past. Somehow it was in her blood. Passed onto her from her grandmother, maybe. How she could possibly know that she couldn't say. But she knew. She knelt and aimed it at them, spell-arrow knocked. Now it came to it. Liam watched enrapt by what was transpiring. Then he looked at the soldiers.

His expression shifted to concern. "Oh, that's dirty. A sneak attack," he said, "with conjury. That's dark."

She couldn't tell if it was a criticism or not. Maybe he didn't know. She raised an eyebrow. "Are you ok with this?"

His scowl suggested not. "We can debate the morality of it later, after we've saved those people." She wasn't convinced. But she was less interested in playing by the rules. She nodded and aimed, but still hesitated. This was a lethal spell. That much was clear. Was it right? Even with these obvious scumbags? Did she really want to be a killer? A lifetime in Midworld never harming anyone, and a few days here and now she's a murderer? Liam placed his hand on her shoulder, neither judging nor encouraging.

She growled. *There's no time to debate this. I must do something.* Every muscle tensed. Loosing would make her a cold-blooded killer. That much was certain. Even justified, she balked at crossing that line. But something within stirred. Deep and old, it arose, not only from this spell, but from a deeper level she had yet to understand. Something in her blood and bones. An inner force swept aside the conflict. She relaxed, a cool rage dominating her now. *They have to pay.* She snarled and loosed.

The glowing arrow shot straight through both men, blowing holes in their mail as if paper, spraying blood. One died instantly. The other dropped to his knees and looked back as Mia stood defiant. "Conjury!" he shouted before slumping to the ground. She smiled at their deaths despite herself, then felt sick, erasing the smile. There was no turning back now.

Horsemen up the slope took notice. "Conjury!" they shouted, drawing axes and swords. Liam crept to a bend in the turf and stone wall near the road.

"*Kianaa.*" She loosed at three. The arrow knocked one off his horse in a spray of blood — injured but alive; another evaded the shot by diving, but the third slammed into a tree, pinned, arrow through his neck.

Deep down, she was horrified. She had killed — not one but many. Where was the remorse? Fear, compassion, and caring had disappeared, incinerated by numb wrath. The urge to weep emerged but disappeared. In the back of her mind, it terrified her, but she pressed on.

The surviving horsemen galloped forward. She thought to keep attacking — but each arrow cost soulfire, expended quickly. Too quickly! She needed to conserve. The ring-shaped mark on her arm began to bleed! She recoiled in pain. The skilled riders neared.

They took out sharp javelins and aimed them at her.

Liam leapt from the wall and with a mighty cleave hacked one of the two riders clean off his horse, mud flying as he crashed into the ground. The other reared as Mia approached, holding more spells to conserve herself. She had no idea how long she could do this. His eyes wide, the other man wheeled his horse and spurred hard toward the growing gloom. Liam snarled and charged the horseman, ducking under a mace swing to grip the man's throat, tearing him from the horse and splashing his head into a stone wall. He then strode to the prone rider and stabbed him through the throat. She came to his side where he stared at the dead men. His eyes drifted to his scarred hand, now stained with blood, sword cracked and useless next to the body. Liam watched the blood drip, panting, hand slightly trembling.

He looked at her. "See what this place does to you?"

"I do. You all right?"

Nostrils flared, he slowed his breathing. Eyes brooding, he glared at the blood and contorted faces. "I don't like the fact that I enjoyed that."

She nodded, unable to respond. But she *understood*. Grateful farmers swept their families back into their homes, pilfering what they could from the bodies. "I think I get why you hacked into the TRNR robot, now."

"You're hurt!" He grabbed her arm tenderly, ignoring his own wound.

She softly swept his hand away. "It's the magic — it's this place. I … don't know what it's doing to me." She tore a piece of cloth from the dead man's tabard, wrapped her bleeding arm and tied it with her teeth and free hand.

He perused the bleeding mark intently, eyes bloodshot, skin pale. "I never learned about magus-born blood." He reached for the injury again but stopped. "Sorry. Not a frail flower."

She raised her eyebrows and nodded. "Thanks. Maybe if we both believe it, it'll be true."

He let out a pained chuckle and turned to the road. "I should have known you were magic."

"Steel your will, men," said a voice from Tarila, behind. Lucius, "no conjuror is taking my courage. We've braved the roads past the Unseelie bogs. We've now braved Tarila. We can face an apprentice sorcerer and a lost boy with a broken sword."

"She's no apprentice," said Damien, now staring at them from his horse, some fifty paces up the slope toward the field with the warning posts. The traces of moonlight glowed upon the clouds in a red maze, then fell upon the grey-brown hills and overgrown brochs surrounding them. Distant mountains disappeared behind the lingering dun fog. "But it doesn't matter. I offered you mercy once, Liam. Never again. Crossbows!"

The hunters loaded quarrels and took aim. Mia panicked. Liam shifted his big frame in front of her, pelt wrapped forward. Behind them, the mottled country crawled wearily westward, choked with boggy swampland and tangled blackthorns.

"Loose!" cried Damien, and the hunters did, but at the same time one was hit with an arrow from the south. His mail turned the shot but threw off his aim. Liam took several hits anyway and cried out, then they both fled into the blackthorn bog.

Once out of range, they whirled. Damien approached, hunters and Lucius behind. Some twenty Nurnian men-at-arms joined them with spears and crossbows, scattered about the rugged terrain like walking weeds, their tabards damp from the light drizzle. Maple ducked a few quarrels, darting through them to hop by Mia's side in the thicket, her bow trained on them.

"Too many," Liam rasped, quarrels sticking from his pelt. She swept it back — the pelt must have been tough — the quarrels left only bruises on his arm and sides.

"Don't do it, Liam," said Damien. "Surviving spriggans is one thing — you'll never survive that swamp. You, little one, talk reason to him."

"Don't you throw shapes at me, you manky chancer!" Maple said, snapping her fingers at him. "You lot of vagabonds and ne'er do wells can sod off!" She turned to Mia. "Come on, I'll help you best I can."

"Where is Lungor?" Liam said, face contorted in pain.

"He got spooked by all the spears, bless him — said he'd come looking for you two later."

"Comforting," said Mia, scowling at the line of Nurnians on the road.

Damien shook his head. "Kill them," he growled.

They bounded into the bogs, men-at-arms shouting behind, horses galloping, quarrels zipping past. They ran recklessly into a cave-like tangle of blackthorns, Liam stumbling, the poison and wounds taking their toll. But his eyes powered forward, and he kept on. Mia pushed forward beside him, the soulfire within her apparently keeping her bare feet from freezing in the cold mud, but swirling in her head, pounding from within. They stubbornly kept moving. The hunters closed in, quarrels slamming into branches. They leapt over rows of hedges and overgrown stone-stacked walls, into knee-deep boggy water overhung with putrid mist.

"Hold, men," said Damien. The Nurnians stopped short at the blackthorns, quarrels knocked, unable to get a clear shot through the web of limbs. Damien sat astride his mount, Larsorn sheathed, scowling. Mia squinted. Their enemies looked southward. Something had caught their eye. She followed their gaze up to the top of a small hill, where a figure crouched in a tree. The rising moonlight lit the fog that crossed a tangled branch, where a seven-hooded figure perched, long axe slung over his shoulder. He carried a horn and brought it to his wolfish snout to let out a low, ominous sound. Her heart nearly stopped. She patted Liam insistently on the shoulder and pointed. "Liam," she whispered, "it's him!"

He swung south and froze. "The Woodsman."

"Easy, men," said Damien, soldiers and hunters backing toward the road, eyes glued warily to the Woodsman, some hundred paces south. "Stay out of the Unseelie bog and they won't bother us … hear that, Liam?" he shouted into the blackthorns. "You have nowhere to run. The servants of the Unseelie King kill any who trespass. You're trapped!"

Liam and Mia glared at each other, nonverbally piecing together something. "Come on," he said, pushing westward, deeper into the blackthorn bog, sweat dripping off his beard. He hefted Maple onto his shoulders to keep her from the mire, wading further in. Mia sloshed beside him.

She helped him climb onto the ruins of a rotted crannog. The gloom deepened as the hunting horn sounded again. Maple hopped onto the dirt and squinted into the darkness behind them, slivers of moonlight piercing the shadows of the bog, blackthorn limbs looming as if to grasp.

They waited in silence. No marching or shouting men behind them. "Think we've lost them?" asked Mia.

Liam winced, holding his injured arm close. "Let's hope. Woodsman, too." He gnashed his teeth. "That Lungor — rockhead! He was a lot of help. Ugh, whatever ... what am I going to do with this," he hissed at the wound. The barbed tip sunk deep into the flesh of his forearm. He took a deep breath and gripped the haft.

Maple stopped him. "Oh, don't do that, now! It'll be far worse."

He grimaced. "Great, so what, I just leave it in?" Blood dripped onto the mound of rotting timbers.

Mia took his hand, curling her lip at the injury. In just a few days she'd seen more blood than her entire life before. It hurt to even look at it.

Maple scrunched her face at him. "I didn't say that!" He scowled. "Now don't *you* be throwing shapes at me, too! My, but you make a bad patient!"

He straightened. "Fine. Do your worst." He held out his arm. She took out a tuft of feathers from a small satchel. He opened his mouth to protest, but she shushed him. Then gently, she slipped the feather into the wound and gingerly tugged. Sweat beaded on his brow, but he stood fast. Mia watched with a racing pulse, grasping his other hand. "Now, just a wee bit more and — there!" Out popped the bloody arrow. She wrapped his arm in a torn cloth.

He closed his eyes and let out a strained snort. "Grrgh! That'll put a spring in your step, won't it?" He held it to his chest.

"Aye, that it will," she said, trailing off.

Mia exhaled and scanned the area. All around the rotted broch swirled foggy shadows framed by tangled blackthorn trunks. Under the branches stood short, mossy, vine-covered stone walls.

"Um ... Maple," said Liam, red lines under his eyes. "What's that?"

He pointed to a faint light in the mist to the south that bobbed in the darkness as it drifted toward them.

Mia's blood ran cold. "A lantern? Soldiers, maybe?"

It wasn't.

Maple turned paler than usual. "Moldy bad luck, I'm thinking," she whispered. "That'll be a will-o-wisp, or I'm a salamander's tongue."

"Friar's lanterns," said Liam, bloodshot eyes wide. "We should go back."

"With those hunters back there?" said Mia. "Will-o-wisps are just spontaneously igniting swamp gasses. You know, from anaerobic decomposition."

Liam shook his head gravely. "We're not in Midworld, Mia. Here those lights have minds. Unseelie minds."

"Oy and spreading their plague of unseelie bogs across all of Kaledon," said Maple.

As if on cue, more lights arose, floating over the black water and muddy fungi-covered rocks in eerie yellow spheres of haze. Behind them, the tall, menacing figure of the Woodsman strode slowly from the darkness, followed by eerie floating snakes with frond-like fins.

Mia inched toward Liam, limbs slowly petrifying with fear at the creature literally from Liam's nightmares. She could feel his muscles as tense as vibrating wire, clamping down on the trembling. The growing lights illuminated countless skeletons sprawled across the bogs. Some half-submerged. Others bent over the stone walls. Still others stretched toward the trees as if fleeing their last. Mia swallowed, suppressing the urge to shiver. Soulfire lurked within her wildly. She clenched her abdomen and forced herself to stay calm.

"Rathchylde clan once lived here," said Liam coldly, eyes on the skeletons. "Good people." He shook his head.

The wisps drifted toward the three of them, the Woodsman stalking slowly behind them. Mia moved into a crouch, ready to sprint. "Ok so this is the part where someone says what we do now."

Liam scowled and stood. "They're children of the Unseelie King himself. We'll have to push *through* the bogs and hope to outrun them."

No one wanted to express how insane that seemed. Even knowing barely anything about them, the sight of them brought ice into her veins.

"Now!" he growled.

They shoved ahead, and the malevolence within the dimly glowing light of the wisps made Mia's marks burn, even from a distance. From here, Mia thought she saw the Woodsman smirk as the wisps gathered momentum and sped toward them. They charged ahead, Liam carrying Maple when the bog became too deep, long shanks striding swiftly, enhanced by Mia's first spell, while she lagged. More wisps rose from dark pools behind, keeping pace. Maple hopped onto a muddy bank and loosed arrows at them, but they swirled out of the way and kept coming. Liam reached for his sword, but realized it was broken and gone.

The wisps closed in, pain coalescing into a voice within and hitting them all, penetrating the gloom, and seemingly coming from within as well. *Plunderers ... grave robbers ... debts you owe us. We serve the Lady of Vathine ... daughter of Vinraith Flame-eye, king of the Unseelie! We shall take naught but lifeblood in payment for your trespass!*

"I didn't take anything! I would never plunder!" Liam shouted, stumbling forward, Maple falling into a roll on a muddy tuft, Mia straining to keep up.

Priests ... invaders ... Myrrdian filth of Briden the convert ... dishonor humans have done us!

Screams and sorrow rose like an evil chorus, clouding her vision, the soulfire within her barely resisting a heavy pressure now upon her mind.

Now we will claim you, said the voices, in eerie unison, low and gut-wrenching.

Liam lurched and shook, his eyes cloudy, expression blank. Then he straightened and bolted into the darkness. Mia caught her breath, heart blasting like a hammer. Liam had become possessed. "Father!" he rasped, as will-o-wisps swarmed about them like cruel fireflies.

The next few moments came in fragments — waves.

Liam, bursting forth at unnatural speed through the blackthorns, over walls and through muddy brush. Mia called after him into the dun fog to no avail. Maple cried for them from long behind.

A force pushed her limbs now, taking control of her consciousness. "Leave us alone!" she cried fruitlessly.

The fire in her blood slowed the infectious pressure upon her mind, but only by a few moments.

She stumbled, and black wings flew over her head as a great darkness loomed before her, dim firelight flickering from within a great structure, hopeless tangles of vines and roots covering the stone of a long-devoured castle.

Her vision went black.

Chapter 13

A cascade of life images crashed into Mia's fevered vision. Curled up on a chair the day her parents gave her up to the Childcare Plex because they were "too busy" to bother with her. The other children spitting on her, calling her "little nothing," and tearing up her fledgling drawings. Being simply *unable* to stop making more in secret. Liam defending her, to the point of bloodying others and being sent to isolation. Making the wooden figurine together, protected against the Monitors who told them they'd have to destroy it — the work of a mysterious administrator. Her years of education to become an animal behavior specialist in a world where most animals lived in containment facilities and were extinct in the wild. The years she and Liam lived together, each year seeing him shut down more and more often, brooding in silence, drinking too heavily deep into the night. Vain attempts to get him to open up to her. Her inability to reach him.

Making her feel useless.

Until that sad day they decided to part as friends.

She opened her eyes. She was curled up on a rug in a dark stone room. Cool, sharp air blew in from a window, hitting the cold mist on her skin. How long she had been there, she couldn't say. The candlelit chamber gaped large and seemed circular, furnished with old wooden odds and ends. She sat up, muscles aching. Behind her stood a musty bed, oval rug beneath patterned into a triple spiral design.

She squinted, puzzled, reviewing the last moments she could remember. To her left sprawled a fireplace full of half-burnt logs, and to her right a jumble of tables and chairs. Ancient tapestries of falcons and wolves hung on stone walls. The ceiling stretched into the shadows. A deep creaking rumbled somewhere.

She fended off the chill with a musty quilt. In the night, creatures howled as the wind swelled through the trees. Each moan sounded lower and more cruel, as if directed at her. Her heart jumped, but with effort she slowed her breathing as Doctor M taught her years ago. Cold sweat beaded on her neck. The window yawned like a demon with metal teeth for bars, and thunder rolled in, followed by rain, a storm overtaking the night like a dark god.

She scanned the room. No wisps. But no Liam either. She clamped down the jitters through sheer force of will. The rain-misty air reflected the flickering orange candlelight, revealing a door on the other side. Nobody here. Drapes undulated by the empty sill.

She approached the door and pulled the opener. Locked. Wrestling with it only increased her heart rate. Groaning, she hit the door fruitlessly with her fist. She sighed and searched for a key, and a nervous scramble turned into a concentrated search. She tackled furniture, mildewy chests. Nothing. She stared out the barred window at the dense forest that had overtaken the outer wall. The smell revealed the hidden unseelie bog beneath the dark canopy. She tapped her cheek. *I'm in the castle I saw before I faded out. But how did I get here?*

She sighed as her stomach rumbled. Time was wasting and if she didn't find a way out of here things were going to get lean. What's more, Liam was probably in mortal danger. The wind mounted. Snorting and snarling noises rose from the forests — or was it below the tower she was in? She grasped the bar of the window as wet wind blew her hair behind her. She gasped. *Something is moving down there!* No wisps, Woodsman or floating snakes out there. What else could it be? She didn't want to know. The treetops tossed, hissing through the leaves, and dim shapes darted among them, as if the forest itself was rousing.

She was thirsty, so she took a ceramic cup and reached through the bars, filling it with rainwater despite the howls, drank deeply, then returned to the door to stare at it. How was she going to get out of here?

"Children forbid," said a voice, "I'm too late and you've gone starkers on me, haven't you, little flower?"

She whirled. Sea Breeze stood perched on the windowsill. Mia smiled in relief. The candle light seemed to brighten a little. "Oh my god, Sea Breeze! Help me get out of here, I'm trapped. Where's Liam?"

"Easy, love, easy. Don't get your pantaloons in a tuck. You all right, there? You had a bit of a long kip — tried to wake you several times, but the will-o-wisp's had you by the throat, you could say."

She patted herself. Still whole. "No, I'm okay. Pretty sure?"

The raven flittered to a table and breathed in and out sharply. "Now listen close." Mia leaned in. "I've bought us a bit of time, flower. The wisps wanted to devour you both, but I bargained with them and ... well, they set a trial for you."

She glanced at the bird sidelong. "A trial? Like a test?"

The bird nodded. "Winners escape ... losers, well ..."

She narrowed her eyes on the bird. "Die?" Sea Breeze nodded. She rubbed her forehead, then shrugged. "I dunno what I was expecting, anyway. A friendly game of Nexwork golf? Ok, so what do we need to do?"

"The wisps destroyed the Rathchylde clan long ago. This was their home fortress. MacTira Moor, they called it. But other things lived here, too. The dangerous beasts they captured for sport."

Mia mulled that over, rubbing her chin. "All right. Anything else?"

The raven bobbed and paced, as if trying to think of how to best say the next part. "That's where it gets complicated."

She crossed her arms. "Don't sugarcoat it, Sea Breeze."

"The creatures trapped here … have suffered a cruel fate. Because it's Unseelie Fairywild now, they're unable to starve and die, but they're imprisoned, so they can't roam free."

"And…?"

The raven stared at her squarely. "They're *between* you and the way out."

Blood drained from her face and she instinctively stepped back. She placed a hand on her chest and closed her eyes, controlling her breathing slowly and forcing herself to stay focused. "So what you're telling me is that in order to escape, I have to run a gauntlet of ravenous, crazed beasts."

"I'm afraid so, love."

She shook her head. "Of course." How the hell was she going to accomplish this? No weapons. No armor. No knowledge of this place. She sat on the stone ledge by the hearth, rocking back and forth. "Why are they doing this, Sea Breeze? These Unseelies … why do they hate us so much?"

The raven flitted down on the ash-dusted stone beside her as thunder rolled outside and a wave of rain swept past the window. "It's their king, love. Vinraith Flame-eye."

She sat up and turned to her, attentive. "Who is he? I need data."

"Listen close, love," said Sea Breeze, voice lower, candlelight flickering in her black eyes, blue tuft wafting in the breeze. "There's ages to that tale, stretching farther back than you could likely imagine. For you see, Erentyr is far older than Midworld. Perhaps someday I will share all of that tale with you. For now we must stay focused, flower. It's enough to know that the Unseelie King is a powerful Remembering One. As mighty as the Fairy Queen Herself. He lives in a dark, tortured valley to the west of Kaledon. For many centuries he kept to his own. But now his infested bogs and groves consume Kaledon year by year, unstoppable."

Despair made Mia's blood run cold. "But ... why? Did Liam's people offend him?"

Sea Breeze scoffed, feathers puffing, "Nay, little flower. It wasn't that. It was Ynwin, Liam's mum, and her desperate move to save her son. When she sent Liam to Midworld with the Dream Stone, that tipped the balance between Vinraith Flame-eye and the Fairy Queen in his favor," she said, unusual sadness in her normally sing-song voice. "He was free to spread forth his wrath against the mortalkinds from the Dark Valley, gobbling up everything in his path, love. He's been slow but relentless, savoring each bite with cruel glee. Soon there'll be nothing left of your friend's homeland."

Mia swallowed and looked down, heavy weight upon her now. She recalled their tromp through Tarila and the spriggan than Lungor killed. "Can the Unseelie King be defeated? Killed? Maybe we can fight him?"

Sea Breeze raised her beak to Mia, eerily slow. "Oh no, flower. His minions, yes, but the Unseelie King himself is a Remembering One. A Kosithi. He is immortal. There is no way to defeat him."

That stole her breath. She suppressed trembling. Mia closed her eyes, breaths rapid. This was way over her head. She let her hair fall in front of her face and sat quietly for a long while. *No way to defeat him. None.* Sea Breeze, seemingly sensing her turmoil, simply caressed her forearm with a gentle wing. It helped.

Mia let out a sharp breath. "I am so out of my depth here," she whispered.

She lingered on that thought. But then, the image of dead Nurnians, falling to her spell-arrows emerged within. Blood splattered. Faces frozen in horror.

A dark presence emerged slowly inside her, like a tiger in a night-soaked jungle. The feeling swept the fear aside and replaced it with smoldering embers. Her breathing slowed.

147

To hell with this. Do or die — that's all there really is here. There was no choice. She opened her eyes. "This is beyond cruel, Sea Breeze. I have no experience with anything like this. Haunted swamps infested with servants of the Unseelie King like the Woodsman and the wisps? God knows what else? But ... I don't care. I'll do it. Whatever it takes."

"That's the spirit, love," she whispered. "I'm sorry you got caught up in all this, flower."

She straightened, tightening her jaw. "I'm not. I put myself here. I'll just have to find a way. Or get ripped to pieces. That's all there is."

"One more thing, love," said the raven, hopping closer. Mia frowned. "Don't die here, or you'll end up like the beasts — your spirit trapped forever."

She chewed her bottom lip and glared at the raven. "Great. This place is insane. Whatever. First thing is opening that huge door." She stood.

The raven nodded with an "*err, err,*" then hopped to the sill. "Yes, about that. Let's just say without a *key*," Sea Breeze lingered on that word and pointed a wing at Mia's hip pocket, "you'll never escape."

Mia felt something in her pocket and withdrew it. An ornate, brass key. Sea Breeze put a wing to her beak and winked at Mia. "See you outside the curtain wall by the ruined fountain, love. I think I saw Maple sneaking about that way, too."

"See you there," she answered, forcing it.

The raven flew off.

Mia gathered herself before the door and stared at it, breathing slowly. Never in her life had she faced anything like this. The characters in the movie-plex shows were always able to do things like this without hesitation. There was always some way to *beat* the enemy. But that was just fantasy — this was real. And seemingly impossible.

Still, there *was* no real choice. Liam needed her right now. The burning, swirling force within her surged, as if "agreeing" with her, like the blood of a restless ancestor ... perhaps the grandmother she never met? That thought gave her a grim smile.

The iron reinforced door loomed, making her feel like an ant at the foot of a fortress. Eyes closed, she put the key in and turned before she could change her mind.

The door unlocked.

She faced the darkness and scoffed. *These 'Unseelies' have a cruel sense of humor. Make her feel useless, just like she always feels. That will break her.*

Jerks. She snarled and lit a candelabra with a flint box. Taking a deep breath, she carefully made her way barefoot down the dusty stone steps. "Damn, damn, damn," she muttered, pushing through fear with each step. *I'm out of my depth. So far out.* Still one foot fell after the other. The stone felt firm and solid underfoot, not as cold as she expected. The glow from the tower room faded behind as the flickering trio of candles and the dim turquoise of her grandmother's ring became her only source of light.

Bestial grunts and scraping emerged from the cool dark. The landing opened into a cobblestone room lined with cages, the air musky. Wolves, bears, and badgers paced and pawed in dirty cells. By their huffing and drooling, she could tell they were agitated — her experience with timberwolves told her how stressed they were. Her heart rate climbed. Her skin became clammy. The cages were closed. On the far end, the path stopped at a heavy door. She forced herself forward, shaky key hand leading the way. "I don't suppose any of you talk? Like Sea Breeze? Anyone?" They gnawed the iron bars. *Ok, then.*

As she approached the door, they quieted, licking their chops and glaring. Turning the key, a clunking noise echoed, followed by the rattle of chains and counterweights. The cage doors opened. Wolves shoved their muzzles under rising bars as bears and badgers pawed at the growing gaps.

Oh shit! Heart racing, she flew back up the stairs.

The door to the tower was closed!

She pounded the heavy planks. "Hey! Open up! Sea Breeze? Are you still there?"

A low growl froze her. She turned to see a wolf stalking up the steps. Her jaw quivered. "S-Sea Breeze? Open the door. P-please."

She squinted through the keyhole. Gold glinted, then the shadow of a human form walked past! Blood drained from her face. She stood up. *What the hell was that? Who is in there?* Didn't matter. "Sea Breeze! I left the key downstairs!"

The raven's voice rang. "You can do this, little flower."

She released her death-grip on the candelabra and set it down in front of her. The wolf slunk closer, eyeing the candles. Her blood pulsed quickly, but she stood firm. The image, gestures and words erupted in her head. She adjusted them the way she instinctively knew how, partially letting it take over. Partially remaining in control. *"Oplarravin,"* she incanted, and the power formed the red bow of Mogdun in her hands, arrow knocked, flames crackling, warming her face. She let out several quick breaths, raising the bow. The creature flinched but then kept creeping forward.

The bow and arrow evaporated and shooting pains wracked her arms. Wizard marks. She dropped to her knees in pain, then, realizing her predicament, she froze, eyes locked on the wolf. It shifted back and forth, clearly unsure of what she was doing. She shook the pain out of her arms and started again. But she paused, then put her hands down. No. Not like this. Then, hearing barks below, the wolf suddenly darted down the stairs. Her wizard marks swirled, stylized beasts loping. She clenched her fists, and her inner fire rose.

Too enraged to care about safety, she padded to the candelabra and marched back down the spiral staircase after the wolf. Thoughts of weariness, of uselessness, of smallness had disappeared.

She entered the large chamber at the bottom.

The cages yawned, as did the door on the other side. Her key still stuck from the lock in the open iron-bound door. She fiercely retrieved her key and shoved the door open to reveal a darker stairway. She could go back up now, back to the safety of the tower with the key.

No. I'm going forward, not back.

She bit her lip and descended into damper air into a low, dripping tunnel.

She passed the threshold. Then a low growl rattled the air and her breath stopped. Tunnels pierced several directions, and a portcullis blocked entry into a cell ahead of her. The wall held a large iron mechanism with a keyhole. Inside the cell a massive wolf lay dead, its skin pulled over starved ribs, unmoving in a reeking puddle, a tuft of white hair across its cheek. Across from it rested a pile of gigantic bones in another cell — perhaps a monstrous bird.

Her breathing ragged, heart pounding her sternum like a jackhammer, she considered moving on. But then she recalled what Sea Breeze told her — the creatures here had been trapped and unable to die. She stared at the bodies of the massive wolf and bird. Silent and still, yet she could almost feel their endless suffering. But so what? She needed to get out of here. *Forget them. Just leave.*

But she couldn't.

Without thinking any further, she unlocked the mechanism, backing away from chain-rattling. The portcullis opened, followed by others. She flushed, a chill overtaking her muscles. Why did she just do that?

The dead wolf sprang up, eyes glowing white, its flesh changing. It hobbled toward her, and she found herself facing monstrous lupine eyes. The wolf stood half again as tall as she at the shoulders. Behind her the bones stirred, forming together into an enormous falcon, new feathers springing forth on newly spindling flesh. The wingspan would have stretched 100 feet, had it not been cramped. The wolf growled down at her, forcing her backward down the tunnel, while the massive white falcon scratched its claws and let out a deafening screech. The sounds cut her to the soul, like death itself might, as two more huge wolves joined behind the leader, freed. She stopped cold, her bare feet in a puddle. The falcon looked as though it could prey on elk without much effort. Even less on tiny morsels such as herself. The wolf's grey and black mane flickered eerily in the candlelight, white tufts along its cheeks. It stepped forth, its paws — each larger than her head — padded forward.

Fear swirled within her, overpowering whatever courage she had mustered. Out of the corner of her eye she noticed a small tunnel in the wall. If she could run fast enough, she could get to it. The wolves stalked with each step she took backwards, and behind them the falcon pushed out of its cell, streaking its white feathers with mud, to close in on her from the other side. How long had they been in here with no food? Obviously waking them up meant they were hungry! The white-tufted wolf licked its lips.

Panic electrified her limbs. She swirled her hands and imagined the complex diamond design in her mind. *This better work.* "*Sheeaza,*" she whispered, and the power of the spell crept down her legs from somewhere deep within her blood. She faked left and turned to bound at uncanny speed down the corridor. The wolf growled and the falcon screeched, and she dove into the tunnel —little more than a gutter. She sloshed in the water backwards and ran into a grating. Trapped. The wolf snuffled at the opening, trying to put its muzzle in and get her, but she was just out of reach. Its hot breath wafted her damp hair back and she suppressed the urge to scream. It would do no good. She squirmed against the bars behind her.

How long she crouched there, water soaking into her dress, the wolves taking turns trying to get at her, she couldn't say, for it seemed an eternity.

After a while, the wolves left, and distant screeches and howls echoed through the stone tunnels.

Dawn light fought to penetrate the stony wet undercrofts.

Silence, save the dripping stone, filled the air.

She gingerly crept out of the culvert. The tunnel stretched into darkness on the left, toward dim light on the right. She scrambled right, to an exit where a huge double door had been smashed open, tufts of fur and massive feathers scattered. Misty air wafted in, carrying the scent of pine.

Elation entered her step, a new surge of energy pushing her to flee. Her bare feet trod on the cool earthen path beyond the stone, into an overgrown courtyard, a dark canopy of walnut and cedar sharply silhouetted against a timid orange sky above. A strange new feeling coursed through her heart, as if she'd unlocked a color palette she never knew existed. She glanced back at the open gate at the foot of the keep. *Did I really just do all that?* She nodded to herself. *Yeah. I actually did.* A mighty, distant howl arose from the west, as a huge shadow soared into the foggy distance. Realization dampened the moment. After all, her escape had just unleashed huge predators that would love to eat them all for breakfast.

She breathed out sharply. So be it. She did what she had to. Rain crept down from the treetops, and she closed her eyes and raised her face to feel it on her skin. Breathing deeply, she held her hands open to the sky as if inviting more to fall. Down came the rain, seeping into her dress, wetting her thick hair, making it wavy and unruly. She should have been cold, but soulfire warmed her. Deep, ancestral, and mysterious, ancient blood lit an endless fire. She opened her eyes, exhilarated and terrified. She was getting stronger ... for better or worse. Deep down, nine more unknown spells still lurked within her, like shadowy stalkers, bloodthirsty and dark. They would have to wait.

She wound the path along the tree roots, wolf-shaped marks on her arm twitching, her grandmother's ring glowing dimly. She found a cobbled path crawling with vines and blackthorn brush. It coursed through tall statues draped in nightingale green. "Sea Breeze?" she called, trying to whisper and shout at the same time. No answer. She entered twisted wet brambles brimming with life, frogs croaking by the hundreds.

She scanned the canopy. "Sea Breeze? Did you find Liam?" Still no answer.

The path opened into a patio wild with mushrooms that quivered eerily, climbing the nets of blackthorn branches. Beyond stood a mighty curtain wall gatehouse that led to a 20-foot tunnel of impenetrable bleeding rhododendrons. A hedge maze? She approached a central pool of murky water in the courtyard, rippling with raindrops. Behind her the brambled castle loomed.

A bubble erupted from the pool. Something was submerged, barely visible. She knelt by the edge to get a better look. At the bottom, amid the skeletons, lay the bodies of Liam and Sea Breeze, still as stone. The sight shot through her body like lightning. She nearly screamed, then without another thought, she dove headfirst into the pool and swam down with all her strength.

Chapter 14

Liam topped a grassy hillcrest. A brilliant green vista swept down before him. Silvery lakes adorned the distant rocky hills, and beautiful flower fields covered the land in a mosaic pattern brighter than anything he'd seen. A jagged line of mighty, snow-capped mountains flanked the valley. Sapphire sky flecked with overlapping layers of cloud soared to infinity. The air smelled of crystal sweet roses, which gently fell across the cascade of glens.

A tall man rested on a rock at the hill crest in a fur-lined tunic, his great cloak wrapped several times about him. The air blew brisk and fresh, tossing the cloak with his wavy red hair. He carved a piece of wood into a circle of intricate knotwork designs. Liam's breath caught. He knew who this was. But how was this possible?

Am I dead? Is this Evensade?

"Father?" he asked, gingerly approaching.

"Come, son," said the man, "sit with me."

Liam did. He stared, unable to help himself. Cormac an Brionglóir smiled and held up the wood carving. A gorgeous crest of the family clan — one that could be hung on the door of one's home with pride. "I think I'm getting better, what do ye think?"

Liam fell mute. What does one say to one's father dead fifteen years? He blinked. His father always wanted to try wood carving. And here he was, that easy rugged smile on his face, that deep, contemplative way. That tremendous strength in his eyes. How could he live up to one such as this? "Why am I here, Father? Is this a dream?"

Cormac shook his head. "No, lad. 'Tis real — more real than Erentyr and Midworld combined, if you can believe it."

That made no sense. But more pressing questions strangled him. He pushed through it. "Is Mom ... here?"

"Nay, son. But then, that's why *you're* here isn't it? Even if for only a short time." His father's voice resonated — comforting, unlike any other voice. Cormac smiled wistfully. "See that village down there?" He pointed with his knife down a path that wound lazily through rocky hills and flowery fields. It ended at a hamlet where smoke twirled from chimneys and herders tended to their livestock. Pipe and harp music, and beating drums carried on the wind, tickling his memory. Liam nodded. "That's where everyone is, now. The whole clan." Liam straightened, but Cormac put a hand on his shoulder. "Easy, there, young one. You cannae go now. But that's where we wait for ye. Your mother still needs you in Erentyr, right enough."

He turned to his father. "Because Mom is a Stoneguard," he said softly.

Father nodded, sweeping his red beard down in the wind. "Aye. If only you could've seen how proud she was when she accepted the Calling Brand from your grandfather, Oisin — she trained for many years for that. She is the one. The one who can save Kaledon." He fell quiet. "I miss her."

He straightened. "I can rescue her, Father. I will fight to the utmost end of my will."

Father patted his back. "Aye, I've no doubt! Never a man to shirk a chance at glory." Liam smiled half-heartedly. Such words felt undeserved. "But you need your gift from me. That dragon at the gate withheld it from ye — a black deed that was, and for certain!"

Liam raised an eyebrow. "He granted us passage to Kaledon from his castle as his boon."

"Ach, that dragon is wily and full of trickery. That was no boon! Drelthun sent you to the Fairywild to die. That other man — Sir Damien, of the Southern Conclave of Ozremorn? The sword, Larsorn, was *his* boon for surviving the gate — one of the fabulous weapons of the Fallen Dream Empire. Uncountably old and made by the gods."

"Are you saying such a weapon is due to me as well?"

He gazed into his son's eyes, pride and deep concern on that weathered face. "Aye. The Fairy Queen granted me this one chance to return it to you — 'tis my old sword, which I gladly give to ye, as you're my only son left in Erentyr. 'Tis a blade to match Larsorn. You've greater need for it than I. But you must promise me something."

Liam's pulse quickened. "Anything, Father."

"You've got to tell my tale, son. You've gone for ages, keeping it to yourself. It's not our way, lad. You must tell how it ended for me. You and your mother witnessed it. You must share it with our countrymen."

That hit him in the stomach. Of all the horrible memories he'd wrestled with, *that* one tore him to pieces — he'd refused to speak of it to anyone, not even the therapy bots back home. "Father … is there no other way?"

His brows furrowed. "You'll do as I say, now, son. It's my right. If you want my sword you'll have to promise."

Liam lifted his chin, swallowing his reluctance. Father was right. It was not optional. He had *earned* such a request. "Yes sir. With pride. I would do it without any reward if that is your wish."

"Aye. Now, I must go. The Fairy Queen did nae afford us this meeting to chatter about. Work needs to be done. Hard deeds are nigh, and you must rise to meet them. You'll do your father proud, I know."

An avalanche of years missing his father crashed down on him. "Father … don't leave me just yet. Can't I stay with you, just for a little while?"

He patted his shoulder, Liam's eyes blurry with tears. "You must let it go, son," he said softly. "It's all right. One day, years from now, we *will* meet again. And what a day that will be! I'll take you down this road to our home here in Evensade and we'll feast at your coming."

He mastered himself, nodded and embraced his father long, as if trying to make up for the thousands of embraces he missed and would miss again. He closed his eyes and tears coursed down his cheek into his beard, their wordless exchange stronger than farewells.

***

When he opened his eyes, darkness surrounded him. Arms heaved him up. Bubbles swirled through his hair. Mia and Maple pulled him from the courtyard pool. Sea Breeze flapped about, coughing and sputtering water from her beak. He sat up and spat water to the side, dripping in the gloomy, boggy blackthorn grove that overwhelmed the curtain wall.

In his arms, sheathed, a sword glinted in the dim orange light of dawn.

Chapter 15

Liam slowly stood, took his father's sword from the sheath and brandished it high — a magnificent claymore with a gold-trimmed hilt and shimmering ogham script upon the silvery blade. It flashed like snake-skin in the rainy dawn.

"Ooh, I recognize *that* sword," said Maple. Mia and Sea Breeze gawked at it. "It's Xanibor. The 'Druid's Claymore' the young ones call it now."

Holding the sword aloft, he felt power emanating from it through the thick leather-wrapped handle into his arm. Pulses of élan, tensing muscle, preparing for an explosion, barely containable. Another Erentyrian surprise. Gripping it double hand, he lowered it at the curtain wall, and the sword seemed to let its will be known. Attack! In response, barely conscious of what he was doing, he unleashed it, and a tangle of new vines and branches sprouted layer upon layer, thorned vegetation surging wildly in an area some thirty feet in diameter. Numbing pain hammered his hands, dropping him to his knees, knocking the wind from him.

Clearing the cobwebs from his head, he heard Sea Breeze, "all right there, Liam? Best not try that too often, right love?"

He marveled at Xanibor. "I never saw my father in action with this weapon. Truly incredible."

"That be a sword from the wars in the early Stones of Time, love," said Sea Breeze. "Made by the Remembering Ones. Best know your onions before you tinker with those."

He nodded and sheathed Xanibor to sling it on his shoulder. "Might need some practice."

Mia turned him to her, eyes full of joy at seeing him alive, and embraced him. It was good to hold her. But before long, he realized how prolonged the hug was getting, and he backed away, embarrassed. Apparently, she had the same thought. Flushed, she cleared her throat as he fidgeted, scratching his head and looking away.

"So," said Mia, gathering herself and tapping the handle. "Where did it come from? The sword, I mean."

He stroked his beard. "Yeah, that's the weird part. I remember running from the will-o-wisps and the Woodsman, then I found myself in this bright green valley. My father was there. He said I could have his sword if I told his story to our countrymen."

She tilted her head. "Wait. *His* story? The one you've never told anyone?"

He straightened, rigid with resolve. "Yes. And I *will* do it, too."

She raised her eyebrows and searched his expression. "I believe you will."

He nodded mutely, appreciating her support, though he did not say it.

"So, you're saying it might it have been a dream, then?" asked Maple, chiming in.

Mia pursed her lips to the side, in thought. "Mm, dreams don't conjure up swords out of thin air."

Liam shook his head. "No, they don't. Though the sword could have already been there and I dreamed the rest — either way, you saved my life. All of you. Thank you."

"And maybe mine, too, loves," said Sea Breeze.

"You're … welcome," said Mia, wringing the water from her long hair, seemingly taken aback by such sentiment. Was it so rare that he expressed appreciation? That thought stung him with worry.

"So," said Mia after an awkward pause, "what now … how do we get out of here before the Unseelies return?"

Maple hopped forward. "I can help with that, now. I came in from the other way, through that gammy maze once we got separated. Took me hours to puzzle it out. But! I think I've got it, now, if you want to follow me."

He crouched to Maple, still worrying. "I don't know what we deserved to get such an amazing friend, Maple, but I'm grateful for it."

Maple blushed, waving him off. "Oh, go on, then. You lot are a tiddly-do."

A deep, staccato howl echoed from the west — deeper, rattling Liam's bones. He put a hand on the sword. "What the holy hell was that?"

Mia rubbed her forehead and closed her eyes. "Yeah ... that was my doing. Giant predators. Long story."

"Well let's stop chin wagging and get on," said Sea Breeze.

"Agreed," said Liam, marching through the gatehouse and into the hedge maze. Maple guided them through foggy corridors of thorny high brush for several hours. The day wore on, light barely penetrating the cold fog. They pushed on silently, exchanging glances at every noise. Every rustling sound in the foliage.

Then a low hum came rising from all around. Malice seemed to ooze through pores in the air. Will-o-wisps emerged from side tunnels, from behind them, much faster this time. They ran.

"Now would be a good time for that spell again," said Liam, breathless, "whatever you called it."

"Windy river. Don't ask me the real name of it — I don't think I could pronounce it." Mia circled her hands and closed her eyes briefly. "*Kolorris*" she said, but nothing happened. Her eyes went cloudy and she stumbled, but quickly recovered with a hand up from Liam. She regained her bearings. "Damn, messed it up!"

"Come on, leg it, you two, no time for that!" said Maple, zipping forward and scratching her head at an intersection.

"Lands sakes, they're angry," said Sea Breeze. She hissed, "their hatred is overpowering." The raven twirled to the ground.

Liam backtracked to pick her up. Three wisps, inflamed with red light, shot toward them. "Go on Sea Breeze, fly out of here, meet up with us later,"

"Sorry loves," she said, flapping unsteadily into the hazy sky. The wisps ignored her and sped on.

They then unleashed a wail that burst within their minds, wracking all with shooting pains unlike any they'd felt before. All three of them dropped, squirming in agony. Liam crawled toward Mia, her cheeks streamed with tears, teeth gritted, face red. With his last ounce of strength he crawled toward her, trying to somehow protect her.

Then her eyes glowed green, and she forced an incantation from her lips, straining with sheer will, circling her hands in a strange gesture. "*Eee-anahhhe!*" She squawked and a wave of spell-force surged through them, extinguishing the pain. The wisps recoiled. The three scrambled to their feet, trying to shake off the brief stiffness, before running again. "Quench-the-fires?" Mia whispered as they ran together.

"Whatever works," he answered.

Maple leapt ahead, then beckoned them on. "This way! Almost out!"

They rounded a corner to a long misty tunnel, cold light against the grasping thorns of the hedge, roots bumpy upon the hard earth.

All stopped hard in their tracks.

At the end of the last tunnel some fifty paces, crimson cloak flowing, stood the Woodsman, blocking their only exit, hand upon the haft of his axe, wolf-snarl poking from the deep layered hood. Icy crystals infiltrated Liam's muscles, clenching his stomach, clamping down on his chest. Mia stood rigid, white as stone, eyes wide. Maple scrambled to string her bow, fumbling with shaky fingers. Behind, Liam could feel the wisps returning.

Through sheer force of will, knowing the others needed him to be brave, Liam stepped forward and unsheathed Xanibor, forcing his breathing to be smooth despite the trembling chest and racing heart.

"I told you, Liam," said the Woodman, hoods pulled low, "you do not belong in my lands." He pointed his axe accusingly at him. "You should have *died* with your family. Admit it!"

Rage battered against the terror inside him. He bared his teeth. "I don't know why I survived, Woodsman. Or why you have chosen to torment me all these years. But I'm not a boy anymore. Let us pass or I'll–"

"Or you'll what?" the Woodsman taunted with a sneer.

Liam's anger mounted. He sharply nodded to Mia and Maple each. They nodded, both quiet and still. He lifted his blade in the traditional Kaledonian salute, then held Xanibor in a high guard, posta di fenestra. "Or we cross blades. So help me, if you don't get out of the way, I will kill you."

The Woodsman raised his axe high and chuckled. "Let's just see if you can," he oozed. Then he charged, axe reared.

Liam closed in, entire body focused, taking long strides but keeping a defensive position. The Woodsman roared, blindly running, hood still over his eyes, yet he still seemed able to see what was happening. His axe stroke circled toward Liam's neck with uncanny speed.

Liam was ready, however, and shifted left, guiding the axe with a high parry and guiding it away, causing it to miss its mark. Then he retaliated with a savage slash across the Woodsman's neck. A sickening thud, followed by the scrape of metal on something sharp left Liam whirling to see the Woodsman stumble forward, his head rolling several paces ahead, wrapped in the cloak and hoods in a bundle which stopped at Mia's feet.

The Woodsman's body then slumped forward onto the ground, still as a stone.

He blinked at the others for a moment. Mia was the first to realize the Woodsman was dead. She and Maple gingerly passed the body and joined Liam as he stared at the dead wolf-man, gasping for breath, flush with rage and pounding pulse.

"I killed him," he whispered, panting. "After all these years. I did it." Mia patted his shoulder, smiling. The rain fell for a few quiet moments, and Liam regained his breath.

Maple squinted at the dead body, monocle in place.

Then the body quivered, forcing them all to take a step back. Slowly the headless body clambered to its feet and strode forward. Liam's breath stole away, blood draining from his face. Leaning without effort, the Woodsman reclaimed the head and placed it back on his body. Then he retrieved his axe, flaring his cloak behind him.

Liam glanced at Xanibor. The blade was not covered in blood as it should have been. No crimson pools lie where he'd struck down the creature, either. Instead, small splinters lined the sharp edge of his glittering sword. Scratches marked the blade that slowly disappeared.

"I told you, Liam," oozed the Woodsman, "you should not be in my lands."

Liam curled his lip in terror, unable to believe his eyes. "What kind of servant of the Unseelie King are you?" he whispered.

Mia swept her hands and with a word conjured up the red, glowing bow in her hands. Maple loosed an arrow, but the Woodsman caught it in midair, snapping it and tossing away the fragments. Mia unleashed her spell, but it stopped an inch before the Woodsman's chest, bursting into a shower of harmless sparks. Spell-bow gone, she raised a hand to cover her mouth in horror, apparently coming to a realization.

"L-Liam," she whispered, "h-he's not who you think he is!"

The Woodsman stepped forward, flipping his axe menacingly, then gripped the edge of his seven-layered hood. "She's right lad," he said with a snaggle-toothed smile, "I'm not a servant of the Unseelie King. I *am* the Unseelie King. Vinraith," he said, lifting his hood to reveal a single burning pupil, fiery blue against his grey wolf-fur, the other eye black as coal. "Flame-eye."

Liam, Mia and Maple stood petrified with terror.

Vinraith lowered his axe into his other hand, blade glinting in the dim light. "And this will be your last warning, mortal. I will answer your question: I followed you because you have yet to justify your existence to me. Your family was slaughtered and you fled. To 'survive'," he sneered. "Well that's not good enough," he growled, pointing at him. "If you enter my lands again, lad, your head will be on my chopping block."

Wisps came at his beckoning, floating down the hedge corridor, oozing malice, their eerie voices hissing on the wind incomprehensibly.

A god in mortal form gave him one last chance to escape certain death. But Liam hesitated. Wouldn't death be *preferable* to any more fleeing? Wasn't Vinraith *right* about him surviving for no good reason?

Mia's eyes darted between him and Vinraith. Maple's teeth chattered, helpless.

No. Not in front of them. Death would come some other day.

He bolted to their right, taking their hands. They snapped out of it and sprinted out of the hedge maze. A horrid howl arose, joined by a cacophony of wisp voices. They charged along a muddy path through the woods and tumbled down a bumpy path.

After what seemed forever tearing through brush and root-strewn trail, they crashed into a puddle on a ravine floor. Behind them the maze blended into the blackthorns, the towers of MacTira Moor now barely visible in the fog.

Liam struggled to his feet and helped Mia up, heart pounding in his ears, lungs on fire. He regained his breath, stretching the bruises and bumps in his shoulders. They stared at the blackthorn lands for a long while, expecting Vinraith and an army of wisps to erupt after them. But nothing came save eerie silence.

Liam knelt down and placed his forehead against Maple's and Mia's for some time, regaining their bearings and their wits, along with their breath. Finally he was able to sit back and survey their surroundings. A misty ravine yawned opposite the ever-misting Unseelie Fairywild. He scanned the grassy gloom for enemies. None currently visible — but something was off.

"What did we stumble into here?" Maple knocked an arrow, squinting. "Feels like an ambush."

"I think so, too," said Mia, straining her eyes in the fog. "Something's not right."

Liam sensed a presence as well — someone watched them, though he couldn't place how he knew it. He drew his father's sword. "All right!" he shouted to the ravine walls. "You can come out already!"

Four shadowy figures emerged: men in hoods and thin scarves over their faces. Another arose seemingly from the soil. A man in a long black gambeson and heavy mail, beneath a tattered red tabard and weather-beaten cloak, pinned with a bronze brooch. Not Nurnian cloth. The man pulled back his hood and scarf. Maple squinted at them from behind Liam, monocle in place. Mia eyed the others suspiciously, rubbing her grandmother's glowing ring.

Liam planted himself before the armed sentries, hiding the pain from his wounds, forcing his mind to clear the harrowing journey they had just endured. The front man approached. His face was rugged, with deep lines and a salt-pepper beard, tired grey eyes below a gnarled brow. He wore a thin bronze torc and a silver livery collar. He was older, but not of great age, and he moved like a younger man. This one wasn't to be trifled with.

"All right, then, lad," said the man, "how about you lay down your arms and surrender. Either that or you can turn back to wherever you three come from."

Liam did not move. "I don't think so. I've come a long way, and this is my home."

"Is that so, then, rolling out of the Unseelie boglands like that? It's been stirring and ill-favored for days now, and then you come popping from it? Just a coincidence, I suppose?" He scowled. "I say nay. State your business! Are ye man or fairy-creature?"

"I am a man, these are my companions, and my business is not yours. Let me pass."

He stepped closer, hands drifting toward an axe in a belt hook. "We'll not. And by your dress I'd say you're from a clan now all dead. So you must be an imposter. What say you?"

Liam unshouldered the baldric and placed a hand on the hilt of Xanibor. "Now look," he said.

The spearmen advanced, and one began to string a bow. Maple lifted hers, defiance on her face.

Mia shot forward, catching Liam off-guard by getting in the man's face and pointing at him. "Imposter," she seethed, "this is no imposter, this is Liam, Seventh Son of Ynwin."

Liam hid a smile at Mia's sudden outburst.

"Liam?" said the leader. The man studied his features, a hand slowing the spearmen behind him. "By the gods," he muttered. The warriors eyes darted between the leader and Liam, suspicion in their gaze.

The leader crossed his arms. "Liam, you say? What be your clan name?"

He furrowed his brow. Trickery? "My name is Liam Trendari Panregon. What of it?"

"As I live and breathe … it really is you! I thought I recognized you. Figured it was a trick of the fog. But of course, you've gotten tall and strong! I'll bet you've got a tale to tell."

The ragtag lot studied him, lowering their weapons. "I'm sorry, do I know you?"

"Well, you don't remember me now. By the faoladhs, you've been away long! I'm Bran O'Halloran, Thane of the Aisling Tuath and Knight of the Black Wolf Order. Your people knew ours. We've ever been friends of the Shoreland Tuath. I knew your mother."

That got Liam's attention. "My mother, you say? Tell me her name, then."

A solemn look fell upon Bran. "Ynwin Panregon was her name. Daughter of Oisin. And a fine and brilliant chieftain she was, 'longside your father, Cormac an Brionglóir. Died in those very Rathchylde lands behind you, they say. May the gods compass him, whatever his fate was." Agreement came from the sentries. "And the rest of your kin."

Liam found no deception in their expressions. His father's face, from that dream — or whatever it was — came to him. He owed his father the telling of a tale. That would have to wait, though. The wind drifted down from the ravine crest and tossed the tufts of brown, withered grass here and there as it passed through the company. The other warriors approached him, and he noticed the feeling of his mother's presence intensified, as if somehow emanating from the Dream Stone in his sporran. Did these men also believe his mother was dead, too? He kept silent.

Mia clasped his hand with questions in her eyes. He returned with a wordless "stay sharp." She nodded, nonverbally responding with "*you* stay sharp!"

"Come on then," said Bran. "Sorry about all this. We have to be careful, now and on, what with the false King Arrius and his faithless poltroons always about." He patted his shoulder, gazing into his eyes. "The Lost Panregon has been found."

There *was* something familiar about Bran. The memory of his face was vague and fleeting, but powerful. It trickled into his mind and stayed there, churning about. "So I truly am home, finally — Kaledon?"

"Aye. I'm amazed you made it through the bogs — you must have been nigh the cairn of Bryn Ducell itself, but never mind that. We've been hearing the calls of the MacTira Moor the last several days, after years of eerie silence. None have heard that sound in ages, I'd wager. Put everyone on guard, but so far no sign of them. You come with strange portents about ye. You're lucky to be alive. But I'm afraid much has happened since you disappeared, young man. Our yokes lack kine and growing seedcorn, and our homesteads stand like forlorn jakes upon the hilltop with none to tend them. 'Tis a blight brought by a cursed king." He spat on the ground. The spearmen grunted in agreement.

He recalled a young Bran pacing the walls of a great castle. He *did* remember him. But then Liam narrowed his brows. Cursed king? That *wasn't* the reason for Vinraith's plague on the land. Why did they not know the truth? "Not a cursed king, Bran," he said. "That's not why our home is being eaten alive. It's because my mother was captured. I think she's in the great stronghold. That's why I'm here. To rescue her. Can you help me find the way? The roads are all choked, and honestly, I don't remember them now. This slow death," he pointed to the encroaching blackthorn bogs, "won't stop until I find her."

"Well," he said, looking him up and down, pondering for a moment, "I can understand why you'd want that, whatever the cause of the curse. We should discuss all that soon." He seemed to be working out what to say next. "It is a long journey," he said at last, "well past the Ring of Brodmar and the passage tombs. And it's dangerous, but ... have no fear, young man. I'll show you the way."

Liam nodded tentatively. Mia looked on with suspicion in her eyes. That was too easy.

"Conal," said Bran, turning to a rugged, younger man in a green, weather-stained gambeson and mail with lined cloak, leather gloves and a damp hood. The man strode down the slope, keeping his blue eyes trained upon Liam. "I'm taking this man here to the camp. Take your equipage to the rounds."

"My lord," said Conal, taking out black cloth hoods. "We should at least precaution with these if you're heading back."

"No need. This man is none other than the Lost Panregon. Seventh son of Ynwin herself."

Conal looked at Mia. "And her? A foreigner? And obvious conjury?"

"She's my friend," said Liam. "Without her I never would have made it back home." Mia crossed her arms, chewing her bottom lip and staying silent, but not backing away.

Bran nodded. "Aye, I believe it. Only strong conjury could have gotten you all the way here from the dragon's castle in Caldbana."

Conal stood before Mia gazing down at her. At first she averted her eyes, but then she raised them again to gaze back defiantly. "Fine," he said. "So it all depends on whether this 'Liam' is who he says he is."

"You can just bet he *is*," said Maple, snapping her fingers. "I'll vouch for him miself!"

Conal ignored Maple and planted himself before Liam. He swept dingy brown hair from his eyes, his sharp-angled face close, barely concealing his contempt. "Meaning no offense, my lord, but how do we *know* this be the youngest son of Ynwin Panregon? Bit of a hard story to believe, don't ye think? We've been fooled by King Arrius's conjury before. We've no good counter-conjury at our avail, and Lamon is a vile sorcerer." He glared at Liam squarely. "Full of trickery."

Sentries nodded in agreement.

"Steady on, Conal. And the lot of you. My sister will have a look at them. And there will be a testing. But I won't leave this unexplored. The Lost Panregon, wandering in my watch from the Fairywild itself, it seems, with strange cloth and even stranger companions. I cannae o'erlook it. Could be the Fairy Queen's work. Her hands are quiet and strange, but gold for those who seek it."

"Praise the Ocean Mother," several muttered. "Praise the Fairy Queen."

Words of doubt from Liam's countrymen cut deeper than swords. "I'm a true man, Lord Bran. I'll prove any test you give."

"Be that so," said Conal, spitting at Liam's feet. "Then where the bloody hell have you been all this time?"

Liam swallowed, scowling. Guilt punched him hard. He had no answer.

"Enough," growled Bran. "There will be time for that tale upon the morrows."

Liam ground his jaw, eye to eye with Conal. *Indeed there will be.*

"Now let's go, Liam," said Bran, "and best keep that fine sword handy. We've more than the growing curse to contend with. Banditry and Nurnian hunters are hard upon this land now, and we've a long journey yet."

Conal looked him over, still suspicious, but then rounded up the sentries and turned southeast, tracing a path they swiftly covered behind them and leaving Bran with them.

Bran nodded. "I cannae wait to hear your story, young Liam — no doubts it's a grand one."

"Me too," said Mia, glancing at him, concern in her eyes.

Liam's smile faded, gloom overtaking him. Bran led through the ravine and up the grassy lumps to open ground that sloped to a wooded crest. There the foggy land turned hilly, and mountains rose beyond that, a heavy cloud ceiling mingling with snow-dappled crags. They silently passed neglected pastures and huts. In the distance rose the misty, 100-foot shadow of a great standing stone of Cwen Dreorig. Mia watched the farms go by with sorrow in her eyes.

"So much suffering," she muttered.

***

They worked their way through rugged Kaledon country over the next few hours to cross a field of moldering weeds. Maple hopped on grassy tufts to avoid the muck, fascinated by the conversation. "Soon you'll be before the knights loyal to Kaledon," said Bran, "and your tale will be judged. *I* believe you're the lad I once knew, but ... the knights must judge by their own hearts."

Liam clicked his tongue and stretched his neck muscles, fighting off worry. "As they should." The cold water deepened as the light dimmed, and unease grew within him. He signaled for Maple to hop into his arms and he carried her as Mia walked unhindered *on the surface* of the water beside him. He made a double-take at her. Her eyes were narrowed in concentration. "Figured out another one, huh?"

"Yeah, don't distract me," she said. "That's five."

"What happens when you figure out the twelfth one?"

She shuddered, almost losing her concentration. "I don't want to think about that."

He wrinkled his brow, studying the marks on her calves and forearms. Her eyes glittered eerily as she walked across the water.

"I'll tell ye," said Bran, eyes watching Mia as they exited the marshy patch and found the road again, "I'm glad I found ye and not someone else. Your story meant something to us, Liam, and to have you return, and with such strange company," he said, casting a glance at the pipe-puffing Maple and the marked Mia and her glowing ring. "We've desperately needed a glimmer of hope."

"So you're a refugee band of rebels," asked Mia.

They turned to hike along a willowy grove, misty in the gloaming. "Aye. Most of the Clans have surrendered to King Arrius long ago, hoping that might lift the curse. But we refuse."

"I like this family," said Maple, bunching up her fists in mock fighting.

Liam chuckled darkly.

Bran stopped and looked at Liam squarely, eyes darting to the other two. Everyone stopped with him. "Now listen close, all of ye," he said, his cropped auburn hair dripping from the mist, "talk of vengeance carries few hearts now. Most fear any attempt at uprising will wind up with us all roaming the boglands like those will-o-wisps you barely escaped. We hide and stab from the dark. It's all we can do — Arrius has a death grip on us and the land itself has betrayed us."

Grim shadows crossed Liam's mood. He shifted his jaw back and forth. "And Caer Lannican? Is there any chance we can take it back? Rescue my mom?"

Bran crossed his arms and gave him a grudging smile. "You're a squire with a *knight's* courage. But the rest of the Clans tell us we're suicidal for even fighting at all. Maybe they're right, or maybe they're bootless lurdans! Me, I'll be damned to the worst pits of Evensade before I bow to that false monarch. He's no king of mine. They want me to spit on the memory of the great warriors and queens of old? It will nae be me." He turned, and they followed, marching closer together now past the willows. He narrowed his brow. That wasn't an answer. Mia was preoccupied, sorting through something internally. That worried him too.

They worked up the foothills into darker, colder country, pensive moods settling on them. They passed hewn obelisks carved in ogham script and scenes of battle. He scowled as Bran drifted ahead of them, his silhouette showing in the fog, weariness causing them to lag behind the rebel leader.

"I know that look," said Mia beside him along the grassy path, flexing her hands as if they ached. Maple trotted ahead, face scrunched as if deep in thought.

"I just can't figure why Vinraith, of all beings in Erentyr, targeted *me* all these years."

Mia switched to rubbing her other hand, still preoccupied. She shook her head. "Don't really have enough data to answer that for sure."

"Yeah, more data. It's very unsettling," he muttered. "I'm just afraid I'm leading us to nothing but suffering."

Mia knitted her brow. "You're not leading anybody. I'm here because I want to be. When are you going to realize that?" She pressed on.

"Perhaps," said Maple, peering at Bran and wiping her misted monocle with her coat, "...perhaps there are worse things than suffering, Liam. Hm?"

He clenched his jaw and glanced at her as she bounded ahead of Mia, wild, frizzy hair waving.

Chapter 16

The sloping country rose to Caer Lannican, though most days it was not visible for the dun mist. They passed through easily missed outcroppings into narrow draws of the west Mondryhten highlands, and by nightfall they reached the rebel camp. Passing sentries via Bran's secret hand signals, they crossed the perimeter amid drooping evergreens guarded by stern-eyed Kaledonians with spears. Mia soldiered on beside him without complaint. He felt guilty for continuing to entangle her more and more in this world. *All this must feel like walking into a hornet's nest for her. All these strangers.* But she continually refused to discuss it. *And she says I am closed off!* He scowled and looked ahead, Bran leading the way deeper in, realizing he was not much less of a stranger than Mia was. Maple they welcomed, however, as a fairy creature loyal to the Queen. They bowed politely to her as she passed.

Bran muttered something to the sentries and turned to them. "Come on. I need you two to meet my sister and the remaining knights." Jaw set, he exchanged a glance with Mia. Her head was tilted forward, arms at her sides, eyes roaming. *Both of us, to be vetted.*

Families gathered in a network of campsites, evoking his father's words. *"Hiding and striking from the wilds was the old way."* His curly red hair wafted in the breeze as snow flecked his beard. *"It may not be knightly, son, but it's necessary. Our ancient ancestors, the folk who fought with bone and antler from island broch in old times, knew this."*

Men, women and children, dirty and hungry, populated the camp. Scouts cycled through returning and embarking on perimeter guard and reconnaissance. Many were missing hands, teeth, or legs. Others were wrapped in blankets, tended by herbalists or family. Nowhere were the perfect skin and coiffures of Midworld. No plastic botoxed beauties or silicon enhancements.

Mia's expression shifted between rubbing her chin, brows narrowed as they passed by hungry children, to mouth gaping, unable to look away at missing limbs and festering boils on the faces of the sick. Liam's chest felt tight as he walked the narrow paths through the camp, stomach tense, edgy feelings resonating through his nerves. *Life in Erentyr is full of continual fear,* he recalled from history class, *and danger of violent death. Life there is poor, nasty, brutish, and short.* But who in Midworld already knew that better than he? Yet *seeing* it again iced his veins.

He forced himself to return to that old way of being he had long forgotten. He reached out to stumbling elders, smiled wearily at curious children, and nodded in respect at the haggard rest that eyed him with suspicion. Mia, apparently mastering herself, pressed quietly on, back straight against the suspicious eyes on her.

She noticed he watched her and leaned closer. "They have barely anything ... yet they cling to each other fiercely. So different from home."

"True. But they wouldn't need to be that way there, would they?"

She gazed steadily at him, a crackling bolt-mark twitching up her neck, seeming to want to say something. She turned back to the rocky path. He furrowed his brow, annoyed that he was still irritating Mia despite trying not to. He moved on behind Bran.

The path opened, and they neared a lit, brick stove in a ruined chapel to St Roan. "Oy, Bran," called one, "Have some stew! O'Connor had a good haul today. Some venison, courtesy of King Arrius' generosity." Weary laughter wafted through the mist, as hungry folks shuffled toward the pot.

Around the stove, scouts and commoners huddled, taking a small scoop in their wooden bowls, and drinking from mugs. Proud knights stood like weatherbeaten statues, wearing the traditional torc atop mail hauberks. Liam found himself looking away when they gazed upon him. Ian, a cloaked knight in beaten mail, passed around ladles of stew and a tiny box of some kind of seasoning. He had wavy red hair, like Liam's, a scraggly, unkempt beard, and a raspy, young voice. He handed a small wooden bowl to a grateful old man. "Here now, grandfather."

"What is that?" asked Bran, eyeing the tiny box. "Salt? Where did you get that?"

"Another 'gift' from the king. Looks to be Sathenite stock by the finery."

Bran squinted at the man. "Caravans along the southern road, Ian? You know how dangerous that is."

"Aye, Caoilte discovered that." Ian pointed to a young man, heavily bandaged about the waist, laying on a bed of straw near the fire by the old altar. "Branwen's trying to help him heal, but she's run down and reached the waning, I'm afraid." Over the pale, wounded youth with curly blond hair, a white-haired woman tended. She wore a faded green kirtle beneath an open coat. Over these she wore an Aisling-make traveling cape with a deep hood. She passed hands swirled in strange thorny markings over the groaning young man. She gave him a drink from a flask and patted his sweating forehead with a russet cloth.

"So," said Ian, chewing a crust of bread, "who are these two?"

Branwen pulled her hood back to look at them, and her face gave Liam a start: faded green and grey markings on her face twitched–animated tattoos, like Mia's, only different from her black, orange and blue ones. She was a Druid — the Aisling tuath had one, he overheard his mother say once. Branwen's expression was kind and weary, like a mother who had buried her own, but her age was hard to judge. She looked like Bran, but a mix of both younger and older than him, and there was a power and energy lurking behind her tired glance. "By the Ocean Mother," she said, her voice youthful sounding and clear, "I know who that is. How in all the lands did you find him?" Caoilte groaned. "Oh! Easy there, lad." She returned to the wounded man.

The name Caoilte triggered a memory. A small boy Liam often played with at the fire festivals. Of course he would be in his twenties now. Bran and Liam rushed to their side. *Definitely him!*

"He has lost much blood, I'm afraid," said Ian, many of the others now gathered, as if mesmerized by a slowly extinguishing campfire. "We couldn't afford the risk of being tracked, so we had to take it slow. The fight was hard for this larder we're eating now."

Branwen laid a hand on Ian's shoulder. "We're most grateful. Had they any conjury?"

He shook his head, chewing. "Nay, not this time. But Arrius is getting wise to our tactics. He's boosting his guards. Judging by the mercenary lot he chooses to hire, he's getting more desperate, and his conjurer seems to have let up! We're getting to him."

Bran scowled and shook his head, "Or he's created new treachery. Can you do anything, sister?"

Branwen sighed, patting Caoilte's forehead. "The king's bondsmen crawl every boreen between here and Cairnford. They're after you, of course. They want to kill you and end the curse, same as always, brother. But Ian's right — most of my conjury has been spent hiding us. I'm depleted right now. It'll be a long while before that changes." She narrowed her eyes and leaned toward the pale youth. "But ... I suppose I could try."

Caoilte's eyes opened, and he grabbed her wrist weakly, stopping Branwen in her tracks. "No," he rasped, "Lady Branwen, don't do it. The family needs you more. Don't use your last spell on me. Time's come for me to wander with the Black Eagle as an old man, selling stories and yarns for a night's rest."

Branwen shushed him, her bloodshot eyes downcast. Nevertheless, she breathed deeply, preparing for a great task. Mia reached out, to find spears pointing at her.

"Hold it, lass," said Ian, dire warning in his rasp.

Liam scowled, enraged, grabbing a spear shaft. "Hey!"

Mia backed away. "I thought I might have a healing spell within me. That's all! I just want to help!"

Branwen squinted at her. "You … who are you? Name your master! You're of Ishanu are you not?"

She blinked, head darting back and forth. "Um … no? I'm … not sure how to answer that?"

"Enough," said Liam, shoving the spear away and taking out the Dream Stone. "Back off your spears," he said through his teeth. "I can explain!"

"Do it," said Bran. The spearmen backed away.

Liam let out a breath. "She's from Midworld, Lady Branwen. Like me. She … she seems to have taught *herself* the craft."

Branwen nodded, eyes wide. "Ah," she said, eyebrow raised. "A rogue. I've heard they pop up now and then." Her eyes searched Mia's now cold expression. "Perhaps we can share information — later."

"Like I said, I'm here to help," Mia shot back, "I'm not the one pointing spears."

"Right," interrupted Liam, holding up the Dream Stone. Several rebels eyed it. "Now, like I was saying. Hold your labor. Both of you save your … spell power, or energy, or soulfire, or whatever it is. Let me try to help him with this, I've used it before."

Branwen examined his scarred hand, tilting her head in surprise. "You actually made it past the Mad Dragon, didn't you? You survived."

Caoilte's breathing weakened.

"Yeah, I did. Look, no time to explain." Liam placed his scarred hand, warm Stone in palm, upon the young man's bandages and recalled the feeling of healing Mia and Lungor. That seemed ages ago. "Hey, buddy. Caoilte, remember me? Fire festivals? We used to race each other. All the time, when we were kids."

Caoilte looked quizzically at him.

Odd. He glanced at the others, who shrugged. *Too weak to remember.* He dismissed it. He poured his will into knitting the man's wounds, and the power of the Dream Stone slowly cooled, but the pain in his hand felt like molten lead. He forced his hand to remain. Caoilte winced, and Ian tried to intervene, but a raised finger from Branwen stopped him. Mia watched with great interest, bird-shaped mark on her arm twitching.

Caoilte's injuries were severe. It seemed, however, that his soul was not quite ready to pass onto the next world. Somehow, he understood — as if the Dream Stone had *told* him — that if that had not been the case, no amount of healing would work. Nor could the Stone heal long-standing injuries. It was possible this wouldn't save the young man. Liam pushed through it, and after an agonizing pause, he recoiled his hand, pocketed the cold Stone, and rubbed his palm — it felt seared by dragon fire, though intact. He doubled over and coughed, a vast emptiness gaping within. He hissed, feeling bit again by Drelthun. Images emerged of fleeing Arrius and entering the briar covered castle, until all of a sudden Bran, Mia, and Branwen pulled him to an upright kneel next to a grateful Caoilte. Color now flushed the blond, young man's cheeks.

"I cannae wait to hear how you escaped all those years ago," said Branwen. "A lash from the gods is normally fatal.

And I must learn of that Stone — looks to be the one your mother had."

"Yes, it was hers. Though it's still a mystery to me in a lot of ways. So Caoilte, remember me now?"

He blinked, seeming to search his memory. "Well, I..." he trailed off, turning quizzically to Mia, gaping. "By the gods, what otherworldly beauty is this? An Elf-shyne lass of the Tali?"

Mia reared back, hand on her chest. "Excuse me?"

"Well, looks like he feels better," said Ian with a laugh.

Liam crossed his arms and raised an eyebrow at him. But then, he had no right to be jealous. The exchange evoked a weary cheer, as Caoilte apologized to them both. Liam and Mia locked eyes for a moment, then laughed wearily.

Then a big lad — a squire by his garb — brought around a barrel-keg and poured ale into eager mugs. The lad came near him but balked. He turned to Bran. "What about these two?"

Liam clambered to his feet and stood tall, and Mia hopped to her feet. Caoilte had left already. He frowned. *We'll catch up later, I guess?* Bran took his mug and filled it for him. He raised his hand to quiet the revelers, "listen here, now. I'll have you know this is none other than Liam Trendari Panregon." A gasp of surprise arose. "That's right. The Lost Panregon we've heard about for all these years. And this lass be," he said, turning to Mia.

"Mia," she said. "The Wild Witch," she added, making Liam raise an eyebrow at her. She winked at him. What was going on with her?

"Incredible," said a sitting, long-bearded old man, "look at him — he favors his mother Ynwin!" Liam puzzled at the old man, wondering where he'd seen *him* before. Images of dancing with him, much younger, popped into his head. "And he's befriended strangers from the far-off islands of Ishanu, or I'm a newborn!"

"He's the Seventh," said another. "The Seventh son of Ynwin and Cormac an Brionglóir — Liam Trendari, the lost little boy."

"He's got his father's hair," remarked an old woman. "He's befriended a wee folk from the Fairywild," she said pointing at Maple, who bowed. "A child of the Queen. That's a good sign!"

"Not a boy any more, is he?" asked Ian, slamming his shoulder with an open palm.

Liam took a huge drink of ale — extremely rich, unlike the pale, bland beers of Midworld. Rough-hewn and questionable, but he cared not. The alcohol loosened his nerves. He smiled at the onlookers. "That's right. I've come home!" he finished the mug and plopped it down with emphasis, and pipes, flutes, and drumming erupted, which encouraged dancing. Mia looked at her mug, shrugged, and downed it in one drink. Then she coughed, eyes wide, and fanned her flushed face, evoking a laugh.

The music arose, and Liam glanced at her, holding out a hand. "How about a dance with an old friend?"

She hesitated, but then smiled mischievously at him. In a way she hadn't done in years.

She took his hand and the two of them joined in the dancing, steps coming to him unbidden, to the accompaniment of many a huzzah, and "Cheers for the Seventh! Cheers for the Lost Panregon!" But the sudden adoration felt *wrong* deep down. He was no folk legend. He was just a survivor. And Mia's behavior confused him. It felt like it used to, but inwardly he worried. He knew they could never make it work, as many times as they had tried.

He didn't care. They danced.

***

In the ruined galleries of St Roan, Maple played chase with the children, to their great delight, helping them forget their troubles. After a while, Ian placed himself before the musicians and they stopped at his signal. He then addressed the assembled family and turned to Liam, sitting by Mia. "So, then! Let us hear the tale! Tell us, Liam, how did you make it back to Kaledon—"

"What's left of it!" shouted a drunk old man in the back, followed by downcast glances.

"Aye," a voice said loudly, but without mirth. Conal stepped forward, his knightly torc glinting in the moonlight. "Let's all hear this tale, finally, before we become drunk and daft."

The moonlight trickled into the old ruins where a few candles burned. Many expectant eyes fell on him. Liam's smile faded. Mia took notice and her face became worried and irritated again. Her eyes darted between him and Conal. She unfolded her arms, and Branwen shot to her feet, a tall staff suddenly appearing in her hand, stern blue eyes blazing. Tension crackled in the air. The situation threatened to spiral quickly. Instantly his whole body tensed, chest tight.

Always in Erentyr, the ever-present threat of violence.

"Enough," said Liam, "Please. My friends, kinfolk ... Mia, Lady Branwen. I will tell my story. I promised my father I would." He held a hand up to Mia. "Please," he said softly to her. She reluctantly stepped back, eyes thin slits at him.

Conal folded his arms and glared. "Out with it, then."

"Well," he stammered, "I ... after I entered that briar-castle all those years ago, getting away from Arrius —" he was interrupted by many groans at that name, along with "False king!" shouts. "Yes. After that, after the dragon bit me," he lifted up his scarred hand glowing with firelight, "I passed into Midworld with my mother's Stone. A place of legend here if I remember right." The confused expressions confirmed his suspicion. "It's a different world, to be sure. Then I ... lost the Stone and couldn't return until now." Many nodded in understanding. "I was hurt for a long time, not only by Drelthun, but by the loss of my family and clan, the Shoreland people." Sorrow cut off his words.

Surely, it's the ale. He cleared his throat. "But now I am back, for better or worse. And I mean to help any way I can."

"Nice story," said a scowling Conal. "Are we to take your word as sooth for it? Squire? Because I heard Liam was naught but a wee boy, running into the Fairywild, only to be run down like the rest of his brothers. 'Twas a sad end of the noble Panregon Clan. I knew them and may the gods keep them. But now you come here, some dark spell on ye? Strange companions," he shot a glance at Mia, who frowned and looked away. "Are we to believe you're truly the Lost Panregon? Nay. I say you're a trickster. I don't believe a word of it." He stood eye-to-eye with him.

More knights stepped out of the crowd and gathered by Conal. One had Xanibor and was admiring it, and another his wrapped-up wolf pelt. Those who murmured objections shrunk under Bran's stern glare. This was the moment Bran had warned him of. He was on his own. Mia's gaze darted between him and Branwen, who shook her head subtly, as if to say "don't try it."

Liam stood under the moon beams, surrounded by frowning, cross-armed knights. The crowd fell still. He put down his mug. Feelings of unworthiness lingered. He returned their accusing stares, a dark serpent coiling within him, of memories he thought he'd never have to speak of, even to Mia. But the image of his father in that fever-dream in the Unseelie bog returned. He'd made a promise. Death would be preferable to not keeping it. "Look, you've heard these good folk attest. I look like both my parents."

"Looks can be imitated with conjury."

Liam moved slowly and deliberately. "Then test me any way you like."

Conal scoffed. "Aye, that's clever. But you know we have no way of doing that, don't ye? The king's conjurer is a skillful one. They say Lamon could infiltrate our camp right under our nose. So try again, lad!"

They seemed at an impasse. Liam stood nose to nose with Conal, neither man backing down.

"Then if I can't prove I'm true with spells," Liam said at last, "perhaps you can follow your hearts. I'll tell you my story. All of it," he said, a storm rising from within he refused to show outwardly, "then judge me as you must."

Conal smiled derisively and backed away. "By all means..."

Liam paced before them, long locked memories bursting from their vaults. "Yes, it has been years. But I can tell you my mother, as Chieftan of the Panregons, refused to convert like so many other Clans did. *None* of the Shoreland Clans acquiesced. And for that, Arrius came."

"We know all that," growled Conal. "Tell us some-"

"I was a little boy," Liam overrode angrily, "a newly named squire, to be a knight like my brothers before me, and my father. But when Arrius came, he surprised us in our home, dragged us to Rathchylde lands."

His throat tightened, and his voice became breathless, yet he stayed strong, eyes blazing. Words seethed from between his teeth. His insides shook. "And there they forced my mother and I to watch as they burned my father alive in Arrius's iron chair. It took hours. They laughed as he twisted and vomited in agony. Laughed. But my father never uttered a sound, save to rasp broken songs to the Fairy Queen in the old tongue." His cheek twitched as a tear trickled down it. "Afterward, so amused, they cast him into a pit. Then Arrius, Lucius, and the rest beat my mother and I both at their whim. I was next to be burned — my tender age no safeguard for mercy. They wanted my mother to watch me die slowly. They bragged of how they would then rape her for hours before her turn on the chair. But by some miracle of the gods, my brothers came. The fight was messy and quick, and we fled the broch into the eastern forests toward Cwen Dreorig — the edge of Kaledon."

The audience froze in silence. Conal and the other knights listened, their faces as impenetrable as stone. Mia's face was still and fierce, like a panther's, but with tears streaming uncontrollably down her quivering jawline.

"I'll never forget that day. I've tried. I wish I *could* forget it. Arrius pursued us with his hunters. My oldest brother, Rendan, gave Mom and me the swiftest horse. At the edge of Kaledon, wise in the ways, she released a hare, making a prayer to the Remembering Ones to guide us. The beast bounded unexpectedly toward Caldbana, where sits the ancient castle of Drelthun upon the purple glow-fly slopes, as you all know. Thus we went, but one by one Arrius's hunters and warlords picked off my brothers. Struck down in blood. Mom was shot in the leg and couldn't run anymore. Shattered her shin bone. Then," he said, "she prayed to the Fairy Queen to protect me, and ordered me to flee into Drelthun's domain. Into it I went, and this," he held up his scarred hand, "was my payment for refuge. There I fled Kaledon, my home, and my kin to be lost in a strange place I only recently returned from. I was there for what feels like a lifetime, and this I say ... with shame. But against that shame," he added, glowering at Conal and the other knights, his abdomen tensed, nostrils flared, his heart white-hot, "I will have vengeance. Vengeance upon Arrius, Lucius, and all his men. Every last one. And I will rescue my mother from Caer Lannican or die." Mia snarled and nodded, fists at her side.

Exhausted, Liam left the central floor without another word and sat down slowly into a chair, steepling his hands and staring, not making eye contact but watching and awaiting judgment, a silent hurricane within him. A long quiet followed, and all eyes watched Conal. Mia swept to his side, defiant eyes challenging anyone who would further question him. He let out a long breath.

Conal studied him, then looked back to the other knights. They exchanged glances. He collected Liam's weapon and pelt.

Crossing the floor, boots heavy upon the stone, he stood before him, paused, then handed the hilt of Xanibor to him, wrapped in the wolf pelt. "Welcome home ... squire."

Liam took his effects, surprised at the show of confidence. Conal turned and left the chapel, beyond the gallery.

"Hail the Shoreland brothers and sisters!" shouted Ian, stepping forward. "And hail the Lost Panregon!"

"Aye," added Bran, "May the Remembering Gods keep the Shorelanders safe in Evensade!" Everyone raised their mugs and drank, including Maple, who had taken a break from the children to puff her pipe. Hope rekindled for a moment. He swam in the emotion, surprised by how much he had recalled.

Mia stood beside him and put a hand on his shoulder. The gesture brought him back from his thoughts. She looked upon him, cheeks tense, eyes wet. "I guess now I know why you never wanted to share that story."

He took her hand and squeezed it. "My father — or his ghost, dream image, I don't know — was right. I needed to do that for him. And for me."

Performers with candlesticks walked into the center of the ruins. His tale demanded more entertainment, and so the Storyteller stepped forth: Branwen. Liam and Mia joined the others, to sit on a pile of rushes and lean against a log. He wrapped himself in the wolf cloak to sip ale, losing himself in Branwen's stories, Mia resting her weary head on his shoulder. She had not done that in ages either. Having her near helped, despite the old misgivings. He let it happen.

Branwen's storytelling was augmented by the performers — an emaciated family of four from Somled, now homeless. It was agreed that today's victory, and Liam's return from apparent decades-long death, called for storytelling. It was most welcome.

He marveled at the tales Branwen wove. Her mastery impressed him, and her stories eased the pain of recounting his own story. Everyone seemed to know her tales — of the ancient crannog wars of Kaledon, to the War of the Tree that happened in the first Stone of Time, unimaginably long ago. The crowd joined in, enacting the scenes, breaking into song, really participating. As the stories weaved, he stared at the Dream Stone. Its depths held him like the tales. *Crafted by the Fairy Queen of Gods Herself. Such a simple, small thing, invulnerable, its age fathomless.* How many universes had this humble rock seen? He shook his head, flipping it in his scarred hand, its weight sturdy and solid. *A key to infinities in my hand? Yet here barely remembered.*

"Incredible," said Mia. "It's not just someone telling a story. It's a whole group thing."

"I forgot how this was," said Liam, sipping ale. "Back in Midworld nobody does this. Everyone just mindlessly stares at their own personalized, AI-generated stuff on their Nexwork-d."

"Yeah," she said with a disturbed expression.

The comparison unsettled him, too — what did it mean? The refugees looked so happy, despite their predicament. *You'd think they were all drinking orinol.* Maybe they knew something he had forgotten.

Branwen next told the story of Techtmaar, the First Druid, who met the Fairy Queen Herself when She emerged from an age lost at sea. Thin and hungry eyes lost themselves in the tales, distracting them from their empty bowls. Bran mingled with the knights and men-at-arms, and Maple played with makeshift toys with the children. Mia fell fast asleep, exhaustion finally claiming her. He resisted the urge to kiss her forehead the way he used to do when they were together. Wouldn't have been right.

In any case, his heart was restless. Two facts turned over in his mind. None said plainly that Ynwin was dead. And none seemed to know why it was so important to rescue her. But he knew: she was the only person who could save Kaledon from the Curse of Vinraith. That lore must have been lost when his mother sent him to Midworld. He breathed in deeply and let it out slowly.

For now it was enough that he had fulfilled his promise to his father. The moonlight glinted on the hilt of Xanibor, leaning against a column next to him. His father's sword was now properly *his*.

Chapter 17

Over the next few days, Liam and Mia stayed with the Kaledonians, helping anyone who needed it with clothing, food, or chores. Mia earned quick respect by having uncovered a healing spell that could relieve minor cuts and bruises — she had to use such spells sparingly, however, for she was depleting herself, her wizard marks fading. After healing five wounds, cuts, and minor fractures, the knights, trained in conjury and counter-conjury, advised her to stop and conserve her soulfire.

Branwen agreed and began teaching her every night near the small fire in the courtyard. Liam watched in fascination as they laughed at the pain the wizard marks caused, or studied an ancient tome written by a certain Azirikhan the Mystic — the only magical tome Branwen had — entitled *Prolegomena for the Apprentice*. Branwen had to translate from the incredibly difficult Elvish tongue it was written in. Most nights he sat near and listened quietly to them as he helped the men-at-arms at garment and mail repair, the squire's duties returning to him after so many years. Anxious to get on with his mission to save his mother, it felt good to patiently build calluses on his hands again while he waited. Bran promised a meeting soon, once the last raiding team had returned.

One night, Liam returned from night watch duties to put the short tallow candle out as both Branwen and Mia had fallen asleep sitting at the table where they studied. Mia had taken the older woman's hand in hers, her grandmother's ring glinting in the waxing moonlight. He smiled and draped blankets over them, trying not to disturb them, his gaze lingering on Mia's sleeping form. Old memories surfaced of their long fights. His head drooped and he took in a steady breath.

"I see how you look at her," said Maple, her soft voice surprising him. She puffed her pipe, sitting cross-legged on the table. Had she been there the whole time? "You love her. I can see that."

Liam nodded gently.

"So what happened with you two, anyways?" she asked.

He sighed and turned to her. She rested her chin on her fists, young-old eyes wide, frizzly hair wafting across her freckled skin. "Maple, sometimes love just isn't enough," he said numbly. "We always ended up fighting. Needed our space, maybe."

"Midworld didn't give you enough of that?"

He pensively watched her sleep. "What, space? Well ... no, I guess not. There were always so many other things. Everyone had their own tailored little digital world they could stay in as long as they wanted to." The wildgnome scrunched her features quizzically. "It's hard to explain, Maple. Connecting like this," he said, waving his hand at the refugees, "nobody does that back home. Easier for a lot of people to feel connected by just buying an ARC ... that's an artificial romantic companion, or stay connected with each other via Nexwork-d."

"Is that not the same, then?" she said, seemingly genuine.

His eyes lingered on Mia's long, dark hair. The twitching marks on her arm. "I don't know. Maybe not. Maybe it's my fault. Any time she asked my feelings I pulled away, not wanting to poison her with all my pain and suffering. I got mad." He wrinkled his nose. "Can't say I was perfect boyfriend material."

Maple chuckled and shook her head at him.

"What?" he asked.

"Take it from me, lad. Perfect is the enemy of excellence. Greatly overrated, for certain." She hopped down and headed for the tents. He watched her bound off, pondering that.

Mia and Branwen awakened sluggishly.

"Aye, what hour is it?" asked Branwen.

"The witching hour," said Liam.

Mia rolled her eyes at him. "Smart ass. You'll have to forgive him, Lady Branwen."

He placed a hand on Mia's shoulder. "Maple has already prepped your tent and gone to bed. See you tomorrow?"

She nodded. "Branwen here has agreed to take me on as her apprentice officially once we win this fight against Arrius," said Mia, eyes sparkling.

It was good to see her smile. He couldn't remember when the last time he saw her so upbeat. He nodded. "May that day come soon," he said, a slight edge to his voice.

Branwen glanced at him, her expression not nearly as hopeful, as if hiding chronic despair behind a quiet smile. "May it indeed. I look forward to that day," she said to Mia, who patted her hand.

***

After a fortnight in the camp, Bran called for all the rebel families to meet at sundown. Something had been brewing between him and his sister and it was time to deal with it. Liam sat with Maple on a log by the central fire. Mia and Branwen had been conversing since morning, drawing strange symbols and practicing hand motions by a new candle. Common men-at-arms, archers, porters, and knights filtered into the courtyard to the central gathering place. Mia came to join Liam.

"So many different clans and families," she said, eyes darting between everyone as she took a seat. "How long have they been starving and fighting?"

Liam glowered at the fire, hands resting on his knees. "Since I left. I'm ashamed I was gone so long."

She crossed her arms, expression turning dark. "Yeah. I don't even have *that* excuse for not being helpful."

A cloud of gloom seemed to pass between them.

Branwen sat beside Mia, hood pulled low, faded marks on her lined face. "What is it?" she asked, noticing Mia's curiosity. "Something odd about our ways?"

She shook her head, her expression lightening. "No, no. You say odd, I say *beautiful.*"

Branwen laughed softly. "We're sickly and hungry … not much else."

"I just wonder," she replied, that study-expression back on her face, wheels turning in her mind, a finger tapping her chin. "Your world has a lot of pain, Branwen. But it's not so … *brutish* … as I'd been led to believe."

Branwen looked quizzically at her. "Well … thank you, I think. I've often dreamed of what Midworld must be like. That is, when Ynwin spoke on't, which was rare. A world of peace and plenty. No war. No want. If only we could build such a place here!"

Liam scratched the back of his tilted head and exchanged a knowing glance with Mia, who raised her eyebrows silently.

The gathering quietened.

Bran stepped forward and his sister joined him in the circle.

"Where is Caoilte?" asked Conal with a frown.

"He left for the perimeter right after he was healed, remember?" said Bran. Conal stroked his beard, eyes squinting into the darkness.

Branwen joined her brother and signaled for silence.

"You start," Bran said to his sister. Haggard families stood proud and defiant or sat against the logs and ruined columns.

"I believe we've had a sign," began Branwen, pointing at Liam. "First, the Lost Panregon comes to us unlooked for, with friendly conjury, and with even one of the good folk besides." Maple puffed on her pipe with a grin. "This is the sign we've awaited. The sign to attack Arrius right at the heart," she said, punching an open palm. Bran scowled in disagreement. "Liam wants to storm the Rock o' the Cliff. I say it's time. Kill Arrius and end this curse on our land!"

"With respect, madam, but are ye mad?" asked Ian. "How many times have we tried? Have ye forgotten?"

"Aye," added Conal. "And it was costly. It's a fool's errand. And you'll be of no help to us without your battle-conjury, begging your pardon, until the Mage Tide comes to you, is that not right?"

"We cannae afford to wait for that," another replied. "The Unseelie bogs creep forth more every day!"

"Aye, and the Nurnians sell us to the slavers of Embrosius to the south," chimed the clan-mother of the Lorwynns.

"Storming Caer Lannican isn't the way," said Conal. "We'll fare better if we can draw Arrius out in ambush." Others agreed. "That will end the curse on our land quick enough. Leave off the castle, says I. Everyone knows it's impenetrable."

Liam couldn't contain himself anymore. He let out a measured breath and raised his hand, and the Druid acknowledged him. He stood and entered the center of the gathering by the hearth. "Due respect to all of you. But as much as I would love to kill Arrius — and I *really* would love to do that — the curse on this land that everyone's talking about has nothing to do with him. We don't have to take the castle. We just need to rescue my mother."

Many voiced disagreement. Bran raised his hand to quiet everyone down. "Let him speak."

Liam cleared his throat, eyeing Conal, who frowned at him. "Look, I know everyone has spoken about the kingslayer curse of Sibne for a long time. I mean, I remember people saying a good king or queen can bring blessings upon the land as long as I remember. But that's *not* why Kaledon is being steadily devoured by the Unseelie. It's because my mother needs this." He held the Dream Stone aloft. Eyes tracked to his hand.

"The Queen's Lament," said a very old woman in the crowd, as if to herself. Everyone turned to her. Having been sick for weeks, it was the first words she'd said since Liam had gotten there. Her daughter stroked her hair and gently shushed her.

"Yes," said Liam, the name triggering more memories, "that's what she called it, though I never knew what that meant exactly. All I know is that my mother took the mysterious Calling Brand from my grandfather, Oisin, to perform a task sacred to the Fairy Queen Herself. The Calling Brand was the mark on her hand," he pointed to the back of his left hand. "And every year I saw the fairy folk speak to her. They respected the mark. They respected the Calling Brand and her status as Stoneguard. Before I ... left," he said, pushing through a catch in his throat, "she told me to return the Stone to *her*, or Kaledon would suffer."

Eyes turned to Branwen, as if to check his story. "Aye, the Stoneguards were a closed-lipped tradition. Charged with a task many swore to secrecy to carry out," she added to the onlookers. "Only the Druid Masters of Techtmaar in far off Tawel Bannon knew of it beyond whispers. I only heard shadows and inklings of it, miself."

"Exactly," continued Liam. "Something to do with going into Midworld and restoring the ancient connection that had been lost." He shrugged. "I don't know. But that's not important right now. What's important is whatever it was, she never got the chance. The Nurnians got to her first."

"Fine, lad," asked Conal, "but how does all this help Kaledon now?"

He paced among the men-at-arms and porters. "I think it's the link between my mother and the Stone. When I left Erentyr, they became separated, and that's when the balance of the gods shifted here. I always heard the Unseelie King kept to himself off in the Dark Valley of Uluth. Right?" Others nodded, except Mia who listened with fierce intensity, eyes narrowed in quizzical concentration, following each discussant with her eyes.

Knowing she was probably thinking about their recent encounter with Vinraith, and at the same time not wanting to bring *that* detail into it, he continued. "Everyone's heard those tales: never go to Vinraith's valley, and you'll never have any trouble. In the old days, we respected the Old Guard of Uluth and we traded with the Arcane Masters beyond Kaledon. We survived with mutual respect for the boundaries. A harsh life, but a true one, my father always said. But when the Stone left Kaledon, the wisps, spriggans and," he shot a glance at Mia, who very subtly shook her head "no" "...and all those servants of the Unseelie King came forth devouring mortal lands, like ours. The only way to stop it," he said, more loudly, holding the Dream Stone high, Ynwin's face staring into his young eyes in his mind, "is for me to bring this back to her. She is the only one who can restore the boundary and tip the scale back in favor of the Fairy Queen. Killing Arrius won't help."

Conal's frown deepened. "Liam, we accepted your tale about your father and kin, but what you're saying now strains credulity, man. Anyways, even if it were true that 'all' we needed was to rescue Ynwin from the castle, it cannae be done. Breaching the castle is suicide."

Liam slowly turned to him. The questioning was getting annoying. "And I'm telling you, it's the truth. I swear on my life as a squire."

The crowd turned to Branwen. Her expression grew sad and weary. "His story has the ring of sooth to it, but I was not privy to Stoneguard lore. Maybe it's true, maybe it's not. But either way, we all know the gravest problem with your plan, Liam."

He straightened, skin flushing. "And what is that?"

She frowned, looking to the others. Everyone seemed to be struggling with something. Something nobody wanted to say.

Mia neared Liam. "Branwen. Is Ynwin not a captive of Caer Lannican?"

Liam gripped the Stone, still feeling his mother's presence with it. There wasn't going to be any arguing about that. His blood began to get hotter. Murmurs arose.

Bran waved the noise down. "Lad," he said.

"No," said Liam, shaking his head. "I'm not having it. She's alive."

"No one has seen her since the day the Shoreland Tuath was attacked," said Conal without pleasure. "She's gone. And so if your lore about the curse is true, we have no hope. You're telling us even killing King Arrius won't help. For all our sake," he added, eyebrows raised, "I hope you're wrong, lad."

"No!" growled Liam. Mia placed a hand on his chest. He shook his head vigorously. "My mother is alive. The Dream Stone — I can feel her presence within it! I'm telling you. Why does everyone find that so impossible to believe?"

"It could be a ruse, son," said Bran softly. Deathly silence. "The king's Royal Conjury-master, Lamon. He's tricked us before." He shook his head to the side, eyes locked on his. "More than once, lad."

"Aye," said Branwen, leaning on the table, eyes downcast. "His power exceeds mine by large measure. I've had precious little time to advance my skill these last many years, while he has the Royal library to study." She pointed to his hand. "Whatever you feel in that old relic, lad, I don't think we can trust it."

Liam glowered, unable to answer that. He knew they might be right. Erentyr had shown him time and again that hardly anything in this world could be trusted. He returned the Stone to his sporran and bowed his head. Mia took his hand in comfort. He breathed deeply. His head pounded and he ground his jaw.

Branwen neared the center. The chapel fell silent again, lamp and hearth light flickering shadows against troubled faces. She turned to her brother. "Bran ... whatever the truth is, we must act now. We cannae wait any longer. We'll die out here, sure as the Gummp's predictions. Hiding and striking from shadow can avail us no more." Bran grumbled and looked away. "How many more years can we hang on like this?" she continued, arms waving. "How long can we endure scraping upon mountain rocks? No yoke for the husbandman? No aliment for our wee saplings? Damn it, we must act!"

Some in the crowd shouted in agreement — others called for silence. "Don't start with me, old beldam," shot back Bran. "We're playing the long game. You agreed to it!" His eyes surveyed the rest of them. "We will wait for the moment to strike Arrius."

"Aye," persisted Branwen, pacing, "and what if *this* is the moment we've been waiting for? One wild chance in a lifetime, seemingly impossible — that is when the Fairy Queen and Her children may come to our aid," she added, pointing at the gathering for emphasis. "A thousand opportunities may go by unnoticed. Let not this one be so!"

Bran shook his head. "I love your passion, sister. And your loyalty to your kinfolk, Liam. And you, Mia — you may be new here, but you're a quick study, right enough. But the warriors must be the ones to decide. Alyia's Children may favor us, but they wrestle with the Unseelie who hate us. We cannae risk an attack on the castle. Not now! The danger is too great, and we don't even know if it will help. Even if Ynwin can stop the curse, she's most likely," he glanced at Liam, concern in his eyes, "well she's most likely gone. You know this. Why would Arrius keep her alive? And if he didn't, our *only* slim chance would be to kill him, and hope that ended the curse and tipped the scales in our favor. Should we throw away such a fragile chance of victory on an impulse? Or scrap of lore nearly forgotten? Did you not agree with my plan when I put it into motion all that time ago now? Can you not trust me?"

Branwen looked down and sighed. "All right, brother. I will let it go."

"I'm sorry, lad," said Bran, facing Liam. "I want to believe you. We all loved your mother. If we had *any* proof she was still alive, I'd say let's chance it. Howbeit, Lamon has caught us in his snares before and made us nearly all gudgeons for the gallows more than once. I have to be sure. By the gods! If we had but one fraction of the Kaledonian knights of old, this conversation would surely be a different one."

"Aye, but we don't," said Conal clanking into the center.

Mia raised a hand, and Bran lifted his eyes to her. "Knights of old?"

Conal furrowed his brows. "It's been going on for centuries, lass. Many of the great knights of old either died in ambuscade, took ill with disease ... or they wandered into the arms of the Unseelie, never to be seen again. It worsened tenfold after the conquest. They're gone. We're all there is now."

Downcast and defeated faces encircled Liam, and he understood that feeling. He turned away from the center and walked to a corner of the courtyard where a small lamp flickered next to a column, rubbing his closed eyes.

"It's all right, Liam," said Mia behind. "We'll find a way."

He shook his head. He did *not* want to give up. Yet what choice was there? His temples pounded. He dabbed his nose; it was bleeding again. His stomach twisted into knots. But it was all hopeless. He let out a long, strained breath, fist clenched tight. "No," he said at last. "They're right." The farmers brought out a trestle table for the knights to plan. "I don't know what I was thinking, coming back to Erentyr. I thought Mom needed me, that Kaledon needed me. But I never had any sort of real plan. Infiltrating Caer Lannican, on the slim hope that Mom was still alive after nobody's seen her in *years*?" His heart fell, as if into an abyss. But he stood firm, watching himself clench his fist open and closed to distract himself. "There's no way she could still be alive. Dream Stone or not. They're right, it has to be a trick. Maybe Damien and this Lamon character worked together and this is just a way to get the Stone."

She tilted her head, eyes seeming to coolly gauge him. "Does that mean you want to give up?"

He glared into the darkness outside the flickering lights of the chapel candles. "I don't know. This world feels utterly damned. We didn't know how good we had it in Midworld."

"Liam, look at me."

He did. Her mahogany eyes narrowed in concern. She placed a soft hand on his bearded cheek. "Something is happening to me here. I can't even begin to explain it. It's terrifying ... but — and I know this sounds weird — I can't help but wonder if I didn't *need* this somehow. I mean, sure — the Magnolents achieved great things. Nobody suffers there like they do here! And there are a thousand entertainments and conveniences. Everyone is perfectly safe and comfortable. So, I mean, I would understand if you wanted to go home. But," she said, chewing on her bottom lip for a moment, "wouldn't it feel wrong to turn your back on these people? They aren't even my kin and I feel like I should do everything I can to help them."

He chuckled in disbelief, shaking his head. "You're right. Of course I don't want to turn away. But Mom was *adamant* that hers was the only way to save Kaledon from Vinraith's curse."

She nodded and pursed her lips to one side, eyes searching. He knew to wait while she did that. "Maybe ... what if we tried my spells, and your muscle–"

"And my craftiness!" added Maple, who had been listening and puffing her pipe beside them, leaning against a ruined stone column. They turned. "Don't think you're going off on your own without me. I'll not be sitting here like a fandangled tiddly-do!"

Mia smiled, eyes lighting up. "Yes, and what if just the three of us sneak about the castle and see if we can learn anything? To my mind, we desperately need more data! From what everyone's been saying, the Nurnians aren't expecting, um, 'counter-conjury' as they call it, right? Maybe we can find a way to sneak in? At least learn if she's still alive?"

"Capture a sentry," said Liam darkly, despair turning into plans, nodding to himself, "and ... interrogate him."

"Right, I don't know. And if we find nothing, we'll know what we have to do: join them in trying to break the curse the way the kingslayer legend says."

Liam punched his fist. "By killing Arrius. That sounds like a fucking win-win."

Maple and Mia enthusiastically agreed. Without another word, he marched before the knights at the table as they plotted their next raid, Mia and Maple trying to catch up. "Lord Bran."

The old knight held up a hand and silenced the gathering. "Come to join us?" The warriors turned their attention to him.

He half-smiled, eyebrow cocked. "Not exactly. Since there is apparently a disagreement on whether *my* proposal is ... viable ... Mia, Maple, and I propose a new plan: just the three of us go on a reconnaissance mission to find out if my mother still lives. If we learn she is lost, and that there is no hope of taking the castle, then I will gladly join you in the mission to assassinate Arrius. I mean, I'll be at the front of that line, trust me. But if there's a way to save her, I *must* try."

Bran smiled. "He's his father's son, is he not?" The older knights and commoners laughed and agreed. "Liam, let me tell you something. We are knights of Kaledon. We are men and women of honor. We keep our oaths, we defend our land, kin, and we keep our faith in the Fairy Queen. Do we not?"

The knights pounded the table. Some shouted "hear, hear!". Others chimed "for the Fairy Queen! For the Ocean Mother!"

"As such," Bran continued, "no man or woman knight here is held to duty that is against their conscience. All are here of their own blood and valor."

Liam squinted at them slightly. "So that means I have your permission?"

"He's saying a knight needs no permission," said Ian, "to do that which is in his or her heart. We are bound by oath and loyalty, but it is ours to decide how we carry out conscience."

"Aye," added Conal, "only there's one problem with you, isn't there, lad?"

Liam straightened, squinting at him. "What problem?"

"You're not a knight," said Bran, who walked around the table and faced him eye-to-eye.

Liam swallowed and looked down. "Hm, yes. That's true, I suppose."

"All right, then," said Bran, raising his voice. "Liam of the Shoreland Tuath and last son of the Panregon Clan. As I see it, foreign shores have scarred your soul. But that matters no longer. Your true home is Kaledon. Look here, now. You see this livery collar?" Liam raised his chin. A chain that hung broadly about his cloak of black pelts glinted, coming to a silver wolf's-head with a ruby encrusted in one of the eyes. It hung below a lean torc of bronze that peeked from under his grey beard. Liam furrowed his brow at it, puzzling over its uncanny resemblance to … Vinraith? Surely not. "This be the insignia," said Bran, setting aside that strange question, "of the Order of the Black Wolf. And this torc is a sign of the Knighthood 'neath it. I'm a Knight of the O'Halloran Clan and the Aisling Tuath, but more than that, I was chosen for the Black Wolf Order. By tradition, only the High King can select us. And even though High King Sibne was a traitor, the order is honorable, and far elder than he. We were once thirty-three. Now our numbers can be counted upon one hand."

Liam clasped his hands behind his back and raised his eyebrows. "So what does this have to do with me?"

Bran stared at him squarely, face grave, thick brows gnarled. "You're nae going to leave us as a mere bootless squire, Liam. If you must hie on to your doom, you're going to do it properly. You must do it as a knight like your brothers and father before you. I dinnae care how destitute and weary we are — a knight is a knight."

"I don't know about that, Bran. I honestly don't feel I've lived up to—"

"This is no request! This isn't about you." He poked him in the chest. "It's about Kaledon. It's about your Clan and your kin-folk, gods keep them. And if I say you're ready to take on this great burden and honor, then you can do it my way, or you'll have me to contend with. Not one foot will you set from our camp until you do it as a knight, proud and strong, are we clear, lad?" Bran's tone brooked no argument. He took a step toward Liam. Ian and Conal stared at him with steel jaws.

Shame became battle-readiness, a feeling like he had when he faced the martial arts robot, memories flooding of when he was a boy and dreaming of such a day. "All right," he said, searching Bran's intent. He was serious. Energy flickered within him, quickening his breath. "If you say it must be so, I will do it. My lord."

"Kneel," said Bran.

The chapel fell utterly silent, save for the distant howling of the winds to the south. A chill crept up Liam's spine at what would now commence. Now it came to it. His heart pounded. He solemnly faced Bran and the other knights. "Fair enough."

He went to one knee.

Chapter 18

The setting quarter moonlight illuminated the chapel. The center of the stone ruins had been cleared save for Bran, Ian, and Conal on one side, and Liam on the other. All the Kaledonians watched. Mia and Maple sat with Branwen. Conal set a bundle of items wrapped in a blanket by a table while Ian lit several additional candles. Bran stood directly before Liam.

"All ready? Good. Now ... know ye the vows of the knighthood?"

He nodded. "Every word."

Bran smiled, nodding. "We'll have to do it the battlefield way."

Liam placed his hands on his one bent knee, and the wind blew wet fog across the cobbled stone columns, the dusk light orange upon the dew. The scent of hazel flowed and distant thunder rolled. He offered Xanibor to Bran.

He admired the blade. "'Tis a mighty sword. Where did you get it?"

He pondered how to answer that for a moment. "When my friends and I were lost in the Rathchylde bogs, I came under a spell from ... the will-o-wisps. I'm not actually sure what happened, but I had a vision there, or maybe a dream, of my father. He gave me his sword, because I agreed to share the end of his story with my countrymen."

"Liam Trendari, the Dreamer," said Ian with a grizzled smile. "Plucks swords out of his sleep." Some in the crowd chuckled.

Bran laughed softly, but then became solemn. Silence fell. "Speak the words."

"I wish," he pronounced loudly, "to be a Knight of the Shoreland Clan." His heart rate rose.

"Swear," said Bran, Ian and Conal looking on, men-at-arms, and farmer families watching. Bran took off his left glove.

Liam swallowed and let out a breath. "As a knight, I swear to honor the Fairy Queen and Her children, uphold my Lord and liege, and protect all those in need."

Bran backhanded him across the face, but Liam made no movement, knowing the ritual.

"As a knight, I swear to seek the greatest Glory, find Equanimity of spirit, and fight for the purest Good."

Bran struck a second blow, this time harder.

"And as a knight, I swear to hunt for naught but Truth, humbly keep the courtesies, and—" he scowled, face hot, "I will avenge all wrongdoing."

A third and final blow nearly turned him around. But he recovered and smiled at Bran. "This final strike, my lord, shall be the last I endure unanswered."

Bran breathed in deeply and set Xanibor upon the squire's shoulder. It seemed to hum with elder power, barely perceptible and deep. Mia winked at him. Maple leaned forward, eyes huge, puffing furiously. "By my faith and honor," said Bran, "as Knight of the Order Black Wolf, Knight of the O'Halloran Clan, and Thane of the Aisling Tuath, I name you, Liam Trendari, Knight of the Panregon Clan. Take this as your own." He removed his bronze spiral-carved torc and placed it around his neck. Liam's heart raced with pride. "Rise, Knight of Kaledon."

He did, ready to face any foe. "Thank you. Finally," he added, nearly to himself, flush with desire to immediately charge the enemy.

"Welcome to our ranks, brother," said Ian.

"Well then," said Conal, "Liam, Dreamer Knight, of the Wolven Fell. Son of Cormac and Ynwin. Whereas before I had many doubts, now I am honor-bound to doubt you no more." He leaned in. "But I am still watching you."

Liam smirked. "I would expect no less from you, brother."

Bran's expression became grim. "I wish you luck, Liam. I'd join you but I've lost too many good men going where you're going. But a knight must obey his conscience. Above all else." The other knights nodded sagely at that.

Liam bowed slightly and set aside the childlike reverie within him, replacing it with focus, straightening his body, feeling as if he'd grown even taller. "Thank you. I'm comforted. Now even if I die, it shall at least be as a Knight of Kaledon."

He turned toward Mia and Maple.

"So," said Bran, "you'll NOT be observing the bestowal of arms?"

He stopped and backtracked. "Bestowal?"

Ian handed Bran the bundle. "Even *you* can't march off in naught but a tunic, lad," said Bran. "Any mother's son with a pointed stick would end you with a wee flick. You need a proper harness. We have battle-gear cleaned and repaired from our fallen brothers and sisters. Take this arming doublet." Liam set down his great wolf pelt and put on a long, tough black gambeson. "Strong, thick linen soaked in salted wine. Very sturdy. And this," he held up a hauberk of mail, "you've seen it before. The armorer worked at it all night. But look at the maker's ring, lad." Liam followed his finger across the five-in-one riveted rings to find the mark. Séamas MacLennan. He looked up. "Aye," said Bran with a gleam. "We took it off a Nurnian thief, but before that, we suspect it belonged to none other than—"

"My father," said Liam, his throat tightening. He put it on, recalling the last day with his father, walking beside him wearing this very mail coat. The rings settled, heavy but not overly so. A hide of metal. He felt nigh-invulnerable. "It's one of the last made by old master Séamas."

Conal raised an eyebrow and tapped the rings with a gauntlet. He whistled. "Cormac wore a fine coat, indeed. Full-proofed against barbed arrows, and even half-proofed against needle bodkins, but at least they won't kill you instantly."

"Aye," said Ian, "they'll kill you three days later," he added with a dark laugh.

"Very funny," said Bran, waving them off. "Now here's the rest. Kettle helmet, only a wee dent. Arming cap, throat standard, and mail gloves. Oh, and one last thing. Not your father's, but it was sewn with your clan crest. With compliments from Bridget, our best seamstress." Bran handed him a blue and black tabard and belt. He put them both on, along with the other items, but he marveled at the crest: a likeness of the two suns and a sliver moon all equidistant, just as he saw them in the sky on his first day back in Erentyr. That seemed a lifetime ago.

He furrowed his brow at Bran as he reclaimed the wolf pelt atop his gear. Mia came to his side, Maple behind. Mia patted the heavy mail and tapped it with a knuckle. "Very handsome. What is this stuff? Doesn't feel like steel."

"Enchanted Torgonite," said Ian. "Stronger and tougher than steel. Troll-delved, like as not. Strong as anything you might find even in the Dwarf kingdom of the far off Bandoren Mountains."

Liam reeled inwardly, turning away, neck muscles tight. This was too generous. Too giving. He hadn't earned all this! "So much labor, just for me ... Bran, how do I repay it?"

He gazed sternly. "Return in one piece. Find out what ye can. Enemies surround us on all sides now, young knight. Mayhaps you can find a way where others could not. When were you planning to leave on this scouting mission?"

He exchanged glances with Mia. She tilted her head to the side, ready to leave. "Immediately," he said. "Cover of night and all that."

"We're ready," said Maple, stringing her bow.

Bran embraced Liam like a son. "Good luck, then, young Panregon. May the Remembering Ones compass you. I can only pray we will meet again."

"Aye," said Conal, pointing at him, "and don't lose that fine gear. When you die like a fool out there, I want it for miself."

Liam's heart became grave, but his newfound resolve remained after having been knighted. He scraped his mailed thumb along his bearded chin. Conal, Ian, and Bran gave him stern looks, respect on their faces. He saluted them. "Farewell, gentlemen."

Branwen clasped Mia's hands and looked her in the eyes. "And farewell to you, too, my new student," she said with a weary smile. "You be sure to come back as well. Don't get too ... distracted," she said, eyes flickering toward Liam, wry smile on her lips, "out there in the lonely dark. You need to stay ... focused."

Liam suppressed a laugh as Mia blushed, shaking her head.

"Now see here, Branwen," said Maple, wagging a finger, but clearly enjoying the innuendo, "you just let them be, now."

"No, no," Mia and Liam both chimed in simultaneously, "we're just friends. We're — that's all we are. Just friends."

Branwen tapped her upper teeth with her tongue and gave them a lingering look. "I'm sure," she said, shooting a wink at Mia before heading back to the planning table.

Liam looked down awkwardly and cleared his throat. "Right, then," he said, whirling.

They set off, and worked their way out of the camp, setting suns, quarter moon and spare stars providing the only light. They kept eyes on the distant silhouette crest of Caer Lannican far up country as they went, and shadowy mists hung stubbornly across the rough lands that climbed to the fortress. They pushed northward as the last traces of sunset bloodied the low clouds. In just a few hours, the night would fall pitch black.

As they evaded the growing blackthorn bogs, Mia moved her hands, brow creased with deep concentration, scowling as they walked. Most likely another spell was forming within her, and she struggled to give it shape. But dread fell upon him at the thought of her unlocking the last spell. Lore spoke of some spell-weavers going mad with spellcraft, so alien was its power to mere mortal minds. He shuddered and put that thought away swiftly. They stopped on a grassy patch surrounded by large boulders. Mia stood still, eyes closed.

She lifted her head and opened her eyes, whites burning unnaturally bright. "*Kwellavatai,*" she said, and the wind shifted briefly. Her eyes returned to normal. Liam exchanged glances with Maple as Mia looked around, as if her vision had changed.

"You all right there, Mia?" asked Maple.

She nodded. "The sixth one."

"What does it do?" asked Liam.

Her eyes seemed to go *through* him. "You can't see them, but there are glowing invisible dragonflies buzzing about us. Three. I feel like they are telling me what *might* happen ... but without words. It's hard to describe."

He clicked his tongue and squinted into the gloom. Vague hills in darkening fog and creeping groves. "Hm. Well ... are they telling us to press on northeast toward the castle? Or go a different path?"

She closed her eyes and nodded. "They don't say where to go — doesn't work like that. More like once you consider a path, they hint at what *might* come." She faced different directions. "I think there. Around that bluff ahead, where the fog lingers. Keep near the foot of the hill."

"That fog is going to make this *really* difficult," grumbled Liam.

"Oh, don't curse the fog just yet, lovelies," said Sea Breeze, making everyone snap to a nearby blackthorn branch. "Might be the Fairy Queen's doing. Oy, Maple, good to see you again, love."

Liam smiled, arms opening toward the bird, as if to hug her. "Sea Breeze! Boy, you're a sight."

Maple snapped her fingers. "Oy, that's the style, bang on, Sea Breeze. Between her spells and your help, we've got a good chance tonight to catch those chancers."

"What happened, Sea Breeze?" asked Mia. She held out her hand, and Sea Breeze perched on it, cocking her head at Mia's unnaturally bright eyes. "Oh, getting the hang of it, aren't we? Uncovered six of the twelve by the looks of ye."

Mia nodded. "And the more I figure out, the more the marks tear at me."

"Best be careful, then, love." She turned to Liam as they picked through dewy grass, moonlit fog rolling down the hillside to their left. "And to answer your question, I've been flittering on for days trying to find you, dodging a giant falcon that's been following the Teralian Timberwolves migrating west. Lungor has been skulking about by night along the boggy roads in Cwen Dreorig — land sakes, he looks like a boulder when he wants! But those spearmen make him nervous, though, don't they? So he's been going slow."

Liam nodded. "I can understand that. But he's all right, last you saw?"

"He'll be fine, but he's hoping to find you again."

"I hope he does too, we could use his muscle, the big lugnut." He paused and stopped. Everyone turned to him. He scratched the back of his head, dreading the question he needed to ask. He let out a sharp breath. "Sea Breeze, can I ask you something?"

"Of course, love. Anything."

He lifted his eyes to her. "Is my mother alive?"

The raven hopped onto his shoulder and looked at him. "What does your heart say?"

He rubbed his temples with a scarred hand. "I wish I knew for certain."

The raven nodded, and Mia's hand touched his elbow. "I say we're going to assume she's alive, until we have more data."

It was the best course. He nodded slowly, then updated Sea Breeze on their current mission to find an outrider and press them for information.

She loved it, naturally, and demanded to join along.

***

After three more hours of plodding along an overgrown road between low rock walls, they rounded the base of the hill and climbed toward a gap where the road forked. One way descended northwest into menacing, dark country. Maple gulped. "That way's the Uluth Valley. Forbidden territory. Home of the Unseelie King."

The high, sharp shadows of that valley seemed to yawn, as if to devour them. Liam forced down a chill that threatened to rise up his spine. "Think he's come home? Even though we left him way back in Rathchylde country?"

"I'd say it's quite likely," said Maple, puffing her pipe, eyes staring at the creepy valley. "They say Remembering Ones can take any form, from crawling beastie to high upon the wing. He could have returned there anytime."

Definitely didn't want to go that way. Liam shuddered and turned to the other path. It swept swiftly northeast toward Caer Lannican's boggy upcountry.

"Look sharp, love," said Sea Breeze, "and mind the fog. I'll see you after — I'm going to try to find Lungor."

"Yeah, good idea, Sea Breeze," said Mia. The raven flew into the night.

Maple knocked an arrow in her bow, and Mia drew a knife she'd gotten from Branwen, serious eyes almost glowing beneath long waves of black hair frizzy in the dampness. She looked more dangerous and unhinged with each step. But then, he felt the way she looked. He steeled himself inwardly. *That's what Erentyr does to you, though, isn't it?*

They had gone far enough, considering the fog and where Mia had felt the scouts' presence. It was time. He could almost sense everyone's tension matching his own inner tightness. He nodded to them. They returned the gesture and faded into the fog. He unshouldered his baldric, put on his helmet and strapped the double-mail standard around his neck. He then pushed ahead, dingy yellow light glinting off his mail, tabard and wolf cloak, gambeson and belt distributing the weight of the heavy gear.

If Mia was right, Nurnian lookouts would not be far, and he welcomed a conflict.

He got into position, just as they'd planned. "Mia?" he called into the shadows ahead, purposefully overloud. "Maple? I lost you. Where are you?"

He took a few more steps. The barest sound of rustling carried from the air ahead. If he hadn't been prepared, he never would have heard it. To the right a cluster of bushes barred the way north, so he had to pass between rock and bush to get to the river that wound toward the castle.

Impressive. I can't see any of them.

A sharp twang came from the pass. A quarrel hit him in the gut. He gripped the haft and resisted smiling through the blunted strike. His mailcoat turned the barbed tip, but he held it there anyway. Poorer metal would have failed — it was a well-made quarrel, but too weak to pierce enchanted torgonite rings made by a master craftsman. He feigned injury and dropped to one knee.

Four scouts arose from the brush and jagged terrain with belt-hook crossbows ready. All deserved death. But that feeling also unsettled him — he had never felt so much rage before. It felt unchained. Dangerous to more than just the enemy. His limbs practically vibrated with a desire to strike. To draw blood. Lots of it.

Then a fifth man in brigandine armor, mailcoat and sword approached from the shadows. Lucius. "Thought we might find you skulking about out here. On your belly, Liam." Breath frosted in the air before his craggy brow.

Liam smiled. "Good evening gentlemen." He tensed like a coiled spring, poised to strike, yet calm, but spoke as if struggling against a wound. "And let's clear this up: it's *Sir* Liam. I have a few questions, and you're going to answer them."

The scouts laughed. A Nurnian approached. "Look here, Lucius, it's a live one. Rogue Kaledonian rubbish by the looks of him."

"I said on your belly," said Lucius. One of the scouts loosed a quarrel that stuck into the ground near his booted foot.

"Where is Damien?" demanded Liam. *Keep them talking.* The silhouette of a branch up the hillside dipped almost imperceptibly behind and to the left, while a tiny light — easily mistaken for a firefly — drifted by a bush to the right. *Mia was very quiet here when she wanted to be.*

Lucius smirked. "He is with ... another hunting band, shall we say. A more pressing issue, mayhap. Much the pity for him. Since your clan scattered like roaches years ago, you're the last hapless cur of that Shoreland rot. The fame of slaying the last Panregon, therefore, will come to me."

Now.

Liam stood up and tossed the blunted quarrel aside. "Will it, though?"

The scouts gaped in surprise, but then recovered and attacked.

Liam gripped Xanibor as he had done in the MacTira Moor courtyard, and called upon its power, aiming directly at Lucius. A line of swaying grass flowed toward Lucius, then spiky, twisted branches exploded from the earth to entangle him, thorns digging into his flesh or piercing between plates of his brigandine. A concussive wave hammered Liam's hands with the use of it, but blood-pounding rage swept the pain away.

Another scout loosed a quarrel at his head. He tipped his chin and let it bounce off his helmet with a rattling impact. Stars burst into his vision, but he suffered no injury. Then a red line shot across the pass from a standing Mia, eyes shining, murmuring an incomprehensible word that echoed in his mind, mouth snarling, teeth bared. The crossbowman and the spearman behind Lucius cried in agony, blood spraying, dying instantly. The second spearman crawled, red rivulets escaping his mouth. Maple dove from a tree, knives in hand, and stabbed under the rim of his helmet. The second crossbowman — now the last Nurnian standing — tossed his weapon and drew forth shield and warhammer to charge Liam.

He set himself and worked out quickly what his enemy would likely do. It was a guessing game. Years of martial arts instincts kicked in. Thoughts flashed through him as if in slow motion. *It always begins with footwork. That shield will limit his ability to attack my right but is still a weapon in itself. I have reach, but he will be able to sweep past a strike and hit me around the shield.*

"Mind the god-forged blade," called Lucius, struggling in vain to escape the entanglement.

Liam shot forward with an exaggerated slash. As predicted, his foe ducked, raised the shield, and prepared to charge in for a hammer to the gut. Liam shifted, however, slipping between the shield and hammer, batted away the weapon and pushed straight in with the blade, then twisted his wrists and slashed across the man's neck above the coat of plates, blade tearing through gambeson and mail, dropping him instantly. His enemy convulsed in a pool of blood, and Liam ended his misery with a stab in the face, then strode toward Lucius, planting Xanibor in the earth, then taking out flint and tinder box and lighting a torch.

Mia, eyes normal now, joined his side, bruising on her neck from the inflamed wizard marks. Lucius followed her approach. "I see your pretty little friend sorted out her conjury, then." Drops of blood trickled down his face where a branch had torn his helmet off and held him fast.

Liam growled, torchlight flickering in the center of the four of them. He brandished the torch, flush with rage, feeling out of control. "So tell me, Lucius," he spat, voice strained. "Think back. Recall that day on the chair with my father. Or perhaps do you need a reminder?" He yanked the man's mail coif off and placed the torch against his cheek. He roared in pain. Liam waited for satisfaction to creep into his veins.

It didn't.

He pushed harder into the man's face. Flesh crisped, and stench filled his nostrils. He noticed Maple cringing, unable to watch. He released the torch. "How now, Lucius? Have you no stomach for it when it's *you* against the flames?"

Lucius raised his chin defiantly, cheek smoking and blackened, sputtering. "Welcome back to Erentyr, lad."

He slammed a knee into Lucius' gut, making him retch. When he recovered, he grabbed a tuft of hair and yanked, forcing Lucius to face him. "Tell me what I want to know, Lucius — is my mother still alive? Answer me truthfully or she'll know." Mia crossed her arms and glowered, fuming. He had never seen her so angry. She seemed just as ready to wreak vengeance as he was. Had his story truly infected *her* as he feared? Didn't matter. He curled his lip at him in derision.

Lucius scoffed. "You think I don't know conjury? There's no spell like that." He spat blood. "Do your worst, Kaledonian filth."

Liam cocked his head, let go of Lucius's hair and straightened. "Have it your way."

He pressed the torch against Lucius's face on the same spot, making him scream.

"Stop, please," said Maple, tugging at his tabard. "Liam, 'tis not you. Don't become like them! Is this the knightly way?"

He stopped, Maple's words impacting, leaving Lucius to hang limp in a bloody slump on the vines, barely breathing. He hesitated, feeling the need to defend himself. He *was* losing control.

Trouble is, he liked it. He chose to ignore that terrifying fact.

"I'm not like them, Maple," he seethed. "Unlike them, *I* torture for a reason." Maple turned away, burying her face in her hands. Bitterness gaped within him. This was wrong. Yet he did not want to stop. The desire to inflict more pain remained, his father's silent agony etched into his mind. "So we're going to do this until I get the answer I like."

Lucius panted, blood dripping, sweat beading.

"Going once ... going twice ..." said Liam, inching the torch closer.

Lucius caught his breath and then sneered at Liam. "Fine, I'll tell you. You're too late," he taunted, "Ynwin's dead. Died the same way we killed your father. Now piss off."

Suddenly Mia clenched her fists and her eyes went pitch black. *"Ayarogoth!"* she shouted, then Lucius let out a silent scream, absolute horror and agony on his face, body twitching, whole frame contorted in sudden contraction.

"Well that's number seven, then, isn't it?" murmured Maple, perched on a rock, aghast, covering her face to the eyes with her traveling coat, as if to hide.

For a long moment Lucius twisted helplessly before them. Liam squinted at Mia, pure wrath upon her face. Eyes glaring down, lips snarling, teeth clenched. Unlike he had ever seen before. Lucius trembled, then cringed before them both. "I-I will tell you what I kn-know," he said. Mia crossed her arms, eyes returning, dark, eye-shaped marks on her arms pulsing and twitching.

Liam gripped the torch. Lucius trembled. "P-please, no more burning. No more spellcraft! I beg of you."

"You pathetic slime," Liam seethed. "How dare you beg for mercy? After what you did to my father?"

"I sw-swear I will tell you everything you wish to know."

Liam breathed sharply through his teeth, his body practically shaking with rage. It took every bit of strength to master himself. But Maple was right. This was not the knightly way. The man had yielded. *Would I reduce myself to the level of a filthy coward?* He pulled the torch away. "Do that and I will grant you a quick death. A knight's death, Lucius."

His face betrayed a great struggle. He clearly feared them but could not resist sneering out the corners of his mouth. Liam pretended not to notice him attempting to cut himself free with a hidden dagger, despite being deeply disturbed by Mia's latest spell, and fighting to master his own trembling. "You're all d-doomed. I might as well tell you everything because you're too late anyway! Lamon and Lord Damien have outwitted the lot of you. He's infiltrated your c-camp, and by the time you return, the rebels will have either been all killed or enslaved. Bran will be put to the sword and lift the kingslayer curse, and they will catch up with you and hang y-you at the nubbing-cheat."

The three of them exchanged horrified glances.

Then Lucius, suddenly surging forth, fought off the vines around his neck. He lunged, but Liam was ready. He grabbed his wrist, wrenched him around, snatched Xanibor, and slashed. The ease through which the blade sliced through flesh and bone shocked him. He let out a ragged breath, vengeance unleashed. Lucius's head fell upon the damp grass, blood splashing, body lumping to the ground.

Nostrils flared, Liam wiped the blood from his cheek. Mia wiped a drop of blood from her arms as the last traces of the quarter moonlight dimmed. How long he stood there he couldn't say. His heart pounded in his head, ragged breathing slowing as the depth of what they learned sank deeper into his soul. The fact that he had finally exacted revenge on Lucius for torturing his father to death hit him hard, too. Within him roiled a hundred emotions, but vengeance rose to the surface. The feel of the metal in his gloved fist, the cold air flowing into his nostrils, and the satisfaction — tinged with regret — could not be denied. He gripped Lucius's decapitated head and pondered it, staring into those lolled eyes as the head dripped blood.

"Liam," said Mia, softly but urgently. He blinked at her. "We have to get back to the camp right now!"

He doused the torch and shook his head, all of them now gray outlines in a blue-black world. "We can't. It's pitch dark out here, and the fog is thick as soup. We'll get lost and be no good to anyone. If any other Nurnians are near, lighting a torch will only draw them to us." He sighed in frustration. "We'll have to wait until dawn."

They hung their heads for a moment, taking that in. "Come on," said Maple, finally, "I know a wee cave we can hide in for the night that might be safe."

The three of them stole away into the darkness.

Chapter 19

Arrius gazed out at the countryside beneath his castle as dawn broke. Each day it seemed the Unseelie bogs grew further from the Dark Valley, through Dreyana north and east into Kaledon. No longer the slow overgrowth of distant farmlands and pastures, the Unseelie curse now crept seemingly a footstep whenever one looked away, tangled blackthorn bogs, heavy mist and deadly creatures of the Unseelie King within.

He furrowed his brow, his frown deepening. All these years of fighting, built on the promise of a kingdom of his own. A rare pang of regret struck him at all he had done to achieve it. And now this accursed plague upon the land. *The Unseelie kept to themselves in Uluth Valley for generations. Why now? Tradition has maintained it was a kingslayer curse ... but is that so? Am I being punished for my sins against the gods?*

But that made little sense. The gods rewarded the strongest, and the one who took the greatest risks. That is how his lord far to the south, Ozremorn, had become Grand Sovereign of the Enclave of Wizard Kings. And to show his support, Ozremorn had sent both his apprentice Lamon as conjury master, and Lord Damien from beyond the dragon's gate. Both formidable allies, ever loyal these long years.

One thing did not add up, however. The Lost Panregon. One stray scrap of a recent folk legend. Dismissible. And yet ... he stroked his beard as light from the two suns emerged from the east. Just how *did* Liam really play into all this? His mother, Ynwin Panregon, emerged in his mind. He recalled that last day in Caldbana when his hunters had caught up with her. *What Druid-taught secrets did you stow away in that world beyond the gate, Ynwin?*

But then, he had his own secret about Ynwin, didn't he? He let out a deep breath, slow creeping boglands catching his eye again.

Lamon joined him on the battlements of the central tower of Caer Lannican. Surf crashed into the sea stacks far below. Arrius glanced sidelong at the Royal Conjury Master. Power seemed to emanate from the bleeding wizard marks. But he knew a power even greater than spellweaving: loyalty. Trained in counter-conjury as a young warrior for Ozremorn, Arrius knew to check the hands and mouth for any unusual movements, to gauge the wizard marks. But especially the eyes. Lamon wove no spells at the moment. He adjusted a bandage on his forearm where a mark had burned him. What a cruel existence it must have been to wield so much power but suffer so much for it. Lamon had proven his loyalty many times, but was it time to share his greatest secret with him? A nagging feeling told him to wait a little longer.

Lamon gazed into the accursed land by his king. "It is done, my liege."

"That is good to hear," Arrius replied. "Was Bran among them?"

"Yes, my king. He was stripped, beaten and locked into the slave wagons, which journey here as we speak."

He nodded, a surge of confidence swelling within him. "It is almost over, finally. After all these years. What of the so-called Lost Panregon? Liam? Him too?"

"He was not there," said Damien, boots clanking on stone as he joined. "On a scouting mission, it would seem." He fingered the hilt of Larsorn. Arrius's eyes dipped to the god-forged blade. Formidable weapon. Perhaps he needed to take it from Damien.

"So he is no longer a concern," said Arrius. "We've won. Let Liam rot, then. He'll never breach the unconquerable Caer Lannican in a thousand years." He patted Damien on the shoulder. "You can return home. You've earned it, young knight."

But Damien deliberated instead of celebrating. Curious. He placed a gloved hand on the battlements and scanned the countryside as the wind tossed his blonde hair about. "Grand Sovereign Ozremorn wants me to tie up this last loose end." Lamon nodded slowly, agreeing, eyes on Damien. "With Ynwin dead and gone, Liam is all that remains of our mission that relates to the Dream Stone. But I still need the Stone itself to complete my task, if possible. Then I'll return home a hero to my own people in Midworld."

Something about that answer troubled Arrius, but he could not place what. The courtyard bustled with the activity of men-at-arms and slaves. That is where he would hang Bran.

"I beg your leave, sire," said Damien abruptly. "I believe Liam is down there," he said pointing to a dark cluster of overgrown and jagged farmland, gripped with fingers of Unseelie bog near the forbidden Uluth Valley.

"How do you know?" asked the king.

Damien glanced at his left hand. "I can feel the Dream Stone. Liam is getting perilously close to the ancient Unseelie dominion. If he is drawn there, the Stone will never be recovered and I would be denied my prize."

"Prize? I thought all you craved was to kill him and go back to Midworld."

He stared at him for a moment. "Of course," he said with a smile. "But, in a perfect world, I would return in possession of the Dream Stone."

He shrugged. "I have it on good authority that we do not live in a perfect world, Sir Damien. But, you have my leave anyway."

With that the knight bowed but exchanged a suspicious glance with Lamon before he left. What were those two up to?

Lamon regarded the king. "Sire," he said. Arrius nodded, and the Royal Conjury Master left too.

Arrius returned to the vista below, now *very* glad he did not share his secret with Lamon or Damien. He breathed in deeply. It was quite a risk, actually, not sharing everything with Lamon, Damien, and hence Ozremorn himself. Those two were up to something. Once this business with Bran was done, he would need to attend to them.

He narrowed his eyes upon the infested countryside, fingers tapping on the stone balcony rail. In any case, the Unseelie curse was spreading daily now. His eyes fell upon the crowded courtyard where prisoners were being processed. Killing Bran should end it. *But if killing Bran should fail to stop the curse ... then thank the gods I kept my one surety.*

The royal equerry approached, a jowly, balding Nurnian, overdressed.

"Gavinius," said Arrius, "did the cook leave a tray on my table in the solarium?"

"Yes, sire."

"Good. Close the door behind me." He left the balcony for a corridor to his private bedchamber. "I will be in my study and I do not wish to be disturbed."

"As you command, my king."

He passed through the empty royal bedchamber, where more than a few Kaledonian slave girls had been taken over the years and entered the solarium. He carried the platter of fruit and bread to the hearth and pressed the stone near the right sconch — as Sibne had taught him before Arrius executed the traitor king. The royal signet ring vibrated briefly. The fire died down and the hearth opened into a hidden stairway. He crossed stones carved in runes to climb a spiral stairway, reaching a landing blocked by a heavy iron door. He unlocked the door and opened it. Within, a lamp flickered atop a heavy wooden table, barely illuminating a windowless and musty chamber. On the far side, a woman curled alone on the rushes. She breathed softly, leaning against the wall.

Arrius placed the platter next to an untouched plate of food and crossed his arms before her bowed and wilted form, grey and blonde hair long and frazzled about her small body.

"Ynwin," he said at last.

***

Ynwin Panregon, thirteenth Stoneguard of the Shoreland Tuath, opened her eyes upon hearing a plate set upon the table. Stripes of lamp light against ancient stone bricks stretched into the darkness. She turned around with great effort, legs and joints burning with relentless aches that never quite left her, the bone in her leg, where she'd been shot all those years ago, having never healed properly. King Arrius, murderer of almost her entire family, and captor these many years, stood frowning, light from the windows filtering up the stairway into her hidden cell. Even after all this time, hate kept her going. Pure, unmitigated loathing fueled her blood.

She glared silently, rubbed the aching Calling Brand on her left hand, the once bright green lines of its knotwork leaf-shaped tear now faded to brown and muddy. Beneath the hatred she shot at him with her eyes, sorrow weighed on her like leaden rain. Her beloved husband and six sons awaited her in Evensade. Only Liam, little red, her last hope, kept her from starving herself to death. But that hope was dead, now. Marks she scraped on the walls with a stray pebble added up to fifteen years. He was never coming back home. Sweet release, now, was only a few days away.

"They tell me you've spurned your meals for a week," said Arrius. She replied with a heavy-lidded glare of disdain. "Do you not care if Kaledon is consumed by the Unseelie curse, then?"

"The kingslayer legend is false," she rasped. "I told ye once already, *sire*," she added with venom. "Stoneguards kept the balance," she said, flicking the back of her hand with the Calling Brand at him. "You still need me alive." Arrius listened quietly, gnarled features weighing her words. She smiled weakly. "But soon I will die, false King Arrius, and nothing will save your stolen kingdom. I hope the Unseelie destroy you *all*."

Arrius sucked his teeth in derision, curling his lip and raising an eyebrow. "You would abandon your home for mere revenge?"

Rage erupted. She raised a manacled fist and pointed at him. "You killed my husband and six of my sons! I dinnae care what happens to me, so long as ye suffer." The corner of Arrius's mouth twitched into the hint of a smile. She had not railed against him like this in years — he was likely enjoying this. She mastered herself rather than give him further satisfaction. "So kill me, kill Bran, it matters not. The Unseelie King will devour you to the quick, and hie on't."

"Fool," he hissed, pounding the table with a fist and making the tray rattle. "Liam has returned, you old beldam. What say you to that?"

Ynwin blinked, pushing through agony to sit up, suddenly trembling. "Y-you lie," she whispered.

Arrius smiled. "Ynwin, you're as cunning as I am cruel and ruthless. You'd know if I lied." He glanced at the food. Two Atrogonian pears, plucked from Nurnian orchards far to the south in the land of the Wizard King Enclave. Fine grazalia cheese and fresh round dark bread. He set a goblet of Atrasian wine next to them, the royal signet ring that had belonged to Sibne, and countless Kaledonian High Kings before, glinting in the yellow light. "Perhaps you should ponder that before you starve yourself. Bran will be here soon. If the curse does not lift when I execute him, I will need you to save my kingdom."

She snarled. "I'll never do that."

He stood up and gazed down haughtily at her. "You have but one son left, Ynwin. A knight known as Damien, from

Midworld no less, where your precious Liam lived for all these years. He hunts Liam down for me even now. I know you won't use your gifts to save *my* kingdom. But I wonder, will you save your only living son?"

Rage, terror, panic, and defiance vied for her soul. She could not speak. She gaped at him, trying to shift into a comfortable position. None were possible. Her eyes drifted to the floor and she leaned back against the wall.

He smiled, huffing a laugh. "I'll leave you to your thoughts." He turned and exited, closing the door with an echoing thud.

Turmoil raged within her weak and dying body. Death, sweet release, was so close. But her son was alive. "Damn that man," she seethed, finally finding her voice, her isolation making conversations with shadows common. But her defiance finally broke. So many years of pain and sorrow. So many years of worrying about her only remaining child, lost in a strange world far beyond this one. A world she sent him to. She collapsed and wept into the stone, for what seemed like hours.

Aching silence returned.

She breathed deeply, forcing each breath. In, out. In, out. With great effort, she sat up and crawled to the chair. She greedily ate and drank the wine deeply, tears streaming down her cheeks. "Hurry my son," she said upon finishing the plate. *I cannot hold on much more.* She stared at the Calling Brand, the lamp light glow falling upon the fading markings as her life slowly ebbed.

Only one thing left to live for.

***

Liam entered the chapel of St Roan. Blue-gray skies sent sprays of rain down upon the devastation. Bodies. Blood. Tangles of corpses. Some burnt. Some hacked and mutilated. Vultures circled the skies, watching. Fires still burned here and there, where before there stood tables, chairs, old furniture, tents. Barrels of precious provisions had been smashed and set to the torch. Smoke twirled from many places.

Farmers, children, yeomen, traders. All dead. The side tunnels, alcoves, shallow caves — the same.

Maple stepped silently beside him, hand over an open mouth, tears welled up in her eyes. She went to a child who had played with her not two days before and knelt, her coat dipping in the pooling blood now beginning to dry. Mia walked stiffly, fists clenched, head down, eyes glaring forward through a mass of hair, frazzled, breath shallow. She turned and vomited onto the flagstones.

Liam shook, breathing through his teeth, tight and forced. A coyote gnawed at the body of Ian, who lay in a pool of blood, eyes glazed over. Other coyotes skulked and sniffed about, nibbling and pulling at feet or hands. He roared and charged at them, grabbing a smoldering plank and lobbing it at the one near Ian. The coyotes backed away, yipping and whining, hungry, but hopping out of reach into alcoves. He went to Ian and closed those frozen eyes, placing his broken knightly sword in a stiff hand.

Mia knelt beside Branwen. The humble Druid's body lay limp on the stone, a huge mark blackened her dead form from foot to chest, throwing knives embedded in charred flesh. Mia's glowing ring hand on Branwen's chest, she rocked back and forth. Liam stood and walked up to her as Maple trotted nearby.

Mia let out a moan, and Maple patted her back helplessly. "Lamon did it," she said at last, shouting at the body. "I can see it. He commands spells of lightning and burning knives. That *smirk*." She curled her lip in derision. "I saw Branwen's last moments. Brave." She turned a tear-streaked face. "She and I were going study together," she whispered, neck muscles twitching. "She was so kind and helpful to me." She dipped her head and sobbed, holding Branwen's stiff form.

Maple scuttled about, nose near the floor just outside the flagstones, on the beaten earth in the shadows of the encircling hillcrests. "Lungor, bless me. Lungor was here, too. Oh dear."

"What? Is he ok?" asked Liam, following the wildgnome. "Did they kill him too?"

Maple shook her head, curly red mass bouncing. "He came to help. But he was hurt. There's blood here," she said, tracing the ground with a finger, "tiny stone crystals — that's giant's blood. His footprints head off north. He must've climbed up to the overhang to escape."

Liam pinched the bridge of his nose and sighed. He plummeted into bottomless darkness inside. His head pounded and blood trickled from his nose. He was far beyond tears. Into numb, frozen horror.

The fog rose, refusing to melt in the dawn. Skies of endless grey and sprinkling rain crept by. "My brothers and sisters," he whispered to no one, his father's torture flashing in his mind unbidden, his brother's bloody slaughter hammering him from within. "So many..." He rested his fist on his lip and looked down.

Mia approached, hands clasped before her, eyes unnaturally steady. "So what do we do now?" she asked, a dark edge lurking beneath her voice. Wizard marks crawled on her skin; her gait oddly calm.

He shook his head. Emptiness was all that was left. "The only thing left to do now is go back to Caldbana and use the Stone. Return to Midworld. Forget we ever came to this forsaken world of death."

"You would ... consider that?" said Maple sheepishly, hands in her coat pockets.

He took out the Dream Stone. His mother's still pained presence seemed to emanate from it. Mia and Maple stood before him in the burning, smoky courtyard, the stench of death heavy. "We have to face the facts. We can't possibly win, now.

The Dream Stone is lying to me — my mother is dead. Damien and Arrius have won. We — we should go home and live our lives in peace. Midworld is safe."

"You don't know that your mom is dead, Liam," said Mia, daggers in her voice. "And even if she is, what about Kaledon? What of her memory?"

"She's gone! There is nothing left."

She stared at him. "If you can let this go, seriously, nobody would blame you. But don't do it for safety, do it because it's the right decision."

He closed his eyes. If he stayed here he would likely die a horrible, painful death. Or … he could go home. Live his life with Mia. A pleasant life. Margaritas at *Circuits*. Just taking orinol if he began to feel grief or pain. No more fighting or killing. No more struggling. No more combat even with robots at the gym-plex. Just vibing. He could grow old. He looked down, drifting into what that would be like. He could, at old age, look back at their long lives. He knitted his brow. *And find them … utterly empty.*

The word resonated in his mind for a long while. The calm before an inner storm.

Then images of his family's death pummeled him like never before, locking up his shoulders and stomach, hammering his head. He saw his father, dragged and beaten, chained to the iron chair in front of him. Helpless as they shoveled hot embers onto the metal. He felt a hand on his shoulder. "Liam?" asked Mia.

No. She *could not* be a part of this. He would *not* poison her with this any more! There was no way she could understand it. This *weakness*. All this death. He opened his eyes, enraged at his woundedness. He growled and yanked his arm away from her, stepping forward toward the courtyard of twisted bodies.

"Oh no you don't!" shouted Mia. He stopped, scowling. "Don't you do this, you fucker. Look at me! Right now!"

Liam turned slowly, smoldering, ready to fight. He glared at her. Maple peeked from behind a chair.

She pointed at him, eyes wide, teeth bared. Her hair frazzled, face flush. "We can't do this here. This walling everyone one off shit that you do. This is Erentyr! You can *not* shut me out now! You don't have that luxury anymore!"

He stepped forward, glowering down at her. "No? And what about you? All those years, every time I tried to get *you* to share with *me*, you changed the subject. Made everything about my pain and suffering! My traumas. My pathetic weaknesses. You pulled away worse than I ever did! What about you?" he shouted, making her flinch.

She clenched her fists, then let out a scream, her eyes becoming pitch black, her wizard marks flickering blood red for an instant. A concussive wave knocked Liam back to one knee, a shock of horror striking his core like a bolt of lightning, making every muscle clamp down, nearly making bones crack. He shook, scarred hand in an open, rigid palm, as if pushing away a truck that threatened to run him over. He gasped, finally able to take in a breath, and tottered his head up to see her on the ground, weeping in terror at what she had done, both forearms trickling with rivulets of blood that oozed from her wizard marks, flowing from between her clenched fingers. She was being devoured by Erentyr. Turning into something he didn't recognize. But then, perhaps, so was *he*.

The moment hung, tense in the air for an unknown time, when finally the touch of a small hand on his open palm, and another on Mia's fist, made them both blink and turn to Maple. "Shh, shh, please," she said, her voice calming. "Listen to me, both of you. Focus on my voice, now." They fought off their trembling and tried to recover their breath. "That's it." They calmed enough to listen. "Now, you both need to learn something. But I can't just tell you. You have to *feel* it. Tell me:

which is stronger? The open palm or the closed fist? Hm? Come now, tell me."

Ready to change the subject, hoping it would help him regain his bearings, Liam said "open palm. Stronger s-structure."

Mia shook her head. "Fist. N-no contest. Strike hard and fast. Right?"

"You're both wrong," said Maple. Liam wrinkled his brow. Mia tilted her head quizzically. Maple brought Mia's fist into his palm. "They're both strong. But not alone. If you stay locked in one or the other, you become paralyzed. Only the hand that can flow *between* them is strongest."

Liam and Mia blinked at each other.

"That's ... really good, Maple," said Liam, finally able to smile.

Mia laughed, letting the tension out and nodding. "I like it," she whispered. "Words of wisdom from Maple Magicwood."

The wildgnome pulled them into a group hug. "Oh, you young ones," she said. "Two fluthered thing-topples, if there ever were!"

Moments passed.

Finally Liam raised his chin and straightened, opening his eyes to stand before the sprawling carnage as the others rose to their feet. "If we returned," he said at last, the gravity of their situation returning, "no one in Midworld would know what happened here." He turned to face Mia. "But there's only one problem."

Mia set those mahogany eyes to him squarely, putting something in one hand from her belt. "And what is that?"

"*I* would know."

Mia smiled, the dark edge returning. "That's the right answer." She opened her hand to reveal the pouch of war paint she'd made all those weeks ago.

He tilted his head at her. "You knew I would change my mind?"

She shook her head. "I said I'd support you, not follow you back." She patted blood from her arms with torn cloth from a tunic. "We're obviously still not relationship material anyway. I think we've proven that. And in any case, I'm not done here — so I'm glad we agree for now. You're still my best friend, despite our differences."

He raised an eyebrow, the truth of her words stinging. He nodded sharply. "Same. I guess I shouldn't have assumed you'd go back. But aren't you afraid of what might happen to us here? This place is eating us both alive. Surely you can see that."

She nodded, her expression humorless, her eyes steady, her stance tense. "Yes. I do see it, Liam. I'm not blind. I'm changing. We both are. But your people took me in and called me friend just like that. No questions, no criticism, even as strange as I am to them." She chuckled grimly. "I should have known — they're like you."

He embraced her tightly, and Maple hopped into their arms and joined in the group hug.

He set Maple down and stroked his beard. "So, maybe it's not time for warpaint just yet. We have to figure out how to salvage this mess before we charge into glorious battle-death."

"Well," said Maple, puffing her pipe as buzzards swooped lower, and coyotes skulked back, "no matter who is king, we've got to save Kaledon from that scribbly Unseelie curse."

Mia tapped her cheek in thought. "Yes. And the only way to do that is to capture Arrius — either to kill him or find out what happened to your mother."

"Or both," he said. "But how can we possibly lay siege to Caer Lannican without Bran and the remaining knights?"

Maple squinted, monocle in place. "I bet that Damien locked up everyone they didn't kill in the slave wagons," said Maple. "I noticed fresh wagon tracks heading north. We'd have run smack into them if we hadn't used me shortcut."

A new wave of energy flushed his veins. Heart beating, he stood. The others followed. "Free them, then," said Liam. "That's a good place to start. Shall we?" He placed his hand in the center of the three of them. Mia placed her glowing ring hand on his, and Maple put her rough small hands on hers.

"Lead the way, Maple," said Liam.

Suddenly they heard a great howl to the south, far deeper and menacing than a normal wolf's. The buzzards scattered. The coyotes whined and fled. A mighty screech tore across the sky. They scanned the low clouds but saw nothing.

Blood left Mia's face, and Maple chewed her fingernails, eyes darting about. A chill crawled up Liam's spine.

"The giant wolves I freed," said Mia softly, her expression tense with fear. "And the great falcon. They smell the blood of the carnage here."

Liam unshouldered Xanibor. "Let's go before they decide we're next on the menu."

Mia nodded enthusiastically and they followed Maple swiftly from the decimated camp.

Chapter 20

Arrius sat upon his throne as grey sunlight filtered into the great hall from high windows. Whitewashed walls hung with Nurnian tapestries and banners of the Southern Kingdoms, and a wide carpet covered the hardwood floor. A statue of Ozremorn in his ceremonial garb as Grand Sovereign of the Enclave of Wizard Kings stood majestically to his left, while to his right stood Myrrdon, Prophet of the Falling Stars, whose influence reformed the ancient Druidic Ways the backward Kaledonians still followed. Hearths flanked the hall, while the trestle tables sat dismantled in the corners. The king brooded on his throne, attended by the royal equerry, quartermaster, and several scribes and officials who discussed matters among themselves.

His thoughts drifted to Ynwin. The end of it all was coming. If she was right, he would have to convince Damien to spare Liam ... at least until Ynwin halted the curse. But how could he force her to? Imprison Liam as ransom?

He nodded. That would do it. He smiled to himself.

"Sir Damien of the Gate," said the herald at the door.

The knight strode in boldly. He knelt before the throne.

Arrius indicated for the knight to stand. "Back so soon?"

"Something troubles me, sire," said the man.

"Do tell."

Damien glanced at his left palm, then rested it on the hilt of Larsorn. "Yes. It's been nagging at me for some time now. Has Lamon returned from the observatory with any news of Liam?"

"He has no news," said Lamon, entering behind him, the herald having missed him. He walked up the dais to stand beside his king. "A certain raven has been flittering about the countryside, thwarting my scrying efforts. Definitely a fairykind in disguise, if I'm any judge, though I cannot say if it was Unseelie or one of the Fairy Queen's minions."

Arrius regarded Damien carefully. Something seemed off with the man — was it his tense posture? Measured speech? Arrius knitted his brow. "Why do you ask?"

Damien placed a finger to his clean-shaven chin. "I carried the Dream Stone for many years, sire. It has many mysterious qualities, having been crafted by the Fairy Queen Herself."

"Of course. And?"

He stepped forward. "When I confronted Liam in the Tarila Wood, I told him his mother was dead, and he called me a liar."

Arrius felt tension climb his torso. He forced a laugh. "The wishful thinking of a man lost." He turned to the Royal Conjury Master, but Lamon stood statue-like, expression impenetrable, sleeves of his open cloak covering his wizard marked arms.

Damien chuckled politely. "Yes, of course, sire. That's what I thought, too. Only he seemed … insistent. As such, I must ask, *did* you kill Ynwin?" His expression slipped into a menacing smile. "As you *said* you did before?"

Arrius shot to his feet, mailcoat rustling under his brigandine and royal coat. The hall fell deadly silent under his wrathful glare. Damien, however, stood firm, cheek twitching, the mask of a smile upon his features.

"You dare question my word?" whispered the king. Damien returned with a cool stare. Arrius glanced at the guards. The royal equerry and attendants backed away, heads turning about in concern. Men-at-arms came forth in mailcoats, carrying mace, hammer, and dagger. Damien still stood nonplussed, disturbingly calm. He did not even reach for Larsorn. "Lamon," said the king, "escort this man from my castle. See to it that he returns to his world in shame."

"I will not yield," said Damien. Four men-at-arms, two of whom had accompanied Damien on his hunting mission with Lucius, brandished maces and shields and closed in on him.

"Lamon," seethed Arrius, "make him yield."

"Aye, my king," said the wizard. His eyes glowed white as he wove his hands, then spoke the word, *"thurikitar,"* then stretched out his hand.

At Arrius.

White flashed in his eyes, and a crackling bolt engulfed the king's body, burning across his torso, muscles suddenly tensed, no aid offered from his fine armor. Arrius dropped, mouth emitting a squeak, energy buzzing across him, pain roaring, unable to move. Barely registering, he slid down the dais as the men-at-arms looked about nervously, Damien drew Larsorn and lowered the tip at him.

Another wave of agony stretched over him like a crashing surf, frost forming on his body, freezing cold overtaking his limbs to the bone. "See," said Damien, boots striking the wood toward his head. "I've been thinking. Lying to me about Ynwin is betrayal, sire." He bent over Arrius and plucked the royal signet ring of Brendan, one of the last High Kings of the Mythic Ages and placed it on his own hand. "Hence you have betrayed our liege Ozremorn as well as myself. Traitorous."

Arrius struggled to speak, pain and cold numbing his muscles. He reached out to one of the men-at-arms. "Help me," he rasped. "I am your king."

Only one man strode forth, mace brandished. Turian, an older soldier from the conquest, beard black and white, scars on his face and forearm. "I'll not abide this treachery!" he said, glaring accusingly at his fellow men-at-arms, then turning to Damien. "You lay down your arms, foreign knight. I care not for your god-forged blade. By my honor, you'll taste my steel."

But Lamon advanced, hands up, eyes still unnaturally white, now turning blue. *"Aharandoth,* my good man," he said, voice soothing, yet still strangely echoing in Arrius's head.

Turian blinked and scrunched his features, staggering momentarily, before calming and straightening. He turned to Lamon. "I'm sorry, sir, what were your orders, then?"

Arrius grimaced. Turian's counter-conjury was poor. Destitute! Yet so was his own. His body betrayed him. All he could manage were weak, slow movements.

Damien, amused, placed the tip of Larsorn to Arrius's vulnerable neck. The king hissed, shivering, and glared up at the traitor-knight. Damien waved the ringed hand. "I hereby proclaim myself as regent of Kaledon, in the name of Ozremorn and by his authority and rule. King Arrius is hereby deposed for withholding valuable information from his subjects. I shall be acting ruler until such time as a suitable heir can be produced." Turian straightened and saluted, while the other men tentatively stood by, neither voicing protest nor allegiance, eyes darting about the room. Lamon surveyed the group, the whites of his eyes returning to normal brightness, silently approving of the knight's proclamation. Damien turned back to Arrius. "As for you, Arrius, I do not expect you to tell me where you've hidden her. And so I will end your suffering now and find her myself. I do not pity you the welcome you'll receive in Evensade."

Arrius tried to burst forth in defense, gripping Larsorn, trying to push it away, but it merely cut his hand, right before the traitor knight shoved the enchanted blade into his spine.

***

Liam followed Maple, Mia close beside, as dusk's light bathed the foggy hills from the west. Maple zig-zagged along the trail, until they reached the pass where the road split. Glittering rain fell in fine droplets. Northeast, the trail climbed toward Caer Lannican, cloaked in mist, but northwest, the trail descended a gnarled path into the Dark Valley of Uluth, a jumble of jagged tree clusters upon twisted hills flanked by cold, black mountains.

Uluth ... heart of the Unseelie of old, and source of the long fingers of bogland that had eaten Kaledon slowly over the last fifteen years. Domain of Vinraith Flame-eye, Unseelie King, Hidden One, Old Man of the Forest. Woodsman. Dread threatened to strangle Liam's ragged breath. The idea of being so near that immortal foe making his limbs leaden and cold. Yet he trudged forward, shoulders hunching, glaring, placing one foot before the other by sheer force of will. Vinraith was not far, now. The Dream Stone somehow knew it and so Liam could *feel* him near. Death ... or worse ... would surely soon follow.

A blood-curdling moan arose from the south. Mia glared back at the sound, uneasiness on her features, twirling her thick hair in her fingers, as if mesmerized. She lifted her gaze to the mottled clouds. In the growing darkness a shape soared high above, barely visible, watching, waiting to strike.

"They found the camp," muttered Liam.

Fluttering settled on a nearby dogwood tree. "Careful, loves. Beasties are barely sated. They're coming this way."

"Yeah, got that," said Liam. "Good to see you again."

"Oy, 'tis herself! Evening, Sea Breeze," said Maple.

Mia lifted a tense wrist for Sea Breeze to flitter and perch to. "Did you find Lungor?"

"Ooh, he fought valiantly," chirped the raven, "but got hurt. Not lethal, mind you — but he's hiding. He fears the Timberwolves and the falcon both."

"Understandable," said Liam, fingers tingling cold.

Mia sighed, her features crestfallen. "I did this. *I* set those creatures loose." She stared at her hands, wizard marks twitching on her forearms. She closed her eyes hard. "So much chaos ... too much!"

"Hey, easy, easy," said Liam, caressing her shoulder. "You're too hard on yourself. The Unseelies forced you into that terrible choice."

Sea Breeze hopped on Liam's shoulder. "Aye, I agree. That's what Vinraith's minions do, little flower. They make cruel games. I wish it weren't so."

She turned to the wildgnome, new determination in her eyes. "The trail, Maple. Are they headed to the castle?"

"Oh right." Maple turned to the road, with her monocle. "So — bad news. The wagons don't turn toward Caer Lannican. They go, um, that way," she said, pointing to the forbidding valley of Uluth.

Liam closed his eyes and let out a breath. He forced himself to stay calm as tingling prickles crept up his neck. "I knew it. Why the hell would they go that way?"

"Maybe a trick of the mist," said Sea Breeze. "Children knows it gets devilish here sometimes. Manys-a-man have wandered into the place by accident, never to be seen after."

Mia joined him, staring in horror at the twisted road. She gripped his arm tightly, other hand in a fist. He shook his head as the dusk faded, leaving the waxing quarter moon to peek behind the clouds into the ancient Fairy domain. He gnashed his teeth. "Hmf! Well, then, I guess this is it, isn't it? If that's the way Bran and the other rebels were taken, that's the way we have to go."

"Liam," said the raven.

He glanced sidelong at her. "Don't try to talk me out of it now, Sea Breeze."

"I was just going to say, that's the dominion of–"

"Vinraith Flame-eye, I know," shot Liam. "We've met. Can't say he's that fond of me, nor is the feeling exactly mutual."

Sea Breeze nodded. "Then you know those knights and everyone on that wagon are probably lost."

Maple twirled her curly hair in her hands nervously. "I'm afraid I have to agree."

Mia crossed her arms. "Sure, but what choice is there?"

His heart rate rose, and he squinted into the dark path that led deeper down. "Look. I get it if no one wants to go there. But Mia's right. There is no choice. Not for me. I understand if you don't wish to follow. There'd be no shame in that. But I'm going in." He turned to the dark, descending path.

Sea Breeze let out what sounded like a sigh. "Of course you are, *err, err*. So be it." Maple scrunched her nose and started along the trail, Mia at her side.

They followed the wagon tracks slowly, eyes darting, misty air cooling the further down they went. Ahead of them an Unseelie forest of strange trees arose. Dark red trunks rose fifty feet to spread into a circle of densely packed branches with emerald-colored needles and cones. The forest would have been considered beautiful, as moonlight began to take over from the waning suns, but for the darkness to come. The fog receded, as if bound by the edge of the Unseelie Fairywild they now entered. The breeze blew crisp and cool.

Liam unsheathed Xanibor, Sea Breeze on his shoulder, her black eyes focused ahead, as Maple strung her bow with great seriousness, and Mia slowly drew Branwen's gift-dagger. They crept through the tall woodland for an hour, before the dragon blood trees gave way to a forest even stranger. Trees climbed from the red-needle floor in columns of gnarled crystal, and the white-yellow moonlight shined through an infinite web of prismatic branches. Maple and Mia gaped in awe, as a sudden wind made the leaves hum like glass-harps in a chord of great mystery, melodic threads blending into each other. Despite the foreboding that hung on everyone's hearts, they could not help but smile and marvel at the wonder of it.

Mia let the rainbow-light fall upon her wizard marks, which seemed to crawl, energized by the forest. She held her hands aloft and soaked in the light of ten thousand beams, taking in quick breaths. Sparks of moonlight shifted on her face. When her eyes opened, the whites burned bright for several moments.

"Isn't there anything like this place in Midworld?" asked Maple.

"Not even close," whispered Mia, eyes returning to normal, voice wavering.

The road stopped winding and straightened through a tunnel of bare glass branches. Sparkling trees grew wilder, unfettered by gravity, twisting into a spiderweb pattern.

"Old minds," said Sea Breeze, voice unusually somber. "Memories old here. Careful, loves. Keep your wits about ye. These were seeded by the Lyrvians long ago."

Liam tried to digest that. They emerged to a red pine-needle clearing, well-lit from the crystal grove. Wagons. Dead bodies. Some Kaledonian peasants, from the camp. Good folk. There were many Nurnians as well. Maple puffed her pipe and examined the grounds while the others waited on guard, peering into the silent shadows. "Looks like the Nurnians fled."

Liam raised an eyebrow at her. "How do you know?"

She pointed with the mouthpiece of her pipe at the footprints. "Atrogonian-style boots. Common with Nurnians."

"What of the rebels?" asked Mia.

Maple squinted beyond the grove. "Seems, the rebel knights went ... *further into* the valley." She pointed to a rise in the trail closely flanked with crystal branches that entered a tall aspen grove.

"Bran, Conal, and the other knights," said Liam. "My brothers and sisters." That thought set a new blaze in his heart. He practically ran further in, setting Sea Breeze's wings aflutter and causing the others to run behind. Moonbeams pierced the canopy of tall quaking aspens to light a leafy floor of glowing blue-gray mushrooms. Liam stopped in his tracks, blade front.

One beam settled upon a fallen log, upon which sat a small, lumpy creature.

He was a dark green man wearing a cloak of goose feathers over a torn cloth kilt. Unseelie — Liam was certain of it. His pulse raced. Bushy green hair of vines spilled over the little man's shoulders and flowed into a thick green beard that tumbled over a round belly. He smiled broadly, revealing shiny emerald teeth. "Greetings," said the creature in a deep, rich brogue. "I am The Gummp, faithful servant of my lord and master, Vinraith Flame-eye, king of the Unseelie. What common and filthy mortalkind dares enter his domain so brashly?"

Mia stood pale beside him, while Maple backed away. Sea Breeze cocked a suspicious eye at this Gummp.

"With respect," said Liam, lips dry, sheathing Xanibor and holding out hands in peace, "I seek the prisoners who came this way. They are my kinfolk. I wish only to take them and leave in peace."

The creature's keen, penetrating eyes went from the pouch that held the Dream Stone, to the raven, then to Mia and Maple. "By decree," he proclaimed suddenly, making Mia and Maple flinch, "and order of King Vinraith the Ancient, no mortalkind may enter this dominion lest she or he be of Kaledonian blood."

Maple shook her head. "Don't do it, Liam. Don't agree to that. The Gummp is a tricky old fandangle. Sharp as a popinjay. Especially don't let him make predictions for you!"

"Better know your onions if you're to face Vinraith's Old Guard and the Gummp, love," whispered Sea Breeze.

He glanced at Mia. She chewed her bottom lip, eyes concentrating fiercely, her expression wan. She swallowed and mastered herself, lifting her chin to him. "Go on, Liam. You've got this. We'll be ok."

That was asking a lot. His head turned forward, then back to her. He could tell she didn't believe they would be "ok" at all. "Mia, what about the giant wolves? The Nurnian hunters? The Unseelie bogs?"

She stared at him, unblinking. "You … need to trust me." A bead of sweat trickled down her cheek. She was forcing herself to do this for him. He could see it. *I don't deserve her.*

Conflict pulled within. Deep down, he knew this would likely be the end. For them all.

He stepped closer to Mia. Sorrow opened inner emptiness that tore at him. His throat tightened, and he gnashed his teeth. All the years they had known each other reeled through his mind. "Mia. I ... we may never see each other again," he said, the words cracking. "I need to say something." He swallowed, breathing through his teeth. "All the times we've tried over the years. All our stupid bickering, all our failed attempts at love. All those fights ... they just feel stupid and frivolous." Tears streamed down her cheeks and she forced herself not to sob as he spoke, standing straight as an arrow, wind tossing her wild black hair about her face. "I don't care about our struggles. I don't care that all we did was fight. All I know is that there will *never* be anyone for me but you." He stood before her and he wrapped his arms around her. She clasped his neck, hanging on every word. "I just want you to know before we both die," he whispered, "I love you."

She pulled him into a tear-stained kiss with frantic desperation, kissing for the first time without reservation in years. "I love you too, Liam," she said, breathless. They both wept as they kissed deeply, knowing their time together was running out.

After a brief respite, they both slowed and pulled away, knowing they had to. Her lips trembled as her eyes remained fixed on his. "I'll find you," she whispered. "I don't care if it's beyond death's door. *I will find you*."

He grimaced and turned, heart pounding heavy, deep darkness upon his soul. He set his jaw and forced one foot ahead of the other. Sea Breeze flittered to Mia's shoulder. She watched him walk away, hand to her mouth in despair. Maple waved at him, worry wrinkling her features, pipe puffing.

He turned and planted himself before The Gummp. "I, Sir Liam Trendari Panregon, Knight of Kaledon, accept."

The creature grinned, then waved his hands, and a flash enshrouded the knight. Pitch black engulfed his eyesight.

***

He turned — nothing.
His heart pounded.

***

Liam's surroundings gradually came back into view. He stood in a grand, grassy clearing, the sky moonless. Some quarter of a mile ahead stood a massive castle lit by burning forests all around. According to legend, the fortress was Vinraith's famous castle of Miren-Senan. Few could claim to have looked upon it and lived. Everywhere the aspens burned high, hitting him with waves of heat and filling his nostrils with smoky dark wind. The smooth walls of stone that, in their day likely burst from the wooded hills to break the clouds, were now mottled cliffs of cobblestone, bearded with ivy and moss, red with the firelight and swirling embers, climbing into pitch black skies. The oldest and largest Midworld castles, Liam recalled from books or pictures, paled in comparison with this stronghold. Not far ahead of him, rising from the short grass, climbed a single-file stairway with a sheer drop on both sides, leading to the castle. Beyond the blaze, the Dark Valley mountains peeked over miles of fire. The fortress loomed over him like a demon's crown of stone towers, perched upon sheer rock walls that flickered in the light.

Blinking away the disorientation, not knowing how much time must have just passed, he turned. The Gummp stood, leaning upon a small staff, wearing a menacing smile. "The die is cast."

He scanned the area for his companions. "Mia? Maple? Sea Breeze?" he called. No answer.

"Silence, young knight," said the Gummp. "They must fend for themselves now. You've made your accession. Now that you're here, name what you seek!"

"King Vinraith," he said, swallowing. "He has my countrymen. So ... I must speak with him, now."

The Gummp cracked a smile. "Then in you must go to yon castle. I can tell you what will happen if you go in there."

He turned, eyes drifting up to the spires of the forbidding stronghold. Terror gripped him — but not new terror. *Old* terror. Deep in his bones terror, from when he was a child. Flashes of memory erupted unbidden. His strong brother, Rendan, the oldest, run through with a spear. An arrow striking his swift, brown-haired brother Arran, huge gashes through the twins Declan and Aidan. His large brother, the dark-bearded Banner, gutted after killing three men, and the musical Ewan, smashed in the head.

He raised an eyebrow. Knowing what would happen could be useful. Might help calm the hurricane in his head. He recalled Maple's advice — don't listen to the Gummp's tricks. His head pounded. He struggled to keep his breathing still as the bloody images of his slaughtered family bashed him from inside. He had to know. "Fine. W-what? What will happen?"

The Gummp lowered his chin and glared at him from under bushy brows. "Are you sure you want to know? I am Kosithi. A Remembering One in your tongue. I *never* lie. My predictions *never* fail. Many choose not to know."

He believed him. He swallowed, forcing his breathing to slow, standing straighter. "Tell me."

"Very well. Brave or foolish? Let us see." The creature closed his eyes, stroked his beard, then opened them, pupils twinkling. "First, you will reach yon castle, but you will not enter it willingly. You will then find yourself in the dungeons, encountering an unexpected enemy. You will defeat the enemy but still lose. You will then get your wish — to be brought before Vinraith himself. But he will not grant you your plea. Instead he will sentence you to execution, whereupon the headman's axe shall fall, with your head upon the chopping block."

Not very comforting. He narrowed his brows and frowned, blood pummeling his temples. He swallowed, absent-mindedly clutching at his neck. "Pretty grim."

"Still wish to enter?" Liam lowered his head, struggling to make sense of all that. Surely this was a trick. The Gummp awaited his response with a disturbing smile. The castle seemed to loom even greater now. Meanwhile the fires burned higher, sending embers to swirl in the air. "Do you decline, young Knight of Kaledon?"

No. That would not do. No matter the flashbacks, no matter the terror surging through him like electrical pulses, no matter the seemingly absolute certainty he will fail. Turning back would simply not do. So what if failure was inevitable? Was the effort not worth it in itself, regardless? He lifted his chin defiantly. "I'll take my chances."

The Gummp stopped smirking and regarded him intently, no longer with smarmy amusement, but perhaps, respect? He was difficult to read. "Very well, then, mortal."

Without a word The Gummp disappeared into thin air.

Liam rubbed his eyes to be sure. Gone. He was all alone, now, before the fortress. He started toward the stairs, dread following heavy on him, seeming to pull down his shoulders. The predictions weighed on him. Kosithi never did lie — that much he'd heard from childhood. But still ... that seemed to allow for all sorts of ambiguity, nonetheless. In any case, if the creature's predictions were true, that meant he now walked into certain death. No escape. He scowled, trudging stubbornly forward. "Indeed, Gummp. The die is cast," he murmured.

Chapter 21

Ynwin leaned against the stone cell wall. Something had shifted ... she could feel it in her aching bones. The Calling Brand burned. She bowed her head, breathing weak, contemplating the meaning of it. Her prayers to the Fairy Queen had sustained her this long, but how much longer? It felt as it had in the past, when the moon itself darkened to the color of ash.

Soon Kaledon would be devoured.

And my son along with it.

Ynwin wept.

The lamp light died. She didn't light it again, preferring to waste away in the shadows. *My beloved Fairy Queen ... Alyia Anundiami Anwei-i ... Ocean Mother ... I pray to You one last time. I asked You to look after my son. To help me live long enough to see him once more. I have asked nothing else. Was all that suffering for naught? My family slaughtered, my kingdom raped, my last son consumed in a wave of baleful beasts and hateful creatures from the Unseelie King, Your husband?*

Why? She pounded the stone with her manacled fist and unleashed a silent scream.

All for nothing! All that sorrow ... meaningless!

She caught her breath.

Meaningless.

She barely noticed the thumping of footsteps climbing the secret stairs. She remained unmoved, uncaring.

The room flooded with yellow candlelight from the stairway. It was not Arrius. Instead a man in knightly mail and rich brigandine walked in, tabard and cloak in royal blue, chevron shield of ash wood and canvas upon his back, extraordinary arming sword at his hip, a bascinet under his arm. His chiseled, fine-arched features, clean shaven, framed blue eyes that studied her thoughtfully. Light struck his blond hair from behind. "And so there you are," he said, letting the words soak into the darkness. "I am Sir Damien, knight–"

"I know who you are," said Ynwin. "At least I know enough. You hail from Midworld don't ye, lad?" He nodded, eyebrow raised, allowing her to continue. "Arrius told me about you. He said you were his loyal–"

Damien plopped Arrius's severed head on the table. She blinked at that twisted visage; those gnarled features having tormented her for so long. Satisfaction from his death cooled her anger. She studied the bloody, dead face, letting his death sink into her depths. Small comfort came. The fact that Kaledon was dying and her son was in the middle of it quickly snuffed any pleasure at it. Vengeance rang hollow. Hope within her struggled for breath. She scowled, noticing the stolen signet ring on his hand. "So what do you want from me, Sir Damien of Midworld? I gather you've taken Arrius's position as usurper king."

"Grant me the Calling Brand, Ynwin."

He was obviously no fool. She narrowed her eyes upon him. "Why would I do that?"

He tilted his head slightly. "Because if you don't, your son is going to die under the Unseelie curse. Pass the Brand to me and I'll end it, and then leave this miserable hell of a world forever."

She shook her head, leaning against the stone. "You dinnae fool me. You're after the Dream Stone — you want to close the gates for all time." She raised a weary finger. "Against the Fairy Queen's will."

He put his fist on the table and leaned toward her. "I'll kill you if you don't."

She chuckled weakly. "You disgust me, lad. You and your 'Magnolent' friends … locking away the Dream Stones. Denying the sharing of knowledge and experience between worlds. Go pound sand, ye gowkish naff! My son comes for me. Harm me and he'll destroy you, sure as the Gummp's predictions. So go ahead and kill me. My husband and children have waited long for me in Evensade. Grant me peace. Do it! Either way, my son will find you and slaughter you like the pig you are."

His eyes narrowed, lips curling in a snarl. He pounded the table. "Erentyr is poison! We have made a society in Midworld free of the toxic horror of this shit-hole. I hate the smell of it. Nothing but war and death and impossible fairy creatures. Magic fueled by gibberish. Incomprehensible mysticism, madmen wielding the power of life and death at their whim. This world of suffering is not worthy to share with mine."

"Aye," she said half smiling, back and hips roaring in pain, "and what have *you* done to relieve that suffering, I wonder?"

He straightened, eyes cool. "I am merely protecting my own, as any good father would. Protecting Midworld from the *infection* of Erentyr. Building a world of mercy and compassion. All we have gotten from this place over the ages is war, chaos, and death. Do you deny it?"

She shook her head slowly. "Nay. But you will find, Sir Damien, that *without* those things, Midworld will become even more terrifying than you can imagine. Lock it away and try to forget it if you must. You'll fail. We can only ever face the darkness, lad, and do our best. We can *never* escape it."

He scoffed, placing his helmet on the table and crossing his arms over the brass-riveted brigandine coat, glowering. Yet he did not retort immediately. He seemed to ponder her words, puzzled disgust on his face. He shook his head. "Everyone in this world is insane. Gladly accepting their daily dosage of agony. Fine. Let Kaledon die, then. I can simply abandon this accursed land for the Southern kingdoms. The Enclave of Wizard Kings would gladly accept my sword in their service."

"Aye," she said, suppressing a smile. She was getting to him. "But without the Stone, you will nae return to your precious Midworld, will ye? Kaledon might die, but my son will still earn the Calling Brand from the Druid order in due time. You have nothing to hold over me, Sir Damien."

The knight regarded her intently for a long while. He lit the lamp. "The prideful words of a desperate mother. Liam is extremely vulnerable. His scars run far deeper than any upon the surface. I've seen it myself. The horrors he's witnessed here have left him weak. But that's all right. Because I've figured out your secret, Ynwin."

She snorted, ribs twinging with pain, turning away. "Oh aye, and what is that?"

"He can sense your presence with the Stone, can't he?"

She locked eyes with him. What was his game? Then she worked it out. "What of it?"

He smiled darkly. "I thought as much."

She curled her lip in derision. "Use me as bait, then. You just better be ready when he finds you, lad. You have no idea the strength he has within him."

The mirth left his face. "His strength was destroyed years ago, before he ever left Erentyr. That kind of trauma is impossible to recover from." He sighed. "I do not envy what I must do, Ynwin," he said, glancing at the severed head. "But you leave me no choice. Your son is hopelessly outmatched, and I will be forced to end his life, take the Stone and leave you to your fate."

The sheer weight of that possibility nearly crushed her soul, choking her breath and draining strength from her weakened frame. She mustered every ounce of will to keep from weeping in front of him. Her expression remained like stone, though a tear escaped the side of one eye as she scowled at him. "And if you succeed, may you carry your *mercy* and *compassion* with you all the way to your precious Midworld."

She turned away, closing her eyes.

Damien clicked his tongue and left without another word, taking Arrius's head with him.

The door closed, leaving Ynwin with even darker thoughts than she had before.

***

Mia, Sea Breeze on her shoulder, followed Maple along the bumpy dirt path to where the road split at the pass, leaving the Dark Valley of Uluth behind as the light dimmed. She jogged, breathing quickening, nearly trembling with panic, grief contorting her face. Nevertheless, she pressed on. Glancing back, a chill crept into her body, for the light of the moon had suddenly disappeared. Precious little starlight peeked through the ceiling of clouds, leaving the land horribly dark. Mia squinted. "What happened to the moon? Is that normal?"

"Oh that's a tiddly-do," said Maple, whistling in awe, "No, not normal at all! Could be a trick of the clouds?"

"I don't think so," said Sea Breeze, anxiety in her voice. "If I didn't know better, I'd say we were all sipping the lemonade, but there it is!"

"So that isn't supposed to happen — ok," said Mia, insides alight with dread, still reeling from her recent parting with Liam. She felt sick. She forced herself to keep going, and beneath her fears skulked the lurking energy of the deepest spells, hiding in the shadows of her emotions, clenching her stomach muscles, tightening her chest with worry. She rubbed her eyelids wearily. "What the hell are we supposed to do now?"

"We've got to crack on," said Maple. "Can ye still cast any spells?"

She stopped and let out a long breath. "I've cast a lot since I first got here," she said, glancing at the raven on her shoulder. "Now I understand what you meant, Sea Breeze. Every time I weave one, I feel more *depleted* somehow. Like lamp oil burning away. That crystal forest helped a little, but I'm reaching the waning ... I don't know how much more use I'll be if I don't conserve my soulfire." A pang of regret touched her. Branwen had taught her how to use that word, "soulfire."

Maple reached up and patted her hand. "Now, don't sell yourself, short, young one," she said. "I believe in you."

She, however, didn't. She struggled to stay focused. Anger, fear, and restless energy waged war inside her. Worse, the spells roamed the shadows of her awareness, threatening chaos, loss of self, now worse than ever. She could feel them tugging at her very consciousness, wanting to erupt.

A red glow rose from deep in the valley, spreading quickly in a circle and lighting the clouds from below. Stiffness gripped her muscles. Her eyes grew wide and her breath shallow. "Is that a ... forest fire?"

Sea Breeze flitted to a rocky perch on the steep hillside. "So it is, love, or I've gone pure starkers for sure. That's in the depths of the Dark Valley, too ... where Liam is."

She huffed in frustration, chewing her bottom lip. She could not afford to speculate about him now. She owed it to him to stay focused on surviving. She made him a promise, after all. "Is it heading toward us?"

"Looks to be," said the raven. "If a strong northerly wind comes, it'll be ill on us, and quick, I fear."

Mia hissed, suddenly furious that Liam was beyond her help. "Damn, damn, damn," she whispered, rubbing her temples.

"Oy," said Maple, her voice ominously low, "I th-think we've got even bigger problems," Mia opened her eyes to Maple pointing to the east. Just past the intersection, dim red lit the road that descended to a clearing of wet grass, bounded by the silhouettes of a tree line and backed by a spur of rocky hills. Cracking wood and rustling noises came from the darkness, bringing shivers to Mia's skin. Fire behind ... something lurking ahead.

She wavered, then regained herself. She scowled and suddenly plunged off the road onto the wet grass, fists clenched. Maple lagged, fumbling to string her bow, and Sea Breeze flew to a bush-covered boulder. Mia's fingers flitted, itching to unleash more spellweaves, though she did not know what.

Several pairs of eyes glinted from the woods, followed by an unnaturally deep, bone-rattling growl. Slowly giant Teralian Timberwolves emerged into the orange-red glow, white-tufted wolf leading. Mia went completely cold with horror. Her limbs refused to move and she began to tremble, eyes glued to the massive approaching beasts. Sweat trailed down her forehead, plastering long twirls of black hair to her face. Then a powerful whooshing sound came from behind them. Sea Breeze darted away with a squawk, replaced by a massive, winged form. The mighty gyrfalcon, talons digging into earth and stone, perched and loomed over them, head lowering as if waiting to swoop.

The wolves approached from ahead, licking their lips. Mia struggled to keep from panicking, but her head bowed, hair covering her face, eyes squeezed shut involuntarily, teeth gnashing, fists clamped down. Flashes of memories erupted. Curled up in a ball at the Childcare Plex, abandonment shooting through her child's heart, right before she met Liam. But he was gone now. Maybe even dead. A tear coursed into her gritting teeth.

Maple backed against her leg.

Sea Breeze whispered into her ear. "Steady, flower. Steady."

The growling rose, and the falcon screeched, preparing to swoop.

Little flower ... that's what my grandmother called me in her letters.

Something shifted inside her. Something immensely powerful. Deep. Unknown. All her life she had been a nothing. Nobody. All her creative energy wasted on nonsense. All her studying, all her obsessive art — when artificial art outdid her technically in every way.

Her fear melted away, replaced with towering rage. Rage at the family that abandoned her. The world which ignored her. At Liam for likely dying on her. Pure, unalloyed power crackled through her body, and the two deepest spells that lurked like drooling predators in the forgotten shadows of her mind emerged into her awareness. Mind-runes swirled and formed, settling on intricate designs. A hundred voices organized into one — her own inner voice. Loud, strong, unyielding. Uncompromising. She opened her eyes.

"Put your bow away, Maple," she said calmly, her outer voice not matching her inner. "Sea Breeze, stay with her."

Maple swallowed. "Y-yes, ma'am," she said, and Mia could see herself reflected in Maple's huge gnomish eyes. The whites of Mia's eyes glowed brilliantly. She took out her pouch of black paint and covered the top of her face, trailing down from each eye and her nose with a snakelike line. The giant wolves slunk closer, teeth bared, growls rising. They towered over her, larger than warhorses, hairs bristling upon their shoulder blades knotted with massive muscle, eyes narrowing on her small form. Behind, the falcon flapped its wings in the rising orange glow, wind blowing, beak clacking.

She raised her black-tipped, gesturing fingers wide before her, flipping her hair behind her, chin high, eyes challenging. "*Awaiakanni! ... Ooolandokana!*" she shouted, daring the world to silence her. Within the chaos roared, flowing all through her. She welcomed it. *Encouraged* it. This would change her forever and destroy who she once was before. And not a moment too soon.

The timid mouse lay murdered.

Wind roared around them. The wolves shifted, eyes darting about, as if not expecting such an outburst from this small upstart. She sensed within them trepidation, where once they thought her a mere midnight snack, barely more concerning than a mosquito. Now she could feel — they saw within her something strange and unknown.

Then the wind died down, and the beasts remained, returning their attention to her, renewing their threatening stance, baring teeth once again.

"D-did the incantation not work?" asked Maple, hiding behind Mia.

"Aye, doesn't look like they're fleeing, love," said Sea Breeze, now on the gnome's shoulder.

Mia lowered her hands slowly to her side. "Making them flee isn't the goal." The falcon spread its wings wide and the wolves encircled them.

The gigantic bird swooped, talons bared, covering them in shadows.

Chapter 22

Liam swallowed. The Unseelie King's castle loomed like a scowling, gargantuan beast. The forest burned higher. He gripped the Dream Stone, flames crackling, heat coming in waves. Sweat trickled along the side of his mail coif and into the throat standard, helmet and gauntlets warming. He pocketed the Stone, then a horrid, two-tone wail arose from the burning woods. Dozens came, riding black, smoking steeds with fiery eyes galloping toward him; the riders wearing billowing white cloaks and hoods with horse skulls, from which great antlers gnarled.

Unseelie riders.

He broke into a run, the strange riders nearing, skeletal hands waving glinting scythes.

He reached the narrow stairway and charged up, but under the shadow of the castle, the riders stopped. Or were they forcing him into the castle? He stood tense, waiting for an attack. It seemed they wanted only to prevent him from turning back.

It appeared he was committed. He strode up and up, often making sure the riders still held their position, but each step was harder than the last, as uneasiness crept into his bones. He pushed through and reached the landing. Orange and yellow fell upon a curtain wall that spread into a great circle before a massive gatehouse. He neared it, portcullis rusted away, landing decorated in a triple-spiral stone mosaic. Same as the image within the eye of the Dream Stone. Strange.

Swarms of bats flew across the grey and green land below, and clouds of smoke hid the bottom of the castle mountain, blowing in from the surrounding forest blaze. The landing went into the castle, but two walking paths also hugged the outside, along the cliff's edge around the mountain. Within the castle, layer upon layer of walkways, towers, and balconies — all riddled with ivy — stretched into the charcoal sky. An idea came. The Gummp said Liam would enter the castle. But he could go along the side path, defying the prediction. He raised an eyebrow and shifted the strap on his baldric. What would that do, he wondered. *Let's find out.*

He half-smiled and stepped along the side path.

But once he did, the stone gave way and he dropped into a tunnel.

Thunderous, pummeling darkness followed. He guarded his head with his arms and tried to slow his descent with his feet. The wolf pelt, armor, helmet and gauntlets buffered him. Finally, he hit the ground, muscles twisting like wounded snakes. As if on cue, a candle lit on a sconce in the deep chamber. Others followed. Aching, he sat up with effort to find brown flagstones in a vine-covered passage. Damp air wafted on his scraped face.

He sighed and grumbled to his feet. "Very clever, Gummp. You said I would 'enter' the ruins, but you didn't say how." He nodded to himself. "And if I hadn't tried to avoid my fate, I wouldn't have met it. Brilliant." But the accuracy and the fact that it seemed to *account* for him knowing the prediction and trying to avoid it disturbed him.

He picked up his sword, irritated, and drew the blade. The shimmering pattern-weld glinted in the candlelight. He limped down the corridor. The tunnel pierced the earth for a while, and his gait evened as the pain dulled. *An unexpected enemy is next, I suppose.* The candles dimmed behind him. He strode between two dark places that failed to penetrate the gloom above.

Eventually, the passage opened and more candles lit a chamber with two doors atop a small landing. Beautifully carved from ancient wood, the doors stood side by side, decorated with one continuous scene. From a flower petal, embellished with knot-designs and spirals, a girl emerged, floating in a fetal position above the bloom under a starry night. The Fairy

Queen, Vinraith's wife and enemy, decorated his very home. Interesting.

The texture and intricacy amazed him, knotworks folding in on themselves like fluid fractals. Then he remembered the next prediction and backed up to brandish Xanibor. One of these doors had an unexpected enemy in it. Which one was it? How was he supposed to figure that out? Trial and error?

He breathed deep and stroked his beard, thinking.

Wait a second…

If I open the first door and there's nothing in there, then the enemy must be behind the second door. But then, he would be expected! So that means he can't be behind that door, and I should expect the enemy to be behind the first door. But then that means it can't be there either because I expect it! Tomfoolery. He scoffed. *It's a contradiction. There can't be an enemy.*

He chuckled uneasily. Surely this prediction was simply impossible.

Confident, Liam opened the door on the left, from which sprung a knight in a coat of plates over mail, with pale, crazed eyes wide within a houndskull helmet. He hissed and attacked Liam with a wicked poleaxe. Liam responded with Xanibor. The knight unleashed a flurry of blows, backing him into the wall of roots behind him and slashing his arm — the mail and gambeson prevented a severing, but not a gash. The knight rasped incoherently, heavy mail flashing in the candlelight, pressing the attack. Reeling, Liam tripped over a root and slammed to the ground. The knight swung down at his chest.

A thousand moments condensed into an instant — he recalled Rendan's squire-training — he would have judged him harshly for losing his bearings so easily. But then, where was Rendan? Dead! That thought grew like an infection — so many dead brothers. Mother missing. Father gone. Probably Mia too. Utterly alone. Memories twisted into anger, becoming an awakened dragon.

He bared his teeth like a wolf and grunted. The world became encircled by fire in his sight, and a spirit of battle-fury erupted like rays of a dark sun. He evaded the poleaxe, sparks flying, and leapt to his feet. He swatted the weapon, then heaved a great arc, slamming the man down, plates splitting, knocking his enemy onto his back.

Not satisfied, he shouted and buried Xanibor right above the coat, through the mail and into the knight's neck, causing a tremor to shake through the fortress as he buried the blade a foot into the stone, instinctively summoning the full power of Xanibor. Pouring his anger, grief, and sorrow into the stroke, he shoved until he could no longer push. Vines, roots, thorned branches, and grasping leaves poured from the ground all around him, expanding into the entire room and down the corridors over a hundred feet from him. Sweat dripped from his face as the sword resonated in his gauntleted hands, pain tearing through him, as if the blade amplified his very life force and poured it into the surrounding growth in a single act of malice. For a split-second, his mind saw his apartment, smashing the wooden figurine he had made as a boy with Mia's help, only now he was still clad in heavy mailcoat and wolf pelt, but then it vanished and he was back in the inner chamber. The rumbling stopped, and he coughed and wheezed.

Regaining his composure, and his wind, he stood up and Xanibor stilled, flickering light hitting its pattern-weld sheen. He snarled. *An unexpected enemy. Fooled me again and predicted perfectly.* His heart sank.

I'm going to die.

He yanked the blade, then gasped, for the sword was cracked. Xanibor crumbled before his very eyes, rune-carved hilt remaining. He gasped, frozen in horror.

"No!" he cried out, dropping to his knees, gaping at the shattered sword. "My father's blade ... ruined!" His throat tightened and he released a moan of agony. "Father," he cried, gazing at the darkness above, unable to speak further. He closed his eyes, holding the hilt next to his helmet. "Forgive me," he said finally, voice tight.

Then he scowled at the enemy, sprawled and covered in choking vines and thorned roots. "You! How is this possible? What are you?" In a fit of anger, he tossed the hilt and removed the helmet.

To discover himself, gaping, pale, eyes still as stone.

But not as an adult. He stared at himself, as a child. He had slaughtered himself as a boy.

He blinked, utterly dumbfounded. What trickery is this? What spell? He scanned the dead boy. He was small, 9 years old, maybe, armor oversized. His head swam.

What is happening?

Beyond the door, a tunnel grown with moss and mushrooms stretched into darkness. Marching feet emerged from the shadows. More doors opened, bringing knights and squires in full battle harness, shields and maces, arming swords, hammers, and axes brandished.

Mind churning in confusion, he stood, weaponless. Fists clenched, heart pounding, he prepared for a fight, but his feet were slowed by the overgrowth. Enemies surrounded him.

Shock struck him. Their tabards revealed clan colors of the Tuaths of Kaledon, but their gear was crusted over with swirling molds, their mail and coats of plates rusted, rotted, and weatherbeaten. Anger turned to despair. The leading knight faced him, raising his visor.

Bran.

Liam's blood became ice. The old knight's eyes glazed, vision piercing right through him without recognition.

"Bring him to the master," said Bran, pointing, voice grave, mechanical.

Conal closed in with a dozen others he did not recognize. Some of the clan colors were faded as if by centuries — in heraldry he did not recognize, nor even heard of. Like Bran, Conal's eyes glazed eerily, swirls of moss on his face. "The Unseelie King demands!"

Liam lowered his fists. A fight to the bitter end would have been acceptable — but not against his fellow knights, spellbound or not. "I will not resist."

Gauntleted hands forced him to his knees. Conal removed Liam's helmet and covered his head with a black cloth. They bound his hands behind him roughly. He gritted his teeth, the inevitability of his fate sharpening into greater clarity. The Gummp's prediction, again, was perfect. *You will defeat the enemy but still lose. You will then get your wish — to be brought before Vinraith himself.*

But he will not grant you your plea.

Chapter 23

The cloth flew off Liam's head to reveal a great circular courtyard under a red-tinged sky. Rain drizzled onto vines that crawled sparsely across ancient flagstones. Knights stood in coats of heavy mail with thick, hooded tabards, emblazoned with clan colors, mud stained and adorned with whorls of fungal growth. Beneath the hoods each knight wore a coif of mail with an arming cap beneath and stared with bloodshot eyes at Liam's kneeling form.

A stone dais climbed to a mighty throne, upon which sat the tall, menacing and muscular Vinraith, covered in white fur and clothed in a resplendent black coat of plates with shining brass rivets and gilded embroidery.

Vinraith Flame-eye, husband of the Fairy Queen, King of the Unseelie, gripped an exquisitely crafted spear, his other arm upon the stone rest. "Greetings," said Vinraith in a deep voice that seemed to echo within his head as well as from the surrounding stone courtyard. It seemed here his power waxed even greater. Encircling them, standing stones climbed into the misty gloom, as crackling light backlit the silhouetted and gnarled trees beyond. Directly before Liam sat a blood-stained chopping block surrounded by four tall torches. "I warned you never to trespass in my domain again, Liam. You did not listen."

"My lord," said Liam, summoning every ounce of courage he could muster, "I come before you to–" A raised hand from Vinraith silenced him.

"You gave ear to the Gummp's predictions," said the Unseelie King. "There is nothing else to speak on, for, as you know, you are to be executed for your failures."

He let out a slow breath but did not avert his eyes. "My failures? Your ancient forest burns!"

Vinraith smiles. "The purging fire brings sorrow, true, but also renewal. You were tasked as carrier of the precious Dream Stone. To return it to your mother. It is you and your people who allowed the Nurnians to come in and overtake your land by force, displaying your weakness." The spellbound Kaledonian knights scowled, eyes unblinking, accusing. "And yet now you enter my sacred wood and disturb the natural cycles of my court. Are you a fool? All Kaledonians of even modest wisdom know *never* to enter my dominion."

"But my lord, the Unseelie bogs–"

"That sin is upon *your* nation and people. You allowed the Dream Stone to languish in the world beyond and have practically begged me to consume and destroy your native land. Have you any last words before your certain death?"

Guilt and shame bore down on him like leaden tears, twisting him from within, infecting him with self-loathing. Vinraith was right. Conal scowled at him. *Where had I been all this time? All those years I wasted in Midworld, meanwhile my home was dying and my countrymen enslaved and murdered.*

He wanted to vomit; instead he prepared himself for death. He welcomed it, for anything — even death — was better than this life of shame. Shame he'd fended off for as long as he possibly could.

He closed his eyes and looked deep within the void growing in his soul.

Empty of honor. Devoid of meaning. That agony stabbed deeper and more cruelly than any mere physical or emotional pain. To suffer in service to something greater could be borne. To serve meaninglessness alone could not be.

But that was just it.

Was it not curious that suffering and even death could be so much *preferable* to shame and emptiness? Were not pain and suffering the greatest enemy?

He opened his eyes.

No. They were not.

"I do have last words, your greatness."

Vinraith regarded him with bemusement and gestured for him to continue. The knights stood with kettle helmets and hand weapons at the ready. Conal stepped closer to his left, heavy boots against stone, while Bran brought forth Vinraith's axe, blade glinting in the torchlight. "It's true I didn't accomplish my mission. But that doesn't mean I failed. I never backed down one inch from my task."

The Gummp appeared next to Vinraith and settled upon a stone slab by the dais, interlocking fingers upon a plump belly.

"What does that matter," asked Vinraith, "if you still lose in the end?"

He winced to hear his own words haunt him. But he kept on. "The courage to press forward is ALL that matters, dread one. All my life I've been running and fretting over vain hopes for good outcomes. But the outcome is *nothing*, lord. It's in the hands of gods such as you. If I've learned anything from your predictions," he nodded to the Gummp, "it's that my ability to foresee the outcome is as frail as the rain. It's beyond my reach. But the fight itself? That's in *my* hands." He smiled grimly, raising his head proudly. "And I *do* like a good fight. And if I fight to my utmost, I refuse to be considered a failure."

Vinraith raised an eyebrow, burning blue eye bright within the gilded black hood. "Well spoken, mortal knight, but it changes not our judgment." His wolfish muzzle snarled into a toothy smile. "Prepare to accept your fate. Place your head on the block."

Liam bowed his head, loathing his impending death. To never see Mia again. To never have a chance to save his mother. These cut him deeply. And yet, there came a strange peace. No longer did the traumas of the past roar so loudly within him. Fear and death stepped back, revealing a deeper knowledge.

"I give you this last chance to plea for mercy," said the Unseelie King.

Liam raised his eyes to him. *Should I? Might he be merciful, if I beg for it?* But he shook his head. "I will not, sire. Your judgment is *your* concern, not mine. I will act with honor, even if the world will not. I have no right or ambition to tell gods what to do, just or not. But I do know what *I* will do." He placed his head on the block. "So carry out your judgment and be done with it. The sin of injustice will be upon your head and not mine."

Vinraith growled menacingly, his thunderous voice echoing across the ancient stones. "So be it, Liam Trendari Panregon." Liam closed his eyes. Vinraith's voice enveloped him. "With this final stroke of the axe, so will come the final doom of your homeland. Heed this moment well."

Liam relaxed, hands still bound behind his back, wet and scarred wood against his cheek. Bran walked toward him, axe brandished. Liam accepted death, and waited for the stroke to fall, as it inevitably would. He furrowed his brow. Heed this moment well ... what did that mean?

***

Ka-chunk went the blade. Liam froze.

***

Strangely, Liam's consciousness remained.

***

He opened his eyes.

Just above his head, the axe stuck from the wood. The torchlight extinguished, he sat up, hand-bonds gone. Steaming trees and scorched wood littered the floor of aspen leaves, and blackened, but intact, pine cones. Already new growth sprouted amid the embers. He stood. The courtyard was gone. Where Vinraith and the dais stood rose a hill where Xanibor glinted — fully intact — planted in the earth with baldric on the ground beside it. The Gummp and others had been replaced with foggy dark forest where live oaks and mountain ash stood blackened but otherwise unharmed by the extinguished fire. Moonlight crept through the breaking clouds, illuminating in beams through the misty forest air.

Liam smiled. The Gummp's final prediction — *The headman's axe shall fall, with your head upon the chopping block.* That turned out to be true, too. *Tricky.* He retrieved Xanibor and marveled at it. It seemed the god-forged blade had repaired itself. *Vinraith was testing me? Does this mean I passed?*

Leaves and wood shuffled in the darkness outside the moon's glow. He brandished Xanibor, body surging in alert, heart pounding as he whirled on the small hill, encroachers coming from all sides. "Who goes there? Show yourself!"

Bran entered the light first, eyes squinting in confusion, a squire in gambeson behind him. Then came Conal, equally bewildered, along with dozens of other knights and squires, tabards and banners bearing heraldry from clans long gone. Squires bore satchels of gear behind their masters, heads swiveling about, trying to make sense of their surroundings. Porters, archers, and others joined them.

"Liam?" asked Bran, approaching. "Is that you?"

He poised to fight. But Bran's eyes were no longer bloodshot. No longer did his harness bear twirling tendrils of fungus. Recognition settled on his gnarled features. Liam smiled broadly. "Bran!" He sheathed Xanibor and shouldered the baldric. Bran joined him on the hill, and the moonlight spread, alighting the crystal forest that surrounded the aspen grove. The air sparkled.

The knights and squires pulled off their hoods and removed helmets. Men and women knights of many ages and heraldries marveled at the crystal woodlands. "Are we dead?" asked one. "Is this Evensade?" asked another. Bran embraced him like a long-lost father. "You did it, son. You broke the enchantment on us."

"So it would seem," said Liam. "And far more than I could have hoped for. Surely now you believe me. Killing Arrius will not break the Unseelie curse upon Kaledon." The others gathered on the hill, Conal patting Liam on the back like a brother, grateful to see him alive. "*So comes the final doom of Kaledon,* said Vinraith before he freed us. I think that means we must hurry to get the Stone to my mother. It's the only way we can reclaim our home, once and for all. Even if we can't defeat the Nurnians, we owe it to our ancestors to try."

Conal nodded, new respect in his eyes.

Bran smiled. "Aye, lad. I believe you now. I should nae have doubted ye. We'll go with vengeance in our hearts."

"Oh hell yes," said Liam, renewed fury flushing his veins. "Vengeance for my family." He clapped Bran on the shoulder.

The old knight snarled. "And for Branwen."

Conal's eyes narrowed, nodding curtly. "And for Ian. And all the others, slain or taken. It would seem you bested the Unseelie King himself in his own home."

"Oh, no," said Liam, finger raised. "No, he saw fit to let me go. That's it. He took mercy on us."

"Aye, because of you! 'Tis an act unparalleled in centuries, brother," said Conal.

A cheer rose up, spreading across the crowd. Many raised weapons or fists to him in respect. It was a good feeling.

Then suddenly a great thumping came from the east. Weapons drew forth, squires handed shields and war-gear to their masters, and all turned to face the new threat. The sound grew louder, and shudders crept up through Liam's thick traveling boots, rattling the laces.

Finally a 20-foot figure, nearly as wide as tall, came into view, torn great sack in one hand, tree trunk slung over the shoulder in the other.

Lungor.

The giant eyed them with suspicion, scars upon his rough skin. His gaze settled on Liam. "Friend," he said. Liam smiled at the giant.

"Good to see you, big guy."

Lungor pulled a scraggly smile. "Me fight too."

***

As dawn broke upon the brooding highlands of Kaledon, Liam sat by one of the fires in the copse of ragged trees before the rugged slope to Caer Lannican, Xanibor's bare blade shining in the cool light. Sparkling patterns along the living kosite, perfectly crafted, rooted him to the spot, hinting at the ages it must have taken to make the weapon. Each perfect fractal pattern perfection within deeper perfection. Forged, Branwen had told him, by a Remembering One named Tul-Bre in the unthinkably ancient First Stone of Time — the Forgotten Ages before mortalkinds even existed. Older than the universe of Midworld. His head spun just thinking about it. How could he even *imagine* anything that old? Fathoming such a mind? *No Midworld machinery could create something like this, no matter how advanced. It lives.* He held it aloft. *Forged by the toil of a god ...* he shivered. The realization struck him to the marrow, like standing on a lake of ice, when a leviathan thumps against the surface from below. *Imagine what power it could summon in their hands?*

He rubbed his shoulder, feeling a cold wind. *The Childcare Plex taught me gods were ideas. Vague abstractions. Not here. In Erentyr, gods are tangible. Heavy. Their blood pumps. Their infinite thoughts echo. Like this blade.*

He sheathed and slung it, shrugging off the vertigo such thoughts brought. *And yet, it came to my father, and then to me.* He cracked a wistful smile. *I miss you, Father.* Cormac's smiling face brought him back to the here and now.

The night had been long, trekking back to the wagons to plunder the supplies left by the Nurnians, to set up camp along the northern reaches of the Uluth Valley, in a dangerous border wood not yet outside the Fairywild. The road to the castle wound through bog-soaked, blackthorn-strangled pastureland up to their goal: Caer Lannican fortress. The Unseelie had pushed even further into Kaledon.

Tendrils of smoke wound from the breakfast campfires, tended by knight and squire alike, with warriors emerging from their tents, still in mailcoats and leather doublets, polishing helmets and gauntlets, tending to shields and sharpening blades, gathering quarrels and arrows. A dull drizzle met the embers. The night had been laborious and full of planning. Many of the knights had been spellbound so long they wept, for everyone they had ever known had died in the centuries that passed from their original capture. Strangers in a kingdom out of their time, they nevertheless recovered because they *had* to, seeing the dire state of their native land. Of the scores of knights, archers, porters, squires, men-at-arms, laborers and yeomen rescued, only Lady Aoife, Knight of Rathchylde, had any knowledge of the Nurnian conquest, for her homeland had been overtaken by wisps a few years after Liam disappeared and became "the Lost Panregon." Tall and blond, a hard, wrathful expression on her face, she ordered her squire about and gathered her war kit.

Liam ground his jaw and tried to stretch the tension from his neck, as if to squeeze the worries from him. *How can we possibly succeed with this suicide mission? Even with these freed numbers, we face a fully garrisoned castle. Bran said it was still three to one against us.* But then he reflected upon the words he'd spoken to Vinraith, and the lessons he'd learned from the Gummp's predictions. He nodded to himself. *Doesn't matter. We give it our all — there is no other option. Kaledon will die otherwise.* He smiled to himself. *We few, we happy few, we band of brothers.*

Slowly they gathered by a large oak when Bran gestured for it. Liam stood, finishing the rabbit stew prepared by the squires last night, and the chunks of meat Lungor had brought in his dubious-looking sack. None complained about the extra provisions, no matter how sketchy they smelled. He adjusted the belt around his mailcoat and the circle of warriors parted for him. He stood by Bran. Lungor sat nearby, looking like a boulder apart from the furry pelt he wore.

Bran regarded Liam as he approached. "I know that look, lad," he said, gazing at him squarely. "She'll be fine. By your account, Mia is becoming quite the adept at conjury."

He forced a smile. "She was always a quick study." But his smile faded as attention left him, and he looked down and frowned, tugging his beard. Worries about her safety nagged at him like a rattling snake. He quelled the likely event that she was already dead as best he could.

Bran calmed the chatter with a raised hand. "Liam." He looked up. "You have led us to this moment. Your courage forged this gathering."

"Aye," said Aoife, in an odd-sounding dialect of Gaelsh, "you solved the riddle of Uluth."

Liam nodded solemnly but knitted his brow. "Now look. The Unseelie King is still hell-bent on destroying Kaledon. Our only chance is to save my mom — then *maybe* she can use the Fairy

Queen's Dream Stone to restore the balance and convince him to stop. We still have a huge fight ahead of us. All I did was even the odds a little." They seemed to understand, faces grave and stern.

"My sister once told me," said Bran, wistful and soft-voiced, "that the Fairy Gods are so mysterious because they're so unimaginably old. This delicate balance between Seelie and Unseelie is one of those mysteries, certainly." Liam nodded with many others. "Their minds, she said, stretch long, before the Bloodening or the peaceful time of Auril Dranne, and Vinraith even more so. For millennia he has captured those who wander into his domains, to release them eventually when his whim desires, sometimes after centuries, like some here." An odd silence fell upon the group. Only the tiny drizzle of rain and distant far-off howls made their way into the cool air. "But whatever the case, you have proven your knightly courage, Liam, and dare I say, leadership."

Liam did not shy from that, but neither did it please him. He took a solemn breath and addressed the others. "Thanks. But I have little experience leading. Nevertheless, I do know this — we will probably fail. But that's not important. What's important is that we won't get another chance, even if it's slim. This is our last. There'll be no ransom for those of knightly rank — to them, we are all stripped of title. As such, no one here would be thought a coward if they were to leave now in the face of such a mission." The knights and squires, young and old, men and women, straightened, lifting their faces, showing no sign of budging. Liam nodded. "That's what I thought."

Solemn nods in agreement.

"Fine then," said Bran. "Does ever a man know his position?"

"Well, my lord," said Conal, followed by many "aye" responses.

Liam nodded. "We all know the ancient legend of Burrham wood, that crept upon the fortress of Lord Mac Beatha during the time of King Brendan of Pirrh. Even in Midworld, this legend is known, though in an altered form. But the Nurnians don't know it. That'll give us an advantage — we will defeat them with a *story*." More nods and a heartfelt "aye" from many. "My father once told me that no battle plan survives first contact with the enemy. We might lose. But let me say this: if we lose, they'll know they fought men of unmatched courage, in this world or any other. Unmatched."

Conal smiled. "This one is truly his father's son."

"Aye," said Bran, "and his mother's."

Liam looked into each of their eyes. Stern, strong men and women looked back. He paced before them. "All right. My only last thought is this: No matter what we do, we must do it with honor, or not at all. That is what my father and mother both taught me, what I forgot in Midworld, and what I found again in the depths of Vinraith's domain. No matter the outcome, we will be remembered for this day. That is as sure as the suns. It must be the knightly way, or nothing."

"Hear! Hear!" some shouted. "For Kaledon!" said others. "For our kinfolk," many said.

Each fighter then spoke solemn oaths of valor and courage before the group.

"One thing remains," said Liam after a time, loud enough to get everyone's attention, backing away from the group to an open clearing among the trees. "Squires!" He drew Xanibor, and the youths, having the go-ahead from Bran, approached. "Great deeds are to come. If it's all right with Bran and the other clan leaders — whoever is left — I will need *knights* after today. Bran?"

He approached, and a stern look made the squires all kneel before Liam. "Why look to me?"

"Come now," said Liam. "If we win the day, and we can feast together in the great hall, if we rise victorious, we will need a new king. We all know it's you, man. There's no contest."

A quick survey of those present revealed no objection. "Well then, I'd say you'll need knights to help manage the long-lost land of the Shoreland Tuath. Have at it."

He smiled at the squires. Youthful faces looked up at him, mud upon their cheeks, some burdened with gear, some clearly as proud as he was on the day he was knighted not long ago. Liam looked up. "Lungor!"

The giant turned glassy eyes to him as fog drifted into the grassy thin clearings past the forest. "Me?"

"Yeah. You too, big guy."

Chapter 24

Dawn bloodied the boggy, overgrown slopes leading to Caer Lannican. To the west, midnight hues stubbornly painted the sky against the suns that peeked through the leaden carpet above. Kaledonians, hidden along the roads by dirt, branches and mud over their war gear, blended with the overgrown boglands. Brush tied to helmets, backs and shields with twine or fresh-cut vines disguised them as bushes and saplings. It had taken many agonizing hours, slowly creeping toward the fortress, not only avoiding detection, but also avoiding wandering into the *real* Unseelie blackthorn groves.

Liam and Bran peered at the castle from behind a line of boulders with Lungor crouched and stone-like, beside. A single raven called *err, err* barely audible. He peered through the dun mists and saw it fly from a rock into the shadows to the south. He thought he saw a blue tuft upon its head. *Was that…?*

"Aoife and the other scouts," said Bran, "say the Nurnians are alarmed at the 'new growth' but have so far dismissed it as Unseelie work."

"Good," said Liam. *Isn't it strange that we have had to become part of the curse itself in order to cure it?* But there was no time to ponder it. "Is there a way to tell if Arrius is home?"

"Aye," Bran pointed to the collection of banners waving atop the sprawling sea-cliff castle. "He's home. The Nurnian banner flies — it's the one with three falling stars."

He breathed out sharply and glanced at the Dream Stone. *Bring it back to me, or our homeland will die.* He pocketed it. "Excellent. All right, that means step two."

"Good luck, lad," said Bran, palm on his shoulder.

Liam gripped the man's hand, dipping his head in affirmation. "Okay, Lungor, we're up."

The giant opened his large sack and Liam climbed into it, bumping into a hard round object that had been stuffed into its own small bag. He looked inside and recoiled — Lucius's rotting head. *Lovely.* He glanced at Lungor and shook his head — *giants collect the weirdest things.* He climbed the rest of the way in. "Let's go."

Lungor hefted the sack and swung it behind, rattling Liam's head. He shook it off and unshouldered Xanibor. His muscles tensed with anticipation, and his blood pulsed. *Only one chance at this. Timing has to be perfect.*

Nurnian men-at-arms called for crossbowmen as Lungor lumbered over the palisades to the front gatehouse. He heard them prepare ballistae as the giant bellowed and pounded the portcullis. Liam gripped Xanibor as the sack dropped like a pile of potatoes — the painful impact against the stone made his heart race for action.

"Go on, you pea brain!" shouted one of the guards, "you'll never get in — can't you see this gate is designed to fend off giants? Bugger off!"

"You bad man!" Lungor pummeled the double-reinforced iron. Liam ignored the stench of the sack as he tied a mid-sized burlap bag of his own. "Go on, Lungor," he whispered, "you're doing great."

"Let me in! You bad man."

"Get lost, you pest!" called the captain at the battlements.

"Should we sound the horn, sir?" asked a man.

"It's just one dimwitted giant. Do you see an army arrayed anywhere? Just get some sand heating and bring a few more windlasses. Get that ballistae loaded and bring spears!"

Just a bit longer.

The captain called "loose at will!" and quarrels whizzed through the air.

Lungor grunted — several hit their mark. "Me come back tomorrow." Then he lumbered away, his footsteps shaking the drawbridge timbers.

"Go on, get after him," said the captain, "anon, cavalry! Spear the brute and see that he ne'er returns."

With a hefty rattle the portcullis rose. Liam lay still, measuring his breaths, ready to pounce. *Not yet.*

The gate raised enough to let a handful of horsemen charge forth. So far, so good. His mother's face entered his mind, a red swathe of blood with it.

"Look lively, there," said the captain, "did that idiotic lump leave his traveling sack?"

Hold...

"Wait," said the captain.

Liam shot out of the sack and darted hard through the gatehouse as the portcullises began to close and shouting arose. He shot Xanibor up and called upon the power of the sword. With a surge of energy through his forearm, thick vines, branches, and thorned plants erupted from the arches, blocking the gates from falling.

"Defenses!" came shouts from above, and crossbow bolts flew from murder holes above. Defenders distributed hatchets and hung over the side to chop at the new growth. Barbed quarrels hammered his mail, bruising but failing to pierce it. Quarrels clanged loudly against his kettle helmet.

"Bodkins," came a shout from above. The battle horn sounded, and more echoed. Liam jumped to his feet as a crossbowman shot a needle bodkin through a hole. It pierced his mailcoat and gambeson into his thigh, though the armor kept it from breaking his femur. He dropped to one knee with a snarl as heavy men-at-arms charged down the stairs with shields and hammers.

Then a roar came from behind — Kaledonians erupted by the hundred from the foggy ditches. Archers shot branch-hacking defenders, causing them to fall. More arrows slowed the footmen. Nurnians crouched behind leather-bound shields of ash. Kaledonian knights and men-at-arms charged the gatehouse with claymores, shields, spears, and maces. Liam rushed the footmen, slamming the top of his shield and thrusting the tip through his face, knocking him back into two more behind before bashing past them, through the narrow tunnel where more quarrels and needle bodkins rattled his helmet and stung his flanks. His father's mail held strong.

He limped across the great bridge spanning the outer and inner gatehouses, where the castle proper stood upon a thousand-foot sea stack. Salty air breezed past as he pushed across the dizzying drop, Xanibor brandished high. Defenders manned the second portcullis and heaved the unlocking mechanism. Others cranked windlasses. Liam led the charge, gripping double-hand to call upon the power of Xanibor once more. This was critical — if he did not stop the portcullis they would all be trapped on the bridge — sitting ducks for a hail of crossbow bolts.

Having called upon Xanibor's power already so recently, he knew this would be costly. Shooting pain winched both arms, pulling the raw life force from him and making him stumble. But his vengeance burst forth in heavy growth, halting the second portcullis. Two needle bodkins, launched from thousand-pound windlass crossbows, pierced his stomach with such force that his legs kicked out, sending him sailing off the bridge.

Roaring in pain, he hung with mere fingers, bolts zipping past, empty air plunging into sharp rocks and surf. Mail and gear weighing him, he gripped the ledge for dear life, hands screaming in pain, body swinging. He pulled, but with three bleeding arrow wounds, and heavy mail besides, he couldn't last. A strong grip came, locking around his elbow.

Conal.

The knight heaved him up, Bran helping. The two knights pulled Liam back onto the bridge as Kaledonians pushed through a hail of quarrels. He climbed to his knees, never so happy to see Conal's wincing face. Half a dozen quarrels pierced the knight. Blood flowed from his mailcoat.

"You'll need this," said Bran, handing him Xanibor. Blood dripped from a cut in his forehead.

Liam gripped Xanibor and patted Conal as he sunk to his side. "Thank you, brother."

Conal nodded weakly. "Go on, ye gobshite, finish them off!"

Liam charged by Bran with the other knights into the main gatehouse.

Pain shot and cut through his body but he forced through it, the mayhem triggering images of his brothers deaths. But this only fueled his rage, making him shove past even his allies into the melee under the gatehouse. Shields met spears, axes and maces crashed into mail and coats of plates. Swords thrust and hacked against helmets. Liam, full of wrath, wrenched ahead to injure many in great arcs of Xanibor, the kosite, ever-sharp blade able to split mail rings when hitting full-force. Many fell under his reddened blade.

"Fall back," came an order from behind the defenders. They retreated, shield wall up.

Bran put a hand on Liam's shoulder. "Easy lad! They're trying to pull us into a wedge so they can surround us. Stand your ground, Kaledonians!"

Standoff.

Nurnians dragged their injured companions from the panting Kaledonian invaders. The portcullis of the outer gatehouse crashed to the ground; the defenders finally having hacked through the branches. The Kaledonians were trapped and outnumbered.

The guard captain, geared in brigandine and furry cloak, stepped forward. He stood nearly at Liam's height, clean shaven and with brown hair. "Well aren't you a tricky lot?"

"Oh, we're full of shenanigans," said Liam. Bran's bloodied eyes darted between Liam and the captain, palm still on his shoulder.

"Well you've gotten in, clever enough, but now what? Eager for the nubbing-cheat, are we?"

Liam stood defiant. "Bring forth King Arrius. Let him face long-delayed justice."

He shook his head in disbelief. "The cheek of this one! How did you get past Lucius anyway?"

He tossed the sack he'd prepared at the captain's feet. "Ask him yourself." Their expressions brought him dark joy as the captain pulled Lucius's head from the sack. The Kaledonians laughed.

Liam advanced another step, beyond Bran's reach, among a scatter of dead bodies as misty winds tossed his hair and red-splattered wolf cloak behind him, his black and blue tabard wet with blood. He pulled needle bodkins from his shoulder and flank, tossing them aside. Pain pulsed through his body, and his blood dripped with his foes. Drelthun's old mark, burning fiercely in his scarred hand, nonetheless allowed him to endure far more punishment than most. Still his vision swam with aching arms, legs, chest.

Above them the main keep rose. His mother would be in that tower. He gripped the Dream Stone in his belt-sporran. Her life-force still weakly pulsing in his mind, he planted himself in the courtyard in full view of the crossbowmen. This would be his final stand. He snarled and grinned blood. "Where is the king?" he shouted. "Let him face the Last Knight of the Panregon Clan, and all my brave countrymen, to answer for his deeds under the morning suns!" Behind, a commotion arose on the southernmost tower. A handful of sharp-eyed crossbowmen peered south, but no one else noticed. "Is he a coward?" roared Liam. "Let this so-called king crawl out from his hiding hole!"

The Nurnian defenders chuckled at some unknown joke, then parted for a younger man, not the king, bald and clean shaven, smirking. He approached calmly, cloak billowing behind, and upon his skin were strange tattoos. His eyes reflected orange in the rising daylight, and he approached bare chested, even on the cold autumn day. He bore a long bronze staff, carved with spiraling engravings. The mist of the high cliffs melted as he stood before the knight. Liam scoffed. *A sorcerer.*

"Not the king," said the wizard, "but his Royal Conjury Master. Lamon of Contavius, apprentice to Ozremorn, at your service. I strongly advise you to lay down your arms, lest you all die upon this courtyard. You are gravely outmatched and outnumbered. Surrender and you'll receive mercy."

Bran and the other knights, wounded and weary, stood proudly defiant. Bran raised an eyebrow at him, as if to ask what he was playing at. Though barely able to stand, Liam's rage would not quench. He planted Xanibor before him and stubbornly glared at this upstart. "I have a better idea. Why don't you go fuck yourself."

Lamon was not amused, clicking his tongue. He put his hands into a curious position, then shouted, *"Ia-marka-rogh!"*

Liam burst into flames and he stumbled backward. He growled, instinctively wrapping the wolf pelt around himself. The fire extinguished, only blackening his skin with smoke. Scorched, he marched back to where he previously stood, planted Xanibor in the ground before him, and rested his hands upon the hilt. He cracked a half smile. "What else you got?"

"Extraordinary," said Lamon, motioning for the gathering footmen to stay back, his glance keeping the crossbowmen still. They looked on with smirking curiosity, windlasses cranked and loaded with needle bodkins. The defenders kept shields and weapons up, but watched with amusement. Lamon sneered. "The Lost Panregon, is it? That's not even original. You're the fourth such Kaledonian riff-raff to claim that in the last few years. But I see you've a god-forged blade — and you're certainly a resourceful lot, mud-soaked and stinking. But you've walked into the lion's den — can't say the last son of the great chieftain Ynwin would have done something so stupid. And what's that accent you've acquired? Doesn't sound Kaledonian."

"I've been on holiday."

"I'm sure." With a word, his staff crackled with blue energy, and he charged, stave whirling.

Xanibor crashed into the enchanted staff. They exchanged blows, Lamon's movements uncannily swift — no doubt he had enhanced himself with a spell. *Tricky.* Lamon barely fended off the savage strokes, then retaliated with an onslaught of his own. But just as the wizard began to gain the advantage, his eyes glazed over with white. He hissed in an unknown language, temporarily blinded, markings on his chest glowing with his eyes.

The wizard marks! Three men-at-arms went to his aid, but he shoved them away angrily, recovering his bearings. "Enough of this!" He walked back into the center of the courtyard. "If you really are him, then my regent, Lord Damien, would chide me for toying with you."

Liam blinked. "Damien?" The garrison smirked at him. Kaledonians murmured. "What happened to Arrius?"

Lamon scoffed. "Lord Damien took his place as master of this accursed mud-hole of a land. And soon," he pointed at Bran, "we will see the Unseelie curse ended when the regent kills that man."

"My lord," said a crossbowman at the southern tower, "something approaches!"

"Let this Damien come forth and say that to me face, dearie," shot back Bran.

Lamon waved off Bran. "Keep an eye on it," said Lamon to the tower. "All that is left of Kaledon is here, and they are trapped." The crossbowman nodded. Lamon returned to smirk at Liam. "Tell me, Liam, does it trouble you that Damien took your vengeance from you … killing the man who so cruelly ended your father and brothers?"

Liam mastered the boiling blood within him, loathing in his heart. "I am not here for vengeance, conjury master." He recalled the day he pressed the burning torch upon Lucius's face, thinking it would satisfy, but only finding it empty. His wrath had merely been unleashed, but without focus or lasting power. "I am here to reclaim my home. Vengeance is just a happy bonus."

Lamon shook his head in derision. "You'll accomplish neither, then." He curled his lip in scorn. "This rabble does not even warrant the regent's attention." He motioned, and the crossbowmen on the battlements aimed at them. Kaledonians held up shields and lowered their heads in preparation for the onslaught.

Bran nodded at Liam for him to join them.

He didn't. *So it ends here.* He smiled at Lamon, then faced the crossbowmen. Dozens trained on him and his comrades, needle-tips glinting in the morning light. He gripped his pelt with his left hand, and Xanibor with his right, and opened his arms before him, inviting them to shoot. He planned a counter-attack — wrap in the pelt and hope it with the armor might turn the quarrels, then charge the battlements.

But they did not attack immediately, for something turned their attention.

"My lord!" came a second shout from the tower, "conjury!" All eyes within the courtyard now rose to the sky.

And there the suns shined bright, against which a splaying shadow flew, and with a screech that tore the air, a massive white falcon soared with sun beams cast through the clouds behind it. Upon the mighty bird rode a stunningly beautiful woman, her diamond-patterned dress flying about her, a great mass of black hair swirling, one hand high in the air. Her eyes glowed turquoise, and the suns glinted off a ring on her raised palm. The top half of her face was painted black, with red snakes slithering down her cheeks. Then came a murder of crows from behind her, blasting the crossbowmen in a storm of chaos.

"What's all this?" Liam asked, as confusion spread throughout the courtyard. He darted toward the battlements to get a closer look at this newcomer, his heart jumping — *Mia?* Then came howls from the rugged foggy land below the castle. Pouring from the stubborn mist came a dozen monstrous Teralian Timberwolves, loping over bog, tuft and rock toward the gate. The men-at-arms braced for the assault, crossbowmen and spearmen scrambling.

Liam thrust Xanibor into the sky and roared as the falcon rider swooped toward the chaos. Crows flew madly about, making aim impossible. Nurnians cried "Conjury! Conjury! Look to the defenses!"

Bran lowered his sword. "Charge!" he cried, and the Kaledonians threw themselves into the courtyard, no longer caring about battle position, weapons flying, shields crashing, blood spraying.

Lamon, steady despite himself, spread his hands and spoke a charm. He rose into the air, new crackling energy engulfing his staff. "Steady men. Do not fear the great wolves. They cannot get through the gate!" But then the clacking of the front portcullis rang from the outer gatehouse. Liam leaned over the wall to see Maple tugging at the winch. Sweating and puffing her pipe, she strained, and the portcullis creaked up in starts. She was stronger than she looked.

The giant wolves shoved under it and bashed into the defenders, pressing them back with tooth and paw, leaping over fallen pack-mates, flinging defenders off the bridge and gutting others as they bounded toward the bridge to the central courtyard.

Laughing maniacally, nostrils flared, Liam leapt down and charged at the mass of the Nurnian garrison, élan overwhelming him, as if *he* were one of the wolves crashed with renewed vigor; seeing Mia filled his heart with renewed bloodlust. She was alive! As Lamon rose above the mayhem to meet the falcon rider, Lamon shot a glance at Liam, swept his staff and a man broke off the melee to attack Liam specifically.

Caoilte, expression blank, charged with shield and hammer.

He fended off several attacks from the ensnared Kaledonian, his old childhood friend, unsure whether to counterstrike, as the melee raged all around him, crows wild, wolves charging.

***

Mia gripped the falcon's steel-like feathers, soulfire spell-blood pulsing in her veins, and they wheeled about the massive castle, clouds of crows swirling about the central fortress before branching to the smaller side-strongholds, each upon its own sea stack. Crossbowmen and ballista crews loosed enchanted torgonite arrows at them, but the crows ruined their aim. High winds tossed her hair about her as the bond between her and the falcon resonated in her mind. She called him Ba'ande, the Newe word for "sky" and she felt the mighty beast's emotions and thoughts and vice-versa, Ba'ande having accepted her spell-enhanced bond of friendship. Below the giant wolves bonded over her rage, unleashing it against the brutal Nurnian conquerors. They shared common wrath, for the Nurnians deserved to be uprooted and cast out of this land. Below Liam fought with the knights of Kaledon in a fierce melee, and her heart raced. She snarled. *I told you I'd find you!*

But Lamon shot toward her, hand glowing red. He flung a whirling fiery dagger at her, and the falcon instinctively whirled, flapping its 200-foot wingspan and tumbling in midair to evade the spell-bolt. The world spun, a dizzying suspension in mid-air nearly flinging Mia into vast emptiness. When they righted, she hooked her legs into a rope she had wrapped around the great beast's chest and summoned forth a Bow of Mogdun, red flames flickering in her hands. Within she felt her soulfire nearly depleted. Many more spells and her power would be gone until the Mage Tide, weeks away.

Lamon, growling, spun around in mid-air and hurtled toward her. She loosed the Bowshot, but he caught the red arrow with his staff, dissipating its deadly energy with great effort. Blue energy then engulfed his staff and he closed in, poised to bash her skull in with it. She drew Branwen's knife and hissed a defensive spell, feeling its drain. As the towers of Caer Lannican sped past them, crows swarming, crossbowmen shouting, Lamon unleashed a flurry of blows, his speed enhanced with spellcraft. But so too was she enhanced. Sweating, she parried the bone-crushing staffblows, matching uncanny speed with speed, then his eyes met hers, and she roared at him, the world blackening for a moment, the spell power piercing his soul. He tensed in agony and cried. She slashed him and he fell to the courtyard hundreds of yards below. She swooped after him, Ba'ande's claws bared.

Lamon barely recovered in time to land softly, the chaos storming around him. He rose to his feet, eyes glowing crimson. He chanted.

Recognizing a powerful spell, she panicked, and shouted "Liam! Look out! Lamon!"

Ba'ande pitched left as Lamon finished with a mighty "*Ahargrata!*", whereupon dozens of red demonic faces erupted from his hands swirling out, hitting only Kaledonians. All those struck burst into flames. A demonic face catapulted toward her, but behind her a voice cried, "Oh no you don't you dodgy varlet!"

Sea Breeze intercepted the spell and burst into flames. The raven spiraled, smoking, into the ocean far below.

"No!" cried Mia, instinctively reaching for the raven, to no avail. She had no time to go after her, for another had been hit. Ba'ande.

The falcon screeched, sending them hurtling to the flagstones, and she unhooked her legs from the rope and dove into a hay-filled cart, bruising her arms and head with a heavy thump. Flames crackled and men screamed. She shook the stars out of her vision and crawled to her feet, limping out of the hay onto the stone, hobbling into the courtyard. Kaledonians burned, screaming and rolling on the ground, as did giant wolves and many crows. The remaining Nurnians fled bleeding from the courtyard. Knife gripped, she placed her glowing ring-hand on Ba'ande, using its last bit of stored soulfire to ease the creature's wounds, not knowing if it would be enough. The ring fell dull. She scowled and hobbled around a tower. There Lamon panted in the courtyard, wizard marks bleeding and faded, a slash across his chest where she'd cut him, staff crackling. He was depleted, too. Liam, pelt blackened, armor smoldering, bleeding and pained, battled a magically ensnared Caoilte.

She only had two more spells until the soulfire was gone. But no choice remained. She raised her ring hand, traced a pattern in the air, and rasped, "*Esoulla.*" The fires all around her quenched at once. For some Kaledonians and wolves, it was too late. Their bodies smoked, lifeless and still. Ba'ande, scorched but still intact, nursed blackened feathers and backed away, knocking down a stables with his great bulk. The remaining Kaledonians arose with effort, her spell having saved them, and they pursued the Nurnians to the south. Lamon glared at her with grudging respect. She stopped before him.

She aimed her knife at him. "Yield," she said, voice cracking, body aching, pulse pounding.

He scanned the devastated area around him and scowled. "I'll not." He then darted into the air and flew south.

Mia gritted her teeth. "Oh no you don't," she seethed, running to Ba'ande. The falcon crouched to allow her to climb on and she laced her legs around the rope. The falcon then surged upward with a massive heave of his wings, causing her insides to lurch as the bird exploded into the sky after him. The castle shrank behind her and they closed in on Lamon's fleeing form through wisps of dissipating fog by the cliffs.

***

Liam struggled against Caoilte, Xanibor entangled with the man's mace, both men weary, dripping with sweat and blood. Blisters roared under his armor, the fine mailcoat and gambeson no protection against Lamon's vile sorcery. Nevertheless, with the wave of Mia's spell, his devastated allies no longer burned. At the same time the fires quenched, Caoilte no longer resisted, and Liam shoved him back, knocking his helmet off as Lamon flew into the sky and Mia tore after him on the gyrfalcon.

Liam limped back toward the courtyard where Caoilte stumbled, sorting out what had happened. He recalled the spell that eased the will-o-wisp pain at Rathchylde. *Mia must have broken Lamon's hold over Caoilte with her fire-quench spell.* Caoilte gawked at the devastation. Corpses, quarrels, blood, giant wolf bodies. Then his face twisted in anguish.

"Caoilte, wait!" called Liam, limping toward him. "You were under an enchantment! But Mia has broken the spell. You're with us again!"

Caoilte shook his head in horror. "I remember it. I remember all of it. I betrayed you and all my kinsfolk."

"You were under Lamon's control — you had no choice."

He frowned and glared at Liam, stepping back, double door to the great keep behind him. "You always have a choice." He withdrew his rondel dagger and placed it against his throat.

"No, don't!" said Liam.

Suddenly the double door opened. Caoilte whirled as Liam labored up the steps, trailing blood, Xanibor dragging.

From the darkness, Damien emerged.

The Magnolent tore the dagger from Caoilte's hand and shoved it into his throat. Liam cried out hoarsely, flashes of his childhood friend racing with him at festivals crowding his mind. But then the chaos died down and his eyesight cleared. Damien wiped the dagger calmly and unshouldered his shield. His eyes darted over the courtyard as Caoilte drowned in his own blood, writhing, then fell still. "Well. I bid you good morning, Liam. You certainly have not disappointed me. I was beginning to wonder if you'd ever bring the Dream Stone back to me."

"I'm not in the mood for quips, Damien. Tell me where my mother is and be gone."

He drew Larsorn. "Don't be ridiculous. There's a reason I sat comfortably in this castle while everyone else slaughtered each other."

Liam cocked his head to the side in sarcasm. "Oh, is that because you're a fucking coward?"

Damien scoffed. "Because I knew that *if* you made it this far, you'd likely be beaten half to death, and I was right."

He planted Xanibor on the stair before him, resting his hands on the hilt. He knew he could not win this battle. Damien was just as skilled as he, but was fresh, unwounded, with all arms and armor battle-sharp. Moreover, Damien was not plagued with visions of death and pain, tormenting him at every turn, screaming at him to flee as quickly as possible. His heart pummeled the inside of his chest, his limbs shook with fatigue, and blood continued to ooze from his many wounds.

The outcome didn't matter. He remained. "Tell you what, your Grace. We can do this the easy way or the *really* easy way. You can leave. Or you can die."

Damien shook his head in grudging admiration and disbelief. "I must hand it to you, Liam," he said, advancing. Liam backed up, raising Xanibor. "In Midworld you're a mid-level nobody. But look at what you are here! You have the makings of a true legend. You even have a mighty sword to boot. Looks to be one of the god-forged blades of the Fallen Dream Empire. Imbued with great powers, I'd wager. Like Larsorn."

"It is. But I don't need any of that to kill you."

But his left leg gave out and he buckled down to one knee, tearing pain from half a dozen quarrel wounds and double that many bruises taking their toll. He spat blood on the flagstone and raised his head. Damien smiled grimly and put on his shining bascinet, glowering down upon him.

Liam caught his breath in the courtyard as Damien approached, shield out, the smell of oiled metal, sweat, torn entrails and burning flesh heavy in the morning sunlight, battle sounds distant beyond the walls. "You do yourself no honor waiting so long to join the fight, your Grace."

The Magnolent scoffed. "Honor is useless if you lose. Besides, who really cares about honor, anyway?"

He glowered. "I do."

"Ah," he said, lifting a finger, "you do *now*. Now that you're lost in this world of twisted ideas. But where was your honor for the last fifteen years?"

That spurred a deep, horrid and wordless scream within him. Agony which had been locked away for many years. But unlike before, now he let it flow freely. He let it creep up from the depths, flushing his bloody cheeks, pulsing in his hands. He stood, but with less effort than he thought would be needed. "That won't work on me. I know I'm not perfect, nor was I ever. I can only move forward, as a good man should."

He shook his head in disdain. "But look at you. You've been *broken* by this world! I don't want to kill you, Liam. You were rehabilitated from this hell hole. Don't undo all that hard work."

Liam furrowed his brow. "You think I would abandon my mother? Mia? My homeland?"

"Mia is lost," he said, pacing about him like a stalking panther. "Watch and see. She has been seduced by this world. By the blood and guts of it. The raw power she now feels, steeped in sweat and pain and bloodlust. I saw her from the keep. The look in her soulfire-glowing eyes. She won't go home, even with you. Erentyr has consumed her — it's happened many times before, Liam. Throughout history — this world infects your soul with darkness. Forget her and all of this. I'll promote you in my company. We'll lock up Dr Morderan and close off Erentyr from Midworld forever. Put it all behind us."

Liam shook his head in disbelief. "You don't get it do you? You Magnolents can't control the tides of the universe, Damien. The Stone is meant to hold us together as one. Light and dark, peace and wrath, joy and sorrow."

He scoffed. "Your mother told you that as a child, didn't she?"

"Is there some problem with that?"

He smiled grimly and shook his head. "It's poetry and sentiment. Nothing more. Used to justify every atrocity known. You'd think *you* of all people would have learned this. Humankind doesn't need this world. It doesn't even need *us*. The idea of a 'noble warrior' is toxic. We are an anachronism. Outdated. That is why the Stone should be hidden away forever."

He snarled. "I know I don't fully understand the Dream Stone and neither do you. The stone or the gates. They were made by *gods*. You have no idea what we need!"

Damien glared at Liam. "Oh, I see. And you do, now that you've managed to survive this world for a few weeks," he sneered. "It didn't kill you, so it made you stronger? Is that it? The trauma 'made me who I am'," he added mockingly.

Liam stood in black, seething silence. "I never said that. I just chose, to the extent I could, to *use* my grief, my wounds, and my sorrow. To understand them. To know them and respect them, like a dangerous animal. Not to be ruled by them. Can you say the same?"

He snorted. "You will never learn, will you? You're just as bad as the lunatic who killed your family."

He lifted his chin to Damien, boiling inside. "Let's be done with this. And let's use skill of sword alone. No summoning the powers in the blade. Just man against man. Metal against metal." He lifted Xanibor before him in a salute to his foe.

Damien seemed taken aback that Liam would salute him. No clever retorts came. Instead he straightened and drew Larsorn. "Very well. I will make it quick."

He lowered Xanibor into a front guard, so as to keep his reach advantage. Damien pulled into a high guard, shield forward, eyes fierce over the top edge of his escutcheon. Tense moments passed, gentle wind wafting the smoke between them, distant surf crashing, fires crackling in the courtyard. Images of death and blood hammered Liam from within. His shattered brothers and father, but also Lucius, whom he tortured, and all the garrison he'd cut down. Swords into faces, hacking off calves, slicing hands, blades into mailcoats. Blood spraying, men screaming.

Death.

Sweat trickled down his cheek.

"You see them, don't you?" said Damien. "Your brothers and father."

Liam glowered in answer. He did not take the bait. Instead he let the furnace coil within him like a spring. He waited.

Damien scowled and charged.

Liam feinted high, drawing his enemy's shield up, then whirled under the shield to stab into his gut. The strike did not penetrate Damien's brigandine and mailcoat, but he heard the man grunt. Damien shoved back, thrusting the shield to bind Liam before he could retreat, then swung at his knee. He instinctively shifted so the blow would hit mail rather than boot, but the force dropped him. Damien then shoved Liam's weapon away and swung at his neck, but he dipped his head and the strike rattled his helmet. A kick to the chest knocked him to the ground several feet away.

Liam spat blood. Burns, bruises, and arrow wounds roared all over. His ears rang, and fatigue weighed on him like stones.

The Magnolent paced. "Even surviving the bite of Drelthun won't save you, Liam. Healing twice as fast doesn't help if you're dead. Plus I survived it too. I'm just as hard to kill as you are. Stop fighting me!"

The images of suffering and carnage continued to assault Liam's mind. Spears shoved in faces. Limbs hacked. His brothers gutted. His father burning slowly. But instead of recoiling from them, he let them flow. Curious about them. Accepting their pain. He climbed with effort to one knee. "Don't you ever shut up?"

The regent snorted and closed in, sword in a low guard. He swung hard. Liam parried one-handed, then grabbed the shield, peeling it away to head-butt his enemy in the face. Damien stumbled, bloody, and barely blocked Xanibor's next arc, then he retaliated with a slash to Liam's forearm. Mail prevented Larsorn from amputating him at the elbow but the force felt as though it could have fractured bone. He gripped Xanibor with his good hand, shoved the guard behind the shield, wrenched it back and swept heel to ankle, knocking Damien onto his back. He then gripped Xanibor half-sword and shoved down into Damien's mailed neck above the brigandine. The Magnolent shifted just enough to avoid a death-blow, but Xanibor pierced his bicep, forcing a scream.

Liam roared in battle rage, shoving harder down, even as Damien bloodied his face with a punch from the shield's edge, and knee smashes bludgeoned his likely fractured ribs. Then Damien gripped Larsorn and unleashed its power. Pain blasted Liam's entire body, on top of an already tortured frame.

Muscles tensed so hard he thought his teeth would crack. He stumbled back, barely gripping Xanibor, head crushing, nose dripping blood, eyes littered with stars. He dropped to one knee and grunted in agony, frost covering his body from the ground up to his face.

Damien wearily clambered to his feet, blood and sweat dripping, eyes bloodshot. The flashes of death and slaughter in Liam's head grew stronger, only now they acted as kindling for an inner bonfire. Liam's eyes grew wild, the years of pain and sorrow unquenched, unattended bursting forth.

Then, through the unrelenting waves of agony, he *smiled* at Damien.

His foe gaped in disbelief. The pain was feeding him. The agony *meant* something. He'd made Damien cheat. Liam drank it like a burning hot whiskey.

Damien had little cause to smirk anymore, as Liam stood before him, frost melting and cracking. Liam's smile faded. "You cheated."

"So?" he said, voice shaking, "cheat back! Engulf me in strangle-vines, if you can."

Liam shook his head. "That's not how this works. I gave my word. Honorable victory, or nothing! Yield!"

Damien's eyes darted about the courtyard, unsure. "Stupid nonsense!" He wiped the blood from his face on a gauntlet. His scowl deepened, then he rushed forward, shield up. Liam swatted away several swings and bashed the shield, keeping his distance advantage, pushing through the pain enough to barely keep his footwork and counterstrike, but Damien's skill kept the slashes at bay. Both men staggered, panting and sweating, as thunder began to roll in from the south. Damien charged again, frustrated by Xanibor's greater reach. But Liam anticipated it. Instead of backing or shifting away, he leaned into the shield, inside the sword arc, and slashed hard against Damien's forearm. He cried in pain, the blow likely breaking his arm, mail rings snapping and flying. Larsorn crashed into his side, forcing a grunt, then skittered across the stone. Liam hooked Damien's head and hip tossed him to the ground, cracking the battered shield into splinters and sprawling his enemy on his back.

Damien raised his hand, wincing, sword arm tucked in close. "I yield, Liam! I yield!"

Gripping Xanibor half-sword again, he prepared to stab, but stopped at the man's plea. "Tell me where my mother is! NOW!"

"Mercy! In exchange for her location! Swear it, or I'll take the secret to the grave."

"No more games," seethed Liam. "Tell me now or die!"

"I will, Liam, I will. You win," he said, scooting backward. Liam, woozy with pain and exhaustion, pinned the man's knee with his boot, making him squirm. "I will tell you nothing unless you give me your word to let me go. You are a Knight of Kaledon — your word is your bond. I c-can see that. So swear it before me and the Fairy Queen Herself."

"*Err, err,*" cawed Sea Breeze, perched on the roof of the smithy. She shook off several drops of sea water, feathers singed but intact. "Not sure you want to do that, love. Children knows, he's not a bit trustworthy. Why not just budge off his crumpet now and be done with him? You can search the castle all you like, then."

"Ah, sure," said Damien, quickly adjusting to the talking raven, "but will you reach her in time? Her life force is failing." Liam caught his breath, snarling in pain. He lifted Xanibor to strike. Damien tilted his head to one side. "I'll tell you where she is right now if you swear to offer me mercy. Then I will leave Erentyr and never return."

Liam snorted and lowered Xanibor. "Fine, then. I swear. On my faith and honor as a knight, and before the Fairy Queen as well, wherever She may be. Now where is my mother?"

Damien removed Brendan's ancient signet ring. "Take this. She is behind the great hall, beyond the royal solarium. The ring will allow you to shift a stone to open the hidden tunnel where she has been imprisoned." Liam snatched the ring. Tense moments passed. "Now let me go. You promised, as a Knight of Kaledon."

Liam pocketed the ring and stepped off his enemy. Sheer force of will kept him standing. Damien waited, clearly aware Liam could cut him down. The idea was tempting. His fingers gripped and loosened from the sword. But he couldn't. He pointed at him with Xanibor. "You, too, made a promise. Never to return to Erentyr."

Damien nodded. "I did."

"If you go back on your promise," he growled, "there will be no more mercy. None asked or given."

The Magnolent agreed. "I understand. I will never again seek the Dream Stone. It is yours."

Liam backed away, giving Damien room to stand up with arm still tucked. "Trust me, Liam Panregon, son of Ynwin and Cormac an Brionglóir," he added darkly, "I will not underestimate you again. You win the day. I'll meet you at Drelthun's castle — give me until a week after the solstice to get there , *on my honor*. There, if you open the gate, I will leave this world."

"Get out of my sight!"

From there Damien retrieved Larsorn, mounted a horse and rode toward the gatehouse. A dirt-covered and bruised Maple trotted up to Liam, watching Damien with suspicion before joining him as he pondered the signet ring.

"Oy! We just letting him go, then?" said the wildgnome.

"Liam gave his word as a knight of the realm," said the raven. "The man yielded, after all."

"Well, then!" said Maple. "Not so on about vengeance, then?"

"I will not shy from it if need be." But vengeance was far from his heart. He put on the signet ring and took out the Dream Stone. His mother's life was nearly gone. "Maple? Sea Breeze? Can you go check on Mia, for me?" He breathed in deeply.

Bring it back to me.

"I'm going to free my mother."

Chapter 25

Mia glared down her nose at Lamon. She drew back a flaming arrow from her final spell, the arrow trained at the wizard's tense face. He was sprawled on his back, trapped between her and the cliffs behind him. To her right, Ba'ande spread his wings and lurched into the air to swoop for hunting grounds far to the west, their alliance finished for now. Lamon tried to scoot away, but froze.

"One more inch and you're dead," she said. He searched her eyes and stayed still. From the fortress, some 50 yards along the cliff's edge, Damien rode, sword arm tucked close. He galloped along the last remaining road, between overgrown and ruined farms. "There goes your fearless leader. Seems Liam defeated him. Damien has abandoned you."

"So, too," said Lamon, holding his hands to show he cast no spells, "it would seem he has been granted mercy, as I have asked of you."

Maple trotted into the corner of her view, followed by Sea Breeze, who perched on Mia's shoulder. She acknowledged the raven but said nothing. Inside her raged a firestorm of conflict. Mercy or not, this man deserved to die. He was part of the invading force, he tortured innocents and used his powerful craft to subjugate and enslave people. He also killed Branwen. But beneath that, she simply wanted to kill him because she *could*. Never in her life had so much power been at her fingertips. It felt intoxicating and dangerous. And now that all twelve spells had awakened within her, she longed to learn more. She snarled at Lamon.

"Steady on, Mia," said Maple. "He's in the waning — no spells. Ye can see that on 'im. Liam let his man go, you can, too."

"I'm not Liam," hissed Mia. Lamon swallowed.

"Aye, love," said Sea Breeze. "Liam followed his heart. What will yours say?"

Mia gritted her teeth. That was the problem — her heart was at war. "How do I know I can trust you? How can I be sure to have peace with you alive?"

No smirk or condescension traced his features. "I will be honest, Mia, as one sorcerer to another. I have lied and deceived — I see no way you can trust me. But I swear I will not come after you. Consider it professional courtesy."

Mia's muscles tensed. She could let him go. But then what? *By his own admission he was a liar.*

Tension mounted, her muscles tight as coiled steel.

Moments passed, sea surf crashing far below, thunderstorm rolling in from the south.

She loosed the arrow.

It shot straight through his head, killing him instantly.

The bow dissipated and she stood there glaring at the dead body, breathing heavily. Maple looked down and away, nervously fidgeting.

Err, err, cawed Sea Breeze.

"Mercy is *earned,*" she said, snarling. She felt simultaneously sick and flooded with empowerment. Disgusted with herself, but also unapologetic. Whatever the case, Lamon could not harm anyone she loved now. If Damien had been there, he'd have gotten the same treatment.

She approached the body and kicked it off the cliff where it shattered in bloody pieces far below. Buzzards broke from their circling above the castle to glide down.

"Oy, there, Mia," said Maple timidly, "one of those wolves is coming."

She turned away from the dizzying drop into the ocean to see the white-tufted wolf pad up to them. "Oohan," she said, using the name she'd given the beast. "Many thanks for your help. You will be remembered always." It lowered its muzzle to nudge her face, then looked to the road where the Unseelie bogs practically spewed dun fog. Further south the sky blackened. Lightning bolts coursed, followed by cracks of thunder. "Go, my friend," she said, "your pack awaits you."

As Oohan left, the remaining Teralian Timberwolves joined and the pack fled Kaledon for the distant forests of Tarila.

"Come on," said Mia to Maple and Sea Breeze, "let's get back to the castle before the road closes up."

The three of them passed quickly from the cliff's edge into the darkening ruined pastureland, the blackthorn bogs practically growing before their eyes, gloom sweeping. Rain flowed on the southern wind as they sped up, Mia's spirit depleted, heart pounding against a weary chest.

They arrived at the gatehouse where Lungor slumped against the stone, many spear wounds in him, broken Nurnian bodies flung about into the growing foliage. He barely breathed, eyes closed. At his feet swampy vines crept over his legs and worked up his torso. Mists invaded. Sea Breeze flew to his head and pecked. "Hey, you big lummocks, no time for a nap, now, is it?" No movement — the giant was deeply unconscious.

"Mia," called Maple, urgently. She followed the wildgnome's curly red hair through the gatehouse to find Bran pulling Conal's wounded body across the bridge to the main courtyard where other Kaledonians gathered. Conal's arm slung over his shoulder, Bran hobbled as fast as he could.

Mia went to the old knight's side, as Maple darted further in. "Is he all right?"

He gave her a stern, unhopeful look. "I'll not leave a brother like Conal here to die by the bogs. It will nae be me."

She nodded, then entered the crowded courtyard. Yeomen, traders, fishmongers and craftsman, now freed, huddled together with the remaining knights and men-at-arms. They squinted in the light. Some whispered that the end was near. The keep towered above them, balcony opening to the air.

She pushed her way past the crowd and climbed up the wide stairs to the open double door. "Liam?" she called, her voice echoing into the candlelit halls. She padded through several passages and climbed a spiral stair to the antechamber which connected to the balcony. She stopped short at the stone guardrail. "Oh my god..."

From the south, storm clouds gathered and swept in, blackthorn bogs smeared with columns of rain from the coal-ash ceiling. Creeping growth covered Lungor to his neck. Tendrils of fog slipped over hill, rock, and stone wall, darkening the remaining pastureland.

Will-o-wisps emerged, like terrible fireflies, emanating hatred and malice with their growing pulses. Floating snakes slithered behind, oozing venom. Spriggans darted through the foliage, weapons drawn. Green and black crept over the gatehouse, covering it in mere moments and growing across the bridge.

Mia's breath shook and she trembled. "Liam please hurry," she whispered.

***

Liam limped up the stairway, then opened the cell to find a dark stone chamber, where a woman in a torn and ragged kirtle curled up on the floor. As blood pounded in his ears, he pushed through his screaming wounds to shove the table and chair aside to go to her. A frail, thin, almost ghostly remnant of his mother turned weakly to him, barely recognizing the much larger, stronger man her youngest son had become.

"Little red?" she rasped, reaching a hand to wipe his face.

"Mom," he said, voice choking. "I'm here. C-can you stand?"

She shook her head, reaching to point to her legs. The old arrow wound had scarred over now, but it had shattered her bone. "Too long in darkness. Bones weak and frail. I almost starved myself for release, but I held on for you to find me. And you found me," she said, smiling and coughing. "Praise the Fairy Queen after all."

He crouched to hold her. "Mom, we need you. Kaledon is nearly gone. Here," he said, scrambling to bring out the Dream Stone. "I-I brought it back to you."

But she did not take it. She met his eyes with hers. "I am sorry, son. I'm far too weak for that. You must do it," she said, holding a trembling left hand open, fading Calling Brand upon the bony back surface. "Take the Bond, then link yourself to the Stone with your blood as I did long ago."

"No," he said, "I can heal you! The power of the Stone–"

She closed his hand on it. "It is too late for me now, my son." She wheezed, out of breath. He held the warm Stone next to her heart, but it would not impart its power to her. Within he felt her life force fading.

But she was not sad. He could feel, deep within his bones, her body was devastated, longing to rejoin her husband and children. She'd prolonged her agony for his sake alone.

"Mom," he said, tears forcing themselves from his eyes, holding her close, as she drifted. "Don't die on me now! After all this? I need you! I'm sorry I took so long to come back. I..." he couldn't speak. Short staccato breaths escaped him. Drops fell on her face.

"Here," she whispered, opening her eyes. "Take my hand now, son. My prayers kept me alive long enough for ye to find me, but now they're fulfilled and I must go. You must be the Stoneguard now. You've proven your worth."

"No, Mom, I'm not worthy. I'm–"

She placed a trembling finger on his lips. "Dinnae say that. You're worthy. Take my hand."

Panic stabbed his heart. He resisted taking her hand, for he knew what it meant. It meant letting her go. At long last. After so many years of loneliness and torture. Her body broken. Her mind weary with sorrow.

He knew what he had to do.

He took out a knife and cut a lock of his hair. Then placed it in his hand and took hers.

"Thank you," she whispered. "I'll wait for ye, son. I will see you again, many years from now. Go and restore the balance. Save our home."

His hand warmed, and suddenly the Calling Brand shined, the knotwork Tear of The Fairy Queen, Ocean Mother of the Remembering Ones, filling the dark chamber with brilliant light. Calming, fierce energy flooded his spirit, knitting wounds, staunching the flow of blood and mending his fractured bones. He gasped, and it was done. The Calling Brand had seared itself onto his hand now. Ynwin lay still in his arms, calmness upon her haggard face.

She was gone.

The grief and loss struck him like a blow to the stomach. He sobbed into her hair. *Mom. Mom. I'm so sorry. I took too long. I'm not ready to lose you!* He tried to cry out, but only hissing grief exited his lips.

How long he knelt there with his mother in his arms, he couldn't say.

And after what seemed like an eternity, he felt a hand upon his cheek.

Mia, tears in her eyes, embraced him. "I'm so sorry, my love," she whispered.

"All things being equal," he rasped, "I'd rather be holding a double shot of Jameson in my hand, right now."

"I know, baby," she said. "I know."

Together they wept freely.

Then finally, he bowed his head and stopped, drawing in a deep breath and letting it out slowly. "It's time.."

Mia caressed his shoulder in comfort. "It doesn't seem fair. We came all this way only to lose."

He shook his head. "No. We haven't lost yet. Come on. I'm taking her out of this horrid cell."

He stood up, Ynwin in his arms, and left the chamber. His boots echoed in the stairway. Mia gently followed, bare feet on stone, carrying the candle. They made their way to the balcony where the rainy air wafted across his cheeks. A dying beam of light from the suns fell upon Ynwin's cheek before the incoming clouds snuffed it. This triggered a wave of light to flow down her form, sparkling, crackling bolts leaping across her body until finally, she disappeared in a swirl of dissipating light. Liam and Mia gasped. Ynwin had passed completely on.

"Farewell, Mom," said Liam to the wind. He blinked at the sky, recentering himself.

He approached the balcony's edge, Sea Breeze looking on from a gargoyle in the wall. Bran and the Kaledonian knights pointed and murmured upon spotting him. Maple sat on Bran's shoulders, anxiously fidgeting. He straightened before the vista of death below. Kaledon crawled with blackthorn bog. All roads choked with vegetation and gloom, and the bridge swelled with foliage that crept into the courtyard, pushing the crowd against the stables. Spriggans chittered among one another, red eyes flashing as they scrambled along the vegetation. Riders with horned, skeletal heads floated along the fog, scythes bared. The Kaledonians retreated into the side fortresses on the sea stacks, their last refuge. The will-o-wisps arose, floating on stormy air toward him by the dozen, pulsing with hate and disdain. Then, before him on the balcony, several wisps coalesced into the form of Vinraith Flame-eye.

The Unseelie King rested his hands upon the long axe, his burning blue eye regarding them coolly, more wisps gathering around him. The great crimson cloak tossing in the growing storm-wind, hood waving in the gathering darkness around him, a golden crown upon his head. "The time has come, Liam."

"Yes. It has," he replied. He slowly raised the Dream Stone before him, placed the knife in his palm and sliced his hand. Blood oozed from the wound and soaked into the Stone. The Calling Brand pulsed white. He felt himself bond with the Stone, like his mother before him, and power resonated along the bones of his arm, filling his heart with dreadful energy.

The will-o-wisps slowed when he did this, the light flickering off the Unseelie King's wolfen gaze, as if this act somehow thundered in their spirits, making them pause. "Hear me, oh great Vinraith, and all the Unseelie children," he said, his voice imperial, rising above the wind, "Rymindron. Haters of mortalkind. I am Stoneguard of this realm. I have the Dream Stone of the Fairy Queen Herself, Mother of all gods. Come before me and judge me if you will. If you accept me as Stoneguard, as my mother was before me, I call upon you to uphold your ancient troth with the Fairy Queen and return from whence you came." He looked up at the mighty king of the Unseelie. "Return to your abodes and leave us in peace!"

Thunder rattled the very air, and rain poured. None moved, even to take shelter. All froze, terror paralyzing them, knowing that with a mere blink, the Unseelie would annihilate them. They drifted closer, and their voices erupted within his mind. Vinraith stepped toward him, but Liam stood fast, as did Mia, firm before the Master of the Dark Valley.

"You do not know what you have in your hands," said Vinraith, voice piercing the gathering gale. "If you knew, you would cast yourself from on high and destroy yourself now. Is this truly your wish, mortal?"

Liam remained still. "I have no illusions of greatness or destiny, sire. I will do what I can, and what I must. The rest is in the hands of the gods. But for my part: I will not retreat one step from what has been handed to me from my elders."

The crowd inched back from the wisps now surrounding Liam and Mia. The balcony nearly crackled with tension.

Liam stood fast, fist raised, Mia beside him, hand in his, chin high. They awaited destruction from the rising, circling winds.

Vinraith narrowed that terrible flaming eye on them. Liam's blood surged, flushing in his face, heart hammering. Then the Unseelie King scowled, eye tracking between him, the Dream Stone, then the Kaledonians. A faint smile curled against his fangs, and he nodded with grudging respect. He gazed down at both Mia and Liam and laughed darkly. "Now it would seem you have become what you always were."

Then the wisps dimmed to a glimmer before disappearing with their king, spriggans hissing and snarling before turning to flee into the blackthorn tangles amid the floating serpents and fleeing skeletal riders.

The wind dissipated, along with the storm clouds. Within minutes the black ceiling broke and the light of late autumn suns returned, shining from the west upon the slopes of Kaledon.

Then the bogs burst into flames, splaying across the landscape like a mottled sea of fire. Liam and Mia recoiled, exchanging glances. Then they ran to the balcony's edge.

Flames swept across the land.

Then just as swiftly, the fires extinguished.

The next few hours went by as if a dream. Fog scattered and disintegrated. Bogs wilted and pools drained. Blackthorn groves withered and cracked, to blow away into wisps of ash. Gentle seaward gusts sent the vines covering the bridge and gatehouse of Caer Lannican into crackling streams of particles. Liam held Mia close and kissed her hair, resting his cheek upon the wet tangles. She pulled him close and kissed his chest.

Bran and the remaining knights of Kaledon charged up to the battlements, cheering with many a loud 'huzzah!' as the peasants meekly made their way across the bridge to enter the new green land that remained. Pastures now grew, bright and full, stronger than ever and nearly glowing in the golden afternoon. Farmland sprawled between the stalwart stone walls, interweaving the pastures like a great quilt of rocky, hilly land, cascading down the countryside to the misty forests to the south. Beams of light settled upon crystal lakes, and small cloud shadows drifted across the verdant quilt-work countryside.

"The purging fire brings sorrow, but also renewal," muttered Liam as he drew in a crisp, deep breath and breathed out in relief.

Kaledon was reborn.

Chapter 26

Damien opened and closed his right palm, the feeling having only recently returned to his fingers after Liam fractured his bone, leaving a huge gash in his arm. But the mark of Drelthun flowed in his veins just like Liam, and so the wound was healing quickly. His boots echoed against the stone of the dragon's dark castle.

A chill fell on him, and it seemed the night shadows deepened. Two purple slits opened in the gloom past the overgrown courtyard, where thorny vine-covered fountains rusted in the dusky moonlight. A dim beam descended into the central chamber that held the now-invisible and closed Dream Gate. "Sir Damien," said the great beast, "thy return boasteth no victory."

"It's true," he replied. "Liam bested me," he said reluctantly. "Erentyr did not break him as I thought it would. Quite the opposite it would seem." His brow furrowed, his mind troubled. Nothing had made sense since that day in the courtyard of Caer Lannican, a fortnight ago.

The dragon loomed nearer. "Thou hast fled from thy castle?"

He raised an eyebrow, looking at the grey flagstones on the floor. "I did. I'm not exactly proud of it. I even bargained for mercy when he had me dead to rights."

"Not proud?" said the beast, a line of teeth flashing into a smile in the dim light, "Why? What careth thee for pride or battle-fame?"

Good question. He scowled. *Erentyr seems to be infecting me as it has Liam and Mia.* Despite himself he had to admit they had become *much* stronger. But that was to be expected. That was the allure of this world — though not usually to such a degree. "Liam has offered to return me to Midworld once he gets here after the solstice."

"Ah ... but is that thy true desire?" Drelthun crept forward, towering over him now in a great shadow of slick dark scales.

Damien tried to avoid thinking about being defeated by Liam, or the unsettling presence of the dragon. "Why would I want to stay in this nightmare world?"

The dragon laughed, a deep, unsettling and bone-rattling laugh. Uneasiness flickered about the Magnolent's body. "Midworld hath done thee no favors, Damien. It hath made thee soft and dull of mind." Damien scowled away the insult. "But ... If thou stay," continued the beast, "and place thy loyalty in me, I shall teacheth thee the way of *Erentyrian* power and domination, such as thy world has yet to see, even at the height of its bloodiest empires."

He gazed up in wonderment at the beast. "What do you mean?"

"Nay," he said, trailing off, now winding his massive bulk about him, tail swirling. "Thou must come with me and pledge thy loyalty to me forever. Then wilt thou know."

The idea was ludicrous, of course. He knew he should say no and await Liam and the Dream Stone. He scoffed in disbelief. *Imagine staying here. Ridiculous. Returning to Midworld would be so easy — all they would do is retire me from the Magnolent Exploration Corps and leave me to manage ComCorp City 335 — a slap on the wrist. All my houses and apartments I'd keep. Wanting for nothing. Unlimited orinol. Endless women and song.*

In exchange for what? A deal with the devil and a lifetime of toil and struggle, only on the promise of glory.

Glory.

He smiled sardonically. The idea conjured pictures of him ruling far more than ComCorp City 335 — a city which ran itself, in all honesty. AI programs had fine-tuned its function into all the optimal flow points. There was little to manage, and much time for leisure pursuits. *But here...* He placed a hand on the hilt of Larsorn, the blade Drelthun himself had given him as reward for surviving his sadistic "test."

Here there was something Midworld could never offer him. Pain ... with the promise of domination. A chance to undo his failure. The fact that he *cared* about that truly bothered him.

No mercy.

The risks soared high. The possible rewards, unthinkable. His heart rate climbed.

The dragon chuckled again, now softer. "It cometh to this one moment, Sir Damien, Knight of the Conclave. Wilt thou choose a life of leisure and idle fancy, or one of struggle and challenge, but where glory, lordship, and mastery reach their zenith?"

He drew in several breaths. "It-it would be going back on my word to Liam."

"As hath I, against the Fairy Queen, for ages now. In this, I would betray Her bond even more deeply. Come with me now, make thy choice to bond with me as Liam hath bonded with the Stone. If thou so choose, thou will become greater. *Much* greater."

Temptation overwhelmed him. Swirling, intoxicating. To regain the honor he had lost to Liam, and command fear and respect among the Conclave. "I'll do it," he said, immediately wondering what he had just done.

But now it was too late. He could not un-say it.

Drelthun lowered his head and nodded. "Thy heart finally speaketh for thee." He slid something metal from the shadows with a massive claw. "Taketh this mask. Bond it to thy helmet and come with me."

He picked it up. The exquisite carving glinted in the waxing moonlight, revealing a stern, handsome face with a single tear flowing from one eye. Eldritch power emanated from it, making his fingers tingle through his gauntlets. "What will it do to me?"

Drelthun slowly neared, his massive draconic head now only inches away. "It shall make thee nigh immortal."

The idea was outrageous — yet he knew, in Erentyr, such an offer from a Remembering One was fully real, and absolute. "Why would you offer something like this to me, your Greatness? Don't you see me as a failure?"

His eerie purple eyes narrowed upon him. "Thou art merely untried. Thou hast strengths that a lifetime in Midworld hath left untapped and unmined. I offer this only once. Never again wilt thou see such a chance in ten thousand lifetimes. What say thee?"

All his life he had fought to wall off Erentyr from Midworld. To uphold the Magnolent Mandate. And here he was considering staying. No less a being than Drelthun had offered an alliance that simply could not be cast aside. He knew, should he refuse, he would regret it for the rest of his life.

He placed the mask upon his helmet. A subtle pulse flowed through his body, healing his injuries, filling him with terrible power. Then it submerged into his soul's depths. He gasped and shuddered with its force.

"The die is cast. Thou hast chosen well, young one." The dragon lurched forward, and Damien walked beside him. Massive black wings blotted out the sky of the courtyard. Then the dragon settled down, the air of his movement tossing Damien's traveling cloak back. He swung his great head back to the Magnolent knight. "Long hath I dwelt in this castle against the Fairy Queen's wishes, immobilizing the Dream Stone and gate, guarding against those who would pass. Tormenting them. No longer. Liam may have won the battle, but he will lose the war."

Damien felt sharper and clearer, mind pulsing with icy cold precision. He knew what to do next, and gripped Drelthun's obsidian-like horned hide. He climbed to where his forelegs widened into massive muscular shoulders. The horned hide formed a seat of sorts, and he gripped it tightly.

Then the dragon surged forth, tearing across the bridge into the purple glow-fly meadows that swayed their tiny lights in the night wind. With a powerful thrust upward which made Damien's insides shift, the ground disappeared quickly and the clouds soared past.

They swept south and flew into the night, toward the domain of ancient Atrogonia, seat of the Conclave of Wizard Kings, and their Grand Sovereign, Ozremorn.

Chapter 27

At the autumn fire festival, all the highlands ranging from the great cliffs to the standing stones of Cwen Dreorig, were alive with bonfires. At the Druid's circle, Liam and Mia stood at the gathering by the funeral pyre where they honored those who had fallen in the siege of Caer Lannican. Caoilte, Branwen, Ian, and many other knights, men-at-arms, and commoners of all walks of life were honored together as heroes.

As the mourners sang traditional ancient songs for the dead under a night brilliant with stars, Liam and Mia stood quietly with Bran and the remaining knights. They lost themselves in the music as they watched the flames crackle and dance, spreading warmth on a cold evening. Liam's mind lingered on all his fallen companions, but most of all Conal.

He recalled that day when the land was restored, and he went to Conal's side, the knight's body pierced with arrows, his body broken on the bridge. In the bustling activity, he offered to use the Dream Stone's healing powers on him, but he shook his head weakly.

"I'm afraid I'm too far gone for that, lad," he said with a weary smile. "Save it." Then his smile faded, and his eyes drifted down in shame.

"What is it?" asked Liam.

He gazed at Liam squarely. "You must forgive me, brother."

Liam cocked his head quizzically ."Forgive you? You fought valiantly. Hell, you saved my life! There is nothing to forgive."

"I never should have doubted you."

He laughed softly. "Conal, I would have doubted me too. It's all right, my brother. You followed your heart, as a knight should."

Conal put a hand on his shoulder. "I tell you truly – you are the greatest knight I have ever known, Liam. May the gods compass you from now until the end."

He gripped Conal's hand, stomach tightening. Liam tensed his jaw and kept a strong smile up for his dying friend. Slowly Conal's grip loosened until it fell limp completely.

Liam closed his eyes, funeral pyre warming his face. "You will never be forgotten," he whispered. "None of you who have fallen for Kaledon will." He stayed with his fallen brothers and sisters for a long while.

***

The next day Liam stood by Mia in the courtyard of Caer Lannican where he defeated Damien. Many gathered to celebrate the coronation of the new High King, Bran O'Halloran, once Thane of the Aisling Tuath. The remaining Knights of Kaledon — including those who had been freed from being spellbound in the Dark Valley of the Unseelie King, chose Bran to ascend the vacant throne. All stood proudly by the king-elect on this auspicious day, each wearing their bronze torcs atop the finest war gear they could muster. Ian, Caoilte, and Conal were missed, but Aoife and the other knights, new and old, nodded in respect to him as brothers. Conal's respect for him was shared by the knights for all he had done.

Bran led the hand-fasting ritual between Mia and Liam, though his sister should have been the one to do it. The ritual blazed in a euphoric whirlwind, the wedding a prelude to the coronation. There Bran stood, stunningly outfitted in brilliant blue gilded brocade and waistcoat, beneath a royal mantle of many colors and silk robes. Many said the crashing waves rose like voices of the Sea Gods, welcoming the union and new king.

Bran raised the silk cloth that would bind them together. All that remained was to hold hands. He offered his to Mia. "Think we can do this, now? After all we've been through?"

She smiled, the barest hint of wicked mischief in her eyes. "It's like Dr Morderan said. All about trust." She placed her wizard-marked hand in his.

He nodded slowly, the depth of that thought bringing him a new calmness. "I trust you, Mia. I will never shut you out again. Never."

Her eyes shined on him like stars. "Same," she said after a pause, laughing and wiping a tear from her cheek.

Bran encircled their hands together. He swam in bliss. In a word, the king-elect proclaimed them joined before the Remembering Ones and the Druid Elders (Bran their temporary representative), and all who could attend, gathered on every spare spot on the battlements, on the balconies, and in the courtyards. Liam embraced his new wife and they kissed to a cheer. Everyone shouted a loud huzzah, pipers blared, drummers pounded away. Aoife, the other knights, and even Lungor, with several children upon his shoulder, raised many hails.

The giant, now knighted, wore his torc as an earring. Everyone loved it and cheered when he emerged from Loch Bruana outside the Lorwynn silver mines following the vigil. He bowed to the newlyweds.

Maple hugged them both. "It's about time, you fluthered thing-topples!" she said with a tearful smile.

***

Then the moment came to crown the king and they watched Bran as he knelt before the people of Kaledon — a rag-tag bunch finally home after suffering so long. Liam took the royal pendant of the ancient, legendary King Brendan and placed it around Bran's neck. Then he took the signet ring Damien had given him and placed it on the old knight's hand; finally, he put the golden crown upon his head. Bran rose, and all went to one knee.

Voices rose in a thunderous "Hail High King Bran! Long live the king!"

After the crowd calmed to a raised hand, the king strode forward to speak. "Here on this day, we proclaim our beloved kingdom is restored to its proper place. But as first act as your new king, we think a new tradition will begin. Our two loyal subjects, Liam and Mia," happy eyes fell upon them both and a cheer rose, "they have suggested we make a new name for ourselves, so that we are reminded of our great victory and rebirth. We look back to the great Brendan of the Lowland Pirrh Tuath, whose royal effects I wear now. Long ago, in a time of war, he was decapitated, but when his head was placed upon a Holy Well at Stirh, he was miraculously restored, after which he fought hard to bring together the Tuaths of Aisling, Othlain, and Somled under a single banner. On our knight, Liam of the Wolven Fell's suggestion, we proclaim our kingdom henceforth to be the land of Brendane, to honor our new life!"

"Hail, Bran, High King of Brendane!"

He raised his hands, "rise, people of Brendane. Except you, Liam."

"How may I be of service to you, my king?" he said, savoring the words.

Bran smiled in a fatherly manner, the bright noon suns glinting off his crown, new torc, and livery collar. "There is a second act that must obtain on this day. For we see our royal court depleted of its station in these days renewed, in that we alone remain the only Knight of the Elite Order Black Wolf. I dinnae wish that to continue. Therefore," he said, drawing his sword, giving him a chill of realization, "we must choose among the Knights here to ascend. We choose you, Liam."

He fell speechless, able only to bow.

"What is your answer?" asked the king.

"I humbly and gracefully accept, sire," he said, as if any other response was possible, heart pounding, beaming with pride.

"Then we name you now, Liam Trendari Panregon, Knight of the Order Black Wolf. A rogue and a lost wolf you became, yet now may you wander no more. For you are home. Here," he said softly now, so that only he could hear. He removed his livery collar with the wolf's head amulet. "As you have my old torc, take you now my old livery collar as well, and know your father would be proud. Rise."

He stood up, his father's proud smile flashing in his mind. Bran placed the collar upon him. "By my faith and honor I will defend the name of the Order until death."

The knights approached and congratulated him, slapping him on the shoulder, or making mock-grave warnings of the increased duties he had purchased with his new title. Each of the knights tapped his vibrant new brigandine of sea-blue and black.

"And so," said the king, "we will have one last request, hearkening back to the great sovereignty of Auril Dranne, in the yester-age, when the people of the Fairy Queen's footsteps chose among their kindred, a mystical advisor. We humbly ask you, Mia Milandre Kimama of the lands beyond the gate, if you would be our Royal Conjury Master. Is there any here who would object to this request?"

A thunderous "nay!" arose, nearly breaking the clouds.

She flushed with excitement, all eyes eagerly awaiting her acceptance. She stepped forward before the crowd. She then bowed to the king and shouted "I humbly accept!" A riotous cheer followed, Liam's voice rising above all others.

She returned to his side and he caressed the soft, wizard-marked cheek of the woman he loved. The countryside swept beyond the battlements where they stood, now greening with burgeoning wood and quickening streams where Lungor stood importantly as gate guard. They embraced amid the cheering crowd, the renewing of the kingdom and the renewing of the land beneath the suns. Liam and Mia had come home once and for all.

***

After the ceremonies, the crowds dispersed into ongoing merriment, including games, music, food, and revelry. The newly married couple made their way to the balcony of the great keep to simply soak in the day. After so much toil and death, the victory was sweeter than anything they'd ever felt in Midworld.

"Oh, that reminds me," said Mia, retrieving something from her satchel. She took out the two tor-heedrom fruits they plucked from Tyaku all that time ago. The pink light of the lamp-shaped, bristly fruits shined on her mischievous smile. "Remember these? Ready to be trapped in deadly Erentyr forever?"

He smiled. "I can't believe you saved them. They actually keep for years before they go bad." He opened his palm. "So bring it."

She made a nose-wrinkly, playful smile and sank her teeth into the fruit, handing him his. The odd flavor of cherry, kiwi-fruit, and fig exploded in his mouth, extinguishing the glow. "Trapped forever now," she whispered.

He chuckled, worries about the truth of the old belief buried in the joy of the moment.

Maple joined them, arrayed in travel gear, pipe out, satchel about her shoulder.

"Leaving us, then?" said Liam, finishing off the tor-heedrom.

"Well, I don't really want to," she said, wiping her nose, "Oh, banjax it, I'm such a blithering fizzle-fazzle. But, well, we did it, didn't we? We set things right."

Mia nodded. "We did, Maple. Couldn't have done it without you."

"Aw," she said, fidgeting back and forth, puffing her pipe.

"You know," said Mia, "back in Midworld they say smoking is harmful for you. I've noticed you puff on that thing every day."

"Every day? She says I smoke everyday?" Maple tapped and put away her pipe. "I'll have you know that's almost not true!" She crossed her arms, indignant. Then she laughed.

"Can't you stay with us a while, Maple?" asked Liam.

"Thanks, but I've really got to go back to Tarila wood now. Me grand-da is still nosing around there looking for the Great Feathered Fluffawump, I'd say, and I know grand-ma is tired of waiting for his tomfoolery to be done."

Liam exchanged glances with Mia. "Well, good luck, to you. I hope to see you again, Ms Magicwood. You are truly one of the Fairy Queen's finest servants."

She smiled broadly and hugged them both fiercely before turning with a sniff and trotting off.

"I'm definitely going to miss her," said Mia.

"Oh, and what about me, love?" said a voice. On the stone railing of the balcony, Sea Breeze eyed them both, blue tuft of feathers shining in the sunlight. "Smashing good job, by the way. You saved the kingdom and did much more than you ever thought you could, didn't you? I'd say the Fairy Queen is most pleased."

Liam smiled. "I certainly hope so. Pity I never got to meet Her." He took Mia's hand.

"Yeah ... how is it we never met this mysterious Fairy Queen?" asked Mia, eyebrows raised.

"Queen Aliya lives far away to the west," Liam answered. "Beyond the halls of Techtmaar. I understand, it's fine. I mean, She *is* the Queen of the gods."

"Ah, Liam," said Sea Breeze, "the Fairy Queen has always been with you. One way or another. One form or another. Even in Midworld. Your mum saw to that with her sacrifice." He nodded softly, and Mia squeezed his hand. "Well," said the raven after a silence, the sounds of merriment rising on the winds. "I must be off now. With a new Stoneguard, many things will change. Much to do in accordance with the Fairy Queen's will. And you've got much to learn. You're fifteen years behind in your Stoneguard training. Best get to it, you dishy gallant."

He lifted his chin proudly. "Have no fear, Sea Breeze. I will."

"Will we see you again, Sea Breeze?" asked Mia.

Her eyes briefly swirled with stars. "Sooner than you think, love." She turned to Liam and seemed to wink at him. "See you later, honey."

Then she disappeared into thin air.

Epilogue

Liam rode to Caldbana from the Shorelands, where the knights he had dubbed in Uluth worked to restore the land in the old Kaledonian manner, modified for the new estates of Brendane. These "forest knights," after the manner in which they were promoted by Liam, Knight of the Wolven Fell, began to rebuild the Shoreland Tuath once again with brochs, crannogs, pastureland and most of all, fishing villages. His heart burst with pride attending the bestowal of arms ceremony to each of the new knights. On the day of the winter solstice, along the snowy beaches where Drelthun had transported him and Mia in what seemed a lifetime ago now, he restored the old Shoreland lands to the people and their champions. With the Dream Stone, Liam was able to negotiate with the many strange fairy creatures of Tyaku to allow him and his people passage through to Cwen Dreorig, province of Brendane.

Mia, new Royal Conjury Master, availed herself of the Royal Library in the topmost tower of the northernmost side-fortress of Caer Lannican. She stayed there most of the time, her Mage Tide-imbued wizard marks dark and sharp, new marks slowly forming as she learned more spells, her ring glowing once more. Now that Brendane grew strong, High King Bran negotiated with foreign kings for the return of Brendane's many slaves and refugees.

Finally the time had come for Liam to return to his mission as Stoneguard and meet Damien at Drelthun's castle, as promised.

He passed the snowy, blue standing crystals of Drenhai, and came to the purple glow-fly meadows of Caldbana in the gloaming of a cold winter evening. His thoughts returned to that fateful day fifteen years ago when he climbed up the meadows toward the castle as a small boy, his family annihilated, his mother seriously wounded, to enter the dragon's abode. The spicy-sweet musk of the strange glow-fly plants permeated the air as he rode. The sights and smells triggered those horrible memories, but somehow now they were tolerable, mitigated, placed in the larger tapestry of his life in a way that made them less insistent and harrowing. His heart raced for a moment, and a bead of sweat formed on his brow. But nothing else came of it.

His mind often wandered to Mia and her new role. She had plunged herself into it, just as he expected she would. But something nagged his mind, worrying him. She seemed *too* engrossed in learning sorcery. He reprimanded himself, however. It was not his place to stifle her, not after a lifetime of Midworld.

He neared the dragon's castle, its ancient stone walls red with the sunset, the vines and overgrowth withered, the tops of the towers and keeps completely gone. What had happened here?

He dismounted and unsheathed Xanibor, then entered the abandoned castle. No dark tunnels, no high galleries, no overgrown fountains. The place was a ruin. He furrowed his brow, ears open, eyes peeled. He entered the previously dark hall where the gate opened and the dragon once dwelt.

No one was there. No Damien. No Drelthun. Nothing.

Liam snorted. Bastard … it just figured he wouldn't show.

But it did not matter. Part of him had not expected Damien to keep his word anyway. *He knows the consequences. No mercy from this day on.*

In any case, he had Stoneguard duties now, and it was time. Like Sea Breeze said, he was fifteen years behind. He lifted the Dream Stone and gazed at its contours, losing himself in the unthinkably ancient, invulnerable stone. *Ironic. I once longed to escape Erentyr. Felt happy it was safely sealed from Midworld. Dreaded re-entering it. And yet here I am.*

But Damien's absence still nagged at him. Something wasn't right. He straightened and lifted his eyes to the ruined wall.

He focused on the Dream Stone's power, now coursing in his blood after having bonded to it with the Calling Brand. The gate opened swiftly, to reveal not the aspen grove of ComCorps City 335, but a clearing on a hill surrounded by lodgepole pine forest that sprawled into the distance like a swelling green ocean. He wrinkled his brow quizzically. Dawn glimmered on the horizon in Midworld as the suns fell below the horizon in Erentyr.

What's all this, now?

He strode through the gate, and suddenly the air felt warm, heavy and thick. His limbs leadened and senses dulled. He entered the clearing of gravel. The woodland surrounded him into the hazy distance. He squinted, his eyesight poorer in Midworld, and took a moment to regain his bearings. In his jeans he found a wallet, money, keys. He carried a backpack with a laptop computer and wireless Nexwork link, along with several key cards and NW3 quickdrives.

The Dream Stone remained unchanged. Liam pocketed it. Part of the power of the gates, it seemed, was to change one's garb and gear. That would take getting used to again. Then he noticed something on his neck. He reached up and held the old wooden figurine, hung from a leather string around his neck. He chuckled to himself. *Appropriate.*

He put it back and peered into the distance in several directions. The gravel clearing led to a road that wound toward the sunrise and into the forest. *The duty of the Stoneguard was to carry out the Fairy Queen's long-term mission. Whatever that is.*

As if reading his thoughts, a familiar voice called out behind him. "And that is why She sent me here to meet you, lad." Liam whirled. A tall, greying man hobbled on a cane as he rounded the corner of the gravel road.

Dr Morderan.

"Doctor," said Liam. "Good to see you again."

He regarded Liam intently. "You've changed."

He nodded slightly. "It was a hell of a journey."

"Where is Ms Kimama?" asked the doctor, suspicion in his one good eye.

Liam pondered how to answer that. "She decided to stay in Erentyr," he said flatly. "Much to do as Royal Conjury Master of Brendane, you see." Morderan nodded slowly, seemingly holding back comment.

Liam finally remembered what had been nagging him. Damien's words.

The allure of Erentyr is very powerful. But it leads to nothing but misery, Liam. Mia is lost. She has been seduced by this world. By the blood and guts of it. She won't go home, even with you. Erentyr has consumed her.

He would have scoffed and smiled cynically at the irony of Damien's words, considering the same seemed to have happened to Damien as well … if he hadn't worried that it could be true. That was deeply disturbing. If those two weren't aware that Erentyr had changed them, what might that say about himself?

"Well," said Morderan, seemingly reading his turmoil. The doctor cleared his throat. "Hearken, then. And come. I have parked down this road a bit. As you can see, we are no longer in ComCorp City. There is much to do and explain. You saved your home and righted a great wrong. You should be proud. You are ready now to carry on your mother's mission. Follow me."

"Let's do this," said Liam, gripping the Dream Stone tightly and following the doctor. A gloom settled upon him for a moment. *The Magnolents thought Erentyr is poison for Midworld. I once agreed with them. Now I am pouring the poison. Funny world, isn't it?* But he didn't laugh. He put it out of his mind and caught up with Dr Morderan.

Just then, something flickered out of the corner of his eye.

Deep in the woods, just for a moment, he thought he saw a red-hooded figure roaming among the lodgepole pines, long axe slung by his neck, snout flashing with a toothy grin.

***

Then a blue-tufted raven flittered from somewhere in the canopy to rest on his shoulder.

***

Liam squinted and blinked, and they were gone.

Author Bio

Erik Goodwyn is a psychiatrist who has listened to the dreams and fantasies of suffering people of all walks of life, in both military and civilian settings. He is also a published scholar, on subjects such as anthropology, dream analysis, mythology, ritual, philosophy, and archetypal psychology among others. As a lecturer, he has been invited to give talks in Ireland, Switzerland, Italy, Germany, and all over the United States. His passion is the imagination, in all its manifestations.

Previous Titles

Non-fiction books by Erik Goodwyn:

The Neurobiology of the Gods. (Routledge, 2012.)

A Psychological Reading of the Anglo-Saxon Poem, Beowulf: understanding everything as story. (Mellen, 2014.)

Healing Symbols in Psychotherapy: a Ritual Approach. (Routledge, 2016.)

Understanding Dreams and Other Spontaneous Images: the Invisible Storyteller. (Routledge, 2018.)

Archetypal Ontology. (Routledge, 2023.)

A Jungian Analysis of Toxic Modern Society: Fighting the Culture of Loneliness. (Routledge, 2024.)

Note to Reader

Thank you for purchasing *King of the Forgotten Darkness: a Raven's Tale Fantasy*. I hope you enjoyed it as much as I enjoyed creating it. If you have the time, please consider adding a review of this book at your favorite online site for feedback. Find me online at my author website www.erikgoodwyn.com and sign up for my newsletter for news and information on my upcoming works, as well as Raven's Tale maps and info!

Sincerely, Erik Goodwyn

ROUNDFIRE
BOOKS

FICTION

Put simply, we publish great stories. Whether it's literary or
popular, a gentle tale or a pulsating thriller, the connecting theme
in all Roundfire fiction titles is that once you pick them up you
won't want to put them down.
If you have enjoyed this book, why not tell other readers by
posting a review on your preferred book site.

Recent bestsellers from Roundfire are:

The Bookseller's Sonnets
Andi Rosenthal

The Bookseller's Sonnets intertwines three love stories
with a tale of religious identity and mystery spanning
five hundred years and three countries.

Paperback: 978-1-84694-342-3 ebook: 978-184694-626-4

Birds of the Nile
An Egyptian Adventure

N.E. David

Ex-diplomat Michael Blake wanted a quiet birding trip
up the Nile – he wasn't expecting a revolution.

Paperback: 978-1-78279-158-4 ebook: 978-1-78279-157-7

Blood Profit$
The Lithium Conspiracy

J. Victor Tomaszek, James N. Patrick, Sr.

The blood of the many for the profits of the few... *Blood Profit$*
will take you into the cigar-smoke-filled room where American
policy and laws are really made.

Paperback: 978-1-78279-483-7 ebook: 978-1-78279-277-2

The Burden
A Family Saga

N.E. David

Frank will do anything to keep his mother and father
apart. But he's carrying baggage – and it might
just weigh him down ...

Paperback: 978-1-78279-936-8 ebook: 978-1-78279-937-5

The Cause
Roderick Vincent
The second American Revolution will be a
fire lit from an internal spark.
Paperback: 978-1-78279-763-0 ebook: 978-1-78279-762-3

Don't Drink and Fly
The Story of Bernice O'Hanlon: Part One
Cathie Devitt
Bernice is a witch living in Glasgow. She loses her way
in her life and wanders off the beaten track looking for the
garden of enlightenment.
Paperback: 978-1-78279-016-7 ebook: 978-1-78279-015-0

Gag
Melissa Unger
One rainy afternoon in a Brooklyn diner, Peter Howland
punctures an egg with his fork. Repulsed, Peter pushes
the plate away and never eats again.
Paperback: 978-1-78279-564-3 ebook: 978-1-78279-563-6

The Master Yeshua
The Undiscovered Gospel of Joseph
Joyce Luck
Jesus is not who you think he is. The year is 75 CE. Joseph
ben Jude is frail and ailing, but he has a prophecy to fulfil ...
Paperback: 978-1-78279-974-0 ebook: 978-1-78279-975-7

On the Far Side, There's a Boy
Paula Coston
Martine Haslett, a thirty-something 1980s woman, plays hard
on the fringes of the London drag club scene until one night
which prompts her to sign up to a charity. She writes to a
young Sri Lankan boy, with consequences far and long.
Paperback: 978-1-78279-574-2 ebook: 978-1-78279-573-5

Tuareg
Alberto Vazquez-Figueroa
With over 5 million copies sold worldwide, *Tuareg* is a classic
adventure story from best-selling author Alberto Vazquez-
Figueroa, about honour, revenge and a clash of cultures.
Paperback: 978-1-84694-192-4

Readers of ebooks can buy or view any of these bestsellers by
clicking on the live link in the title. Most titles are published
in paperback and as an ebook. Paperbacks are available in
traditional bookshops. Both print and ebook formats are
available online.

Find more titles and sign up to our readers' newsletter, visit:
www.collectiveinkbooks.com/fiction

Printed and bound by CPI Group (UK) Ltd, Croydon, CR0 4YY

20/01/2025

01823143-0008